Linda Holeman is the author of the international bestseller *The Linnet Bird, The Moon* [barcode] well as eight previous books [illegible]. She lives in Toronto.

Acclaim for Linda Holeman's previous novels:

'A stirring tale of one woman's search for fulfilment' *Woman & Home*

'Compelling and exciting. On-the-edge-of-your-seat reading. Physical and sensual. A novel in which you can lose yourself' *Globe and Mail (Toronto)*

'An epic story of passion and determination' *Good Book Guide*

'This tale of love, loss and redemption is impossible to put down' *Yours*

'Compulsive reading . . . [*The Linnet Bird*] succeeds in being more than just a historical saga; it is a rites-of-passage tale with a very convincing and resourceful heroine' *The Lady*

By Linda Holeman

The Linnet Bird
The Moonlit Cage
In a Far Country
The Saffron Gate

The Saffron Gate

Linda Holeman

headline
review

Copyright © 2009 Linda Holeman

The right of Linda Holeman to be identified as the Author of
the Work has been asserted by her in accordance with the
Copyright, Designs and Patents Act 1988.

First published in 2009 by HEADLINE REVIEW
An imprint of HEADLINE PUBLISHING GROUP

First published in paperback in 2010 by HEADLINE REVIEW
An imprint of HEADLINE PUBLISHING GROUP

1

Apart from any use permitted under UK copyright law, this publication may
only be reproduced, stored, or transmitted, in any form, or by any means,
with prior permission in writing of the publishers or, in the case of
reprographic production, in accordance with the terms of licences issued by
the Copyright Licensing Agency.

All characters in this publication are fictitious and any resemblance
to real persons, living or dead, is purely coincidental.

Cataloguing in Publication Data is available from the British Library

ISBN 978 0 7553 3113 0 (B Format)
ISBN 978 0 7553 5988 2 (A Format)

Typeset in Bembo by Avon DataSet Ltd,
Bidford-on-Avon, Warwickshire

Printed and bound in Great Britain by
Clays Ltd, St Ives plc

Headline's policy is to use papers that are natural, renewable and recyclable
products and made from wood grown in sustainable forests. The logging and
manufacturing processes are expected to conform to the environmental
regulations of the country of origin.

HEADLINE PUBLISHING GROUP
An Hachette UK Company
338 Euston Road
London NW1 3BH

www.headline.co.uk
www.hachette.co.uk

To my sister Shannon, who brings joy to my life.

Night brings out stars as sorrow shows us truths.

Philip James Bailey

CHAPTER ONE

Strait of Gibraltar April 1930

WE WERE CAUGHT IN the levanter.

I heard this word as a small knot of Spaniards huddled on the deck, pointing and shaking their heads. *Viento de levante*, one of them said loudly, then spat and said a word with such vehemence I knew it could only be a curse. He kissed the crucifix hanging about his neck.

The Spaniards moved to the wall of the ferry, crouching on the balls of their feet, their backs against the building as they cupped their hands around small rolled cigarettes in an attempt to light them. The air had a sudden texture, one of moist, thickening fog. This, as well as seeing the Spaniard kiss his crucifix, seemed a troubling portent.

'Excuse me,' I said to the middle-aged man standing beside me at the railing. I had heard him speaking English to one of the porters as we boarded, and knew he was, like me, an American. He looked as though he had lived a life of excess, with his rather puffy, florid cheeks and pouched eyes. We were the only two Americans on board the small ferry. 'What are they saying? What is *levante*?'

'Levanter,' he said, buttoning his topcoat. '*Levante,*

1

Spanish for east. *Levanter* is to rise. It's a terrible wind blowing in from the east.'

I knew of siroccos and mistrals, the winds that haunt the Mediterranean. But I had never heard of the levanter.

'Damn,' the man said, and then, immediately, 'pardon me. But these things can really hold on. We may have to turn back if we can't outrun it.'

In spite of the wind I smelled his cologne, too flowery and powerful. 'Outrun it? Will it not just blow over us?'

'Can't tell. Reaches its maximum intensities here, on the western side of the strait.' His hat suddenly lifted as if by unseen hands, and although he grabbed for it, it swirled briefly in front of us before disappearing into the air. 'Damn again!' he shouted, his head back as he scoured the low, heavy sky, then turned to me. 'You must forgive me, Mrs . . . ?'

'O'Shea. Miss O'Shea,' I said. My cape billowed up and then swirled around me as though I were a whirling dervish; I clutched it against my chest with one hand while I held on to my own hat with the other. Even with a number of hatpins woven through my hair, the felt hat was lifting in an unsettling way, as if it might, at any moment, be torn from my head. I couldn't catch my breath; it was partly the wind and partly fear.

'Could . . . could the boat . . . overturn?' I couldn't bear to say *sink*.

'I again apologise for my manners, Miss O'Shea. Overturn?' He looked over my shoulder, towards the stern. 'Doesn't happen too often any more, ships going down in the strait. Not with the sturdy engines these ferries are equipped with now.'

I nodded, although somehow his words didn't calm me as I'd hoped. I had recently sailed from the port of New York to Marseilles, and then from Marseilles to the southern tip of Spain, and hadn't encountered anything worse than a day or two of rough waves on the Atlantic. I hadn't considered that this brief stretch of sea could be the worst.

'This climate is so unpredictable,' the man went on, 'and at times infuriating. Levanters usually last for three days, and if the captain makes the decision not to go ahead, we shall have to return to one of the terrible little port towns in Spain and wait until at least Saturday.'

Saturday? It was Wednesday. I had already been forced to wait far too long in Marseilles. Every day that passed added a layer to the slow, yet ever-growing panic that had been building since the last time I'd seen him, seen Etienne.

As the wind blew a salty spray into my face, I rubbed at my eyes with my gloved fingers, partly to clear my vision and partly to attempt to wipe away the image of my fiancé. Wherever he was now.

The man added, 'You'd better get inside. This spindrift . . . you'll soon be soaked by both the sea and the very air itself. You don't want to be falling ill as you arrive in Tangier. North Africa is not a place where one wants to be ill.' He studied me further. 'North Africa is a place where one must keeps one's wits about one at all times.'

His words did little to comfort me. I thought of lying in the narrow bed in Marseilles, less than ten days ago, feverish and weak. Utterly alone.

The man was still studying me. 'Miss O'Shea? Have you travelling companions?'

'No,' I shouted, the wind suddenly rising to a shriek.

'No, I'm on my own.' *On my own*. Had it come out louder than I meant? 'Do you know Tangier?' I realised how ridiculous we must appear to the Spaniards as we attempted to be heard over the wind. Slightly protected by the overhang, they had managed to light their cigarettes and were smoking intently, their eyes narrowed as they watched the sky. It was obvious that a levanter was not new to them.

'Yes,' the man yelled back at me, 'yes, I've been a number of times. Come now, come.' He touched the small of my back, directing me towards the door of the ferry. As we stepped inside the narrow passageway leading to the main salon, the door slammed behind us, and I realised what a relief it was to be out of the wind. I pushed back the hair stuck to my cheeks, and adjusted my cape.

'Could you recommend lodging in Tangier? Just for a night or two; I need to get to Marrakesh. I'm not sure . . . I've read varying reports of the route one takes from Tangier to Marrakesh, but whatever information I could find was a little confusing.'

He studied my face. 'The Hotel Continental in Tangier would be the appropriate choice, Miss O'Shea,' he said, rather slowly. 'It's the most fashionable; there are always a number of decent Americans and Brits there. Quite favoured by wealthy European travellers. It's within the old city walls, but a safe haven.'

'Safe haven?' I repeated.

'You'll most certainly feel a little wary in Tangier. All the narrow, twisting streets and lanes. Quite disorienting. And the people . . .' He stopped, then continued. 'But the Continental has a definite old-world colonial feel. Yes,

I'd heartily recommend it. Oh,' he said, as if just remembering something important, 'and thankfully no French. If they don't have family to stay with, they congregate over at the Cap de Cherbourg or the Val Fleuri.'

I didn't respond, but he went on. 'The lounge at the Continental gets quite lively most evenings. Lots of cocktails and often a sing-song. If you like that sort of thing,' he said, eyeing me further. 'It's not the place for me, but I sense it would suit your needs.'

I nodded.

'But you said you're going on to Marrakesh?' he asked. 'All the way across country?'

Again I nodded.

His eyebrows rose. 'Surely not on your own. Are you meeting friends in Tangier?'

'I hope to take a train,' I said, not answering his question, but as his expression changed, I added, 'There *is* a train to Marrakesh, isn't there? I read . . .'

'You don't know North Africa, I take it, Miss O'Shea.'

I didn't know North Africa.

It was also abundantly clear now that I hadn't really known Etienne.

When I remained silent, the man continued. 'Not a journey for the faint-hearted. And especially not a journey I'd recommend for a woman on her own. Foreign women in North Africa . . .' He stopped. 'I don't recommend it at all. It's a good distance to Marrakesh. Damn country. You never know what to expect. About anything.'

I swallowed. Suddenly I was too hot, the dull light in the corridor blurring into a brilliant white as the sound of the wind and the thudding engines receded.

I couldn't faint. Not here.

'You're not well,' the man said, his voice muffled by my light-headedness. 'Come and sit down.'

I felt his hand under my elbow, pressuring me forward, and my feet moved involuntarily. With my leg as it was, walking on board a ship presented its own difficulties for me even when the sea was calm, and in this case it proved even more tricky. I kept a hand on the wall for support, and at one point I leaned against the man's solid upper arm to avoid stumbling. And then there was a firm push on my shoulders, and a hard seat beneath me. I leaned forward, my arms crossed against my stomach and my eyes closed as I breathed deeply, feeling the blood thud back into my head. When I finally sat up and opened my eyes I saw we were in the narrow, smoky salon, lined with metal chairs bolted to the floor. It was half filled with a mix of those identifiable as Spanish or African by their features and dress, as well as many more that I found impossible to name by physical description alone. The man was sitting beside me. 'Thank you. I'm feeling better.'

'You're not alone feeling ill in these conditions,' he said. I grew aware of the moans around me, the cries of children, and realised that many of the passengers were experiencing the effects of the violently rocking ship.

'Now. You were asking about the train,' he said. 'You're correct: there is a train that goes into Marrakesh. The tracks were just laid the last few years – but it's unreliable at the best of times. Besides, it doesn't run from Tangier. You'll have to first get to either Fez or Rabat, and board it from either one of those cities. I don't recommend going to Fez. It's far inland and quite out of the way; Rabat is a safer bet.

Even so, you'll have to hire a car and driver to get you there. Why don't you stay in Rabat, if you want to leave Tangier and see Morocco?'

'No. It must be Marrakesh. I must go to Marrakesh,' I repeated, trying to lick my lips. My mouth was so dry; suddenly I was incredibly thirsty.

'To be honest, I really wouldn't count on the train from Rabat to Marrakesh, Miss O'Shea. Unreliable, as I've said: the rails are always shifting, or are blocked by camels or those infernal nomads. Best to hire a car and drive all the way there, really. Then again, the damn trails that pass for roads – well, the French are proud of them, but in places they're as isolated and bone-rattling as anything you might imagine.'

I blinked, sitting straighter and trying to keep up with so many details. And all of them negative.

'You'll surely run into problems even on the roads, and be forced to take the old routes, simply tracks in the sand made for camels and donkeys and not much else. Now look,' he said, 'as I keep saying, there are other cities closer to Tangier. And you should stay nearer the sea, for the cooling winds. It's coming on full summer in Morocco; terrible heat. If you're insistent on leaving Tangier, as I said, stay in Rabat. Or even go on to Casablanca. It's much more civilised than—'

'Thank you for the information,' I told him. He was trying to help, but he couldn't possibly understand my urgency in reaching Marrakesh.

'Think nothing of it. But really, Miss O'Shea, Marrakesh. I take it you have family there. Or at least friends. Nobody goes to Marrakesh unless they've someone there. And they're all French, you know. You do have someone there?'

'Yes,' I said, hoping I sounded confident, when I didn't know whether I spoke the truth or not. The answer would only be revealed when I arrived in Marrakesh. Suddenly I didn't want to hear anything more, or answer any more questions. Instead of making me sure that I could and would do this thing – travel across the expanse of North Africa on my own – the conversation was filling me with even more uncertainty and dread. 'Please, don't feel you have to sit with me any longer. I'm fine, really. And thank you again,' I said, attempting a smile.

'All right then,' he said, standing. Did I see relief in his face? How must I appear to him – so alone, so uninformed, so . . . desperate? Did I appear desperate?

As he left, I noticed a Spanish family with three small children sitting across from me. The children's eyes were huge and dark, their narrow faces solemn as they studied me. The smallest one – a girl – held up a tiny doll, as if to show it to me.

I was overcome with an unidentifiable ache, and told myself it was caused by thirst and worry.

The levanter grew worse, and because of the roughness of the sea I couldn't tell whether we had turned back, as the American had suggested we might, or were still going ahead. The ferry forced its way through the waves blown up by the wind, and we rose and fell with a rolling regularity that made me feel even more ill than I had previously. Others did as well; some hurried out to the deck, where I assumed they hung over the railing to be sick, and with no warning, the little Spanish girl leaned forward and emptied her stomach on the floor. Her mother wiped the child's mouth with her hand and then pulled her on to her lap, stroking her hair. The smell in the room grew worse, and the heat increased. I ran my sleeve across my face, grateful now that I had eaten nothing all day. If only I had thought to bring a flask of water, like most of the other travellers. Everyone was now still, bodies rising and falling with the ship, and, in contrast to the earlier cacophony of voices when we left Spain, silent. Even the youngest of the children were quiet, apart from the whimpering of the little girl in her mother's arms.

Again I thought of the ship capsizing. And again I realised what a position I'd put myself into, with little thought for safety.

When a particularly deep roll of the ship tipped me on to the empty chair beside me, knocking my elbow on the hard seat and wrenching my hip, I involuntarily cried out, as did others. And yet still no one spoke; they simply righted themselves and sat, silent as before. I put my hand over my mouth, swallowing and swallowing to keep down the burning bile that rose up my throat and then slid back, echoing the swelling of the waves. I closed my eyes and tried to draw deep, calming breaths, tried to ignore the howling of the wind as it whistled around the deck windows, tried to not breathe in the smell from the reeking puddle on the floor.

And then, so slowly that I wasn't at first aware of it, the heaving of the ship grew less severe. I sat straighter, no longer able to see the sea rising and falling through the windows. The floor beneath my feet was once more solid and familiar, and my stomach settled.

As relief came over me, one of the Spaniards from the deck opened the door and shouted, 'Tangier. *Ya llegamos!*' and a low rumble of relief went up. I assumed he meant that he had spotted the city, or that we were approaching it. So we had managed to outrun the levanter, leaving the winds to continue churning through the centre of the strait. I closed my eyes in thankfulness, and when I opened them again, some of the children had rushed to the windows. The babble of languages started as a murmur, rising in pitch as what felt like a mild euphoria went through the stifling room. And then everyone stood, stretching and moving about, chattering as they gathered children and packages. The family across from me left, the mother carrying the little girl, who still clutched her doll. I stood as well, but immediately felt light-headed and nauseous again, whether a lingering result of the rocking of the vessel, or my thirst and lack of food that day, or from my recent illness.

I sat down.

'Miss O'Shea? Pity you didn't get out to the deck to watch our arrival. Quite magnificent, with the sun . . . Oh. But you're still feeling under the weather, I see,' the American said, frowning, and I knew my face must be damp and pallid. 'Can I help you find—'

I shook my head. 'No, no,' I said, interrupting him. Although his offer to help me was tempting, I was embarrassed by my weakness. 'I'll just rest another moment, and then I'll be all right. Thank you so much; you've been very kind. But please, go on your way. I insist.'

'Very well,' he said, 'But watch out for the touts. Lots of them hanging around the docks. Take *un petit taxi*, or, if there are none, a cart. And pay half of what they demand. Half. They'll give you a story about their ten hungry children, their ailing mother, but stay strong. Pay no more than half,' he repeated.

I nodded, now wishing he'd leave so I could again shut my eyes to stop the spinning.

'Goodbye, then, Miss O'Shea. I wish you luck. You'll need it, if you do truly go on to Marrakesh on your own.' His footsteps were slow and heavy as he walked away.

After a few more moments, hearing only muted shouting from outside the boat, I shakily stood in the empty salon. Then I went out to the deck, into warm sunshine. As soon as I stepped through the door my head cleared; the air was fresh, smelling of the sea and also something else, something tangy, perhaps citrus. It was a clean scent. I breathed deeply, feeling stronger with each intake of breath, and looked at what I could see of Tangier.

It was indeed magnificent, as the American had said. There was the sense of an amphitheatre, white houses rising up from the dock amidst a sea of palms. Minarets stood high above, the sun gleaming on their towers. There was a foreign beauty, unlike the teeming and industrial docks of New York or Marseilles. I stood, gazing at the gently swaying fronds of the palms. And then, drawing my eyes from the city, I looked at the people moving about the docks. It was only men – where were the women? – and I thought, for one odd moment, that there were monks everywhere . . . yet how could this be? Was not Tangier a city of Muslims? In the next instant I realised my mistake: it was simply the hooded robes the men wore. What were they called? The name escaped me. But I assumed they had the hoods up against the hot sun, or perhaps because it was the custom. The hoods extended on either side beyond their faces.

For an inexplicable reason, such a simple thing as these hooded robes that rendered their wearers faceless filled me with a sudden ominous sensation.

I was a stranger here, with no one to welcome me.

I made my way down the gangplank, holding the thick, hairy rope along the side.

There were no guards, no border inspection. I knew Tangier was a free port, an open zone called an international protectorate, and there were no restrictions on who might enter or leave.

As I reached the bottom of the gangplank I spied my luggage, wet from sitting on the ship's deck, the identifying chalk markings now blurred and smudged. My two heavy cases sat alone; I was the last passenger to leave the ferry. As I went to them, wondering how I would find the strength to lift them, a small dark man with a filthy white turban arranged like a tangled nest on his head came towards me, leading a shaggy grey donkey attached to a cart. He spoke to me, but I shook my head at the unknown language. Then he spoke in French, asking me where I wished to go.

'Hotel Continental, *s'il vous plaît*,' I told him, because I knew no other name, and he nodded once, putting out his hand, palm up, as he quoted me a price in French sous.

I thought of the portly American's warning words: *North Africa is a place where one must keep one's wits about one at all times.* What if this man, nodding so quickly, had no intention of taking me to the hotel? What if he were to take me to some hidden spot and leave me, driving away with my money and my bags?

Or worse.

The enormity of what I had done – travelling here, with no one to call upon should I need assistance – came over me again.

I looked at the man, and then at the milling crowds of other men. Some of them looked at me openly, and others hurried by, heads down. What choice did I have?

I licked my lips and named half the price the small man had asked for. He slapped his chest, frowning, shaking his head, speaking again in the unknown language, and then named another price in French, halfway between his first offer and mine. He didn't meet my eyes, and I didn't know whether this because he was shy or shifty. Again I thought of the risk of putting my faith in him, and again argued with myself. I was almost woozy with the heat, and knew I couldn't carry my own luggage more than a few steps at a time. I reached into my bag and pulled out the coins. As I placed them on the man's palm I saw, with a small start of surprise, that there was a fine line of dirt under my fingernails.

It appeared that this dark continent had become a part of me from my very first footsteps on its soil.

The man lifted my two bags into the open back of the cart with amazing ease. He gestured to the seat beside him, and I climbed up. As he lightly slapped the reins against the donkey's back and the cart rolled forward with a jerk, I took another deep breath.

'Hotel Continental,' the man said, as if confirming where we were going.

'*Oui. Merci,*' I answered, glancing at his profile, and then stared straight ahead.

I had arrived in North Africa. There were many miles still to travel, but at least I had made it this far – to the beginning of the last part of the long voyage.

I was in Tangier, and the architecture, the faces of the people and their language and clothing, the foliage, the smells, the very air itself, were all foreign. There was nothing to remind me of home – my quiet home in Albany in upstate New York.

And as I looked back towards the ferry, I knew also that there was nothing left for me in America – nothing and no one at all.

CHAPTER TWO

I HAD BEEN BORN ON the first day of the new century, 1 January 1900, and my mother named me Sidonie, after her grandmother in Quebec. My father had wanted Siobhan, in remembrance of his own mother, long buried under Irish soil, but he acquiesced to my mother's wishes. Apart from their shared religion, they were an unlikely match, my lanky Irish father and tiny French-Canadian mother. I was born late in their lives; they had been married eighteen years when I arrived, my mother thirty-eight and my father forty. They had never expected to be so blessed. I heard my mother give thanks for me every day in her prayers, calling me her miracle. When she and I were alone we spoke French; when my father entered the room we switched to English. I loved speaking French; as a child, I couldn't describe the difference between it and English, but my mother told me, when I was older, that I had used the word *curly* to describe how the French words felt on my tongue.

And as a child I truly thought myself to be a miracle. My parents fed into this belief when I was young: that I could do no wrong, and that anything I wished for might some day come true. They had little to give me in terms of material possessions, but I felt loved.

And very special.

All through the uncharacteristically warm spring of 1916 – shortly after my sixteenth birthday – I imagined myself in love with Luke McCallister, the boy who worked in the feed store on Larkspur Street. All the girls in my class at Holy Jesus and Mary had talked about him since he'd arrived in our neighbourhood a few months earlier.

We argued amongst us who would be the first he would talk to, go for a walk with, or share an ice cream with.

'It will be me,' I told Margaret and Alice Ann, my best friends. I had imagined the scene in my head over and over. Surely it wouldn't be long before he became aware of me. 'I'll make him notice me. You watch.'

'Just because you always have the most dance partners doesn't mean you can have all the attention whenever you want, Sidonie,' Margaret said, her chin lifted.

I smiled at her. 'Maybe not. But . . .' I brushed my hair back with my fingers, running a few steps ahead of them and turning to walk backwards, facing them, my hands on my hips. 'We'll see,' I added. 'Remember Rodney? You didn't believe me when I said I'd get him to take me on the Ferris wheel at the fair last year. But I did, didn't I? He didn't choose any other girl but me. And we went twice.'

Alice Ann shrugged. 'That's just because your mother is friends with his mother. I'll bet Luke talks to Margaret. Especially if she wears her pink dress. You're beautiful in pink, Margaret,' she added.

'No, it will be you, Alice Ann,' Margaret said, obviously pleased by Alice Ann's comment.

'Think what you will,' I said, laughing now. 'Think what you will. But he'll be mine.'

They laughed with me. 'Oh, Sidonie,' Alice Ann said. 'You always say the silliest things.' She and Margaret caught up with me then, and we linked arms and leaned against each other as we walked along the narrow street, our hips and shoulders touching as we matched our steps.

The three of us had been best friends since the first grade, and they always counted on me to tease and surprise them.

I found many reasons to walk down Larkspur Street, waiting for Luke to glance in my direction as he tossed huge, heavy bags of grain with apparent ease. I rehearsed what I would say to him, commenting on how strong he must be to make the bags look as though they contained nothing but feathers. I stole glances at him, imagining what his gleaming muscles would feel like under my hands, on top of my body.

I knew, from the lectures of the sisters at Holy Jesus and Mary, that the desires of the flesh were evil, and must be fought against, and yet I seemed as powerless to stop them as I was to change the predictability of the seasons.

One steamy Sunday at the beginning of June, at Our Lady of Mercy church, I prayed so hard to the Virgin Mother for Luke to fall in love with me that I was suddenly overcome with a strange sense of leaving my body. My neck had been stiff that morning when I awoke, my head aching to such a degree that my stomach churned. I begged my mother to let me stay home, but she refused.

It wasn't uncommon for me to try to find a way to avoid church.

As we walked the mile and a half to Our Lady, my mother admonished me, more than once, to keep up, but it seemed as though I was walking through water, the current making it difficult to move easily. Once inside the dim church, the light filtering through the stained glass made a strange yet beautifully illuminated spinning vortex whenever I moved my eyes.

My body, usually light and quick, was heavy and cumbersome as I knelt alongside my mother, and it was then, with my own fingers interlaced, that everything grew confused: the rosary clicking between my mother's swollen fingers appeared to be dozens of small moving creatures, the smell of the incense was overpowering to the point of making me more nauseous, and the incantations of Father Cecil were as garbled as though he spoke in other tongues. It hurt the back of my neck to lower my chin to pray, and so instead I stared at the saints along the walls, pious and tormented in their narrow niches. Their marble skin glowed, alabaster and pearl, and when I looked at the Holy Mother I saw tears, like glass, on her cheeks. The Virgin's lips parted, and I leaned forward, my chin on my arms on the back of the pew in front of me, my knees numb on the stone floor.

Yes, Mother, yes, I begged, *tell me what to do. Tell me how to make Luke love me. What can I do to make him want me? I beseech you, Holy Mother. Tell me.*

I had to close my eyes against the sudden brilliant light

in the church, but on the insides of my eyelids I saw the Virgin Mary reach her arms to me. And then, effortlessly, I was flying towards her. I soared over the nave and the confessional, the rows of pews, the altar boys, the candles. There was Father Cecil at the pulpit, with his slightly humped back under his robe, and the bowed heads of the congregation. And then I saw my own body, slumped oddly to one side. The church glowed in beatification, white and shimmering. I knew the Holy Mother had heard my prayer, and had deemed that yes, I deserved this wish. She would answer my prayers.

She let me see Luke's face, and then I was no longer flying but falling, unafraid, for my body was as free as the wild rose petals that rain down with the evening wind. I was falling as slowly as a diamond through still water, or a star trailing through a dark and lustrous sky. I was falling towards Luke, who put out his arms to catch me, a gentle smile on his beautiful mouth.

I smiled back at him, my lips parting to touch his, and the colour and heat and light all became one, and I was overcome with a rapture I had never known.

When I awoke, I was in my own small bedroom. The light was still too bright; it hurt my eyes when I blinked, trying to focus.

A woman in a white dress stood near the window, humming my favourite lullaby. I hadn't heard it since I was a child. *Dodo, l'enfant, do.* Sleep, child, sleep.

I thought it was another vision of the Virgin Mary, singing the French song my mother had sung to soothe me when I was small. Then the woman stepped away from the window and bent over me, and I saw, with dull surprise, that it was only my own mother. But there was something wrong with her face; she looked different, so much older. I felt, for one moment, that I must have slept through months or even years.

'*Ah. Ma petite Sido,*' she said, and her voice was as unfamiliar as her face. It was thick in her throat, as if she spoke through flannel.

I tried to open my lips, but they were stuck together. My mother gently swabbed them with a damp cloth, and then held a straw to my mouth. 'Come, drink,' she said, and I drank, the liquid so cold and somehow fragrant that it seemed to me I had never before tasted water.

But the effort of simply swallowing was so great that I had to close my eyes. I must have fallen asleep again, for when I next blinked, the light in the room had changed, and was softer, shadowed, and I could see more clearly. My mother still – or again – stood over me, but now, strangely, my father was at the open window, looking in.

'Dad?' I whispered. 'Why are you outside?'

His face folded in on itself, his chin quivering in the oddest way. I suddenly realised he was crying. He put his hand on his forehead in a gesture that looked like defeat.

'What's wrong?' I asked, carefully moving my eyes from him to my mother, and finally back to my father.

'It's the infant paralysis, my girl,' he said.

I tried to make sense of it. I wasn't an infant. Paralysis I understood, and although the word sent a shiver of horror through me, I was too weak to do more than close my eyes again.

That summer, the polio epidemic of 1916 raged through the state of New York. Although the doctors could identify it, there seemed to be no prevention or cure. Most of those who contracted it were children under ten; some, like me, were older. Nobody knew where it had started, although eventually I heard that many believed it was brought in by immigrants.

So many died. And I was told, by my parents, that I was one of the lucky ones. *It's another miracle*, my mother had whispered into my ear, the first day I understood fully what had happened to me. *Another miracle, as you were, Sidonie. We must pray to give thanks.*

It was well known that polio was contagious; I was in quarantine. My mother stayed with me, for she had been with me when I fell ill. But my father didn't enter our house again for a number of weeks; he needed his job, chauffeur to one of the wealthy families who lived throughout our county.

Margaret and Alice Ann and other friends from school left small presents – a book, a stick of striped candy, a hair ribbon – on our porch, at the foot of the door marked with a paper from the state to indicate the quarantine. For those first weeks my mother kept saying that soon I would be better, that the strength would return to my legs. It was only a question of time, she said. She followed the recommendations given out by the health service nurse, agreed upon by the doctor who had come to see me. She daily bathed my legs in almond meal. She made endless poultices of camomile, slippery elm, mustard, and other nasty-smelling oils, putting the hot plasters on my legs. She massaged my thighs and my calves. When I found the strength to sit up for a few moments, she pulled my oddly heavy legs to the edge of the bed, and put her arm around my waist, trying to help me stand, but it was as if my legs didn't belong to me. They wouldn't support me, and I wept with anger and frustration.

'When will they be better?' I kept asking, expecting that I would simply wake up one morning, throw back the covers, and walk briskly across my bedroom as usual.

My mother murmured, 'Soon, Sido, soon. Remember how you ran about the yard as a little girl, pretending you were a princess, like the ones in your books? How you twirled about, your dress billowing around you like a beautiful flower? You will be this again, Sidonie. A princess. A beautiful flower. My beautiful special flower, my miracle.'

The fact that her eyes filled as she said these things only made me believe in her conviction.

For the first few months I wept often – tears of impatience, tears of disappointment, tears of self-pity. My parents were sympathetic and did what they could – in both word and deed – to make me feel better. It was a long time before I could understand what an effort this was for them: to put on a positive face and attitude when they must have been as shattered and grieving as I was.

After some time I grew weary of my own burning eyes and the headaches brought on by the crying, and one day I simply stopped, and didn't cry again.

When the quarantine had passed and I felt well enough, my friends came to see me. It was the beginning of the new school year, and during those initial visits, when my life felt like a strange, disturbing twilight from which I couldn't quite awaken, I listened to their stories, nodding and imagining myself back in school with them.

Every Friday my mother picked up my schoolwork from Holy Jesus and Mary, and returned it the following Friday; with the aid of the textbooks I was able to complete the weekly assignments and tests.

One Friday, along with my new assignments, my mother handed me a sealed envelope from one of the sisters who had formerly taught me. When I opened it, a letter and a small prayer card, edged in gold, fell from its folds on to the blanket.

The sister's writing was difficult to read, the script small and tight, as though each black letter was painfully forced through the nib of the pen.

My dear Sidonie, I read. *You must not despair. This is God's will. You have been predestined for this test. It is simply a test of the flesh; God found you wanting, and so chose you. Others have died, but you have not. This is proof that God has protected you for a reason, and has also given you this burden, which you will carry for the rest of your life. In this way, He has shown you that you are special to Him.*

As a cripple, now God will carry you, and you will know Him with a strength that those with whole bodies do not.

You must pray, and God will answer. I will also pray for you, Sidonie.

Sister Marie-Gregory

My hands were shaking as I folded the letter and put it and the prayer card back into the envelope.

'What is it, Sidonie? You've gone pale,' my mother said.

I shook my head, carefully placing the envelope between the pages of a textbook. *As a cripple*, the sister had written. *For the rest of your life*.

Even though Sister Marie-Gregory had also said that I was special to God, I knew, with a sickening thud of reality, that it didn't mean, as my mother told me, that He would let me walk again. But I also knew that the polio wasn't a test sent by God, as the sister had said. I alone knew why I had contracted the disease. It was punishment for my sinful thoughts.

Since Luke McCallister had come to Larkspur Street I had stopped praying for forgiveness for my own transgressions. I no longer sent healing thoughts for others in our community who were ill or dying. I had not prayed for the end of the Great War. I had not prayed for the starving brown children of far-away lands. I had not prayed for my mother's hands to know relief from their endless ache, or for my father to be able to sleep without the old and haunting nightmares of the coffin ship that had brought him to America.

Instead I had prayed for a boy to take me in his arms, to put his mouth on mine. I had prayed to know the mystery of a man's body against mine. I had explored my own body with its unexplained heat and desire, imagining my hands were Luke McCallister's. I had committed one of the seven cardinal sins – lust – and for this I was punished.

A week after the sister's letter, I was again visited by the doctor from the public health services. This time I was alert, as I hadn't been on his first call, and read on his face that he had seen far too many victims of polio in too short

24

a time. Openly weary and speaking with a sighing resignation, he agreed, after moving my legs about and testing my reflexes and having me try a few simple exercises, with Sister Marie-Gregory's written prediction. He told me, my parents standing behind him, their faces grey with sorrow, that I would never again walk, and the best I could hope for was that I would spend my life in a pushchair. He told me I should be grateful the disease had only affected my lower limbs, and that I was better off than many of the children left alive but totally paralysed by the epidemic.

After the doctor's visit I resumed my prayers. But this time they had nothing to do with Luke McCallister.

Heavenly Father, Gracious Mother, I repeated, over and over, week after week, month after month. *If you allow me to walk I shall have only pure thoughts. I will never again give in to the desires of my body.*

During that first long year I was forced to remain in bed, propped up by cushions; it hurt my back to sit upright for longer than a few minutes. Margaret and Alice Ann still came to see me, but it was not as before. I began to see that they – these girls I had once laughed with, shared my secrets and dreams with – had, in a few short months, grown taller and brighter, while I had shrunk and lost colour. I listened to them, but now, instead of cheering me, their stories only made me see I was missing out on life. It soon became apparent that they sensed this as well, for they began speaking more haltingly, sometimes stopping in the middle of an anecdote about what someone at school had said or done, or talking about an up-coming dance, or who was sweet on whom, as if they too suddenly realised that

25

they were only reminding me of a life that was no longer mine. Would never be mine. There would be uncomfortable stretches of silence when they would glance at each other, their eyes showing quick flashes of what I saw as desperation or impatience or outright boredom. After some time I dreaded a knock on the front door, not wanting to see my mother jump to her feet far too quickly, and the hopeful smile she gave me as she went to open the door. I was embarrassed by the way she fussed about, bringing kitchen chairs into my bedroom for the girls, followed shortly by a tray with glasses of lemonade and a plate of cookies or slices of loaf cake. I was, for the first time, ashamed of her heavily accented voice – a little too loud – as she tried to make my guests comfortable, or perhaps encourage them to stay longer and come again. She spoke to them more than I did; I had little to talk about. My life now consisted of the walls of my bedroom.

The visits eventually grew less frequent. Although I knew my mother was saddened by my lack of visitors, I was relieved when, after a month of no one knocking on our front door, I knew I wouldn't have to worry about another strained afternoon.

Every week after she picked up my homework, my mother walked another eight blocks to the lending library on Weatherstone Street. She took out the maximum of four books for me. I didn't care what she chose; I read everything. My father bought me a box of watercolours and brushes and creamy paper and a book of photographs of the flowers of upstate New York, and encouraged me to paint. He spoke of how I had shown promise as a child, and how one of my teachers had told him and my mother that I had an uncanny eye for colour and design and perspective. I had never known, before now, what the teacher had said, and it surprised me. Although I had always enjoyed drawing and painting during the weekly art class, I'd never had the patience to sit too long, preferring to be outside.

My parents brought me a coppery kitten. I named her Cinnabar, and quickly realised that she was deaf, for she didn't turn at any sound, small or large. But it didn't matter; perhaps it made me love her more. The rumble of her purring and her warm fur under my fingers gave me comfort when I read or just lay, staring at the small window on the wall across from my bed, trying to recall the sensation of walking, of running.

My parents also bought a gramophone and phonograph cylinders of Grieg's Peer Gynt, with its two four-movement suites. My father would play one of the cylinders each morning as he got ready for work, and I would awaken to the strains of 'Anitra's Dance' or 'In the Hall of the Mountain King' or 'Solveig's Song'.

At some point my mother directed my father to bring in the old daybed from the porch and put it in the kitchen, so that we could be together during the day while she worked at her sewing machine on the kitchen table.

Every morning before he left for work, my father carried me to the makeshift bed. My mother put the small table holding the gramophone and cylinders beside me; I could reach it should I want to listen to Grieg's music. She also arranged my books and painting supplies on the table, and set Cinnabar on my bed. Then she pulled a straight wooden chair up to the table where she worked the hand-operated sewing machine, adding pockets and inserting sleeves and hemming men's suit jackets, piecework for a small company. I read and painted and played with Cinnabar. After a while she had me do the basting for her, and if she made a mistake, I picked out the incorrect stitches. In this way she was able to complete more jackets than usual.

If I wasn't playing the gramophone my mother sang while she worked, French songs learned as a child in Quebec. At other times she asked me to read aloud. It took me a while to realise, after my reading to her became a routine, that the books she was now bringing home from the library were books she would have read if she'd had time. Some of them were in French. I had to speak in a loud voice, to be heard over the rhythmic clicking of the sewing machine, and to make it more enjoyable I began reading in the tone of the voice of the character. Sometimes, when I read a particularly moving or exciting or humorous passage, my mother's hands would stop, and she would look at me, her head tilted to one side, with a surprised or worried or pleased expression, depending on the novel.

'You have such a lovely speaking voice, Sidonie,' she said one day. 'So expressive and melodic. You could have been—' She stopped abruptly.

'I could have been what?' I asked, carefully setting the book on my lap.

'Nothing. Go on, please. Keep reading.'

But suddenly I couldn't continue. The phrase 'you could have been' hit me with an enormity that shook me.

You could have been. What was she about to say? Did she

remember that when I was young, perhaps ten years old, I had announced that I would become a famous actress, and they would come to see me on a Broadway stage? I thought of the long-ago plans Margaret and Alice Ann and I had made: how we might one day move to New York City, and live together in a walk-up apartment and find jobs at Saks Fifth Avenue, selling fine leather gloves or heavenly perfume to the beautifully dressed ladies who strolled the wide aisles of the store. Margaret went to New York with her mother regularly, and it was she who had told me about Broadway plays and the department stores.

But of course now none of those dreams could become reality. Not for a girl who couldn't rise from a bed. Not even if that girl became a woman who sat in a pushchair. I could never live in a walk-up. I could never even live in a house with stairs. I could never stand behind a counter and sell gloves or perfume.

Now what would I be? What would I become? A small, cold voice entered me; it was similar to the black, tightly written words of Sister Marie-Gregory, calling me a cripple. I suddenly knew that my life might not move beyond this daybed, beyond this kitchen, beyond this house and yard.

For the next week I told my mother I had headaches and didn't wish to come out of my bedroom. I had her pull the curtain over the window, saying the light hurt my eyes, and that the music from the cylinders pierced my ears. She sat beside me, her hand with its slightly twisted fingers cool on my forehead. 'Shall I have the doctor come? What is it, Sidonie? Do you have pain in your back again?'

I turned away from her touch. What was making me

sick? Only the fact that I had seen the door close on my future. Only that.

I suddenly blamed her for making me understand this, with those four simple words: *you could have been.* The cold, unemotional voice I heard in my head now told me there was little point in anything: I stopped painting, saying it no longer interested me. I stopped helping my mother, saying that picking out tiny stitches was difficult; perhaps my eyes had been weakened by the polio. I stopped reading to her, telling her it hurt my throat. I turned from her gaze, thoughtful and intelligent.

It wasn't her fault; I understood that fully. And I didn't want her to know the truth. I didn't want to hurt her further by telling her that she had inadvertently held a mirror to my life. Surely I would have held up that mirror at some time – maybe the next week, or the next month.

But I hadn't. She had, and for this I was angry with her.

When twice a day my mother pulled back the blankets and massaged my useless legs, pushing them into the exercise positions shown to her by the health nurse, I stared at the ceiling. She bent and pulled, bent and pulled. I knew there was no use, but I saw it gave her some purpose to believe she was keeping my legs from atrophying, her mouth firm and her arthritic hands – which surely ached even more than usual from the additional movement – seeming to find new strength.

Now when I told her I needed to use the metal pan kept under the bed – and with her help, and me doing my best to lift my legs with their new and frustrating dead weight, we managed – I couldn't look at her. I thought I saw pity in her face, a false cheeriness, as if she didn't mind carrying the noxious pan away to dispose of. I thought of her doing this for the rest of her life.

Eventually I resumed my spot on the daybed in the kitchen, for the boredom of my bedroom made me want to scream with frustration. I said I felt well again, and went back to the old routines of helping my mother and reading aloud, for it was better than lying alone in my room.

I don't know whether my parents were aware that something had changed, had perhaps broken, inside me. They acted in the same way as always.

When my father returned at dinner time and he and my mother sat at the kitchen table, cleared of the sewing machine and the piles of jackets and sleeves and pockets, I ate my supper from a tray on my lap. But now, instead of giving Cinnabar small nibbles of my food, or taking part in my parents' conversation, I silently watched them. I looked at my father's greying head, bent slightly forward over his plate, and the mark at the back of his neck where the stiff collar of his chauffeur's uniform had formed a dark band of red. The rest of his neck looked vulnerable against the darker welt of skin.

My mother clutched her knife and fork awkwardly because of her swollen, knobby knuckles. As before, they spoke of small events, of local gossip and the latest price of pork or tea. They also spoke of the ongoing horrors of the Great War, and the fear that our boys might soon be going to join the fight. But when they tried to bring me into the conversation, asking what I'd been reading, or making unimportant conversation about the weather, or which of

31

my friends they'd seen, I answered only in syllables and phrases.

They spoke as if the world was the same place it had been before polio. Before *my* polio.

Don't you see? I wanted to shout at them. *How can you pretend that nothing is changed? How can you sit there, talking and eating as if it were a normal day?*

My life would never again be the same. I would never run down our quiet road, my hair blowing out behind me. I would never sit on my old childhood swing in the back yard and pump myself high into the air, feeling the satisfying rush of air and delightful dizziness when I closed my eyes and put my head back. I would never pirouette before a mirror in a pair of pretty high-heeled shoes. I would never stroll down a busy street with my girlfriends, stopping to look in store windows as we planned our lives. I would never again dance encircled in a boy's arms.

I would never live a normal life, and yet my father and mother pretended they weren't thinking about it. They pretended they were ignoring the fact that I sat like a propped-up doll in the corner of the kitchen, and for this I was angry with them.

I knew they loved me, and did all they could to make my life as pleasant as it could be. And yet I had no one else to be angry with. I couldn't be angry with God; I needed Him on my side. And so I was quietly angry with them, every time they laughed, every time they looked over at me, smiling. Every time my mother showed me a pattern, asking if I'd like her to make me a new dress. Every time my father held one of my paintings near a window, shaking his head and saying he didn't know where my talent had come from.

And not even that – the painting – gave me pleasure now. I had grown to love the feel of the brush in my hand, the way the soft colours bled on to the thick paper, the way I could create shadow and brightness with a subtle shift of pressure. I loved the sense of accomplishment I felt as an image moved from my mind to my hand, emerging on the blank paper.

The only small satisfaction I took now was in stroking Cinnabar, whispering to her and holding her against my chest as though she were a baby, and I her mother. Yet another of the *you could have beens*. I would never cradle my own child.

By the end of that first year I became the new Sidonie, the one who put away all hopes and dreams. I saw them as bright, pulsing lights, with the lid of a wooden box closing on them. The lid was rigid and hard, unmovable.

CHAPTER THREE

THE SECOND YEAR PASSED, and slowly, changes came about. I was finally able to sit up without assistance, and I moved from the bed into a wheeled chair. This gave me a certain freedom; after many attempts and many falls I learned to pull and swing myself from my bed into the chair without help. I no longer had to wait for my mother to come and assist me in bringing the pan or washing myself; I could wheel myself to the bathroom and into the kitchen. I could eat at the table with my parents. If my father or mother pushed the chair over the high doorway sill, I could sit on the porch in pleasant weather.

With this my spirits rose. On the porch one warm evening, I laughed at Cinnabar, seeing her leap straight into the air, frightened by a large cricket that hopped over her paws. My parents came to the doorway, and I told them about Cinnabar and the cricket.

My father opened the door and walked to me, standing behind me and putting his hand on my shoulder, squeezing it. 'It's the first we've heard you laugh since . . .' he said, and then stopped, turning away abruptly and going into the house.

In that instant I understood how much my parents had

wanted – and waited – for that most simple and human response: my laughter. I understood how they waited for me to smile, to talk about ordinary things, to paint with passion. They wanted me to be happy.

I knew how much they had done for me. I was now past seventeen. Even if I would never accept what fate had handed me, I could pretend, for their sakes, that I still found pleasure in life. I owed them this, at the very least.

The next day I asked my mother to teach me how to use the sewing machine, telling her I could help her with the piecework when she was tired. Her mouth trembled, and she put her hand over it, the fingers so twisted. I suddenly saw that her hair was now completely white; when had this happened?

I took up my paintbrushes again, and had my mother bring books on gardens and botanicals from the library.

And within a few months I had learned something valuable: that at some unseen moment, what starts out as a forced behaviour may become an involuntary one.

Now I found myself singing along with my mother as we sat together at the kitchen table. I did all the sewing, as her hands caused her such torment, and yet the income generated from the piecework afforded us small extras. She always sat with me, watching my left hand push the fabric under the needle, my right hand turning the wheel, and sometimes now it was she who read to me.

We talked of the Great War, our boys sent over, and she told me news of those I knew from school – which ones had already left in the first waves.

By the end of that second year, I proved the doctor –

and Sister Marie-Gregory — wrong. It may have been a combination of reasons: one exhausted doctor's quick prognosis, my body's own strength and resilience, coupled with my mother's endless work on my legs, my determination to rise from the hated chair, and perhaps, I told myself, just perhaps, all the praying.

I was fitted with heavy metal braces from ankle to thigh. They bit into my skin, but they kept my legs from buckling. And with the aid of crutches, I was able to pull myself out of my chair. At first I did little more than drag my legs behind me, my arms growing tight and muscled, my armpits callused from bearing my weight on the crutches, but eventually I was able to swing my legs from the hips, putting pressure on the bottom of my feet. My right leg was now shorter than the left, and so sturdy boots with one built-up sole were made for me. It was only a parody of walking, but I was once again upright, and able to move about, although very slowly.

I stood, I walked. My prayers had been answered. But the cold voice that had taken root within me stayed. In body I was more like the old Sidonie. But inwardly she was gone.

And life was altered in another way. I didn't want to leave the yard. I never resumed my old friendships, for by now, over two years later, and approaching my nineteenth birthday — all the girls I had gone to school with had left Holy Jesus and Mary. Although neither Margaret or Alice Ann had gone to New York as we'd once planned, Margaret was in training to be a teacher, I heard, and Alice Ann had a job selling hats in a fancy shop. Other girls were learning the skills to be nurses or typists; a few were already married. The Great War was over, and some of the young men returned to Albany. Some didn't.

Although I now found great pleasure in my painting, spending hours every day executing botanicals, I hadn't finished my final year of school, although the teachers offered to bring the exams and supervise while I wrote them. I simply lost interest in doing the school assignments. Besides, I told myself, what difference would it make? I would never go out into the world – or even into the main streets of Albany.

My father had been aghast when I told him I didn't care about achieving a high-school diploma.

'I didn't come to this country – nearly dying on the journey in the hold of that stinking, cholera-infected ship – to have my own child refuse the education handed to her. What I would have given to have your opportunity . . . don't you want to *be* something, Sidonie? You could learn to use a typewriter, and work in an office. Or become a telephone operator. Or, Lord knows, you could work in a sewing factory. You're already a top-rate machine operator. There are many jobs where you don't have to walk or stand for long periods. You would make your mother proud, learning a trade. Wouldn't she, Mother? Wouldn't she make you proud?'

I glanced at my mother. She didn't answer, but gave a small, encouraging smile, her gnarled hands curled in her lap.

'She could be anything,' she said.

I held my lips together tightly. Of course I couldn't be anything. I wasn't a child, and I was a cripple. Did she think I still believed her? I opened my mouth to argue with her, but my father spoke again.

'Just until you marry, of course,' he said.

I frowned at him. Marry? Who would marry me, with my heavy black boots, one built an inch higher than the other, and my noisy, dragging limp? 'No. I don't want to work in a sewing factory or be a secretary or telephone operator.'

'What is it you might like, then? Don't you have some dream? All young people should have a dream. *Leprechauns, castles, good luck and laughter; lullabies, dreams, and love ever after,*' he quoted. He had so many clichés about life, so many useless Irish sayings.

I said nothing, picking up Cinnabar and burying my face in the thick coppery fur of her neck.

What was my dream?

'You don't have an excuse now, Sidonie,' he said, and I lifted my face from Cinnabar's neck and stared at him. 'Even though not like before, you can now get yourself about. There's no reason for you to go no further than the yard. I know Alice Ann is having a party tonight. As I came home I saw all the young people on her porch, laughing and talking. It's not too late. Why don't you go, Sidonie? I'll walk over with you. It's not right, you sitting in the house with your paints and books.'

Of course I wasn't invited to Alice Ann's; I hadn't spoken to her since those uncomfortable visits almost two years ago. But even if I had been asked, I was deeply embarrassed of the way I had to swing my legs into position with each step. The braces announced my arrival with a loud clanging. The crutches sometimes hit furniture or slipped on uncarpeted floor. And I felt oddly out of touch; I didn't know how to talk to people any more. I couldn't imagine being at a party. Suddenly I felt older than my parents. How could I ever again be interested in silly jokes and gossip?

'I just don't want to, Dad,' I said, turning away.

'Don't live with regret nailed to your shoulder, my girl,' he said, then. 'There's a lot worse off than you. A lot. You've been given a new chance. Don't waste it.'

'I know,' I said, steeling myself, certain he would launch into his old story about the famine in Ireland, and the corpses piled like logs, of boiling the last of their own rags, all they had left to cover them, and eating them just to have something to chew. 'I know,' I repeated, and, still holding Cinnabar, went out into the back yard, where I sat on the old swing with the cat in my lap, idly kicking myself back and forth with my stronger leg. I remembered the dizziness of swinging high into the air. Now there was no dizziness; I simply swung a few inches back and forth.

I put my head back to watch the evening stars come out. The fall night was cool, and the stars, emerging in the evening sky, were like points of a knife, hard and sharp.

It was the beginning of the many arguments I would have with my father over the next few years.

'You should go out into the world, Sidonie,' he told me, more than once. 'It's no life for a young girl, living with her old mam and da.'

'I like it here, Dad,' I told him, and by this time I truly meant it. After a time I had been able to walk without dragging my legs. I was slow and awkward, still using the crutches, leaning forward a tiny bit at the waist, my legs stiffened by the braces. I eventually exchanged the hated crutches for canes. And then, after wearing the full leg braces for two more years, my legs growing stronger all the time, I exchanged them for small metal ankle braces, which could be almost hidden by the high leather boots. My left leg was now quite sturdy, but I was unable to walk without dragging my right leg in a limping gait.

I knew that earlier I had felt sorry for myself, embarrassed at my affliction and, as my father had said, regretful to the point of bitterness. But those feelings passed, and now I accepted my small, quiet life. It suited me; everyone in our neighbourhood knew me, and there was no need to explain anything. I was Sidonie O'Shea: I had survived polio and I helped my mother care for the house on Juniper Road, and grew perennials so magnificent that people walking by stopped, gazing in delight at them.

I loved our little house, which we rented from our next-door neighbours, Mr and Mrs Barlow. For me the house had a human quality: the watermark on my bedroom ceiling looked like the face of an old woman with her mouth open, laughing; the boughs of the linden tree brushing against the living-room window sounded like soft-soled shoes dancing on a sandy floor; the cellar where the potatoes and onions and other root vegetables were kept for the winter had a rich and loamy smell.

As my mother's arthritis continued to cripple her, I took over the running of the house. I cooked and baked, I did laundry and ironed and kept the house clean. The piece-work ended when a new sewing factory was built on the outskirts of Albany, and although I knew it meant a smaller income, I was secretly relieved, as I found the piecework terribly boring. I was glad for the old sewing machine, though, since I had begun making all my own clothing. I still had to get my father to borrow Mr Barlow's truck to drive me to buy fabric and notions, but at least I didn't have to go into the local dress shops, where I might run into the young women I had once known – either as they shopped or as they served customers.

In fall I cleaned the garden of its dead and frost-blackened leaves and stems, heaping straw over the roots of some of the more fragile plants at rest for the winter. I planted more corms and bulbs, anticipating the new growth the following spring. Through the winter I studied gardening books, painting my visions of new designs for the garden, which had now filled most of both the front and back yard. As soon as the last of the snow melted in the spring, I walked among the pebbled paths I had had my father lay, exulting over the first crocuses and snowdrops, and then the hyacinths and tulips and daffodils, willing the first tiny pink shoots of the peonies to stretch into the warming air.

In the summer I persuaded my father to again borrow Mr Barlow's truck to drive me out to the marshes of nearby Pine Bush, where I sketched the flora and wildlife, so that I could create watercolour paintings from my charcoal renditions.

And through every season I kept my vow. I had promised, in my endless prayers, that in return for being able to walk I would have no unclean thoughts. After a number of years had passed since that first prayer, and I knew that much of my recovery had to do with my body's strength and my own determination, a small part of me was still superstitious enough to believe that should I not keep my promise, I might be forced to pay in some other way.

I managed to quiet the desires of my body, but it wasn't easy. I wanted to know a man, know what it felt to be touched, and be loved.

I knew I would never meet anyone, living the way I did, and yet I wasn't sure how to change that. And it certainly wasn't as though a man ever came to the door of our house on Juniper Road, looking for Sidonie O'Shea.

Shortly after my twenty-third birthday my mother became ill. First it was bronchitis, and then a virulent strain of pneumonia that would clear up but kept recurring. I nursed her as she had once nursed me, feeding her, brushing her hair, gently massaging her hands and feet to help with the pain, lifting her on to the metal pan, making plasters for her chest. Occasionally, on the days when her breath came easier, she still tried to sing her French songs, in a hoarse, low voice, and my father and I couldn't look at each other at those times.

Once more my father brought the daybed from the porch, only now it was my mother who lay on it, propped up by pillows. She watched me as I prepared the meals, and took particular pleasure seeing me cutting out patterns and making my own clothes.

After one terrible bout of pneumonia, the doctor told us that it was now only a matter of time; her lungs couldn't take any more.

My father and I sat up with her that night, after the doctor left. My father spoke to her, and although she was incapable of answering, it was clear from her eyes that she understood. Her chest rose and fell with a painful rattle like the crumpling of paper. At times my father hummed, leaning close to her ear. And I – what did I do? I walked about their bedroom, walked and walked, feeling that my own lungs were filling with fluid, that I was drowning like my mother. It was difficult to swallow around the solid burning pain in my throat. My mouth hurt. My eyes hurt.

And then I understood. I needed to cry. I hadn't cried in eight years, since I'd wept as a sixteen year old in the aftershock of polio.

I didn't know how to cry any more. So overwhelming and tight was the feeling in my eyes and lips and throat, and in my chest, that I felt as though something must give way, must burst. My head or my heart.

I went to the bed and sat down beside my mother, picking up her misshapen hand. I remembered how her hands had cared for me and soothed me. I lowered her hand back to the coverlet, but kept it in my own. I opened my mouth, trying to let the pain in my throat out. But nothing came, and the pain increased.

My father touched my arm. I looked at him, seeing tears running freely down his cheeks, and I whispered, in a choking voice, 'Dad,' wanting him to help me. My mother was dying, and yet it was me asking for help.

He shifted his chair closer and put his arm around my shoulders. 'Cry, Sidonie. *A rain of tears is necessary to the harvest of understanding,*' he said, with something that was like a twisted smile. Another of his Irish quotes, but I needed it at that moment.

'Dad,' I said again, a strange whimper in my throat. 'Dad.'

'Tell her,' he said, nodding once at my mother. 'Tell her.'

And then I knew what I had to do. I lay down beside

my mother, and put my head on her shoulder. I lay like that for a long time. Her breaths were tortured, and far apart. Mine were rapid, aching.

As I lay there, needing so desperately to cry, I asked myself why had I never told my mother that I loved her. Why had I never appreciated all she had done for me – not just when I was a child, or when I lay in bed unable to care for myself, or even later, when I was as recovered as I would ever be but still relied on her? Why had I never told her I knew how my affliction, and subsequent attitude, had affected her? Had I simply assumed she would understand?

I had been her miracle. She had hopes for me, hopes that I would go out into the world. That I would take chances, and learn new things. That I would find satisfaction in a job, in helping others, in nurturing friendships. That I would marry, and have children. Instead, I had taken what had happened to me and turned it inward. I had been her miracle, and yet I had grown closed, and quiet.

I had taken no chances.

As I began to whisper to her, whisper all that I needed to say, my throat loosened. Finally I cried. I cried and whispered to her until she died, just after midnight.

And after that I couldn't stop crying.

My father and I mourned in our separate ways: I with outbursts of uncontrollable sobbing, which I tried to stifle in my room, while Cinnabar watched me calmly from the end of my bed. My father mourned in silence, often sitting on the back steps, simply staring at the fence. Once, when I went out and sat beside him, he said, as if I'd interrupted him mid-thought, 'She wanted to design dresses, you know.

But instead she married me, and left her home and every-thing she knew.' He picked a splinter of wood from the step and studied it, as if it held some insight. I'd never known about her dream. 'You're so like her, Sidonie. Sensitive, and imaginative, and determined.'

It seemed anything could bring me to tears. I cried at the beauty of the sun shining through Cinnabar's deaf ears. I cried when I saw a young couple walk past the porch pushing a baby carriage. I cried when I found the tiny foetal skeleton of a bird in a broken shell under the linden tree. I cried when we ran out of flour.

I cried daily for three months. I cried every second day for another two months. I cried every week for two more months, and then I cried every second week, and eventually I stopped crying, and a year had passed.

My father was a gentle man, with a beautiful lilting Irish voice, but he spoke less and less after my mother's death. We found an easy comfort being with each other. My father and I created new routines that suited us both, and we moved through the house as though we were parallel wisps of smoke, never touching and yet somehow graceful in our harmony. Every evening, after dinner, we read: the daily newspaper, as well as books. I continued to read novels, and he biographies and history. We sometimes spoke about what we read, perhaps commenting on a piece of news, or about a particularly insightful passage from our respective books.

We were all we had.

But my mother's demise had diminished my father in ways not only emotionally, but also physically. He seemed to grow smaller and more hesitant in his movements. And then – whether it was his reflexes or something about his eyesight, even with his eyeglasses – it was soon evident that his vision wasn't strong enough to continue his chauffeuring. His first minor accident was simply brushing against a lamp post when he attempted to park his employer's expensive, gleaming car, but that was quickly followed by nudging the front of the car into the closed garage door.

After this his employer told him he couldn't keep him on any longer. My father understood. What good was a driver who couldn't be trusted to drive safely? But the employer was a kind man, sorry to have to let my father go, and had given him an unexpectedly large dismissal package. We lived frugally, but managed.

My father had loved driving, and owned a 1910 Ford Model T. He told me that it was the true sign of a successful life in America to own a piece of land and an automobile. But even with their hard work and meagre lifestyle, my parents were never able to buy land or a house, and my father often mentioned how good it was of Mike and Nora – Mr and Mrs Barlow – to let us live on and on in this house, paying as little as we did for rent. And although while still employed he had purchased the Model T at an auction, it didn't run and there had never been enough money to repair its engine. My father long held on to his dream to one day drive it. But that never came about; by the time his eyesight deteriorated he had given up the idea of driving the Model T. Still, he kept it in the shed behind our house, and every Saturday, in pleasant weather, we would take out buckets of soapy water and rags and a chamois, and clean it from its hood to its thin tyres. Some evenings he sat in it, smoking his pipe; I sat in it too, reading, in the summer months. There was something comforting about its smooth wooden steering wheel and its warm leather seats.

One day my father brought home an old copy of *Motor Age* from the barber shop. He started talking about his love of cars, and, seeing him enthusiastic about something for the first time in so long, I bought him the most recent copy of the magazine the next time I was buying groceries, and we looked through it together, sitting side by side on the sofa. For an unknown reason I enjoyed looking at the beautiful, sleek new cars being manufactured.

And then he found a Boyce Motometer hood ornament in a weedy lot, and polished it until it shone. A few weeks later he came home with a Boyce Motometer radiator cap he'd turned up in a second-hand shop. This became our hobby; we went into Albany together on Saturday mornings, hunting through second-hand stores and asking at garages. We pored over the auto magazines together, looking for opportunities to purchase the gleaming Boyce hood ornaments and radiator caps, sometimes writing away for one, with a small payment enclosed. The collection grew. Once a month I took them all out of the pine display cabinet in the living room and polished them, laying them on the kitchen table. My father would sit on the other side of the table, watching and occasionally picking one up to study it further.

We went to car auctions together, just to be part of the excitement of all those cars and the frenzy of bidding. We also started laughing again.

The years passed. The seasons came and went, and both

my father and I grew older. Little changed until a late March day in 1929, when an icy rain blew in from the east, and all that I knew disappeared for ever.

CHAPTER FOUR

A s I WAITED AT THE front desk of Tangier's Hotel Continental for the key to my room, I saw that the American on the boat had described it accurately: the other guests were fashionable in an elaborate, formal way, and the hotel itself was quite beautiful – a combination of European and Arabic influences. I wandered to a plaque on the wall near the front desk stating that Queen Victoria's son Alfred was one of the first patrons. As I ran my fingers over the plaque, I again noticed the line of dirt under my fingernails.

I was shown to my room by a young boy wearing a maroon fez; the fabric was discoloured where it sat on his head, and the tassel was a bit ragged. He nodded and smiled broadly as he set down my bags. 'Omar,' he said, patting his chest. 'Omar.'

I put a few centimes in his hand.

'Thank you, Omar. Is there somewhere I might get something to eat at this time of day?' I asked him, and as he studied my lips carefully, in the way one does when trying to understand a language one is not comfortable with, his head continued nodding. '*Manger*,' I repeated, touching my mouth.

'Ah, *oui*. Downstairs, madame, downstairs,' he said, backing out, still nodding and smiling. Suddenly the smile left his face. 'But please, madame, not to go on roof,' he told me, in tortured French. 'Roof bad.'

'*Oui*, Omar,' I said. 'I will not go to the roof.'

When he'd left, I went to the narrow windows. They overlooked the port and the strait beyond, fed by both the Atlantic and the Mediterranean. The strait was perhaps only eight miles across, but it divided two continents and an ocean and a sea. And it was as if Tangier itself was caught somewhere in the middle, belonging to neither European Spain nor African Morocco.

Suddenly I shivered, overcome with melancholy and some-how chilled, although the air coming in the open window was balmy, smelling of the sea. It was unexpected, this odd sense of isolation. I didn't like crowds, and avoided situations where I would have to make simple, unimportant conversation, yet now I didn't want to sit alone in my room. And, most importantly, I had to speak to someone about renting a car and driver to take me to Marrakesh.

I went back down the winding staircase to the lobby, remembering the lounge I had passed. I hesitated at the doorway, the old sense of discomfort at meeting strangers arising as I surveyed the shadowy room. There were people at different tables, some with heads together in corners, other laughing loudly as they sat at the bar. I took a deep breath and stepped in.

I had never before gone into a drinking lounge. I sat at one of the small round tables. Almost immediately a man in a short white jacket bowed before me, setting a tray with a glass of reddish liquid and a small carafe of what appeared to be aerated water on to my table. Even in dim light, filtered by the tall half-opened shutters, I could see three black insects in the water.

'*Non, non*, monsieur,' I said, shaking my head at the man. I had planned to order a mineral water.

'Campari, madame,' he said, firmly, as though I'd asked him what it was, or had expected him to serve it to me. He pointed to a line on the paper he handed me, and rather than argue further, I signed my name. Then he left. I stared at the water, watching the insects trying to escape the carafe. One had made it part-way up, clinging desperately to the side of the glass, while the other two were moving in a sort of swimming walk, although very slowly, as though the water was molasses. Surely all three would soon perish.

Nobody noticed me, and in an attempt to appear that I was used to these situations, I breathed deeply, sitting back and taking a tiny sip of the Campari. It was bitter and had an almost medicinal quality. I thought the strong flavour would have been lessened by the addition of the fizzy water. But I wasn't sure what to do about the insects.

A shadow fell over the carafe as a woman passed my table. She walked in long, easy strides in flat leather shoes, and wore a rather mannish shirt tucked into a simple skirt. She had her hair bobbed, and it curled on to her nape. She glanced at me, and then away. I watched her go to a table and join four others – another woman and three men. They all greeted her with a burst of enthusiasm.

She looked like the type of woman who would know about hiring a car.

I touched my fingertips to my lips; they were burning from the Campari. I rose from my chair and went to the group, aware, as I grew close, that they had turned to watch me. I stumbled, slightly, on the heavy carpet in the high-ceilinged room, lit by long rays of light from the arched windows. A silence fell as I stood to one side of the raw-boned woman.

'Excuse me,' I said.

'Yes?' There was something slightly unfriendly in her manner. She openly studied my hair and my face, her eyes lingering on the scar on my cheek. I fought not to raise my palm to cover it.

'I . . . I'm newly arrived in Tangier. Just a few hours ago, in fact. And I'm in need of hiring a car. I thought perhaps you could help.'

As I spoke, her demeanour changed. 'Well, hello,' she said, extending her hand as if we were men. I responded, putting my hand in hers; it was big boned and strong. She squeezed my fingers in a firm grip, making my knuckles ache as she gave my hand one abrupt shake and then let it go. 'Elizabeth Pandy,' she said, adding, 'from Newport, Maine. And you?'

'I'm Sidonie O'Shea.'

'O'Shea. Hmmmm. Of the Boston O'Sheas? I knew old Robbie. And his daughter Piper.'

'No. No,' I repeated, shaking my head. 'I'm from Albany.' I stuttered on the last word, aware they were all watching me. My forehead felt damp.

Now she smiled. She had a short upper lip, and a great deal of her gum showed. 'Well. New York. I wouldn't have—' She stopped herself. 'Look, when I first saw you I thought you were French. You—' She stopped for the second time.

I knew why she had made this distinction. But the way she spoke – her tone, especially – made me realise that it might be better not to tell her about my mother's background.

'Join us, why don't you, and have a drink.'

'Oh, I already have one, thank you. A . . .' I looked back at my table. 'A Campari.' Again I touched my stinging lips. 'Although I didn't order it.'

She nodded in a knowing way. 'I don't know why these bloody boys think that every foreigner in Tangier drinks Campari. Come now, and have a proper drink with us.'

She raised her chin at one of the men, who immediately stood and pulled a chair from the next table in beside hers. Elizabeth Pandy was unmistakably a woman used to telling others what to do.

'I . . .' I looked behind me, at the doorway of the lounge. How could I leave without appearing impolite? But these confident men and women made me so uncomfortable, so aware that my life was nothing like theirs. That I didn't fit in. 'I really . . . I'm hoping to hire a car, as quickly as possible. And a driver, of course. I was wondering if you knew how I could go about this. I need to get to Marrakesh. I was told . . .' I thought of the American, 'that it would be best to first get to Rabat.'

Elizabeth Pandy dismissed my question with a wave of her hand. 'Marrakesh? Don't be silly. I'm sure there's nothing to see there. Come, now,' she demanded, 'do have a drink. Marcus, order Miss O'Shea a whisky sour. Isn't it lovely being away from the tedium of Prohibition back home? All that silly clandestine behaviour. So tiresome.'

There seemed no alternative without appearing horribly rude to Miss – or was it Mrs? – Pandy. As I manoeuvred myself into the chair, she glanced down. 'Have you turned your ankle on the terrible streets here? I noticed you limping heavily.'

'No,' I said. 'No, I haven't. It's . . .' I stopped, unsure of how to continue.

'Well, never mind, sit down and take a load off. And look, here's your drink.'

Elizabeth Pandy introduced me to the men and one woman, although the only name I remembered was Marcus. His hair was slicked back with shining oil, and was an artificial shade of dark red. All of them, including Elizabeth, were in various stages of intoxication, and it appeared, from their casualness with each other, that this was not an unusual circumstance.

One of the men asked me which room I'd been given, and the other woman – wearing a short pleated skirt and striped jersey, her hair in the same style as Elizabeth's – interrupted him, asking in a demanding voice how long I was planning on staying, but I had no time to answer before the conversation swung away from me. A glass was set in front of me; upon trying it I decided it was more pleasurable than the Campari, and occasionally took a very small sip.

The talk and laughter grew louder, and after a while it took on the quality of quacking, punctuated by animal roars. My temples throbbed and finally, when my glass was empty, I stood to leave.

The alcohol had gone to my head; I wasn't used to it, and for a moment I felt as though I were back on the sea, swaying the slightest and bracing my legs.

Elizabeth grabbed my wrist. 'Don't go. We haven't learned anything about you yet. Always good to have new blood from home,' she said, her mouth opening in a soundless laugh, and I thought of the excitable yawning of some large African beast.

I sat down again, partly because of Elizabeth's tugging on my wrist, and partly because I feared I might topple over.

'Well?' she demanded. 'What has brought you to Tangier? Nobody comes to Tangier without a story.' Again, the open mouth. A string of saliva stretched between her eyetooth and a bottom tooth. The others laughed as well, too loud, too loud.

'Story?' I repeated, sudden panic coming over me as all their eyes turned in my direction.

'Yes, yes,' Marcus encouraged. 'What's your story, then, Mrs O'Malley?'

'It's O'Shea. And Miss. Miss O'Shea,' I told him.

He barely appeared to notice the correction. 'Come, then. What brings you to Tangier?'

I looked at him, and then back at Elizabeth. The other faces receded into pale ovals and inverted triangles. 'I'm going to Marrakesh.'

'I've told you, my dear, it's nonsense. No point going way down there. Stay up here; Tangier is rather mongrel at the moment, but it certainly has its intrigue. Or at least go to Casablanca,' Elizabeth said. 'Now Marrakesh, well, it's such an outpost. Nothing of interest, I'm sure,' she said again. 'Although who was it — Matisse, I believe — who worked there some years back? And there are a few odd artist types — painters and writers and so on — who seem to find inspiration away from civilisation. But on the whole, Tangier has much more to offer in terms of entertainment. There are all sorts — as well as being into all types of things—'

Here she was interrupted by someone's coy murmur: 'What with it being so ungoverned.'

The others joined in, a rumbling chorus of agreement.

'No. I must. I'm . . .' I stopped. In the momentary silence Marcus snapped his fingers, and a boy with a tray appeared. Marcus whispered into his ear. 'I'm looking for someone. In Marrakesh,' I said, unnecessarily.

'Ah. I see,' Elizabeth said, her eyebrows arching. 'Gone off and left you, has he? Perhaps he's a spy. Is he a spy, Miss O'Shea? The country is awash with them, you know. Spies and touts. Everybody looking for someone or something.'

I stood so suddenly, pushing back my chair in one swift movement, that it caught the passing waiter in the hip. He uttered a small, surprised yelp, but kept going.

'No. No. He's not a spy. Nor a . . .'

'A tout, darling. You know, the endless pedlars who won't leave you alone. The Tangerines are quite forceful. Everyone wants something from you,' she repeated. 'We must be quite firm.'

'Yes,' I said. 'Well. Thank you. For the drink,' I added, and then left the lounge, feeling that all eyes were on my limp, surely more pronounced by the unfamiliar sensation of the alcohol swirling in my empty stomach.

★

I lay on my bed in the shadowed coolness, my head still pounding from the whisky, annoyed by the idiotic way I must have come across to Elizabeth Pandy and her friends. I didn't know how to share the easy camaraderie they possessed, nor how to make small talk so openly.

I remembered standing on the deck of the ship that had taken me from New York to Marseilles such a short while ago, and the similar feeling that had come over me.

It had required all my mental and physical strength to remain composed as I waited for the ship to pull away from the dock. I watched the crowd below, mostly waving, smiling, calling out *bon voyage* and *safe journey* to those, like me, sailing abroad. I noticed a few more sombre people in the crowd: a woman with a handkerchief against her mouth, another young man and woman supporting each other as they watched with furrowed brows, a few crying children. But in general the ambience surrounding the dock, and the ship, was one of joy, of holidaying and exciting adventures.

My own sensation, standing on that planked deck, watching the receding faces of the well-wishers, was sheer panic. I had never dreamed that I would step foot on a ship. I had never thought of leaving America. I had never been outside of the state of New York. I was thirty years old, and as anxious as if I were a child on my first day at school.

Panic had given way to sudden fear. The distance between the ship and the dock gaped like an abyss. It was loss I was feeling, loss of all I knew, all that was familiar. But I knew I had to go.

As the ship slowly moved further from the dock, I could still see waving arms and open mouths, but the sound faded. My heartbeat slowed. I grew aware of someone beside me; an elderly woman, her hands, in yellowed, crocheted gloves, gripping the railing.

'Is this your first time at sea?' she asked me, in halting English, and I wondered if all I was feeling was so clearly written on my face.

'*Oui*,' I told her, recognising her accent. '*La première fois*.'

She smiled, showing large, badly fitting dentures. 'Ah, you speak French, although of course not my French. Paris is my home,' she said. 'Do you go on to Paris from Marseilles?'

I shook my head, but didn't say where I was going. I saw her looking at my ungloved hands, resting on the railing.

'You have family in France?'

Again I shook my head.

'You travel to meet a lover, then?' she asked, with a smile that verged on slyness.

At that I blinked, and my mouth opened, but I was at a loss for words.

She nodded, looking pleased with herself. 'I see it. Yes, you are meeting a lover.'

I stared at her for another moment, and then, surprising myself, said, 'Well, yes. I am travelling to . . . to find someone.'

The woman nodded, studying me. Her eyes lingered on my cheek, then dropped down my body. That morning while brushing my hair with trembling hands in front of the mirror, I saw that my face had an unfamiliar hollowness.

'Ah. *La grande passion*. Of course, my dear. A woman always must follow the undeniable. I myself have experienced a number of grand passions.'

Now her smile was roguish – her head tilted and her chin tucked down. In spite of the powder caught in the creases of the deep wrinkles around her eyes, and the thinness of her lips pulled back over the dentures, I knew she would have, when much younger, possessed an attraction to men. And yes, certainly she would have inspired passion in them.

Surely she could see I was not such a woman.

I smiled politely at her and excused myself, going to my cabin, not waiting to see America – my home – growing ever smaller in the distance. I had stayed in my tiny cabin for most of that week of sailing, not feeling well enough to eat much or even walk about the deck, not wanting to have to talk to anyone, afraid that if I ran into the old woman she would pressure me for answers. I had no answers, only questions.

I had trays of plain food brought to my cabin, and spent my time alternately trying to sleep or read. I had little success with either; I was too distraught to sleep deeply or concentrate on the printed page.

I felt a deep sense of relief when we docked at Marseilles. I had made a promise that once I was across the Atlantic there could be no turning back. To have come this far spoke of determination, I told myself. I would not use the word desperation.

But now, in Tangier, I didn't want to think of Marseilles, or anything that had happened before then. I couldn't.

I rose swiftly, pressing my fingers to my temples for a moment. I drank a glass of the bottled water on the dressing table, and then, despite the boy's earlier warning, went out into the hallway, looking for the stairs to the roof. I wanted to see Tangier from above; my vision of it, feeling ill and disoriented as we went through the narrow streets from the docks, had been as if I observed this new world through a long tunnel. I may well have had the same blinkered view as the donkey who pulled the cart, unable to see left or right, only straight ahead.

I found the stairs at the end of the hall, behind a closed door with a simple latch. They were steep, with no handrail. Such steps usually presented difficulty for me, but still I set off up them, thankful the passageway was so narrow that I could help pull myself along by planting my hands firmly on each side of me. There was a strong smell of sewage wafting from somewhere, but when I reached the top and stepped up into blinding light, the darkness and odour were washed away, and I could smell the sea.

The climb had left me panting, and I had to lean over, my hands on my knees. But when I straightened, what I saw threatened to again take away my breath. On one side of me the sea tilted away, glinting in the sun, and on the other I saw mountains. The glorious Rif mountains, the setting sun staining them a blood red.

Standing alone in the sweet breeze, Tangier encircled me, the buildings blinding white in the late afternoon sun. Unfamiliar feathery and broad-leafed trees, as well as palms, stood in variegated shades of green. There was a clarity to the scene in the play of light that made me think of the most brilliant of paintings – the colours were not blue and red and yellow and green, but cerulean, indigo, they were vermilion and crimson, amber and saffron, celadon and olive and lime.

My leg ached; I looked for a place to sit down, but there was only the narrow edge of the roof. I understood the boy's earlier cautioning; one small misstep would be disaster. Had someone else, perhaps someone like those in Elizabeth Pandy's group, come up here after too many glasses of alcohol, and tumbled to certain death?

I closed my eyes and opened them, each time letting the small thrill run through me. I thought of Pine Bush, the barrens a few miles from my home, or the nearby lake, or simply the countryside in Albany County. I had spent so much time in those places, walking and sketching the flora and the wildlife. I thought of my own botanical watercolours, the muted greens of the shade-loving ferns and mosses, the delicate lavender of the speedwell, the shy, nodding pink of the moccasin flower, the modest jack-in-the-pulpit. But here! I knew my box of paints, stored away on the bedroom shelf of my small house across the ocean, could never create such colours.

When the ache in my leg abated I walked, slowly, to the far end of the roof and peered down into a shadowy labyrinth of streets, surely the medina, the oldest part of the city. There the crowds milled in a kind of frenzy; there were calls and shouts and the braying of donkeys and barking of dogs and the occasional roar of a camel.

And then came a sound I hadn't before heard; a high and yet carrying voice, coming from somewhere behind me. I turned to see the spire of a minaret, and knew it was a muezzin, calling the Muslim believers to prayer. Suddenly another voice joined in, and then another, as voices from the various minarets throughout Tangier called out. I stood on that roof, surrounded by the sonorous, rhythmic phrase that to me sounded like *Allah Akbar*, watching the scarlet-stained mountains.

Was Etienne hearing these same sounds? Was he looking at the sky, at mountains, at the sea? Was he thinking of me, at this lonely hour, as I was of him?

I had to close my eyes.

When the echo of voices ended there was a sudden quiet, and I opened my eyes and drank in the sense that the foreign prayers had somehow reached inside me. Without thinking I crossed myself in the old, reflexive habit.

And then I made my way down the narrow, malodorous stairs. I was impossibly hungry. I went back to the lobby, passing the doorway of the lounge.

From the laughter and boisterous voices it was obvious Elizabeth and her friends were still there. The lounge appeared dark and blurred, formless and colourless after the brilliant beauty I had just witnessed. Like the prayer, I felt that the colour I had seen had touched me, and that as I passed the doorway surely Elizabeth and Marcus and the others would stop their drinking and gossip, and instantly grow quiet, staring at me in wonder. In that short time on the roof I felt as though I had become part of the mosaic of Tangier, a fragment of sound and colour.

But as I walked past the lounge nobody turned, nobody noticed.

Out on the spacious terrace – empty but for me – with its gently swaying potted palms and wooden furniture and views of the harbour, I ordered a pot of mint tea and a *pastilla*, which the server explained was a kind of bird – I couldn't understand if he was saying partridge or pigeon –

mixed with rice and chopped egg in layers of the thinnest pastry.

While I waited, I laid my head against the tall back of the chair, listening to the far-off, muted babble of unknown languages, to the nearby cooing of a dove, to the even softer rustle of the palm fronds in the warm early evening breeze. It was lovely, Tangier, although, as I knew from both my reading and the boisterous Elizabeth Pandy, also dangerous and uncontrolled, a free port, ungoverned by any country. I was weary, and overcome with a listlessness that was not unpleasant. But I would not – could not – stop and rest in Tangier. I sat up, shaking off the languor that had set in. Tomorrow I would set out to find a driver to take me to Rabat, as the American on the ferry had instructed.

When the tray was set before me, the server lifted the small brass teapot. He poured the tea in a thick amber stream, holding the pot high over the small painted glass in a silver holder. I expected the tea to splash out of the glass from that height, but he filled it with the foaming liquid without spilling a drop. He then dumped the tea back into the pot, poured it again, and repeated the process a third time. Finally he set down the teapot, picking up the glass with both hands and extending it to me with a slight bow.

'*Très chaud*, madame,' he said. 'Wait, please, for it to cool.'

I nodded, holding the glass by the silver holder, and lifted it to my nose. The odour of mint was almost overwhelming. I took a small sip, and it was intensely sweet, and like no tea I had ever tasted, but it was delicious.

I thought of home, on the outskirts of Albany. Of my garden and the silence of this time of evening. If I didn't venture through the gate on to Juniper Road, days might go by when I saw no one, spoke to no one. I thought of the long, dark winter nights.

It all seemed so far away. It *was* far away, geographically, of course. But it wasn't just the distance. It was what had happened to me since those days, those endless, quiet days when I thought my life would always continue in that way. When my life consisted of small, certain pieces of a larger, but basically simple, puzzle.

When I was certain that I always knew where each piece fitted.

CHAPTER FIVE

I T WAS TWO YEARS EARLIER – 1928 – when my father received a letter from a lawyer.

'Read it for me, darlin',' he'd said, anxiety on his face. 'I can't think what I've done wrong.'

'It doesn't mean anything's wrong, Dad,' I told him, opening the letter and scanning it.

'Go on, then. What does it say?'

I looked at him. 'Dad. Mr Harding has passed away.'

'Well,' my father said, sitting at the kitchen table. 'Poor auld soul. I knew he'd been ill some time.'

Mr Harding had been my father's last employer, the one who had been so kind when he had to terminate my father after fourteen years.

'And why would a lawyer be writing to me about it?' he asked.

I licked my lips, trying not to rush. I was sorry, of course, that Mr Harding had died, but he'd been ninety-two.

'You remember his car,' I stated.

'Which one, now? For he had quite a fleet of them,' my father said.

'Dad. The one you loved to drive the most. You always talked about it.'

He lifted his chin, smiling now. 'Ah. Yes, that would be the lovely Silver Ghost, wouldn't it? Such a thing of beauty. Driving it was like floating on a cloud.'

I well knew about the 1921 Rolls-Royce, with its British right-hand drive, its leather retractable roof, its drum headlamps and tubular bumpers.

'A long, sleek white body with oxblood trim,' my father went on now, smiling unconsciously. He picked up his pipe and tapped it on the ashtray; a clump of dottle fell from the bowl. 'I did love to drive that grand thing,' he said.

'Dad?' I stood, unable to keep my own smile from my face any longer. 'Mr Harding has left it to you. It's in his will, Dad. The car is yours.' My voice had risen with excitement.

But my father grew very still as I spoke. I waited for something – an exclamation, a burst of laughter, something – but he didn't move.

'Aren't you happy about it, Dad? You just said—'

He nodded. 'I know, my girl. I know what I said.'

'So why aren't you—'

Again he interrupted me. 'It's too late, Sidonie. The time for me to own a car like that is gone. You know I can't trust my own eyes.'

'You could still drive it in the day, when the light is bright,' I argued.

He looked at me. 'No. No, Sidonie. Even with the spectacles, I know I can't see well enough.'

I sat down, running my fingers over the embossed letterhead. 'But it's yours,' I said.

'What would I do with it?'

66

I sat straighter. 'I could drive it, Dad. You could teach me, and I could drive it for you. Wherever you want to go.' I was speaking quickly, thrilling myself at the idea. 'Just think, Dad. We could go wherever we wanted.'

There was silence.

'Dad? I could drive it,' I repeated.

'No, Sidonie,' he said, filling his pipe.

'What do you mean, no?' I watched as he tamped the tobacco into the round bowl with his thumb. 'Of course I can learn to drive. It can't be that difficult.'

'It takes coordination, hands and feet. Feet, Sidonie. You have to be able to use the pedals – the gas and brake and clutch. You'd have to be able to bend your knees freely. I don't think . . .' He glanced at my built-up shoe.

My mouth twisted. 'I can learn,' I said, loudly. 'I want to. I want that car.'

My father looked surprised. 'Well. It's a rare day I hear that tone from you.'

I knew my voice was loud. But it excited me – the thought of driving. I realised nothing had challenged me for so long. In fact I couldn't remember the last time I had learned something new. Had felt proud of any accomplishment.

I lowered my chin and tried to modulate my voice. 'It's just that . . . it's been given to you, Dad. If you don't want it, I'll have it.'

He shook his head. 'As I said, you couldn't—'

'I could. And I will. You'll see,' I said. I thought, suddenly, of my mother, and how I hadn't told her how much I appreciated all she'd done for me until she lay dying. 'And Dad?'

He was busy with his pipe again, but stopped and looked at me.

'Can't you let me do this for you? Drive you where you want to go? See you enjoy being out in a beautiful car? You spent most of your life driving other people. You've spent all your life doing things for me. Now I can drive you. Let me drive you, Dad,' I said. 'Please. Let me do something for *you*.'

He didn't answer, but his expression changed, softened, and I knew then that the Silver Ghost would be mine.

Once the car was delivered to our yard, my father did teach me to drive it, and I took pride in the fact that he was obviously surprised at how quickly I mastered it. It was true, as he'd said, that I had a certain difficulty because I didn't have a lot of strength in my right leg, and the knee didn't bend freely. But even though he saw that I could manage, my father still worried, knowing my foot's reflex was poor.

Immediately I discovered that I loved driving the Silver Ghost, and from the first time I took it out on my own I felt a sense of power I had never before experienced. Behind the steering wheel I forgot my heavy limp; with the top down and my hair whipped loose, I achieved the almost forgotten pleasure of moving quickly. Perhaps it reminded me a bit of running.

That first summer of owning the car I ventured out frequently, not only through the country, but also into the heart of the city, where people didn't know me. The car drew attention, and I developed a new and rather proud smile, nodding at those whose eyes lingered on the sleek outlines of the car and then looked at me. I felt an undeniable pride in not only owning it, but driving it proficiently, and suddenly I wasn't just Sidonie O'Shea, the woman with the limp who lived with her father on the outskirts of the city.

In the height of that steamy summer I drove deep into the countryside, waving at children walking along the ruts of the dusty back roads of Albany County. I'd leave the car at the side of the road and tramp through the tangled thickets and marshes, sometimes coming to one of the ponds that dotted the area. I sat at the edge of the water and sketched the bulrushes and the wild flowers. I watched the beavers in all their industry, the squirrels and rabbits working their way through the underbrush, the birds swooping and nesting. Frogs gulped and insects whirred around my head. I found new flora, wild plants I had no name for, and I sketched them with quick, rough lines so I could identify them from the pages of the growing pile of botanical books in my room. By the time I returned to the car, my clothes would be streaked with perspiration, burrs caught in my hem and my hair damp and wild from the humidity.

I couldn't wait to get home so I could paint what I'd sketched. And there was a difference in my paintings that summer. Something about driving had made my wrists and fingers and even my shoulders looser, so that my brushstrokes were freer. The colours I chose were richer, deeper.

Once, as I finished a painting of an Eastern Phoebe on its nest of mud and moss, I stood back from it, studying it.

And what I saw so pleased me that I picked up Cinnabar and did a shuffling movement about the room. I think I was dancing.

I know I was happy.

When the first heavy snow of winter came, it was too difficult to get the car out of the yard, and I had to give up driving for those long, dreary months. I spent the winter longing for the throaty rumbling of the engine, the slight vibration of the wheel beneath my palms, and the new-found freedom the Silver Ghost had given me. I dreamed about driving her again.

It was the very tail end of winter when my father told me he was going to the next county to watch a car auction. He said he would go with Mike Barlow.

'No, I'll drive you,' I said, immediately standing, the old excitement surfacing. 'The snow has melted enough; I looked at the yard this morning, and I know I'll be able to get the Ghost out. Last week I took the tarp off and started the engine and let her run a bit. She's all ready to go, Dad.'

'There's no need, Sidonie. Mike has said he'll take me in his truck, and the roads are icy after yesterday's wet rain and then the freezing. With your leg—'

'Stop fussing about my leg. And I want to go as well. We haven't been to an auction in months.' I didn't mention my desire to drive. Later, when I understood more, I would realise the thought of getting behind the wheel again had been akin to lust. I put on my coat, glancing at myself in the mirror over the sideboard and smoothing back my hair. 'I'm taking you, and that's all. It'll be fun, Dad,' I added.

Something was different now; I had a new confidence.

My father shook his head, his lips tight, but he put on his coat and his galoshes.

I didn't want us to leave with bad feelings, and put my arms around him, hugging him, then pulled away and smiled. 'Wear a scarf, Dad,' I said.

'*No man ever wore a scarf as warm as his daughter's arms around his neck*,' he quoted, and again I smiled.

This time he smiled back at me, nodding.

We both had to shovel the last mounds of slushy snow out of the driveway, and by the time we were done I was flushed and hot, and took off my coat, tossing it between us.

'Sidonie. You'll catch cold.'

'Dad,' I said, shaking my head but grinning. 'Just get in.' Nothing could diminish my joyful anticipation.

While it was indeed wonderful to drive the Silver Ghost again, I hadn't ever driven on anything more challenging than surfaces wet from summer or fall rain. As my father had predicted, the roads were slippery, and if I accelerated too quickly the car's thin tyres slid to one side, just enough to surprise me and make me turn the wheel sharply to line up the car again. My father said nothing, but I could hear his teeth working the stem of his unlit pipe.

My body cooled, and I grew chilled, my shoulders tight. I was sorry I'd taken off my coat, but didn't want to admit it. I shifted gears slowly, and occasionally one would grind. Each time this happened I saw, from the corner of my eye, my father's head turning sharply towards me, but I ignored him. Even though it was just past noon, as we drove out of the city the sky was growing grainy.

It was easier to keep the car steady on the deserted gravel road. Wet fields stretched out on either side of us, and I forced myself to relax, dropping my shoulders and loosening my grip on the wooden steering wheel.

'Turn on the lights, Sidonie,' my father said, picking up my coat. 'Pull over and put on your coat and turn on the lights.'

I shook my head, the concentration I needed making me tense. 'It's not dark, Dad,' I said, annoyance in my voice. Later I would remember that my last words to him had been in this slightly strident tone. 'It's just your eyes.'

'But it's growing foggy.'

'There are no other cars on the road,' I said, looking at him, seeing him holding my coat against his chest, and suddenly his expression changed. I thought it was anger I saw, and shook my head at him. 'I'm quite capable of—'

'Sidonie!' he yelled, and I looked back at the road. A truck loomed on the other side of us, pale as a phantom in the gloom, and its unexpected presence startled me so that I gasped, wrenching the wheel sharply away from the truck. When I relived this split second and my reaction, over and over and over, in the ensuing days and weeks and months, I saw, in my head, that there had been no need; the truck was on its side of the road, and we were on ours. It was only that I hadn't seen it coming as I looked over at my father, and my reaction was an instinct born of surprise.

The land blurred, and there was a sickening spin of the car as I fought to get it under control.

'Don't brake,' my father yelled. 'Downshift. Downshift!'

I tried, but my foot, in its heavy shoe, slipped off the

clutch. The wheel whirled beneath my palms. There was the unbelievable sensation of flight, and then darkness.

I don't know how long it was before I opened my eyes. The view through the windshield was odd. I kept blinking, trying to understand what I was seeing. Finally I realised the car was on its side, my cheek against the side window.

'Dad?' I whispered, moving my head. There was an odd crunching under my face, and a dull bite in my cheek; I raised my hand and touched something unfamiliar, something embedded in my cheek. I pulled it out, feeling no more than a slight sting, and dully looked at a long shard of glass covered in blood.

'Dad,' I said again, dropping the glass and looking for him. He wasn't in the passenger seat. For a brief moment I thought perhaps he'd gone to get help, but as clarity came back I saw, with horror, that his side of the windshield was completely smashed. Blood clung to the splintered edges of the glass. I struggled to pull myself up. The side of my head hurt, but it was just a dull throb. In order to get out of the car I had to climb over the stick shift and drag my lower body across the passenger seat, fighting to open the door straight up into the sky. When I was finally able to swing it open, I pulled myself out, the uncooperative weight of my lower body similar to my earlier days of polio. I clambered out, falling the short distance from the open door to the ground. The car was half on the road and half in a shallow depression leading to a field of frosted stubble.

I pushed myself into a sitting position, peering through the wispy fog. 'Dad!' I called, my voice low and hoarse. I got up and wandered into the middle of the road. I saw a still, small dark animal ahead of me; when I came closer, it was my coat. 'Dad,' I cried, turning in a slow circle, 'where are you?'

And then I saw a mound in the ploughed field a number of yards from the car, and knew with certainty it was my father. When I reached him I kneeled beside him, saying *Dad, Dad, Dad*, and stroking his bloodied face. He lay on his back, one arm thrown over his head, but other than the wide gash on his forehead and so much blood he looked as still and calm as if sleeping. A tuft of coarse wet winter grass was caught in his collar. I pulled it out, laying my cheek against his chest. It was warm, and I felt it rise and fall, slowly.

It was only then, knowing he was alive, that I cried.

'You'll be all right, Dad. You'll be all right,' I said, over and over, weeping as the cold, damp air swirled around us.

Something woke me, and I lifted my head in a hopeful rush. But my father still lay unmoving in the hospital bed, and in the next instant I knew that what had woken me was a painful throbbing in my cheek. I reached up to touch it, and felt gauze and tape. I explored it for a few seconds, only mildly curious, and then again took my father's hand, as I had when they first allowed me to come into his room. The skin on the back of his hand was papery. Veins, thin and blue, created a tracery of webs under darkened spots. When had my father become so old?

His breathing caught for a moment, and I squeezed his hand, looking at his face. A spasm passed over his features, but in the next instant both his face and his breathing settled, and I sat back again. My mouth was dry. I lifted the metal pitcher of water from the small table beside the bed, and saw my distorted reflection: my hair hanging around my face in long tangles, my eyes pulled to an odd shape in the metal, my thick eyebrows, the white bandage on my cheek, my lips parted as if in a question.

I put the pitcher back on the table. 'Dad,' I said, quietly. 'Dad. Please.'

Please what? Wake up? Don't die? Forgive me? I took his hand again, holding it against my unhurt cheek.

'You should rest while he sleeps,' a voice said, and, dully, I looked over my shoulder. It was a man, a doctor, I assumed, from the stethoscope around his neck. I put down my father's hand and stood.

'Can you tell me anything?' I asked. 'What . . . will he be all right?'

The doctor looked at my father, then back at me. 'There were many injuries. Internal.' There was something vaguely familiar – perhaps the word was comforting – about the man's voice. 'And because of the age . . . it's . . . Miss O'Shea, yes? You must prepare yourself.'

I sat down. 'Prepare myself?'

'You would not wish to go home for a while? The man and woman who brought you and your father here – did you know them? Could you call them to take you home?'

I shook my head once. I had only a vague recollection of a car stopping on the road, of a man lifting my father into the back seat, a woman pressing a handkerchief against my cheek, putting my coat around me. 'I'll stay with him.'

The doctor was silent for a moment. 'Has someone

called your mother?' he asked. 'Or perhaps a brother, sister . . . You tell the nurse, and she will phone for you. You have family, someone—'

'There's only me,' I interrupted, my voice hoarse. 'Only me,' I repeated.

'The medication,' he said then. 'It has helped?'

I looked at my father. 'I don't know.'

'No,' he said. 'Your face. It pains a great deal?'

I reached up to touch the dressing as I had a few moments earlier. 'No. I . . . I don't remember . . .'

'It's the deep cut, Miss O'Shea. There were many small pieces of glass; I took them out and stitch it for you.'

I suddenly heard his accent, and his slightly incorrect grammar, and understood what had created this familiarity; his English was similar to my mother's. I had a recollection: the stinging smell of disinfectant, this man's face close to mine, a tugging at my flesh, which was cold, and unfeeling. 'No,' I said. 'It doesn't hurt.'

Why was he talking about my insignificant injury? It was my father he should be attending to. 'Can't you do something? Is there some surgery you can perform, something . . . something to help him?'

The doctor shook his head. His face reflected something – was it sorrow? 'I'm sorry,' he said, and it was clear that he meant it. 'Now it is only the time we wait.' He glanced at a round watch he pulled from his waistcoat pocket. 'I must go now, but I return in a few hours.'

I nodded. His expression was, in spite of his profession-alism, concerned. Perhaps even kind. And his voice . . . Again I thought of my mother, and felt more alone than I had ever felt in my life. I didn't want this man to leave; at that moment even a stranger would have been a comfort.

'Miss O'Shea. It is better for you that you sleep. It's been many hours you sit like this. And the medication for the pain – for your face – it make you tired.'

I thought of the doctor who had tended to me when I had polio, of the doctor who had come to see my mother in her last days. Those men were surely at the ends of their careers; they had appeared so old, so worn, as if they had had a lifetime of passing on sorrowful news. 'It's my fault,' I said, not sure why I felt the need to confess to this doctor. His forehead was high and intelligent, his cheeks ruddy. He couldn't have been a doctor too many years; he was surely only a little older than I. 'He told me not to drive.'

He didn't reply, but kept looking at me, his hands in the pockets of his jacket, as if waiting for me to continue.

Again I lifted my father's hand, this time pressing it against my forehead.

'I am Dr Duverger,' the man said. 'If you wish to speak to me about your father, or your face, you ask the nurse for me. Dr Duverger,' he repeated, looking at me intently.

But I was suddenly so weary, so overcome, that I simply nodded, and turned back to my father.

My father died just before sunrise, without regaining consciousness, without forgiving me. I was there, in the room with him, but at the moment of his death I was asleep.

It was a nurse who came in and discovered he was no longer breathing. She roused me with a hand on my shoulder.

'I'm sorry, Miss O'Shea,' she said, when I stared at my father, and then at her. 'There's nothing more to be done.'

I kept looking at her, as if she spoke a foreign language.

'He's gone, dear,' she said, her hand still on my shoulder. 'Come now. Come and we'll get you a cup of tea.'

I wasn't able to understand how it could have happened this way. So quietly, and so unnoticed. Didn't my father deserve more than this, from life, and from me?

'Come now,' she said again, and I rose and followed her, glancing back at my father's body.

I remember sitting in a small room with a cup of tea in my hands, and the young doctor – what had he said his name was? – speaking to me. But I couldn't understand him. I walked from the room, but the doctor followed me, putting something – a small container – into my hand. Then he draped my coat over my shoulders. I smelled my father, the scent of his tobacco, and swayed for a moment. The doctor put his hand on my wrist to steady me.

'You must put the ointment on your cheek,' he said. 'The ointment – there, in your hand. Put it on every day. And a clean bandage. Come to see me in one week. How will you go home?' he asked, and I looked from his hand on my wrist to his face. 'Who will take you to your home, Miss O'Shea?' he said. 'There is someone to take you, and to be with you now, so you are not alone?'

I wasn't thinking clearly. 'Home? I . . . I don't know. The car . . . my car . . . is it . . . where is it?' I asked, as if he would know.

'I don't know about your automobile, but I think it is better if you do not drive. We will find someone . . . It's very early . . . Where do you live, Miss O'Shea?' he asked then.

'Juniper Road,' I said.

'I will try to find someone to drive you,' he said. 'You may have to wait.'

I stood there, trying to process his words. He *was* kind. 'No,' I said, my senses returning. 'My neighbour, Mr Barlow. Mike Barlow. He'll come and get me. He'll take me home.'

'He has a telephone?'

I nodded. All I wanted to do was leave this place, with my father's lifeless body. 'Yes,' I said. Suddenly I was very cold. Shivering. 'But . . . I can't remember the number. I can't remember it,' I said, putting my hand to my mouth. 'I know it,' I said, through my shaking fingers. 'I know it, but I can't . . .'

The doctor nodded, moving his hand from my wrist to my shoulder. 'It's the shock, Miss O'Shea. Please. Sit here. Mike Barlow on Juniper? I will find this number,' he said.

I sat where he indicated, my teeth chattering, and watched his back as he left me, going to a nearby desk and speaking to a woman there. She looked at me, nodding, and then he looked back at me as well.

'Put on your coat, Miss O'Shea,' he said, his voice carrying across the small space. 'Keep yourself warm.'

CHAPTER SIX

WE DROVE THROUGH THE THIN early morning light. The sky had cleared and the rising sun shone tentatively, as if unsure of itself. Mr Barlow rolled down the window, and there was the sweet smell of the promise of spring. Suddenly my cheek throbbed so terribly that I drew in my breath and closed my eyes.

'You all right, Sidonie?' Mr Barlow asked.

I opened my eyes and looked at his stubbled face, suddenly remembering that when I was a child his gingery eyebrows had reminded me of caterpillars. They were threaded with white now, although still as thick and bristly. 'You all right?' he asked again, and I nodded, looking away from him to stare through the windshield.

And then I saw it. The beautiful Silver Ghost, overturned. There was an overwhelming sense of sadness about it. It lay as though it were a great hulking white beast, beaten and defeated, in the muddy gravel. The sun caught its side mirror, reflecting so that I was momentarily blinded. I covered my eyes with my hands.

'Your dad was a good man, Sidonie,' Mr Barlow said.

And I killed him. I killed him, I thought.

★

It was Mr Barlow who drove me back to the hospital three weeks later. He came to the door, turning his cap in his hands.

'Nora says you got a phone call. You're supposed to go back to the hospital. They say you missed your appointment.'

'My appointment? For what?' I asked, holding Cinnabar against my chest.

Mr Barlow cleared his throat. 'Most likely about your face, Sidonie,' he said, touching his own cheek.

Mr and Mrs Barlow had been good to me for the last few weeks. They had helped with the funeral arrangements and Mrs Barlow had brought me something to eat every day. Sometimes I ate it, sometimes I didn't, and sometimes I didn't remember if I'd eaten or not.

Mr Barlow had taken me to the lawyer's office in Albany, and sat with me while the lawyer explained that my father had left a simple will. He had managed to put away a small amount of money, left to me. I looked at Mr Barlow as we left. 'Is it enough for the rent?' I asked, not able, at that time, to understand what the sum meant.

'Don't worry about that, Sidonie,' he said. 'It will keep you for a little while. But . . .' He stopped. 'Don't worry about paying any rent,' he said, and I nodded. 'You'll have to open your own account, at the bank,' he added, and again, I simply nodded. Nothing made sense, those first weeks.

Occasionally I attempted to read, but couldn't concentrate; I tried to paint, but the colours were flat, my brushstrokes lifeless. I would decide to make tea, put the kettle on to boil, and then forget about it until the piercing scream made me jump, and I realised I didn't want tea after all. I would take up a pen to write down what I needed to buy when I next went to the grocery store, then stop, the pen halfway to the paper, forgetting what I had planned to write. I even wondered why Cinnabar followed me about the house for an hour one day, until I saw, with a guilty start, that her food and water dishes were empty.

The house, without my father, was so still.

When my mother died, I had mourned. The mourning was passive, and took the form of thinking of her, and weeping for her. When my mother died I still had my father. But with his absence I couldn't mourn, couldn't sit and weep. It was a different sensation; as opposed to mourning, I was grieving, and it was active. I had too much energy, but it was misplaced. I needed to keep moving, to find things to keep my hands busy.

I missed our weekend searches for hood ornaments and radiator caps. I missed hearing his whistle as he shaved each morning. I missed ironing his shirts, and seeing the pleasure on his face when he slid his arms into the fresh-smelling and lightly starched sleeves.

I went out to the shed and scrubbed the winter dust off the old Model T. I took all the hood ornaments and radiator caps from the pine cabinet and polished them over and over. I pulled my father's cleaned, pressed shirts from his wardrobe and rewashed them. When they were dry, I unpinned them from the clothes line and ironed them, the iron thudding, the steam rising to dampen my face.

But more than anything I missed talking to my father; he had been the object for my thoughts. So at any time during every day for those first weeks, that first month, I would spontaneously open my mouth to call out to him, something as insignificant as that I'd heard a mouse gnawing between the walls during the night. And then I'd remember he was gone, gone for ever, and we would never again share anything, as small as a mouse in the walls or as large as a crisis in the world.

Still, through all of this I couldn't cry. It was guilt. I couldn't let myself forget what I had done to my father. If I cried, it would be for myself, to soothe and comfort myself. I did not think I deserved any comfort.

I experienced a small epiphany one dark night, sitting on the front step and looking up at the constellations.

Beyond the faint outlines of the bare treetops across the street the cloudless ribbon of night sky was familiar. Predictable. There was only a tiny sliver of moon, a scattering of stars. I found Orion and Cassiopeia, the North Star, Ursa Major. They were always there, old friends, when the night was clear. I had studied the constellations, learning their shape and design from the pages of books over that long-ago polio year of first hopefulness, then bitterness and resentment, and finally resignation. That year there was no view of the night sky from my bed-room window, and the stars were only paper constellations then.

And now the thought came to me that I lived much of my life through the pages of books as well. That perhaps I, too, was only a paper figure. A cut-out, a silhouette. Flat.

I always thought I knew the shape of my life. Of course I thought I knew *about* life, thought I knew all I needed — or wanted — to know. And yet, like the opening left when a burning star falls from its perch, now an unexpected hole was left in what was once a solid curtain of understanding.

What had I planned for myself once I was alone? Even though my father's death had come too early, it was, after all, inevitable. What future had I seen for myself after he was gone and no longer needed me to care for him?

Had I thought that my quiet, safe life was like a thread, running through me and attaching me to the earth? That I would continue on with my routines – caring for the house and garden and painting botanical images, reading on the dark winter nights when the nor'easters blew in, wandering through the countryside in the summer – as surely and predictably as the sun rose and set each day? That this thread would remain sturdy, and invincible?

Now I knew the thread had been abruptly broken, and a huge, dark longing came over me. Sitting under the cold stars, I understood that it was death that made me recognise life, and the existence, or perhaps the non-existence, of my own being. I suddenly realised what my father had tried to tell me, years earlier, about going out into the world. I saw that my own life was so small – no, tiny; as minute as one of the billions of stars that created the hazy band of the Milky Way. Or perhaps it was presumptuous to even view my life as the most minuscule of stars; maybe it was more appropriate to think of it as one of the specks of dust that also littered that celestial sphere.

I thought again of my father's wishes for me, that I'd marry and have my own family.

Although he had long ago given up on the notion of me having a job, he'd started a tiresome rant not too long after my mother had died, telling me that there was a connection between man and woman that couldn't be duplicated in friendship or in familial ties. That only when that connection was broken by death did you understand its strength. 'I want you to know it, Sidonie,' he'd said, too many times for me to remember. And each time I felt a combination of anger and embarrassment; anger towards him for badgering me, and embarrassment within myself for not being able to tell him that he was blind to the fact that no man would ever want to marry me.

As I sat on the steps, remembering his words, the lights in the Barlows' house went out, and suddenly I remembered Mr Barlow saying not to worry about the rent as we left the lawyer's office. I went inside and took the letter I'd brought home that day out of the drawer in the sideboard. I stared at the amount of the inheritance, understanding, only then, how small it was. I thought about what I paid for weekly groceries. The coal for the furnace over the winter. My painting supplies. There was money for little else. And even with Mr and Mrs Barlow's generosity of living in the house without paying rent, what would I do in a few years, when there was nothing left?

And then I realised that although yes, my father had wanted me to find happiness, he'd also worried about what I would do when he was gone. How I would live. He had wanted to know I would be looked after, as it appeared I hadn't done anything to learn to look after myself.

A quiet panic filled me. I climbed into bed, still in my coat, cradling Cinnabar. But even when she grew restless and too hot under the coverlet, struggling to free herself, I clung to her as though she was a lifeline to shore, and I was adrift in a small boat.

It was four days later that Mr Barlow came to the door to take me back to the hospital.

He was still standing there, his cap in his hands. 'Sidonie?' he said, and I jumped, lost in thought.

'Oh. Yes, sorry. When am I supposed to go to the hospital?'

He shrugged. 'Nora didn't say. Just that you missed your appointment and you should go. I can take you today.'

I set down Cinnabar – she was thirteen years old and heavy now – and pulled my coat from its hook behind the door. As we walked out into the spring sunshine, I put my hands in my pockets, and felt something in the left one. It was a small vial and a folded paper. I had worn my coat since the accident – to the funeral, to church, to the lawyer's office, when I sat on the porch, and when I walked to the store – but hadn't discovered these things before. Had I fingered them without even the curiosity to pull them out and look at them, or had I not put my hands into my pockets?

The vial was the ointment the doctor had given me the day my father died, and the paper gave instructions to use it three times a day. It could be renewed if more was needed. There was also a date for me to return to see the doctor. It was for two weeks earlier. On the top of the paper was a small letterhead: *Dr E. Duverger, MD.*

We drove in silence, and when I got out, Mr Barlow touched my arm.

'I'll wait for you,' he said.

I nodded, and went up the steps of the hospital. But at the door I stopped, thinking of the night my father died, and the next morning, coming out into the weak early light to Mr Barlow's truck. A wave of nausea ran through me. I couldn't go through those doors again; I turned away and started down the steps. But Mr Barlow was already parking the truck. I could see the back of his head through the window.

I couldn't let him see me so weak, couldn't go back to him and ask that he take me home, admit to him that I was afraid to go into the hospital.

I took a deep breath and turned, going through the door. My stomach churned, and I looked for a Ladies', but didn't see one. I gave my name at the front desk and was shown into a small room, and after a short wait the doctor came in. Dr Duverger. I remembered his ruddy cheeks. His hair was very dark, as were his eyes. Like mine.

'Good day, Miss O'Shea,' he said, smiling, a very slight smile, and studying me. In the next instant the smile fled, and a line appeared between his brows. 'I phone to your friend – the number you give me for your ride home – because I look at my active patient records, and see that you have not return to have the stitches remove,' he said.

He was standing over me, and I was looking up at him. I was still trying to quell the rolling pain in my abdomen. 'You should have come back when it was the time. Miss O'Shea – did you not see what was happen?'

'Happen?' I echoed, rather faintly. 'What do you mean?'

'The flesh grow over the stitches, and the wound, it turns . . .' He said something in French just under his

87

breath, his voice too low for me to hear the words. Then he said, in English, 'Keloid. It become keloidal.'

I lifted my shoulders a fraction. 'What's that?'

'The tissue – it grows too fast. Look,' he said, pulling a round mirror from his desk. He held it so I could see my own face, and his fingers running up and down the red scar. 'This mound is the formation of fibrous scar tissue. Your own tissue was too overactive, growing so quick. Too fast. We could have stop it. Did you not feel the itch, the pull?'

I shook my head. 'It doesn't matter.'

He stared at me, and something in his expression suddenly shamed me. I put my hand over my cheek. It was hot. 'My father . . . the funeral and . . . and everything. I . . . I forgot. Or . . . I don't know,' I finally said, not wanting to admit my altered state these last weeks since my father's death.

The doctor's face softened, and he sat down in a chair across from me. 'I understand. It is the difficult time. I have lose my own parents,' he said, and with those words, from this man I didn't know, my eyes burned. I hadn't been able to cry at the funeral, or afterwards, when neighbours from the street and my father's old friends had come to the house, the women hugging me and the men pressing my hand or patting my shoulder.

I had stayed strong for the last three weeks. I had stayed strong as I washed the Model T and polished the hood ornaments, as I ironed my father's shirts and wetted his shaving cream with the brush and breathed in the lather, as I put his pipe between my lips and tasted the faint bitterness of tobacco, as I lay on his bed and saw one silver hair on his pillow. I had stayed strong, telling myself I had no right to cry for my own pig-headedness, for my own fatal error in judgement.

So what power did this man have, to make me feel, so unexpectedly, that I wanted to lean my head against his chest and weep? That I wanted him to put his arms around me? I swallowed and blinked, and was relieved that my eyes remained dry.

'You are all right, Miss O'Shea?' he asked. 'I see . . . I should tell you to come another time, perhaps. But already it is too long for your face. Let me look again.' I lifted my chin, and again he leaned closer to me, his fingers gently exploring my cheek. I smelled disinfectant and perhaps, underneath, the tiniest whiff of tobacco. Again I thought of my father. The doctor's fingers were firm, and yet gentle.

'You're French,' I added, and then immediately felt foolish. I had no idea why I made that obvious proclamation.

But he just sat back in the chair, putting on a pair of spectacles and looking at my file. '*Oui*,' he said, reading.

'My mother was French. Not from France. From Canada.'

'*Je sais*,' he murmured, still reading.

'You know?' I asked, surprised.

He put the folder on the desk and took off his spectacles. This time he smiled again, that small, slightly unsure smile. 'Not about your mother. But I hear you pray in the French of this country. And singing. I hear the French song.'

'Singing?' I asked, surprised a second time.

'*Dodo, l'enfant, do*. The night . . . when your father died.

When I pass the door I hear you sing this . . . what do you call the night song for children?'

'Lullaby,' I said.

'Yes. My mother also sing this lullaby to me. Very traditional,' he said, his smile unselfconscious, warm and sincere. In the next instant it faded. 'Miss O'Shea. You wish your face to be better?' He picked up the small hand mirror and extended it to me for the second time.

I took it, and looked at myself. The scar was angry and red, raised and lumpy, and ran vertically from my cheek-bone all the way to my jaw. I was startled at its ugliness. How had I not seen it like this before? Surely I had looked at myself in the mirror, when I carefully washed my face, avoiding the painful wound, or when I brushed my hair and twisted it up into its usual knot at the back of my head.

Again Dr Duverger touched the scar lightly, with the tip of his index finger, but I could feel nothing. 'If I do the very small surgery, I can correct it. There will be new stitching, but it will leave a less noticeable scar. Finer, and more flat. Do you wish to have this done?'

When I didn't immediately speak, Dr Duverger said, 'Miss O'Shea?' and I looked from my own reflection to him.

'It is not an expensive procedure.'

I put down the mirror.

'If this is the reason for your hesitation.'

I stared at him. 'No.'

It was obvious that my reaction puzzled him. I looked down at my handbag, still in my lap, and fiddled with the straps.

'I don't understand. What stops you, then? Is it you are

90

afraid of the operation? But there is no need. It is straight-forward, and there will be no complicat—' He stopped, and, still holding my handbag, I looked up at him. 'Perhaps you would choose another doctor?' His expression had closed.

He couldn't see the great guilt I carried. It was so heavy. And ugly, like the scar.

'I can recommend one of my colleagues. Even to have a second opinion. This is natural, Miss O'Shea.'

I didn't want to be here. The antiseptic smell of the hospital, the sounds of the nurses' rubber shoes on the floors, the occasional quiet cry from behind a door . . . it was too real. I never wanted to come here again. I just wanted to go home, and stay within the security of my own walls.

'I'm not afraid,' I said. My voice was a little too loud, my words a little too fast. Did he hear it, know that I was lying? I sensed he was very astute. 'I just don't know if it's worth it – the time and energy – to bother with. It doesn't matter to me, and it surely doesn't matter to anyone else. I have no vanity, I can assure you, Dr Duverger.'

His eyebrows rose. 'You don't feel you are worth it, Miss O'Shea?' He waited for an answer, but I was silent until he eventually shrugged. 'If this is the case, of course it's your right.' He stood. 'I'm only sorry you care so little for yourself. To carry this mark for ever is not necessary.'

He left then, and I stayed where I was. After some time I lifted the hand mirror and again studied my reflection. Eventually I put the mirror back on the desk, and went outside to Mr Barlow's truck.

There was no way to explain to the doctor that while

yes, part of the reason I didn't want the minor surgery was because I really was afraid – not of pain, but of the horrible memories and feelings the hospital brought back – more importantly, the scar would be my reminder. A reminder of the kind of person I was, and what my stubbornness had wrought. It *was* necessary to carry it.

CHAPTER SEVEN

I SPENT A WEEK IN Tangier.

It was quite clear that word travelled quickly throughout the twisting alleys and bustling souks, for apart from Elizabeth Pandy, I had mentioned only to Omar – the boy who had carried my bags to my room my first day in Tangier – that I was looking for someone with a car to take me to Rabat. But almost immediately a seemingly endless array of men came to the front door of the Hotel Continental. They were stopped by the doorman, and not allowed inside the grand lobby. They waited until I was called and came to meet them.

Most of them immediately proved unsuitable, for they didn't possess a car. They assumed I would provide it, but I explained, either in French, or through Arab translation provided by Omar, that I did not wish to find a car and attempt to purchase it.

I needed a driver *and* a car, I stressed over and over.

During those first days I learned a great deal about the North African attribute of persuasion. Some said they had a cousin with a car; others said they would find me a car. One arrived who said he didn't yet know how to drive, but surely, once he was actually in a car, he would figure it out.

A few did own a vehicle, or had at least borrowed it. But when they showed me the automobile, always with considerable pride, I politely and firmly thanked them but told them it would not work out.

Some of the cars were so rusted they had little floor left; most had no doors or roof. The tyres on all of them were dangerously flat. One enterprising fellow had hitched two donkeys to the front of a car with no engine.

The early summer days were warm and fragrant, the scent of orange blossom everywhere. But I was overcome with frustration and anxiousness. Each day I didn't leave for Marrakesh was another day wasted, and when I couldn't bear to sit in my room or the lobby for another minute, I distracted myself by going to Le Grand Socco – the Large Square. I was told by the concierge that while it was safe for me to walk about the main streets during the daylight hours, I would be better off not to go into the souks on my own, and also to avoid leaving the hotel after nightfall. He also warned me to stay away from Le Petit Socco, which, I deduced from his frown and sniff of disapproval, speaking of the bad women there, was a centre of prostitution or at least immoral business.

Le Grand Socco swarmed with people in the bright sunlight – mainly Europeans, Americans and British, for this was where foreigners to Tangier spent their time. Dressed in fine clothing, they sat under crisp awnings or on café terraces, eating and drinking deep green absinthe or vermilion wine from small glasses. The women smoked cigarettes or thin dark cheroots in decorated holders, and the men had their cigars or sucked the mouthpiece of a winding tube leading from a huge bubbling container that sat on the floor – *sheeshas*, they were called. Many of them also smoked *kif*, with its distinctive sweet grassy odour and form of intoxication that gave its smokers a sleepy, pleased expression. In the squares the shops had signs announcing their wares in English, French and Spanish, and the visitors shopped for overpriced items to take home. There was the atmosphere of a holiday, and also, as Elizabeth had spoken of, a certain laissez-faire attitude amongst these men and women who had come to Tangier for their own reasons: a sense of everything and anything being acceptable. I saw that some of the women wore clothes far more daring than I had ever witnessed, and sometimes, inadvertently, I saw these same women leaning against men – or other women – in doorways. I always looked away, and yet I was drawn to watch as they murmured and touched each other so openly in public places. And more than once I witnessed young men walking about holding hands, also stopping to kiss in the open streets.

This was what I saw. I could only imagine what took place in the hotel rooms and the back rooms of the cafés. I wondered what the people of Tangier thought of these bold foreigners. It was clear the Tangerines preferred to stay in the narrow, darkened souks leading off the bright and busy squares; this was where the real life of Tangier throbbed, for the souks were the heart of Arab life. More than once I wondered at their chaotic thrum, wanting to venture in even for a few steps, and yet, mindful of the concierge's warning, and my own insecurity in this very new world, I stayed where I was safe.

I also spent a great deal of time on the roof of the

Continental. With the calls from the minarets echoing around me, I looked at the towering Rif mountains, the setting sun turning them the same blood red every evening. Somewhere, far beyond the mountains and into the heart of the country, was Marrakesh.

And in Marrakesh was Etienne.

I grew ever more impatient and nervous. I had to get there.

Although I regularly saw Elizabeth Pandy and Marcus and other Americans, I tried to avoid them. I found their constant drinking and loud voices and laughter exhausting. One afternoon I sat in the empty lounge, partly hidden by a high banquette, sipping a mineral water as I attempted to understand a rough map of Morocco I had purchased in Le Grand Socco. I finished my water and folded the map, but before I had a chance to stand I heard Elizabeth and her crowd enter. They had come from Rue de la Plage, where Elizabeth and one of the other women had braved the wild Atlantic waves and plunged into the frigid water.

'Marvellously refreshing,' Elizabeth said, her voice carrying. I was desperate to leave, but didn't want to be seen and to then have to stop and talk to them. I reopened the map, again studying it and hoping they would have one drink and leave. I tried to ignore them, but found it difficult to concentrate, and finally sat back, idly listening to their uninteresting chatter and gossip. But I stiffened as I heard my name.

'I wonder if she's found a way to get to Marrakesh yet,' Marcus said. 'She's determined, it appears, if nothing else. After all, she even has some sort of trouble walking.'

'Quite peculiar, and rather repressed, wouldn't you say? Not unattractive, in spite of the scar and her outdated clothes and heavens, those shoes, but such a plaintive expression,' Elizabeth said. 'One doesn't like to be nosy, but I would like to find out. Such a peculiar young woman,' she repeated. 'I really can't think what she imagines she's doing, traipsing off to Marrakesh.'

'Oh, it's a man she's after. There's no other reason, is there? And it appears she views herself as quite the tragic heroine of her own story, whatever it may be,' another woman said, and there was a snideness to her voice that made a wave of heat wash over me.

Was that how they viewed me? A peculiar, pitiful figure?

I knew that in my neighbourhood in Albany I was thought of as unconventional. Certainly everyone knew me to be a woman who kept to herself, who sometimes tramped in the barrens and dunes, and chose to live her life caring for her father rather than marry. Although not traditional, I was not, at least in my mind, odd enough to be seen as something to be discussed so negatively by others.

I wanted to go back to my room. I rose in a half-crouch, seeing, over the banquette, Elizabeth now standing and taking her bag. I sat down again, waiting for her to leave. If she left, the others would soon follow, and I could escape.

But at that instant Elizabeth walked around the banquette, and stopped when she saw me.

'Well, hello, Sidonie,' she said, and my cheeks flushed. 'What are you doing sitting here by yourself? I'm off to the Ladies'. Actually we were just discussing you.'

'Really?' I said, unable to look up at her.

'Go over and join the others. I'll be back in a moment,' she said.

'No. Thank you, but I'm . . . I must go to my room.' I stood.

She shrugged. 'As you wish,' she said, and then added, 'Oh, have you managed to find a car and driver yet?'

I shook my head.

'I was speaking to a British fellow at the Red Palm Café today. He told me he had just been driven up from Casablanca, and the fellow is on his way back down south tomorrow.' She opened her bag and dug around in it, finally pulling out a crumpled paper and handing it to me. 'Here's his name. Ask one of the boys to locate him; he's staying somewhere in the medina. But if you do find him, hire him for all the way to Marrakesh. From what I've heard, you could end up waiting days for a train in Rabat. There's little sense of punctuality among the Africans.'

Now I didn't know how to react. In spite of her brashness and lack of sensitivity, Elizabeth Pandy had just provided what I had been waiting for. I took the paper and unfolded it. *Mustapha. Tall. Red vest, yellow Citroën*, was scrawled on it.

'Thank you, Elizabeth,' I said, tentatively.

'We all must stick together, mustn't we?' she said, lifting her hand in a kind of salute.

I nodded and smiled, and then left the lounge, stopping to talk to Omar on my way through the lobby. Finally something was happening.

★

Mustapha presented himself to me on the veranda the following morning. I was relieved that he could speak a smattering of French. He was, as the note had described, tall, and wearing a decidedly filthy red vest over an equally dirty, once white robe that was frayed at the hem and hung over the pointed toes of his woven sandals. A very short man, his djellaba hood down and a small round white hat on the crown on his head, stood beside him. He stared at me with one brown eye, the other a disturbing empty socket, slightly puckered.

Mustapha gestured at two other men at the bottom of the steps. They both had their djellaba hoods pulled forward, and I couldn't get a good look at their faces. He spoke to Omar, and Omar thought for a moment, frowning, then brightened.

'Ah. Yes. He brings friends to speak for his purity,' Omar said.

'His purity?'

'Yes. He is pure man.'

I realised then that Omar was trying to tell me that Mustapha had brought references. I glanced at the men, but they turned their backs to me.

'Not to talk to woman,' Omar said, and went down the steps. As he spoke to the men, Mustapha clapped his hand on the shorter man's shoulder. A puff of dust rose from his djellaba.

'*Mon cousin*, madame,' he explained. 'Aziz. He go always with me.'

I nodded at both men. There was no point in correcting Mustapha's use of the title madame. All Arab men referred to non-African women in that way.

I didn't want to get my hopes up; I had seen too many men like Mustapha and Aziz. Still, they did come with a form of reference, from the British man Elizabeth had spoken of. I smiled at Mustapha, although his expression didn't change. 'May I see the car, Mustapha?' I asked, hoping, beyond hope, that it would not be like those I'd seen so far.

'Oh yes, madame, very fine auto. Very fine.' His chest seemed to expand under the red vest as he spoke. 'I very fine driver. Very fine. You ask. Everybody say Mustapha very fine. Auto very fine.'

'I'm sure it's . . . fine,' I said, as obviously this was a word beloved by Mustapha. 'But please. I must see it first.'

'What price madame pay?'

'I need to go all the way to Marrakesh, not just Casablanca. And first I must look at the auto, Mustapha.' I spoke softly, smiling at him, knowing, from this one week in North Africa, that he would have difficulty dealing with a woman giving him instructions. 'May I look at your auto?'

He waved his arm down the street, pointing at a lemon-yellow Citroën. It was covered in dust, its wheels caked with mud. Even from the short distance it appeared that the car had been submerged in water for an indefinite length of time, and then brought to the surface. It was rusted and dented, its ragtop torn in spots, but compared to the others I'd been offered, it was more promising. I followed Mustapha to it and peered inside. It was filthy, littered with scraps of rotting food. An ancient, musty red and black striped djellaba was draped over the passenger seat. There was a particularly bad odour – worse than the djellaba – as I leaned in the open window. It was a three-seater; the third seat was in the rear in the middle. I remembered seeing this kind of car in one of my father's automobile magazines. What was it called, with this strange third seat, forcing the passenger to put his feet between the two front seats?

On the floor beside that middle back seat was a stacked pile of goatskins. Shreds of dried flesh still clung to the undersides, and the pile was alive with flies.

It was a Trèfle, this Citroën. A Cloverleaf, I suddenly remembered.

It would do. This car would do. I didn't want to appear overanxious, or too excited.

Aziz came up beside me. 'What you are thinking, madame? It suits you?' he asked, speaking for the first time. His voice was surprisingly deep for such a small man; his French was better than Mustapha's.

'I have two large cases.' I glanced in at the skins again. 'Will there be enough room?'

'We make room, madame,' Aziz said, and spoke in Arabic to Mustapha.

'Is very fine car, *oui*, madame?' Mustapha repeated.

'Yes, Mustapha. Yes. I would like you to drive me. You will drive me, all the way to Marrakesh?'

'*Inshallah*,' Mustapha said, the phrase – God willing – already familiar to me. I noticed the North Africans said it about every single thing, from the weather to food to their own health. God willing, I thought to myself, nodding at Mustapha. And then the necessary game of haggling over the price began.

★

101

We set out the next morning, Aziz crammed in the back, one of my cases on either side of him. I don't know why Mustapha wouldn't put them in the trunk; he had simply shaken his head when I'd suggested it with gestures, and instead had unceremoniously shoved them into the back seat. Although the car was far from clean, he had removed all the rotting food, and had dutifully strapped the skins to the roof with long strips of rag.

Before we drove away, Mustapha and Aziz had walked around the car, reverently touching it and murmuring.

'This auto already has *baraka*,' Aziz said. 'It has made many journeys. No trouble. It has much *baraka*.'

'*Baraka?* What is that?' I asked.

'Blessing. It is fine auto, very fine,' Mustapha said. I was beginning to think this was the extent of his French vocabulary. 'And I fine driver.'

'Oh yes, madame,' Aziz said. 'The very best. It is difficult, very difficult, to drive an auto, madame. Very difficult for the man, impossible for the lady.' He stood straighter, but was still shorter than me.

I looked at the steering wheel, knowing what it would feel like beneath my hands.

And then I clenched my fingers into fists, burying them in the sides of my skirt. I had vowed never to put my hands on the steering wheel of a car again.

CHAPTER EIGHT

As I LEFT TANGIER WITH Mustapha and Aziz, the rising sun turning the white buildings various shades of pink and red, I let out a long, shaky breath. I was on my way to Marrakesh. I had come this far.

You have come this far, I told myself, looking through the scratched and spattered windshield. *You have done this*. I let a sensation of relief wash over me, but in almost the next instant I asked myself if I really knew what I was doing, setting out in a car in a foreign land with two men about whom I knew nothing more than that they had an automobile and could drive it. I was trusting my life to unknown men based on a scribbled note handed to Elizabeth Pandy by a stranger.

Nobody could identify who I was with – apart from Omar – and even though Elizabeth and her friends were aware I was going to Marrakesh, I hadn't seen them as my bags were brought down and I settled my bill, and so hadn't told her I was actually leaving.

And yet . . . and yet . . . somehow I had a perhaps misguided belief that it would be all right. That *I* would be all right, and would uncover what I needed to find. Or maybe it was more a sense of faith – perhaps a new, unexpected faith in myself. Hadn't I crossed the Atlantic, coped with Marseilles, survived the Strait of Gibraltar in a levanter, and managed to hire these men to transport me to my final destination? I, who had never left Albany, who had never even played with the possibility of a life anywhere but familiar. Anywhere but safe.

The men spoke to each other in Arabic as we drove off, and I wished I could understand what they were saying. Both men wore the same clothing as the day before, although instead of the round white cap, a red felt fez was now perched on Aziz's shaved head. He had taken off his sandals and put his bare feet in the space between Mustapha and me. I glanced at his toes and thought of Etienne's feet: long and narrow, the skin on the top surprisingly soft.

As we left the city on the bumpy macadam road built by the French, the striking peaks of the Rif mountains were on our left, while the blue Atlantic sparkled along the right. The breeze from the sea was fresh and cheering, and because of the early hour, the sky had a pearly haze. There were faint outlines of gulls skimming low over the water, fishing for their breakfast.

There were few other automobiles on the road, although occasionally one passed, so close on the narrow road that I tensed, waiting for the sides of the cars to scrape. More often there were caravans of dromedaries, small, one-humped camels, led by draped figures. The beasts were loaded with goods, or the form of a woman, covered from head to toe apart from a slit for the eyes, balanced on top. Often a child peeped through the folds of the women's robes. Even though we drove at a slow pace, I wished to stop and get out and stare at these passing caravans. I knew it was an impossibility, and my actions would surely be viewed as a foreigner's rudeness, and yet it was as though my eyes ached to see more than what I was allowed.

As in Tangier, I hadn't expected to be so moved by these new sensations. Or perhaps, when I left Albany, I hadn't thought of what I would see, and how it would affect me. My only thoughts were of Etienne.

The road turned and weaved, and we would lose sight of the ocean for a number of miles, and then suddenly, over the top of a dune or at an estuary, it would spread out before us again. This region of Morocco appeared to be a paradise of sea, with long stretches of sandy beach punctuated by sudden groves of olive trees or flat agrarian land. We passed many tiny villages, each one walled, each with the spire of a minaret rising above its parapets.

When we finally stopped, a few hours outside of Tangier, and stepped out of the car, the air had changed. It was thick, almost milky, the sun's rays searing and yet somehow filtered through the air that reminded me of my home's winter fog – but this was, in essence, a hot fog. I stretched, standing outside the car, and the men went to a grove of palmetto palms off the road, the wind from the sea ruffling the fronds with a soft metallic sound. Curious, I watched them, but as they turned their backs to the car, I quickly looked away, realising what they were doing. This had also been a concern for me for the last hour, although it was too embarrassing to speak of with these strange men. But when Mustapha and Aziz sauntered back to the car, Aziz pointed at the palms and said 'Allez, madame, allez,' and I did as he said, going behind a thick cluster of the trees, hoping there was enough privacy to ensure my dignity.

I felt acutely uncomfortable returning to the car, wondering how I would face them, but Mustapha and Aziz were leaning against the car with arms crossed, talking and occasionally gesturing down the road. It was my own American sense of modesty that was distressing me in this wild land; the men were completely unconcerned.

Just before I got back into the car I saw, silhouetted against the mountains, the line of a moving frieze, dark against the lighter vegetation. It was another caravan, but this one of donkeys or horses with bulging packs and the tiny forms of children running alongside.

Where were these people moving from, or to? I tried to imagine a life of endless movement and change. Mine, until so recently, had been one of stillness.

When we again stopped, this time on the outskirts of a village Aziz identified as Larache, I opened my door.

But Aziz shook his head. 'No lady go,' he said. 'Bad for lady.' He gestured in a circle in front of his own face, and I knew he meant that it wouldn't be proper for me to go in to the town with my face exposed. 'Stay in car,' he said. 'And look children do not take skins.' He pointed to the roof of the car. 'Mustapha and I go for food. Come back soon.'

I had to content myself with looking at what I could see through the open gates of the walls surrounding the town. The buildings were all painted a brilliant blue, with red-tiled arced roofs, giving the small town the rather charming look of a Spanish mountain village. Donkeys were tethered outside the walls, standing in the shade with their heads down. As I sat there, little boys, the oldest no more than eight or nine, slowly gathered at the open gates, and then, as if daring each other, left the safety of the walls and came closer and closer. They were dressed in ragged robes, their heads shaved and feet bare. Eventually they clustered around the car, arms touching, silently staring in at me, frankly studying my face. I thought of all the little boys who had clustered around the Silver Ghost on the streets of Albany, curious and admiring. Perhaps little boys were the same everywhere, I reasoned, with the same curiosity for what they hadn't seen before, the same wonder, the same tiny acts of bravery.

Maybe I was the first white woman these children had seen.

I smiled at them, but they didn't lose their serious gaze. Finally an older boy took one step closer to the car, unexpectedly reaching in and touching my shoulder with his forefinger. Before I could react, he darted back as if he'd been burned, his finger still extended, grinning proudly at the others. They all looked at him with a combination of awe and surprise, and took a step back. Did I look so strange, then? I put one hand out through the window, palm up, smiling again to encourage them to come closer, to show them that they didn't have to fear me, but there was a sudden shout, and the boys scattered, throwing up dust.

It was Mustapha and Aziz, coming back to the car. 'The boys are bad?' Aziz asked, looking at the small crowd as they raced back through the gates, and I shook my head.

'No, they're not bad. Just . . . boys,' I said. 'Just boys,' I repeated, realising how true it was. And wishing I could see their sisters and their mothers. Their fathers. I wanted to see them within their walls.

I took the thick round of aromatic bread and a waxy paper of soft white cheese, the sticky figs in a paper cone and the cashews Aziz handed me. I wasn't hungry, but ate it all, licking the last bits of cheese and fig from my fingers, keeping the cashews in my lap and nibbling on them as we drove on.

I needed to stay strong, and to keep my wits about me. I needed to be ready for Marrakesh, and for finding Etienne.

We continued along the road, moving a little further inland at times, so that I could no longer see or smell the sea. There was sometimes a cluster of mature trees I didn't recognise, and I asked Mustapha what they were. He pointed at the few cashews still in my skirt.

My back ached from sitting so long and continually bumping along the rough road. I tried not to think about the evening: where would we stop? Where would I sleep? I was covered in dust; would I be able to bathe? If I hadn't been allowed to go into Larache because of my uncovered face, how would I be accepted in other places? I again thought of the wide eyes of the boys studying me through the open car window, and felt a sudden thud of loneliness. Of being a stranger.

It had been different in Tangier; it was a city welcoming those from abroad, a city filled with all manner of peoples: Africans and Spaniards, French and German and American and British and many more with language and clothing I wasn't able to classify. I thought of Elizabeth Pandy calling it mongrel, filled with diverse mixtures of humanity.

But I had left Tangier, and it was rapidly appearing that in the middle of Morocco I would not just be another woman from the Western world. Here I was an anomaly, an outsider, one who might easily offend or repel.

How would I be treated in Marrakesh? My hurried planning for this voyage had been, I realised as we drove along the dusty road, one of singular notion and narrow vision – of finding Etienne.

I wanted him now. I wanted to feel safe. I wanted to feel I belonged with someone, that I wasn't alone. I wanted to once again feel the way I had with Etienne.

As I shifted, turning my shoulders and stretching my neck, there was a subtly different smell to the air. I felt I should know what it was. The terrain gradually changed, the mountains no longer visible. We drove past a thick forest. The bark of the trees was stripped to a height taller than arm's reach, leaving the bottom of the trunk brown and smooth, while the remaining bark above was whitish and lumpy.

'What are they?' I asked Aziz, gesturing at the trees, and he said, 'Cork. The forest of Mamora,' and I realised then what I'd been smelling. We drove up through the trees, on to a rise, and ahead lay yellow land and the jumbled outline of a city, and beyond that, the misty blue line of the Atlantic again.

'We come city Sale, and river – Boug-Regreg,' Aziz said. He leaned forward to see more clearly, resting his arms on the backs of the seats. 'And on different side of river, Rabat,' he added. 'Sale and Rabat like . . .' he touched Mustapha's shoulder, 'cousins. Or the brothers.'

As we drew closer to the city, I recognised fig and olive trees. Sale, also a white city like Tangier, was walled, terraced, and spiky with minarets. In the distance, south, was another city, this one with the same walled appearance and silhouette against the early evening sky, although its buildings were all a tawny colour: Rabat.

'We take you to house, you eat and sleep,' Aziz said.

House? Did he mean a hotel?

'And how much further is Marrakesh from Sale?' I asked him.

'Tomorrow we come take you, drive past Casablanca, stay one night at Settat. Next day, Marrakesh. *Inshallah*,' he finished.

'You come take me? What do you mean? You aren't staying in the house?' I felt even more alone now, frightened at the idea of the only two people I knew leaving me in an unknown place.

He shook his head. 'Oh no, madame.'

We drove through the massive arched gates into the city, past a market shaded by trees, where I saw rough white wool hanging from ancient scales on tripods. In the next souk were stalls rich with melons and figs and olives, with bright red and green peppers and purple onions and the sizzle and smells of cooking meat. In front of the stalls, covered women argued with the vendors, shrieking, I could only reason, about the thievery of their prices. Surely it was part of the game of the Moroccan culture, for the women did indeed buy the goods, and the sellers, although shaking their heads in a parody of anger and disappointment, handed over the purchases. I looked down narrow alleys, seeing tiny alcoves where young boys hunched, weaving fine matting and baskets, or portly merchants chatted with each other as their goods swung over their heads from hooks.

I was leaning out the window, and as I stared at one of the merchants, he looked back at me with an expression of animosity, frowning, and then his lips pursed and he spat a glistening globule towards the car. I immediately pulled my head in, sitting as far back as I could so the line of the car hid my profile. I was again filled with unease. Even though Sale was a good-sized city, I didn't see any foreigners – men or women. Nor did I see anything that looked vaguely like a hotel.

As I was worrying about this, Mustapha stopped in front of a splintered, locked gate, and Aziz got out, gesturing for me to come as well. He carried my bags to the gate, putting one of them down to pound on the wood with the palm of his hand. If it was a hotel, it was unlike any I had ever seen.

Through a small grilled opening came a feminine murmur, and Aziz spoke into the metal lattice. There was another answering murmur, and the gate was opened by a woman in black, her face covered but for her eyes, which were downcast. 'You go inside,' Aziz said, and I did as he said. He followed me into the tiled courtyard, bringing my bags. Unlike the shabby, unpainted door, the courtyard was lovely, filled with beds of roses and orange trees.

'Woman is Lalla Huma,' Aziz said, setting my bags on the tiled floor. 'She give you food, you sleep, give her only one franc,' and then he turned to leave.

'What time will you be back for me?' I called. I don't know what I had expected, but I was filled with a new surge of fear at being left here, alone, with the silent woman.

'Starting time, madame,' he said, and uttered one sentence to the woman. She picked up my cases – she was smaller than I but lifted them with apparent ease – and climbed a set of stairs that ran up one of the outside walls of the building.

As the gate shut with a clang I stood alone in the court-yard. Then I hurried to follow the woman up the stairs, to a tiny room on the second floor of the house, the one window with an elaborately decorated wooden grille overlooking the street. There was nothing in the room but a hard pallet on the floor, with a thick woven blanket folded neatly in the middle. At the foot of the bed was a bowl covered with a wooden lid, which I thought must be a chamber pot. There was a candle in a little decorated jar on the windowsill; beside it a box of wooden matches.

I had barely time to wonder what I would do – how I would communicate with Lalla Huma – when she left for a few moments and then returned with a large ceramic bowl of steaming water and a long strip of clean cloth. As soon as she left again, I took off my shoes and stockings and began unbuttoning my dress to wash, but stopped, going to the door to lock it. There was no lock.

I washed hurriedly, dressing again, as I had no idea what was expected. In a short time Lalla Huma again opened the door and entered, this time carrying a tray with an earthenware plate of unidentifiable shredded meat and long fingers of cooked carrot and a pot of mint tea. The pot was made from some kind of bone.

She took the bowl of water and the damp cloth and left.

I never saw her face, and she never lifted her eyes from the floor as she did these things.

I ate and drank, my eyes heavy, and then put on my nightdress and lay on the narrow pallet, pulling the heavy blanket over me. The street outside was quiet, although as darkness fell I heard the call from the minarets: *Allah Akbar* – God is Great. I had, since I'd arrived in North Africa, become accustomed to the calls, which came five times a day.

The sound, so familiar now, only increased my loneliness. 'Etienne,' I whispered into the darkness.

I was awakened at dawn by the first call to prayer, and rose, glancing through the wooden grille. Parked below, in the still street, was the dusty Citroën, and outside it, their foreheads pressed to the ground, were Mustapha and Aziz. I quickly dressed and, without waiting for the mint tea offered by Lalla Huma, who appeared silently out of a door when she heard my feet on the tiled steps, hurried out to the car. Mustapha and Aziz were back inside, but were asleep, snoring in tandem. I thought perhaps I'd been mistaken. Maybe it hadn't been them I'd seen praying. Mustapha was on his back with his head under the steering wheel and his feet sticking out the opposite window, the red and black striped djellaba over him. Aziz was turned sideways in the single back seat, his arms wrapped around himself and his legs doubled up against his stomach. There was an assortment of sacks and bags on the floor; perhaps food for the rest of the journey. When they had left me at Lalla Huma's I hadn't considered where they would spend the night, but now wondered if they'd slept in the car.

I rapped on the roof of the car – the skins were gone – and Mustapha raised his head with a start, banging it on the steering wheel. '*Non, non*, madame,' he said, grimacing, rubbing his head, and Aziz mumbled, 'Too early for start time.' Both men settled back, and I returned to the house and had my tea, along with the now familiar rounds of unleavened bread and thick fig jam.

I waited until after seven o'clock, when the streets were noisy with men and pushcarts, camels and donkeys, and boys tapping goats with short sticks to keep them moving, and again went out to the car. I couldn't believe that Mustapha and Aziz could sleep through the cacophony. When I finally managed to rouse them, they both sat up, looking disgruntled, but Mustapha retrieved my bags and again put them in on either side of Aziz, who, although upright, still had his eye closed. He seemed to have grown an alarming amount of stubble through the night; I thought that by the time we reached Marrakesh it would be a full beard.

As we drove away, I asked Aziz if they'd slept in the car all night.

'Some time, madame,' he said. 'First we sell skins. We get petrol, we eat, we visit friends. Is good night,' he said. 'Lalla Huma is good? Your night is good?'

'Yes,' I said, smiling. 'Yes, thank you, Aziz.'

I had been able to wash off the worst of the dust and grime from the road, I'd eaten a hearty meal, and had a deep sleep. I'd been lonely, and sad, but I had felt that every night since the last one I'd shared with Etienne.

'Where does your family live, Aziz?' I asked him.

'Settat,' he said. 'Same Mustapha.'

I didn't know how big Settat was, and wondered if there would be another house like Lalla Huma's for me to stay at, or whether I would stay with Aziz or Mustapha's family.

'Today I see wifes, children. I don't see one month. I am driving many places with Mustapha.'

Had he said wifes? Did he mean wife, or wives? I knew from Etienne that Muslims could have up to four wives. 'How many children do you have?' I asked him then.

He smiled proudly. 'Six. Four from wife one. Two from second wife. But she is young, second wife. More will come, *Inshallah*.'

'And Mustapha?' I asked, looking from Aziz to the driver. 'Mustapha? You have two wives?'

Mustapha understood me, shaking his head, his lips turned down, and held up his index finger.

'Mustapha has bad luck. No money for second wife. But maybe soon fate gives him another wife.' Aziz said something to Mustapha in Arabic, and Mustapha gave a wry smile.

'Your husband,' Aziz said to me then, 'why he lets wife go alone to Marrakesh?'

'I don't have a husband,' I told him.

He frowned, shaking his head. '*Quoi?*' he said, drawing out the word, sounding incredulous. 'What?' he repeated. 'Why no husband?'

I took a deep breath. 'Maybe . . . maybe bad luck, like Mustapha,' I said. It was a question I'd never been asked outright before.

Aziz nodded sadly. 'This is not good. I pray for you, madame. I pray for you for husband. You like we take you to shrine? We pass shrines on the way to Marrakesh.'

'No. But thank you, Aziz,' I said, and turned my head to look out the side window. Aziz understood the gesture, and sat back, not saying anything more.

We drove downwards from Sale, the road sloping to the mouth of the river, where I could see what looked like a steam ferry moored.

'We must cross Boug-Regreg,' Aziz said, and as we inched towards the landing stage for the ferry, I stared around at the crowds who had also gathered to cross the river to Rabat. There were the usual camels and donkeys and goats, as well as crowds of women in their voluminous robes, babies peeping from the front or the back, small children clutching their mothers' skirts. A large man, in splendid robes of burgundy and blue silk, sat on a donkey far too small for his weight, and a tall man with skin black and glistening, in a simple white robe, held the donkey's bridle.

When the steam ferry was packed so tightly there wasn't room for another man or even goat, we were transported across the brown river. The short trip was noisy with the babble of animal roars and grunts and brays and bleating, mingled with the cries of children, the high, quick voices of the women and the lower rumbling of the men. We were the only car on the ferry, and I was viewed, much like at Larache, with open stares. One woman stooped to look in the window and hissed something through her covering, her dark eyes narrowed.

I drew back, leaning to one side, so that I was away from the open window and closer to Mustapha. 'What did she say?' I asked Aziz.

'Womens think you bad, show face to all men,' he said, and after that I kept my eyes fixed straight ahead, looking neither right nor left, and was relieved when we docked on the other side of the river and headed on the road to Casablanca.

The Rif mountains had died away before we reached Sale, but now I saw the outline of others far to the east.

'Atlas mountains,' Aziz told me. 'But not big Atlas. Smaller. Big is later, near Marrakesh. High Atlas,' he said.

The road continued to run alongside the Atlantic. I watched the sun dance on the water, the gulls swooping. There were more olive gardens and orange trees, and the smells were fresh and clean. The plains looked fertile.

'Will we go in to Casablanca?' I asked, and Aziz shook his head.

'No Casa. Too big, too many peoples, hard to drive,' he said. 'The road is beside city.'

We passed Casablanca on the edge of the sea, white, huge and glorious, all spires and towers and ramparts. We left the magnificent white city, turning away from it and the Atlantic, ready to move inland towards my destination, Marrakesh.

An hour past Casablanca we stopped beside the walls of a tiny mud village. 'We eat,' Aziz said, gesturing for me to get out of the car.

It was only then that I saw a small structure with a corrugated tin roof. Two men stood over a grill; going closer, I saw eggs bubbling in an inch of grease in a blackened pan. Clouds of blue flies flitted dangerously close to the heat. An old camel sat on its callused knees nearby, gazing at us with a look of haughty grandeur, occasionally grumbling and spitting. His smell was stronger than that of the frying eggs.

I stood beside Mustapha and Aziz, holding my tin plate and sopping up the grease-laden eggs with tough wedges of unleavened bread. Mustapha went back to the car and brought out a bag of sticky figs and another of dry olives. The men at the grill made us mint tea; I drank it from a dented tin cup. Then we were back in the car. Mustapha and Aziz appeared to have greatly enjoyed the meal, patting their stomachs and burping. I couldn't lose the oily taste of the eggs, even though I ate all of my olives and figs.

'Now in three hours, maybe four, we come Settat,' Aziz said, smiling, and I knew how anxious he was to see his family.

But a few miles from the village where we'd had lunch, the macadam road came to an abrupt end, blocked off by stacks of uprooted, rotting cacti and rusting barrels. Beyond the blockade the road had caved in, and there were jumbled chunks of macadam as far as I could see.

'Aaaaahhhh,' Aziz breathed. 'Not good. Road is broken,' he said, and then spoke to Mustapha in Arabic.

Mustapha turned the wheel sharply, on to simple hardened tracks that ran away from the macadam. The tracks were sandy soil woven with some sort of tough vegetation. Without the cooling ocean breezes, the hot wind blew through the car as though an oven door had opened, covering us in a thin film of dust. Mustapha pointed to the narrow ruts that led into what appeared to be a blank canvas of earth and sky.

'*Piste*, madame,' he said.

I turned to him. '*Pardonnez-moi?*' I said.

'*Piste, piste*. No road. *Piste*.'

I shook my head, looking back at Aziz.

'We drive the *piste*,' he said. 'The tracks of caravans. Roads no good, drive *piste* through the *bled*. Maybe road come back, maybe not.'

'*Bled?*' I repeated.

'*Bled*,' he said. '*Bled*, madame. No city. Country. Big.'

I nodded, thinking how lucky I was that Aziz could speak French well enough to explain the features of the landscape and to tell me, in the most basic terms, where we were and what we would do next.

We rattled along the rough *piste*. Here the land was occasionally dotted with circles of mud huts with roofs made of woven rush. There was always a well and corrals of a sort – defined by low hedges of cacti or wattled thorn – containing hundreds of piteously bleating goats. Under their shade a group of swathed figures sat; I assumed them to be men, as there were no children about. These villages, Aziz said, were called *nourwal*. When, some miles further along the road, we passed dozens of tents made of dark hair – goat or camel – perched on a rocky slope, Aziz said *douar*. After the different forms of habitat had sprung up a few more times and Aziz had again named them, I understood that the mud hut villages were permanent, with the wells and the ancient trees, while the skin tents, with children guarding small groups of camels and goats, were nomadic villages.

When we had first started on the *piste* it had appeared that the countryside was flat. But I was mistaken. We suddenly plunged downwards, and then almost immediately upwards again. This went on for what felt like an interminable time. I clutched the dashboard, aware that my hairline and collar were damp with perspiration and gritty with sand. My stomach rolled with the landscape. It was almost like being at sea again, sailing up and down on the waves. Had this land once been under water? Were we indeed driving on the bottom of some ancient ocean?

I closed my eyes, grimacing as my stomach heaved. I tasted the oily eggs in my throat. Finally I opened my eyes and turned to Mustapha, letting go of the dashboard and sitting up straight, clearing my throat. I didn't want to let these men think me weak. They already pitied me because I was unmarried.

'Mustapha,' I said, 'will we be able to get back on the road soon? So that we can reach Settat before nightfall?'

Mustapha didn't answer.

'Too far from road now,' Aziz said. 'Better we stay on *piste*. And tonight, sleep in *bled*.'

'Here?' I asked, looking around at the empty expanse.

'Sleep in *bled*,' he simply repeated, and I stared straight ahead, willing my stomach to remain still. I thought of how disappointed Aziz and Mustapha would be, so close and yet unable to get home after a month away from their families.

But I was also thinking about a long Moroccan night in a small car with two men, in the middle of nowhere.

CHAPTER NINE

THE *BLED* WENT ON in a great emptiness, and yet I began to find beauty in the late afternoon sun on the parched earth, the rocks, the sudden stands of scrubby palmetto palms. Eventually I forgot about my stomach, and told myself to stop worrying about the night ahead, as there was nothing I could do about it.

Instead, I concentrated on looking more intently at what I had thought was empty land, realising I was actually seeing things where I thought there had been nothing.

A few times another wreck of a car drove by us; one of us had to idle, slightly off the *piste*, to allow the other to pass. The other cars were always driven by Arabs, and Mustapha and Aziz waved and called loudly to the drivers, who responded in the same way. I didn't know whether the men knew each other or this was simply the way of the *piste* in Morocco.

I was staring at a white rise in the distance, which I knew, from Aziz pointing out others previously, was a saint's tomb where the nomads stopped for prayer – and where Aziz had offered to take me to pray for a husband. These occasional tombs broke up the monotony of the desolate stretches of now red earth and stony ground reaching out on all sides of us.

When we suddenly dipped lower and I lost sight of the bit of white ahead, the car hit a hole and bounced to the left. Mustapha yelled, turning the wheel, but the car slid off the *piste* and into a deep rut of sand.

The engine roared as Mustapha tried to drive out of the sand. Then both men got out of the car, walking around it and arguing with each other in Arabic. Mustapha motioned for me to get out as well, and he got back behind the wheel. I stood to one side as Mustapha stepped on the gas and Aziz pushed from behind. He shouted at Mustapha, and Mustapha turned off the engine. They took out my cases, and then repeated the process. The tyres spun in the sand, digging deeper. I went to the back of the car, putting my hands on the Citroën beside Aziz's and pushing while the car roared again, spitting sand and dust into my eyes and ears. I could taste it on my tongue. I closed my eyes and turned my face to one side. Still the car didn't move. Mustapha, leaving it running, came and stood with his hands on his hips, surveying the situation. Then he reached into the car, drew out the mouldering djellaba and tore it down the middle. He placed a piece under each front wheel, again spoke to Aziz, and the two men exchanged places.

It was the same as before. Even the added traction of the cloth was of no use. Aziz turned off the engine and came and stood beside us. 'We need more push,' he said.

I licked my lips. 'I'll drive, and you both push,' I said.

They stared at me.

'All right?' I asked.

Mustapha shook his head and spoke one long angry phrase to Aziz.

'My cousin is afraid of the woman drive car,' Aziz said. 'She will take away the *baraka*.'

'I can drive,' I said. 'I have driven a car. In America.'

Aziz spoke to Mustapha in an argumentative tone. Finally Mustapha threw up his hands and walked away, muttering. He walked in a tighter and tighter circle in the scrubby dirt for a few moments, then came back and stared at me.

'Fine you drive. Go,' he said, and I got in behind the steering wheel. I put my hands on it, and then turned the key, slowly pressing on the gas and clutch. I closed my eyes for a moment at the unexpected pleasure it brought to just hold the steering wheel and feel the car rumble under me. I thought of the Silver Ghost. It spite of the tragic outcome of the accident, the car itself had suffered very little damage. Once its broken windows were replaced and the dents and scratches smoothed and repainted, I had Mr Barlow sell it for me. I never wanted to see it again.

It had fetched a surprisingly large sum of money. When Mr Barlow handed the thick envelope of bills to me I shook my head. 'I don't want it,' I said, looking at the envelope as though it contained something poisonous. I felt the money was dirty, *was* poison. 'You can keep it, for the rent,' I told him, but he shook his head.

'Come now, Sidonie, you're not thinking straight. You've got to plan for the future,' he said, and left it on the kitchen table.

I had made a wide berth around the table for the next two days, as if the envelope of bills was some live thing that might jump up and bite me if I came too close. But finally I had taken the envelope and hid it in the back of my closet, relieved that I no longer had to look at it and think about what it represented.

It was only when the banks crashed, a few months later, in October of that year, that I thought about the money, safe behind my hatbox.

And now it was that money, added to what had been left in my bank account, that was financing this journey.

'Go, madame,' Aziz cried, and I shifted the clutch into first gear, the car rocking under me in rhythmic bursts of the engine roar. In a moment the front tyres caught, just the slightest, and inched forward. I pressed harder on the gas. I could hear the grunts and groans of Mustapha and Aziz as they pushed with all their might. And then the front wheels made contact with a patch of pebbly sand and suddenly there was a lurch and the car sprang ahead. I pressed the pedal almost to the floor, quickly shifting it into second gear and steering it back on to the firm *piste*. I meant to step on the brake and shift back to neutral, but I didn't. Instead, I kept going. I don't know why, except that it was as though a force greater than my own was keeping my hands on the wheel, my foot on the gas. I drove on. Behind me I could hear the panicked shouts of the two men. I didn't glance in the cracked rear-view mirror, but knew Mustapha and Aziz would be chasing me, waving their arms, their mouths black squares of shock. Still I kept going, feeling, somehow, that I was out of my body, although I was aware of the car, rattly and stiff and noisy. It was nothing like the smooth ride and velvety purr of the Silver Ghost, but nonetheless it brought back memories of freedom, of lightness and hope, my own body with its cumbersome gait forgotten. I sped up, slipping into third gear, not willing to relinquish the old joy. The gears and pedals moved cooperatively at my will. I felt as if I could drive for ever. Now I looked into the rear-view mirror, but this time only at my own reflection. I was smiling. When had I last smiled in this unconscious way?

But the sight of my own smiling face, streaked with dust, my hair wild around my head, also brought me back to my senses: what was I doing? I immediately down-shifted, and at the next wider stretch on the *piste* put the car in reverse and carefully turned it around. Then I slowly drove back to meet Mustapha and Aziz, who were walking towards me.

When I reached them I stopped and stepped from the car. Both men's faces were covered in sweat and a fine layer of dirt, and Aziz's one eye was twitching.

'You take fine auto,' Mustapha shouted, staring at me with open suspicion. 'You drive *folle* – crazy. You crazy? You thief?'

I wiped my mouth with the back of my hand, feeling the grit on my lips. I saw how furious he was. 'I'm sorry, Mustapha. And Aziz. I'm sorry,' I repeated, seeing, immedi-ately, how I had betrayed their trust in me. 'I wasn't stealing it. I was just . . . driving it.'

'But for why?' Aziz asked, his voice more reasonable than Mustapha's. 'Why you drive away from us?'

'I . . . I don't know,' I said. 'I like to drive. That's all. I like to drive.' I looked from Aziz to Mustapha, and back to Aziz. I hoped my voice and expression showed them how contrite I genuinely felt. 'I really am sorry. It was wrong, I know. But it . . . it felt good.'

Mustapha said something to Aziz. Aziz nodded, turning to me and spreading his hands in front of him. 'Now is problem, madame. Now my cousin says maybe you not crazy thief, but much worse. Maybe you *djinniyya.*'

'*Djinniyya?*'

'Evil spirit. Woman. Sometime *djinniyya* pretend is beautiful woman. Trick man. Mustapha says you trick him, and steal car.'

I looked at Mustapha. 'Again, I'm so sorry, Mustapha. I'm not a *djinniyya*. I don't want your car. I just want to get to Marrakesh. Please forgive me,' I repeated, as earnestly as possible, not knowing how much he understood. I lowered my gaze then, realising he would be even further angered by a woman with an uncovered face staring at him. I was aware how idiotic my little stunt had been. Perhaps I'd shamed them, or somehow made them lose honour.

Mustapha grunted something to Aziz.

'Mustapha does not like to drive you to Marrakesh any more,' Aziz said.

I licked my lips. 'But . . . we're nowhere,' I said. 'I . . . what will I do? Please, Mustapha,' I said, but he looked at me with such anger that I was frightened. I was completely vulnerable here, entirely a victim to his whims. I could communicate with Aziz more easily.

'Aziz? You understand that I didn't mean to upset Mustapha in this way? Tell him. Explain to him that he can't leave me here. *You* wouldn't leave me here, would you, Aziz?' I instinctively reached my hand to touch his arm, but immediately knew that would be a further mistake, perhaps even an insult, and dropped my hand back to my side.

The men murmured back and forth, and finally, with an angry grunt, Mustapha walked towards the car. Aziz didn't look at me or speak, also walking towards the car. I hurried behind him, and when he opened the passenger door and climbed into the back, I pushed in as quickly as possible, relieved as I sat in my own seat. I didn't know what would happen next, but at least I was in the car; for a moment I had imagined them driving off without me, leaving my cases sitting by the side of the *piste* where they'd unloaded them earlier.

We sat in the car for what felt like a very long time. I knew it was best if I didn't say anything, but found the silence and stillness disconcerting. Flies buzzed around me with a steady, monotonous drone, lighting on my damp skin. I knew the men would be insulted if I offered more francs; this wasn't about money, but about their honour. I was a woman – a foreign woman – and I had offended their sensibilities.

I stared ahead. The immensity of the situation loomed. I had no idea where we were. The land was featureless, the red stony earth bleak and solitary and somehow oppressive. How long would we sit here? Although neither man seemed violent, the possibility that they might force me out was a tangible threat. They might take all of my money and leave me here, alone on the *piste*, and drive away. What was stopping them, except their own principles – whatever they were. What did I know about the workings of the Arab mind?

I was frightening myself further. Slowly, I took my small

sketchpad and pencil from my handbag on the floor. I made some lines on the paper, imagining I would draw some of the trees and cacti I had seen, to calm myself. But instead, human forms emerged from the charcoal tip. A man. Another man. I had never attempted people, and yet it came quite easily. When I was done, it was a drawing of Mustapha, in his vest over his robe, and Aziz, with his fez at a jaunty angle. The men stood side by side. I felt that in this quick rendering I had managed to capture their essence in their expressions and the way they held themselves.

I wondered why I had never drawn people before, only nature.

I looked up from the drawing, gazing at the *bled* through the fly-spotted and filthy windshield, and instinctively tore the sheet from the notebook and handed it to Mustapha. He looked down at it, studying it, then took it from my outstretched hand. He looked at it further, then passed it back to Aziz. The silence continued for a few more minutes, and then Aziz spoke in Arabic in a low voice, giving Mustapha the drawing again. Mustapha answered in a few guttural words.

'My cousin say all right, maybe you not *djinniyya*. But you don't drive again.'

'No, no, of course not,' I said, looking at Mustapha. '*Shukran*. Thank you, Mustapha.' I inclined my head in a respectful bow, wanting him to know I appreciated his decision.

He still wouldn't look at me, but carefully folded the paper and tucked it inside his robe. He started the car and drove back to where my cases lay beside the *piste*. He got out and shoved them in beside Aziz, slamming them against him. Aziz muttered, pushing the cases away from him. Then Mustapha got back into the car and stared at me.

'We go Marrakesh,' he said, with an injured air.

'*Inshallah*,' I said.

Before darkness fell, Mustapha stopped the car under a stand of palmettos just off the *piste*.

As the men opened the trunk of the car I got out, trying to ease the kinks from my hips and back. They pulled out some old rugs, taking them to the smaller palms, and somehow fashioned a draped shelter, one rug on the ground and two more creating the roof.

'You sleep,' Aziz said, and I smiled my thanks at him, grateful that I didn't have to sleep in the car. I sat on the rug and watched as they took a lantern and a tin box from the trunk. Aziz emptied the box on to the sandy earth; it was coals. Next Mustapha pulled out a can with a spout and poured some of its contents into a battered teapot.

Now I understood why they hadn't put my cases into the trunk of the car; it was filled with their travelling necessities. In the sudden darkness as the sun dropped behind the distant mountains, they lit the kerosene lamp and made mint tea. In the circle of light we chewed strips of salty dry meat and ate bread and more figs and olives and drank our tea.

The men stayed around the glowing coals, but I went back to my shelter. I sat in the opening, hearing their quiet murmurs. The sky was like nothing I had ever seen, not at home and not at sea and not in Marseilles or Tangier. I lay on my back, looking up at the starry dome over me.

I thought of the time I had stared at the night sky from

my porch steps, thinking of my life as a mere speck of dust in the Milky Way. And yet here . . . the glorious sky made me feel differently. The stars seemed so close in the absolutely silent night that I felt I could hear them, a distant, muted humming, similar to the sound of holding a shell to one's ear.

In the shell we think we hear the ocean; in this desert I felt I heard the sky. I counted three shooting stars. I felt a strange gravity, as though the starred sky was pushing me into the belly of the earth.

And then there was a soft, rhythmic pattern, a kind of squishing, plopping noise. I listened, trying to understand what it was. 'What is that sound?' I finally called into the darkness.

'Only wild camel, madame,' came Aziz's voice. 'Walking, walking, looking us and smelling us.'

I smiled at the thought of that lone creature, circling our car and the shelter in interest and perhaps wonder, its clumsy-looking feet so sure on the sandy soil. Then I pulled one edge of the rug over me and watched the stars until my eyes closed.

The next day, after morning tea and bread, we set off.

'This day finish we are Marrakesh, madame,' Aziz said.

I swallowed. *This day finish we are Marrakesh.* Tonight we would be in Marrakesh. I had come all this way to find Etienne. Shouldn't I be excited, and relieved? But instead, a strange unease came over me. I didn't understand it.

It was a long one, this final day, with only a quick village stop for some *harira* – a thick lentil soup – and then the seemingly endless *piste*.

As the sun lost its intensity in the late afternoon, I saw something far ahead on the tracks, shimmering in the waves of heat as if a mirage. At first I could only determine that it was a solitary human figure, but as we drew nearer, I made out blue robes. They fluttered out from the figure like a semaphore, signalling something important, although unknown. Closer still, I could tell it was a man. But as we drove straight towards him, he didn't step to the side of the *piste* for us to pass. He continued towards us, forcing Mustapha to stop the car. Aziz murmured something to Mustapha.

The man stood tall and unmoving in front of us. He was covered from his neck to his ankles by his long pale blue robe, and had a dark blue turban around his head, one end covering his nose and mouth. Backless leather sandals were on his feet.

Mustapha went out and faced him; they spoke, then Mustapha came back to the car and said something to Aziz. Aziz dug in the bags at his feet and handed Mustapha a round of bread. Mustapha gave it to the man, and the man put something into Mustapha's hand.

When Mustapha returned, the man in blue passed on my side of the car, staring in at me. I could only see his eyes and the aquiline bridge of his nose, but a small shiver went through me. His dark eyes were expressive and somehow challenging, a mixture of grace and menace. He stopped for a moment, saying something without taking his eyes from mine. I thought he was speaking to me; did he think I could understand him? His voice was quiet, muffled further by the wrapping over his lower face. I finally had to lower my gaze, unable to look into his eyes any longer. He spoke again, and this time Aziz answered, and again I looked up at the man. He stared at me for another long moment, and then walked on, down the road behind us, straight and dignified, almost haughty.

Mustapha tossed something on to the floor near my feet. It was a beautifully ornate tile, painted with an abstract geometric design in greens and blues.

I wanted to know what the man had said about me to Aziz. 'That's lovely,' I said, picking up the tile.

'You take this *zellij*,' Aziz said, leaning forward. 'Is only trade for bread. Always l'Homme Bleu give something for trade.'

'A Blue Man? You call him this because of his robe?' I asked, studying the tile. A *zellij*, Aziz had called it. It was warm in my hands; it must have been against the man's body. I ran my fingers over its smooth face, its sharp edges.

'Tribe is Blue Man. His . . .' Aziz pulled back his own sleeve, rubbing his forearm. 'This. The . . .'

'Skin,' I said.

Aziz nodded. 'All life they wear robe and turban made blue from indigo plant. After many years indigo is in their skin. *Et voilà!* They are blue.'

I put my head out the window, looking behind the car to watch the Blue Man's straight back as he walked down the road. 'They're Arabs?'

'*Non*. Berbers. But different Berbers: Tuaregs. Nomads, from Sahara. Speak like us, but also separate language. They have the camel caravans, bring goods forward and back. Salt, gold, slaves. Walking always in desert. They walk all Morocco, more Africa. Far. To Timbuktu.'

'And they're Muslims as well?'

Aziz shrugged. 'Some, but more not care Muslim. The woman show face, the man cover face. They are like . . .' he searched for a word, 'like backward side Muslim. The Blue Man and their womans do what they want. They are the desert people. No king, maybe sometimes God, sometimes no God. Desert people,' he repeated.

I wished I could have seen the man without the wrapping of his turban covering most of his face. I would like to paint a man like that, I thought, holding the tile between my palms and trying to visualise his features. A Blue Man.

I was still thinking about him an hour later when Mustapha took one hand from the wheel, pointing ahead of us. 'Madame. Marrakesh,' he said, and I leaned forward, peering through the dirt-encrusted windshield.

Then I stuck my head out the open side window. A hot wind whipped my hair around my head. In front of us a wall of red rose up. Suddenly my breath came too quickly in my throat, and my heart beat in hard, rapid thuds, knocking against my chest. I sat back, pressing my hands to my chest, trying to calm my breathing.

I had arrived. I was in Marrakesh, the city where I hoped to find the answers I was seeking. Where I hoped to find Etienne.

CHAPTER TEN

Two months after Dr Duverger had talked to me about the scar, and I'd told him I wasn't interested in having it operated on, I thought I saw him on the street as I shopped for my groceries. I held my breath, realising I didn't want him to see me. But as the man looked into a store window and I saw his profile, I was again surprised by my reaction: this time disappointment. It wasn't the doctor.

I didn't want him to see me because I knew what I looked like. Yet in a strange and contrary way, I did want to see him. More than once, in the last few months, my thoughts had returned to Dr Duverger, and his touch on my face.

I knew the scar was dreadful, and a far greater disfigurement than my limp. Of course it drew notice; people looked at it, then quickly turned away, either embarrassed to have been staring or else revolted, surely. I had never wanted attention, and now I was purposely inviting it. As I had told Dr Duverger, I had little vanity, and yet one recent morning knew that I was avoiding looking at my own reflection, because it was disturbing. Did I wish to go through life like this? Yes, the scar was a horrible memento of what I had done to my father, but now I questioned whether I needed it to be so obvious. The actual weight was within me. I carried it as though it were a heavy earthenware pot of water. I had to walk through my days carefully, so as not to let it spill over. It was my own personal burden, not necessary to be shared with all who looked at me.

That evening I studied my face in the bathroom mirror. I imagined my body's reaction as I walked through the hospital doors. It still made my mouth dry and my stomach spasm, but then I again thought of Dr Duverger's fingers, lightly exploring the deadened scar tissue. I thought about the concern in his eyes, and the way he had tried to make me feel that he understood when he saw my distress in his office, telling me he'd also lost his parents.

I thought about the ruddiness of his cheeks, and the smoothness of his forehead.

The next day I used the Barlows' telephone, making an appointment to consult with Dr Duverger about the surgery. When I met with him a week later I wore my best dress – a soft green silk with a wide fabric belt – and took special attention with my hair. I told myself I was being ridiculous. It was only my scar he was interested in, and all he would notice. I was simply one of his many patients; surely he had the same manner with all of them. But no matter what I told myself, my fingers were damp with nervousness when he shook my hand, and my lips trembled the slightest as I smiled. I hoped he didn't notice.

'So. You have change the mind?' he said, returning my smile and gesturing for me to sit.

'Yes,' I said. 'I needed time, I suppose. To think about it.'

He didn't respond.

'Unless . . . it's not too late, is it? Have I waited too long?'

He shook his head. 'No. But it requires more work now, I'm afraid, because you leave it longer,' he said. 'And you must understand, Miss O'Shea, you will always have a scar. But as I first tell you, it can be much finer, and in some time more smooth and without such . . . the colour. Discoloration.' He started to talk about the procedure, but I stopped him.

'I don't care to hear about it,' I said, with a small, apologetic smile. 'Just do what you can to minimise it.'

He scheduled me for the operation in three weeks' time, and on a muggy, late June day, it was done. I hardly remembered anything about the operation itself, or Dr Duverger, due to the ether I was given to put me to sleep.

When I awoke I had a thick bandage on my cheek, and Dr Duverger told me that I must return within ten days to have the stitches removed.

'This time I will definitely be back,' I said, my tongue still thick from the ether, as he stood by my bed once I'd woken. He smiled, and I attempted to smile back, but the numbness from the medication was wearing off, and the new stitching throbbed.

Ten days later I was at the hospital, again wearing my best dress, again asking myself why I was acting like a silly schoolgirl. Mr Barlow insisted on driving me. 'You go on home,' I told him, as he dropped me off. 'I'd like to walk back. It's a beautiful day.'

'You sure? It's a good hike,' he said.

'Yes,' I said, and waved my thanks as he drove off.

While I waited for Dr Duverger, I took out the pencil and small sketchpad I always carried in my bag, and worked on my rendition of the Karner Blue butterfly. They lived in Pine Bush, and were an endangered species, difficult to spot. And yet I had finally caught a glimpse of one last summer; it was a stunningly beautiful little butterfly with a wingspan of only an inch. It was a male, as the topside of its wings was the clearest azure blue. I knew the females were a darker, greyish hue. Their lives depended on the wild lupin, also blue, with pea-like flowers. My goal was to paint the Karner Blue perched on the wild lupin, both butterfly and flower in different and yet powerful shades of blue, but I couldn't get the sketch quite right. When Dr Duverger entered I put the pad and pencil on the chair beside me.

'Now, Miss O'Shea,' he said, 'we will see the result.'

I nodded, licking my lips.

'Don't be worry. I think you will be happy.'

He gently pulled off the gauze covering, and leaned close to remove the stitches. I didn't know where to look with his face so close to mine. He had put on his glasses, and I could see myself reflected in them. Once he glanced from my cheek to my eyes, and I immediately looked down, embarrassed that he might think I was staring at him. And yet where was there to look with our faces so close together? This time I didn't smell disinfectant or tobacco, but only the faint clean scent of his crisp shirt and stiff collar.

Suddenly I realised he might be married.

As Dr Duverger removed the stitches there were tiny clipping noises and a slightly painful jerk with each one, making me wince occasionally. Each time I did, he murmured *pardon* in an unconscious way. And then, with the last stitch removed, he sat back and studied my face, moving my chin from side to side with his fingers. They were dry and warm.

'*Oui. C'est bien,*' he said, nodding, and I noticed his unconscious use of French.

'It's good?' I repeated.

'Yes,' he said, and again nodded, looking into my eyes this time. 'It was success, Miss O'Shea. Good success. And it will continue to heal with time, and within one year it will be less; it will fade. And you can cover it with . . .' he hesitated, 'the powder, or what the woman wears on the face. Look. You see.'

He handed me the round mirror.

'Thank you very much,' I said, looking at myself for a moment, then giving the mirror back. 'For the surgery. And for . . . for suggesting it. You were right.'

'I'm happy you agree to it,' he said, standing. I also rose, and we faced each other. He stared at me then, not just at my cheek, but somehow more deeply. It was only a moment, but it was somehow awkward, and suddenly my stomach clenched. But it wasn't the sick spasm I had experienced over initially coming back to the hospital. This was different.

'Well,' I said, needing to fill the silence that was both uncomfortable and exciting, and Dr Duverger said *très bien* at exactly the same time, echoing my word.

We both smiled, and then Dr Duverger said, 'So. Good day, mademoiselle. Please call if you have a question, but I think it will go well now.' Almost immediately he repeated himself. 'But please, if you have a question . . . or any pain . . . you will call, *oui*?'

'*Oui*,' I agreed.

I left the hospital and walked home in the warm late morning sunshine, thinking about the effect the doctor had on me. I tried to understand the sensations I had felt, standing close to him in the noisy hospital. I hadn't had a similar feeling since . . . I stopped. Had I ever felt this way? I thought back to my adolescence, and the fantasies I had entertained about Luke McCallister. But I had been a young and silly girl then, not a woman who lived a practical and quiet life, with no room for whimsical daydreams.

It was all in my head. Dr Duverger hadn't looked at me a moment too long, and he hadn't felt the same strange confusion as I.

It was all in my head.

The next evening I opened the front door to let Cinnabar out, and saw a car slowly pull up in front of my house. It stopped, and Dr Duverger stepped out.

It was so unexpected that I didn't have time to think about how I felt. As he walked towards the house, I saw that he carried my sketchpad.

'You leave this,' he said, coming up the steps. 'I look at your address on the file, and see that I have to drive nearby to visit a patient, so think I will return it.' He held it out to me.

'Thank you so much,' I said, taking it. 'Yes, yes, I looked for it this morning. I couldn't remember where I might have left it . . . there's a particular image I've been working on, but I can't quite get it right, and . . .' I was speaking too quickly, perhaps babbling. 'Well. Thank you,' I said again. 'It was more than kind of you to go out of your way to return it.'

'I look to your work,' he said, glancing down suddenly. Cinnabar was twining around his legs. Then he looked up at me again. 'It is good. The work.'

'Thank you. But they're just line drawings,' I said, embarrassed and yet pleased at the thought of him going through the pages.

'But you like this. To . . .' He stopped. 'My English,' he said, then licked his lips. 'To draw. The . . . the . . . talent to draw is obvious.'

'Thank you,' I said, feeling ridiculous repeating *thank you* over and over, my mind darting about for something else to say. If he spoke about my face I would have felt more at ease. But he didn't, and I grew more and more anxious and awkward, running my fingers up and down the spine of the sketchbook.

'Would you care to come in and have a cup of coffee?' I asked, when I couldn't bear the silence any longer. As soon as the words were out of my mouth I wanted to take them back. What was I doing? Now it would be more uncomfortable when he found a reason to decline politely. Or . . . if he didn't decline.

'Yes. I would like to take *le café. Merci,*' he said, and I had little recourse but to step inside.

After he drove away I sat on the porch, staring at the street. I was twenty-nine, and this was the first time in my life I had been alone in my own home with a man who wasn't my father or a neighbour. As Dr Duverger had followed me through the living room into the kitchen, my heart was racing and my throat woolly. But once he sat at the kitchen table and I busied myself preparing the coffee, I realised there was something different about Dr Duverger today. It only took me a few moments to notice that while he was professional and calm in the hospital – the place where he seemed to belong – on my porch and in my kitchen he appeared slightly ill at ease, his English faltering and his face more expressive. As a doctor, with his files and stethoscope, he was in control. But away from the hospital I recognised in him an insecurity, as though he was as unsure of himself as I was when I left the safety of Juniper Road. And seeing this filled me with something I hadn't felt before, some very small confidence.

He's a doctor, but he's also just a man, I told myself.

He asked more questions about the sketches in my notepad, struggling with some of the words, and I told him to please speak French if he wished. 'It's very different from the French my mother and I spoke,' I told him, 'and I haven't used it since she died six years ago, so I'll answer in English, but I like to hear it.'

He nodded, smiling as he sipped his coffee. 'Thank you,' he said in French. 'Even though I speak English daily, and am usually comfortable with it, sometimes . . . in some circumstances . . . it fails me,' he said, and even that small confession gave me more confidence. Did I make him nervous, as he made me, and if so, why?

We talked a little about my painting. I asked where he was from in France, and he told me he'd studied medicine in Paris.

He had been living in America for over five years now, he said.

After half an hour and two cups of black coffee, he rose. 'Thank you for the coffee,' he said.

I followed him to the front door. He opened it and stood there for a moment, looking at me. Suddenly it was hard to breathe.

'I'm glad you made the decision about the operation,' he said, finally. 'Now you will again be beautiful.'

Before I could respond, he went out into the deepening dusk. When he opened his car door he looked back at me.

'Perhaps we will take coffee again,' he called, and I didn't know, by his tone, whether it was a question or a statement, and just nodded in a dumb way. Later I asked myself why I didn't smile gaily, saying *yes, of course*, as if I were used to being asked to have coffee with French doctors.

I watched his tail lights until they disappeared from Juniper Road, and then sat on the top step while darkness fell around me.

Beautiful, he had said. *Now you will again be beautiful.* I thought of his expression as he had told me that, and couldn't remember it, or perhaps it was that I couldn't interpret it.

Surely it had simply been the doctor – not the man, but the doctor – speaking, pleased with his work on a patient. Surely, for I had never been beautiful.

I went back into the house and turned on the light over the bathroom mirror, looking at myself, tracing the pink but smoother and narrower line of the new scar.

Had he said *perhaps we will take coffee again* in a

nonchalant way, knowing we never would? Or had he meant it?

I turned out the light, my reflection in the mirror now just a shadowy oval.

I had no idea how to interpret a man's words or actions.

For the next four days I was in a state of anxiety. I didn't want to walk to the store to buy groceries in case Dr Duverger came when I wasn't home. Every day I wore one of my two good dresses – either my green silk or a deep plum that emphasised my waist – and periodically checked that my hair was held back securely. I put a good cutwork cloth on the dining-room table. I made a spice cake. I constantly went to the front window, thinking I heard a car door slam, thinking I heard footsteps on the walk up to the porch.

By the fifth day I was so annoyed with myself for my stupidity – of course Dr Duverger hadn't really meant it when he talked about having coffee again – that I cut up the drying cake and threw it out for the birds. I took off the tablecloth, snapping it a little harder than necessary as I folded it into a neat square and returned it to the linen cupboard.

And then I put on my overalls with the muddied knees over an old shirt of my father's, rolling up the sleeves. I braided my hair into one loose plait, and went out into the back garden and started on the weeds; in the steamy summer heat everything grew so quickly. After neglecting the garden for the last few weeks, the tangle was overwhelming. I hacked and cleared, attacking the coarse thistles and twining bindweed. The sun on my bare arms was warm, and it was satisfying to stab at the earth, the green growth yielding under my hoe. I was angry with Dr Duverger for acting as though he might really be interested enough to come again, but also angry with myself for four days wasted on daydreams.

I shook my head to drive away the thoughts, and instead imagined the delicate wings of the Blue Karner. Of asking Mr Barlow if he would drive me out to Pine Bush one day soon. Of needing to buy more ochre paint.

At that I stopped, leaning on my hoe. I had been thinking of things other than my father's death. It was still there, but the overwhelming sadness had been edged out, just the tiniest bit, for short periods of time.

I went back to the weeding.

'I knocked, but there was no answer.'

I jumped, turning to see Dr Duverger standing at the edge of the garden. He had spoken in French.

'I'm sorry to have startled you, Mademoiselle O'Shea. As I said, I knocked . . . then I heard the whistling.'

'Whistling?' I wanted to answer him in French, but didn't. I was sure my French was rusty, and it was so different from his. So much less cultured.

'I think it was Grieg. "Solveig's Song", wasn't it?'

I hadn't realised I was whistling. I didn't think I'd whistled since my dad's death.

'Mademoiselle O'Shea? I can see I've disturbed you.'

'No, no, Dr Duverger. I just . . .' I rolled down my sleeves, seeing smears of dirt on one forearm and palm. 'I wasn't expecting you.' Only a short time earlier I had been angry with him, but now that he was here, I was glad. Excited.

'I know it was rude to just stop by. I had extra shifts this week, but today I unexpectedly had some time off. I did telephone your neighbour, to ask them to call you to the phone, but there was no answer. So I took a chance . . .'

I swallowed, thinking of my tangled hair and the shapeless overalls. I rubbed the back of my hand over my forehead; I was perspiring in the heat. Dr Duverger looked cool, wearing another crisp shirt under his light linen jacket.

'Of course it's all right, yes. But I must wash my hands, and change,' I said.

He gestured at two old Adirondack chairs in the shade under the broad leaves of a basswood tree. 'There's no need. We can sit out here. Please, stay as you are. You are looking very . . .' he put his head on one side, 'relaxed. Very relaxed and, if you will allow me to say, it's a charming effect. Apart from the last time I came, I've only seen you in less happy circumstances. Oh,' he added, 'I am too forward? You appear surprised.'

I half smiled, still aware of the tightness of my cheek. I tried to act as if men regularly came into my garden and called me charming, as if smiling was natural for me again. 'As I said, you just caught me off guard. I . . . I didn't expect . . .' I stopped, knowing I was repeating myself.

'Come then,' he said, making a sweeping motion towards the chairs. 'I'll only stay a few moments. But it's so glorious, this weather. And I'm glad to be out of the hospital, even for an hour.'

I sat on the edge of the seat of one of the Adirondacks, and he sat across from me.

'Do you mind if I remove my jacket?' he asked.

'No. And it *is* a glorious afternoon,' I said, sitting further back. Cinnabar appeared from stalking insects in the grass, jumping rather heavily on to my lap.

'What's your cat's name?' he asked, draping his jacket over the arm of the chair. Without it, I noticed the breadth of his shoulders.

'Cinnabar,' I said. 'She's deaf,' I added, unnecessarily.

'A good name,' Dr Duverger said, smiling, and I nodded, lowering my face into Cinnabar's fur so he couldn't see the effect his smile had on me.

CHAPTER ELEVEN

THE WORLD BECAME A different place. I became a different person. Over the next month I fell in love with Etienne Duverger.

He came to see me twice a week. The day and time depended on his shifts at the hospital, but unless there was an emergency, he would arrive when he said he would.

For the first two weeks we sat in my back yard, or on the porch, or in the living room or kitchen, and talked. Over the following two weeks we went to dinner in Albany twice, and once saw a play.

He always left my house by ten o'clock; it was only after we'd seen each other four times that he picked up my hand as he was leaving and pressed his lips to it. At the end of that first month he put his arms around me as we stood on my front step, and kissed me.

I knew, by the look on his face, and the way he moved closer to me as we said our goodbyes, what would happen, and was trembling with both excitement and anxiety. It was the first time I had been kissed, and I was embarrassed by this fact and didn't want him to know, but I was so overwhelmed by the feel of his lips on mine, of my body against his, that my trembling increased.

After the kiss he simply held me. 'It's all right, Sidonie,' he said, and I leaned my head against his chest. I could hear his heart thumping, a slow, steady beat, as opposed to mine, which fluttered like petals in the wind. 'It's all right,' he repeated, pressing me closer against him, and I knew then that he must suspect my innocence in the matters of man and woman.

But that one kiss awakened my body. I realised it had been asleep all these years; I had forced it into hibernation with first my adolescent prayers about my recovery and then, later, because it was easier to live a celibate life without questioning it.

After he'd left, the night he kissed me, I sat on my bed in the dark, reliving the moment. I wanted to hold on to this feeling of wonder, but I was also troubled in a vague way.

Dr Duverger was handsome. He was clever and witty; he laughed easily. He had an exciting career, and had lived a life out in the world.

I didn't understand why he wanted to spend time with me. Me, with my wild hair and dark eyes and skin. Me, with a built-up shoe and limp, with a permanent, although now less noticeable, seam down my face. Me, with my small and narrow life, lacking experience in so many areas.

Of course I knew about the world from reading, both the daily newspaper and books, and every morning I turned on the radio to listen to the news reports. But as for actually living . . . I tried to hide how little I knew about this world – the world beyond Juniper Road and Albany – by making sure Etienne always talked about himself. By forcing him to talk about himself, with my endless questions and my absolute silence as he answered.

He had an exotic background. Although he'd been born in Paris, and had received his medical training there, he now explained that he'd spent much of his youth and young adulthood with his family in Morocco, in the city of Marrakesh. When he said Morocco, I tried to picture a page in the atlas, but couldn't. I was embarrassed that I wasn't entirely sure where it was situated. The only thing that came to mind when I heard the word was the fine leather cover of an expensive book. As to Marrakesh, I couldn't even imagine how to spell it.

'But how is that?' I'd asked, when he'd first told me. 'Why were your parents living in Morocco?' At his request, I now spoke French with him. My Canadian French was provincial and unsophisticated, including, I now realised, many colloquialisms. So from the beginning I tried to emulate his Parisian French. He noticed me doing this, smiling at me and telling me he found it touching.

'The French Protectorate. They took over the government of Morocco early in the century, and a good number of people from France moved there. My father was a doctor as well, and had actually been involved with Morocco before the occupation, coming and going by sea and helping to set up clinics. He told me that North African medicine was based on sorcery, and the antithesis of rational science.' He smiled. 'But somehow the Moroccans had managed before the French arrived.'

I smiled back, reaching up to cover my cheek. It had become an unconscious habit before the operation, and now Etienne occasionally reminded me that I still did it.

'You shouldn't do that, Sidonie,' he said now. 'Please,' he added. 'I keep telling you, there's no need. You're beautiful.' He stopped. 'You have a melancholy beauty. In fact,' he said, reaching over to pull my hand away from my face, 'it makes you look a little dangerous. As though you have lived a life of intrigue.'

A life of intrigue. I'd had absolutely no intrigue in my life. No danger, no chances taken, no consequences to deal with. I'd known deep sorrow, but no giddying joy. I laughed. 'Etienne. You're not describing my life at all. Please. Go on, tell me more about Morocco.'

He nodded, his hand still over mine. 'You're a good listener, Sidonie. You fix your eyes on me, and your face is so still. I think . . . I believe you're used to listening deeply to the silence around you.'

I nodded. 'That's why I love going out to the marsh – I told you about it – Pine Bush. Why I love working in the garden, or painting. Or sitting on the porch, late at night, when the street has gone to bed. The silence lets me think.'

He smiled. 'There's no silence in Marrakesh.'

'What do you mean?'

'It's a city so full of colour and sound and movement that it all bleeds together. I found the constant hum, underneath it all, soothing in a way that silence isn't for me. It's almost like a thrumming, a vibration, under the feet. And the sun . . .' He looked towards the window; we were sitting in the living room. He was drinking bourbon – he had brought a bottle – and I lemonade. 'The sun has an intensity unlike here. Even the air is different. My first winter in America . . .' He shuddered dramatically. 'Of course I'd spent many winters in Paris, but here the air becomes so thin, so hard to breathe. The smell of snow was like metal. Like the taste of blood in your throat. But the Moroccan sky, the sun . . .' His face had grown animated, his cheeks slightly flushing.

'When were you there last?'

His face changed, and he didn't answer my question, reverting to our former conversation. 'Once the Protectorate was in place, my father was assigned a permanent position in Marrakesh, and of course we moved there at that time, as a family. I was a young boy. My father only treated the French; the Moroccans stuck to their own cures. Especially the women in the harems.'

'Are they really full of hundreds of beautiful women? The harems?' I'd asked, trying not to show how impressed I was that this man had lived such an uncommon life. And that he would talk of it with me.

Etienne raised his eyebrows, smiling again. Most of the time, when he talked about his life in Morocco, his face and voice were passionate, and I knew that he had a deep love for the country that had been his home for much of his young life. 'Most Western visions of a harem are based on highly romanticised novels and paintings. But harems in Morocco are simply the women's quarters within a house. The word harem derives from the Arabic word *haram*,' he said, 'which means shameful or even sinful. But in everyday language all it means is forbidden. No man is allowed in the women's quarters in the home, apart from husbands and sons, brothers and fathers.'

'So . . . they see no men but those they're related to, by blood or marriage?'

He nodded. 'The wives of the upper class aren't even

allowed to leave their homes, apart from certain traditions. It's a difficult life for them; depending on a man's success, he can have up to four wives. It's a Muslim convention.'

My face must have showed my surprise.

'Complex for us to fathom, I know. My father said the women were sometimes driven to what we might call witchcraft by their own need for some attempt at dominance. Some way to regulate the behaviour of their men, and their own status with the other wives.'

'What do you mean by witchcraft? What do they do?'

He looked into his glass. 'I see it as backward nonsense,' he said, looking at me again then, and his face had lost its enthusiasm. 'They believe in the occult, and try to attract power either for their own benefit, or to deflect evil powers sent by others.' Now his voice was almost clinical. 'They make potions they believe will create a certain circumstance, either positive or negative – a birth, an illness, love, even death – or to protect themselves from the harmful spirits they believe lurk everywhere around them. There's a great deal of ignorance and superstition that rules their lives.' His voice had grown hard. 'They're only dangerous to themselves,' he said, 'although they also . . .' He stopped.

After a moment of silence, during which Etienne drained his glass, I said, 'Of course,' as if I knew what he spoke about, even though all I knew about Morocco by then was that I'd located it in my atlas, at the tip of North Africa, and had found, in a history book, a bit of information about the French conquest of the country in 1912. Although so often his descriptions of his life were joyful and candid, there were also times when I heard a definite hesitancy, as though he was sifting through his memories and choosing only those he wanted to share. As if there was something he was deliberately avoiding.

'So the men keep their women secluded,' he went on, pouring himself another glass of bourbon, 'and yet it's perfectly acceptable for them to also have concubines – *chikhas* – if they can afford them.' He spoke now with an impatient air. 'The country is a paradox. There's extreme spirituality, and yet there's a sensuality that defies it.'

'Do you plan to return again soon? Is your family still there?'

'No. No,' he repeated, and I didn't know whether he was answering one or both questions.

'There's nothing left for me there now. It's a place of sadness; my parents and my brother Guillaume are buried there. They all died within three years. One, two, three,' he said, and then sat quietly for a moment.

'Guillaume . . . was he your only sibling?'

'He was younger than me by three years. We weren't alike; he was . . .' He stopped, then continued. 'He drowned at Essouria, on the coast of Morocco. It was a terrible time. After that my mother was suddenly old.'

I remembered my own mother's face, bending over me, when I'd been stricken with polio. My father's face at the window; his air of complete powerlessness.

'And my father had been quite ill for some time. But parents are always changed by a child's death, no matter how old the child, aren't they? The unnatural order of it.'

There was silence; I knew he wasn't yet finished, and sat quietly, waiting.

'I lived with regret for a number of years,' he went on. 'I hadn't spent enough time with him – with Guillaume.

153

He looked up to me, and I . . .' He stopped again, and then spoke rapidly and tonelessly, as if he wanted to end the conversation as quickly as possible.

'The year after Guillaume died it was my mother, and then the year after that my father. No,' he said, with finality. 'There is nothing – and no one – for me in Marrakesh any longer. Nothing but sad memories. Nothing could make me return.'

I felt it would be better to ask no more questions; Etienne's voice was low and dark, and all the light had gone from his face. But I was nevertheless fascinated by hearing about a world completely unknown to me, and every time Etienne came to call, I had more questions.

When Etienne asked me about the botanical and bird paintings on the walls of my home – it was the next time he came to see me after he'd first kissed me – I had admitted, a little nervously, that yes, they were mine.

'After seeing your sketches in the notepad, of course I wondered if you'd painted these. They're very well done.'

'It's just a hobby,' I said.

'Can you show me more of your work?'

I rose from my chair and he followed me into my studio – my parents' former bedroom. I was very conscious of their double bed, against the far wall.

Half-finished paintings lay on the table; I had finally started the Karner Blue butterfly the day before, and it was clipped on to the easel near the window. He went to it and leaned closer, studying it.

'You don't paint anything else, apart from nature?'

'I paint what I see around me. In the woods, and the ponds and marshes,' I said.

'Of course they are very pretty,' he said, and then lightly stroked my forehead with his index and middle finger. I wanted to lean my head against his fingers, wanted him to keep touching me. 'I think there is so much more in here,' he said, putting a bit more pressure against my forehead. 'You understand what I mean, don't you? You see other things. In here.'

I closed my eyes, hoping he would leave his fingers on my forehead. 'Yes. But . . . this – botany, and the birds – is what I've always painted.' I reached up and took his hand in mine, and then brought it, slowly, down my scarred cheek. I couldn't open my eyes; I was surprised at my own boldness.

'Why don't you paint the things in your mind?' he said, quietly, but I had no answer.

We stayed like that for a few moments, my hand over his on my cheek, and then he put his other arm around me and pressed me against him.

'It's enough?' he whispered into my ear. 'For a woman like you, a woman with a wild heart, to live in seclusion, and paint only what is in front of her?'

Was this how he saw me? A woman with a wild heart?

That may have been the moment I fell in love with him.

I wanted him to kiss me again, but he didn't. Still with one arm around me, he picked up a rendition of a Downy Woodpecker on a black oak.

'My field is science,' he went on, 'and I have a limited knowledge of art. But I have always appreciated beauty,' he added, now letting me go, and stepping closer to the window, holding out the painting. 'Because at the centre of beauty is mystery,' he added.

'Mystery?' I said, my heart still thudding from the feel of his body against mine. 'But as a doctor, do you really believe in mystery? Don't you believe in facts?'

He put down the painting and turned to me again. 'Without mystery there would be no search, and no discovery of facts.' We stared at each other for a moment. 'You are a mystery, Sidonie,' he said then, setting down the painting.

I heard my own breathing; it was too loud, too quick. He put his arms around me, and I lifted my face so that he understood how much I wanted him to kiss me. He did. This time I didn't tremble, but my body was suddenly so heavy and yet light, liquid, that my legs were weak.

Still kissing me, he gently guided me backwards until the back of my knees touched the edge of my parents' bed, and I lowered myself, without taking my lips from his. He sat beside me, but as he started to gently push me down, I pulled away, sitting up and straightening my hair. I was too conscious of everything: the sweet whisper of bourbon on his breath, the hardness of his chest against mine, my body's reaction. But also that we were on my parents' bed, the bed they'd shared for as long as I could remember, the bed where I'd seen my mother die.

I stood.

'I apologise,' Etienne said, also standing and pulling down his waistcoat. 'I've acted inappropriately, Sidonie, I'm sorry. It's difficult to be with you and not . . .' He stopped, looking down at me, and the heat in my body increased.

'I'll make some coffee,' I said, turning from him, because I didn't know what else to say or do.

But my hands were shaking so badly that the cups and saucers rattled as I took them from the cabinet.

'I've upset you,' Etienne said, taking the china from me and setting it on the table. 'Perhaps I should go.'

I shook my head, fingering the edge of one of the cups. 'No. No, don't go. You haven't upset me. That's not it.' I couldn't look at him, but he placed his hands on my cheeks and looked into my face.

'We won't do anything you don't wish to do, Sidonie,' he said. 'That was clumsy of me. Again, I'm sorry.' He removed his hands and turned from me, and it took all my willpower not to step towards him and again put my face to his, and this time tell him not to stop.

Did I not have morals? Of course I did. I knew it would be completely wrong, as a single woman, to take Etienne to my bed. And yet . . . I was twenty-nine. He was the first man who had shown me any attention, who had made me feel that I was beautiful, and desirable. And he forced me into nothing. It was me who made it clear what I wished to happen. It was me who, the next time he came to take me out for dinner, drew him through the open doorway, pressing myself against him, kissing him, pushing his arms from his jacket, pulling him towards my bedroom.

He had stopped me, saying, 'Sidonie, I'm not expecting—'

It was me who put my fingers to his lips, who whispered, 'I know. It's what I want,' and put his hands on my breasts, and then moved his fingers towards the buttons on my dress.

Of course he knew it was the first time for me; even so,

I told him, and also told him that I didn't know what to do, and that I wanted him to show me. His body was hard and lean, and his skin, on mine, was heated and smooth.

I felt no fear, no anxiety, just the utter excitement of anticipation, looking up at his face as he held me, his lips so close to mine, murmuring, 'You're sure . . .' and I nodded. He loved me. He would never do anything to hurt me. I felt safe and cared for in a way I had never known.

'Tell me what to do,' I whispered again, putting my hands on his hips, and he showed me.

Later, as I lay with my head on his chest, I wept, and he at first misinterpreted it, stroking my bare shoulder and saying *I'm sorry, I'm so sorry, Sidonie, I hurt you, I shouldn't have—*

But I interrupted him. 'No. You didn't hurt me. I don't know why I'm crying, but it's not regret. It's not guilt. It's . . .' I stopped. 'It's happiness, Etienne. I'm happy. You've made me happy. I don't know what I've done to deserve this happiness. To deserve you.'

He was silent for a moment. 'Sidonie,' he said then, his lips in my hair. 'You're lovely. You're so strong, a woman so sure of herself, able to live as you do. You're curious and confident. But then there's a fragility . . . I wish you could see yourself as I do. Sometimes . . . sometimes *tu me brises le coeur.*'

You break my heart.

After he'd left, I looked at myself in the mirror.

Had any woman been as happy as I, as much in love, as at that moment? Was there any man, anywhere, as loving and thoughtful, as sincere, as Etienne Duverger?

★

Now Etienne and I fell into an easy pattern; over the next months, through the autumn and into December, we spent his free evenings – sometimes once a week, sometimes twice – at my house, or in Albany, eating out or attending concerts and plays or simply walking down a street, looking in the shop windows. He stayed with me for the night, although sometimes he had to leave early, while it was still dark, to go back to his rooms to change for work. He lived in a rooming house – a rather bleak place near the hospital, he told me, but fine for the small amount of time he spent there.

When I awoke alone, those mornings after we'd been together, I lay for a while in my bed, stroking Cinnabar, feeling an appetite for the world that I'd never before known. I could hardly wait to rise, and was hungry in a physical way I didn't recognise. I'd cook myself a big breakfast of eggs and bacon and toast, drinking three cups of coffee. I put on my father's records and hummed along as I did the dishes. Now the music took on a new meaning, as did the books I read. As did the way the sunshine came through the windows, or the way the wind whispered in the trees. Everything I heard, or read, or saw – even my painting – was somehow tied in with my new and unexpected joy.

Of course what Etienne and I had begun wasn't conventional, but then I wasn't a conventional woman, was I? I knew that my behaviour, according to both society and my own religion, was sinful, and yet somehow I wasn't tortured by guilt. It felt right, and besides, although neither of us spoke of love, or the future, I knew that Etienne loved me as I did him. A woman knows these things.

I also knew, with calm certainty, that he would propose marriage, and our wedding would follow, and the sin would be reversed. In schoolgirl fashion I wrote my future name on paper I would later burn in the fireplace: Mrs Etienne Duverger. Sidonie Duverger. It had a lovely rhythm.

Our conversations grew ever more interesting to me. I had never before had intellectual discussions; although my father and I had talked at length about the events taking place in the world, we hadn't disputed anything. Had we simply agreed on everything? I couldn't remember. Or perhaps it was that my relationship with Etienne was passionate. And so it was passion that came into our conversations, the same way it arose as soon as we touched each other.

I found a delightful challenge in our debates. His arguments were demanding, but he listened to my outlook with openness and a willingness to accept my points of view. And his expectations of me indicated a shared intelligence I found flattering.

We were sitting side by side on the sofa one December evening at dusk. Cinnabar leapt on to my lap, and I stroked her, absently running my hand down her back.

'She was born deaf?' he asked, and I nodded.

'I assume so. I've had her since she was a kitten, and she's always been deaf.'

'Hopefully you didn't allow her to mate.'

I looked at him. 'She hasn't. But what do you mean, hopefully?'

'Because of course she shouldn't.'

I stared at him, puzzled.

'Her deafness. It would be wrong to allow her to breed and possibly pass on that trait.' He took another mouthful of his bourbon. He drank it steadily through his evenings with me, although it appeared to have little effect on him. 'She's an aberration, after all. And the problem with an aberration is that if allowed to procreate, it can weaken the species.'

Etienne was particularly fascinated by human genetics, and when he spoke on the topic he grew animated. He could somehow make the study of genes sound intriguing. 'Remember when I told you of Mendel's Unit of Inheritance? That every living organism is made up of half of the paternal genes and half of the maternal?'

'Yes,' I said.

'So it's quite simple. Only the strong, the perfect, should be allowed to create offspring. Think, Sidonie. Think of the possibilities of a world without the weak. Without the sickly, the damaged in mind or body.'

I caught my breath. Did he not realise I was particularly sensitive to this? That I was one of the damaged he spoke of? I looked away from him now. 'But don't you think there can be something attractive in that which has a flaw?'

He knew me too well. 'Sidonie,' he said, touching my chin so that I looked at him again. He was smiling, slightly. 'You had an illness. It's not genetic. And you have been made stronger by it, not weakened. You know you're beautiful to me, in every way.'

He never failed to make me feel precious, and wanted. I leaned my head on his shoulder.

'But your cat,' he went on, his breath, just above my ear,

moving my hair, 'is a different situation. With the rule of Intelligent Mating, the best of the species are joined to ensure that the offspring are the strongest and most clever – creating better species through specific breeding. So it's a good thing that when Cinnabar dies she will not have passed on her unfortunate disability.'

I didn't like him talking about Cinnabar like this. 'But I read, in one of the books you lent me . . . I can't remember which,' I said, 'but it was something about surviving. That it's not the strongest of the species who survive, nor the most intelligent, but those most adaptable to change. Don't you agree?'

'No,' he said, at the same time gently brushing my hair from my cheek and kissing my scar. 'But let's not talk of it now,' he murmured.

Although I wanted to argue further, I didn't want him to stop kissing my cheek. 'All right,' I whispered, because now my body ached for him all the time. I knew it might be four or five days before I saw him again. 'All right,' I repeated, turning so that I spoke against his mouth, and pushed Cinnabar from my lap.

CHAPTER TWELVE

MADAME? HERE IS MARRAKESH, as you wish,' Aziz said, his voice puzzled. 'You are not happy to come Marrakesh?'

I couldn't speak or look at him. Instead, I stared ahead as we approached the outskirts of the city. Grand rows of date palms lined the road, and groves of them stretched out on either side. Mustapha drove with studied concentration and decision, although, like most of the other drivers, he constantly blew the horn – at nothing I could discern – with what appeared to be a ferocious indignation.

'Where are you going?' I asked him. 'Mustapha? Where are you taking me?' I had given him no instructions, and yet he drove with complete purpose. It gave me a certain comfort, for I had no idea where I might stay in Marrakesh. Since he and Aziz had looked after all the other arrangements, I could only hope they would do the same for me here.

'Aziz?' I said, when Mustapha ignored me. 'Where are we going?'

'We go French Quarter, madame, La Ville Nouvelle. There are the hotels for foreigners in the new city.'

The long red parapets of the city's walls were made

richer by the lowering sun. I had no visual image of Marrakesh in my head, other than knowing that many of its building were built of the deep red-brown soil of the countryside, and that there was the newer city, built by the French — where Etienne had lived — as well as the centuries-old one within the walls. French was the official language spoken in La Ville Nouvelle, while Arabic was, of course, the language of the old city.

There was a profusion of trees: olive, lime, pomegranate, almond and orange. In spite of my trepidation, I couldn't help but see that they gave a beautiful and verdant sense to La Ville Nouvelle, with its wide boulevards and small taxis weaving between donkeys and their carts and high-stepping white horses pulling open-backed carriages. Brilliant fuchsia blooms tumbled over garden walls. Etienne had told me that a subterranean network of conduits and cisterns had been constructed centuries earlier, as the city was being founded as an important base for controlling the region and for trade routes connecting it to northern Morocco and on to Spain.

I stared at the trees and flowers, afraid that if I looked at the faces of the people, I might suddenly see Etienne. I knew it was rather ridiculous, imagining I would see him within moments of arriving, but still, my heart wouldn't stop racing.

Mustapha stopped the car in front of an impressive, elegant hotel surrounded by tall, swaying palms. *Hôtel de la Palmeraie*, I read, the discreet lettering etched into the stone overhang of the wide double front doors. The hotel gave the impression of lovely Moorish design, and yet, similar to the Hotel Continental in Tangier, it was somehow

European as well. A dark-skinned man in a pressed red jacket with gold braid and a red fez with a golden tassel stood at attention outside the doors.

Mustapha jumped out of the car and opened my door, bowing low and sweeping his arm towards the building as if suddenly he had acquired new-found manners. 'Hôtel de la Palmeraie, madame,' he said, and, as I stepped out of the car, Aziz hauled out my cases and set them on the ground. The man in red and gold hurried over and took them, bowing to me as well.

'*Bienvenue*, madame,' he said. 'Welcome to Hôtel de la Palmeraie,' and carried my cases up the steps and inside the hotel.

I opened my bag and took out the decided-upon payment, as well as a number of extra francs. I put them into Mustapha's hand, and then took out additional francs and gave them to Aziz, who was standing beside the open passenger door. 'Thank you, Aziz. I appreciate your help,' I told him, and he bowed his head.

'*De rien*, madame, you're welcome, it's nothing. Goodbye, madame.'

As he turned to get into the passenger seat beside Mustapha, who was giving the gas pedal little taps so that the running engine made a rhythm, I was hit with the reality that I would be alone again, in a strange city.

It was similar to arriving in Marseilles, and in Tangier, except that in those cities I knew I was there for only a brief time, only long enough to arrange my voyage to the final city. This one, Marrakesh.

'Will you stay in Marrakesh tonight?' I asked, not knowing why it would make a difference. I would be here, at this grand hotel in the French Quarter, while they would stay elsewhere, perhaps in the old city.

'No, madame. We drive again. Maybe we are home, at Settat, in morning. I think from this way road is not broken.'

'You're going to drive all night?'

'Yes, madame,' Aziz said, getting into the car and closing the door. 'Goodbye, madame,' he said, for the second time.

I stepped back from the car. 'All right. Well, yes, then. Goodbye, Aziz, goodbye, Mustapha,' I said. 'Thank you. Have a safe journey home.'

'*Inshallah*,' both men murmured, and I turned from the car, slapping my skirt to remove the worst of the dust, and attempting to tuck my wind-blown hair back into its pins. When I looked up, meaning to wave to the departing men, the car was already at the end of the drive. I raised my hand, but at that moment the car turned into the busy avenue, and I lost sight of it.

The concierge – a short man, his smile a sly glint due to a gold front tooth – watched me as I approached the front desk. His eyes travelled from my hair down my dress to my shoes.

'Welcome, madame,' he said, although his voice wasn't particularly welcoming. 'You wish to stay with us?'

'Yes. Please.'

He turned the registration book, pushing it across the wide, gleaming counter. 'Certainly, madame, certainly. If you would sign here,' he said, handing me a pen with a flourish. As he watched me write my name, he corrected himself, his eyebrows rising slightly. 'Ah. Mademoiselle. It is . . . Osh . . . I'm sorry. What is the name?'

'O'Shea,' I said. 'Mademoiselle O'Shea.'

'You have taken the train?'

'No. I was driven from Tangier.'

He nodded, his eyebrows lifting even higher. 'A difficult journey, I am sure,' he said, his eyes going to my hair. I was suddenly aware of how filthy I was. I had worn the same clothing for the last two days, sleeping in it overnight in the *bled*, and having no place to wash. I was fully aware of the effects of the wind on my hair.

'Yes.'

'And how long will you stay with us, mademoiselle?'

I looked down at my signature, seeing, on the printed page, the cost of the hotel per night. It was far beyond my means. And yet I had no idea where else to stay. 'I . . . I don't know,' I told him.

His face gave away nothing. 'As you wish, mademoiselle, as you wish. You are welcome at Hôtel de la Palmeraie for any duration. I am Monsieur Henri. Please call upon me for whatever you may need. Our aim, at the hotel, is that our guests not want for anything. May I reserve you a table for dinner? It is served until nine o'clock.'

Did I want to eat dinner? Was I hungry? Did I propose to rush out into the streets and blindly begin my search? I didn't know what I was feeling. I opened my mouth to say *I don't know* again, and then realised I needed to eat, to sleep. To keep up my strength. 'Thank you, yes,' I said. 'I will have dinner.'

'Seven o'clock? Eight? What is your preferred time?'

He waited, the pen poised over another book.

'I . . . seven o'clock,' I said.

He wrote, nodding. 'And now, I'm sure you would like

to go to your room, to relax and refresh yourself after your arduous voyage.'

'Yes,' I said again.

He lifted his hand, snapping his fingers with a series of loud clicks, and immediately a wiry boy in the same uniform as the man who had opened the front doors for me ran over and picked up my cases.

I followed the boy through the rich, thick carpets of the lobby, feeling strange and even more displaced than at any time since I left Albany over a month ago.

My room was sumptuous, with walls of burled wood panels and oil paintings of mountains and Moroccan vistas in thick gilt frames. The bed's white coverlet was scattered with a pattern of rose petals. I picked one up, feeling its satin thickness between my fingers, then brought it to my nose.

A bed covered in rose petals. I could never have imagined such a thing. I went into the attached bathroom, and found a large silver dish filled with more rose petals on the edge of the tub. There were fluffy white towels folded into shapes of flowers and birds, and a pair of slippers of soft white leather, and a white silk robe.

I would quickly have to find a less expensive place. But I couldn't worry about that at this moment; I would stay here the night, and hopefully tomorrow be more clear-headed. I drew a bath, pouring in sweet-smelling oil from one of the containers on a glass shelf over the sink, and then sprinkled the rose petals over the steamy surface. There was mirror everywhere, even surrounding the bathtub.

I lowered myself in and leaned back. My hands and wrists were so much darker than the rest of my body; I turned my head and looked at myself in the mirrored wall beside me. My reflection showed that my face and neck were the same deep colour; my three days of travel in the sun and wind had given my complexion a hue I hardly recognised.

I lay back again, looking at the length of my body. My hipbones jutted out and my knees were knobby.

My abdomen lay flat under the warm, scented water.

After I'd washed my hair I pinned it up, still damp. Then I put on my best dress, the same simple deep green silk printed with tiny white sprigs I had worn when I'd gone to Etienne's office so long ago. It hung to mid-calf and had banjo sleeves. I attempted to shake out the myriad of wrinkles, then took my second pair of shoes from my case: although still ugly, black, with the right sole built up, at least they weren't deeply ingrained with red dust.

I went down to the dimly lit lobby; in the middle was a huge, gently splashing fountain. More rose petals floated on the water. Panels of wood in shades ranging from the palest blond to the deepest mahogany, arranged in a pleasing pattern, covered the walls. They gleamed under the soft glow from the sconces.

'Madame?' A boy, tall and thin, with the first hint of a moustache, appeared at my side. He wore the hotel's red and gold uniform, as well as white cotton gloves. 'You wish the dining room?'

'Yes, please,' I said, and he extended his arm.

I put my hand through the crook of his arm. He started

off rather quickly, the natural stride for a tall, long-legged young man, but feeling my slight hesitation, stopped and looked down at my shoes. Then he lowered his head the tiniest bit, as if in apology or understanding, and walked slowly, so that I could keep an even step with him.

At the door of the dining room he stopped, speaking in a low tone to the maître d', another attractive young man. His hair was slicked back with brilliantine, and he wore a tuxedo with long tails, a burgundy cummerbund, and white gloves.

'Your name, madame?' he asked, and when I told him he nodded once to the boy whose arm I still held.

As soon as I looked into the grand room I knew I was terribly underdressed. The men wore dark suits or tuxedos, while most of the women were in long evening gowns of satin and net, their hair either short and curled, or in elaborate upsweeps, and with exquisite jewels around their necks and wrists.

I stood in the doorway in my creased green silk, my damp hair springing out of its pins on to my collar and around my ears, feeling dowdy, knowing that everything about my appearance was wrong. But the young man whose arm I held gave me a beautiful smile under his new moustache, saying, 'Come, please, madame,' and his smile gave me the confidence to lift my chin and walk through the room with him. I stared straight ahead at the darkening sky outside the long open windows. Thankfully the boy didn't place me in the middle of the other diners, but led me to a small table set for one beside a window overlooking the gardens. He pulled out my chair for me, and I settled into its wide burgundy velvet seat. The room was filled with quiet laughter and chatter, the clink of silver against porcelain, and the soft strains of a harp from one corner. But in spite of this formal and very constrained atmosphere, from somewhere beyond the garden outside the window I was very aware of a distant, muted roar and the rhythmic pounding of drums.

I sipped the mineral water instantly poured for me, and chose a simple ratatouille from the extensive menu held in front of me by more gloved hands, and then looked through the window.

In the dusk I could see rows and rows of trees and tall, flowering bushes with paths weaving throughout. At the far end of the garden was a high wall covered with bougain-villea. And beyond the wall, in a vista that resembled one of the oil paintings in my room, were snow-capped moun-tains: the High Atlas. I heard evening birdsong through the perfumed air.

It was a backdrop of such unbelievable beauty that for that moment I forgot, or perhaps was just distracted from, my purpose in Marrakesh.

I came back to my senses when a server murmured, 'To start, madame. *Bon appétit*,' and set a plate of tiny mille-feuille pastries in front of me. I put one of them in my mouth, and tasted something that reminded me of the *pastilla* I had had in Tangier. There was also a vegetable I couldn't recognise. The noise from outside – the distant din, steady and rhythmic, like a thudding heartbeat – grew in frequency. I looked around the dimly lit, fragrant room, but nobody else seemed aware of it.

'Excuse me,' I finally said to the couple at the next table. 'What is that sound?'

The man put down his knife and fork. 'The main square in the medina – the old city of Marrakesh,' he replied, in a British accent. 'D'jemma el Fna. Quite a place,' he said. 'I take it you've just arrived?'

'Yes.'

'Well, you certainly must experience the medina during your visit. This part of Marrakesh we're in – La Ville Nouvelle – is vastly different from the old city. All new, built since the French took over. But D'jemma el Fna, well . . .' He looked at my single table setting, then back to my face. 'It's purported to be the greatest souk in Morocco, centuries old. But I wouldn't recommend going there – or even venturing into the old city – without an escort. Allow me to introduce myself, and my wife.' He stood, giving a small, dignified bow from his waist. 'Mr Clive Russell,' he said. 'And Mrs Russell.' He extended his hand towards the tall, slender woman with alabaster skin sitting across from him. A thin strand of brilliant rubies encased in gold stood out against her long and flawless neck.

I introduced myself, and Mrs Russell nodded. 'Mr Russell is right. The medina is frightening. And that square – oh, terribly bold. I've seen things there I've seen nowhere else. Snakes and their charmers, aggressive monkeys, fire- and glass-eaters. Ghastly beggars pulling at you. And the way the men stare . . . it positively gave me shivers. Once was enough for me, even with Mr Russell at my side,' she said.

'Its name – D'jemma el Fna – means Assembly of the Dead, or Congregation of the Departed – some such grisly thing,' Mr Russell went on, sitting down again but turning in his chair to continue speaking to me. 'They used to display decapitated heads throughout the square, warnings of some sort. The French put an end to that when they arrived.'

'Thankfully,' Mrs Russell added.

'Have you been here long – in Marrakesh?' I asked.

'A few weeks,' Mr Russell answered. 'But it's far too hot now. We're leaving next week. Off to Essouria, where we can enjoy the sea breezes. Have you been yet?'

I shook my head. The name gave me an unpleasant start; it had been there, in Essouria, where Etienne's brother Guillaume had drowned in the Atlantic.

'Charming seaside town. Charming,' Mrs Russell added. 'Famous for its *thuya* carvings and furniture. The aroma of the wood can fill a whole house. I hope to find a small table to have sent home. Don't you love the design here? I feel as though I'm in a pasha's palace.'

'You haven't, in your time here, run into a Dr Duverger, have you?' I asked, not answering Mrs Russell's question. The hotel was obviously full of wealthy foreigners; perhaps Etienne had stayed here. Or was here now. My heart gave one low, heavy thud, and I quickly surveyed the room again.

'What was the name of that doctor we met on the train?' I heard Mrs Russell say to her husband, and I looked back at them.

Mr Russell shook his head. 'It was Dr Willows. I'm sorry. We don't know a Dr Duverger. But you should ask at the desk if you think he may be here.'

'Thank you,' I said. 'I will.' It hadn't occurred to me to ask the pompous Monsieur Henri if Dr Duverger had stayed here recently. How could I not have thought of such a simple question? And yet I'd been in a small state of shock when we arrived. Perhaps I still was.

'The garden . . .' I waved my hand towards the window.

'It used to be some sort of park, ages ago,' Mrs Russell said, before I had a chance to comment further. 'There are lovely gardens like this all throughout Marrakesh, outside the medina walls. Apparently it was the custom for the reigning sultan to give his sons a house and garden outside the medina, as a wedding gift. Many of the French hotels have been built in the midst of what were once these royal gardens. This one goes on for a number of acres. You must take a walk through it, later, as the scents of the flowers appear to become stronger in the evening, when the heat has lifted. And it's walled, so quite safe.'

I nodded. 'Yes. I will.'

'I'd suggest you try the Napoleon for dessert. It's crafted beautifully; the hotel has a very talented French pastry chef,' Mr Russell said, then, turning in his chair ever so slightly, so that I knew the conversation was over, 'We do enjoy it, don't we, darling?' he said to Mrs Russell.

After I'd finished my dinner, which sat uneasily in my stomach in spite of the fact that it was lightly prepared, I wandered out through huge glass doors into the garden. Many of the guests were now dancing in one of the ballrooms I had passed, and the empty paths of the garden were lit by flaming torches. There were orange and lemon trees and thousands of rose bushes amassed with bright red roses. I thought of the petals everywhere in my room. Nightingales and turtledoves nested in the palm trees that lined the pathways. There was an abundance of sweet-smelling mimosa, and plants that were surprisingly like many I knew from my own garden at home: geraniums, stock, snapdragons, impatiens, salvia, pansies and hollyhocks.

Suddenly my memories of home – and my former life there – were so distant. It was as though the woman who had lived that simple life, so out of touch with the world beyond Juniper Road, couldn't possibly have been me.

Under new skies, I was no longer that Sidonie O'Shea. Since I'd left Albany, the things I saw, that I heard and smelled, touched and tasted, had been unexpected, unpredictable. Some had been beautiful, others frightening. Some tumultuous and disturbing, some serene and moving. It was as if all the new scenes were photographs in a book, photographs I'd captured within my mind. I could look at them as if slowly turning pages.

I carefully passed the images of the hotel room in Marseilles. It was too soon to look back on those images. Far too soon.

And the enormity of my final challenge – the one I had journeyed this distance to confront – still lay ahead. The thought of how I might face it, perhaps as soon as tomorrow, filled me with such anxiety that I had to sit on one of the benches.

After a while I looked up at the night sky, listening to the quiet rustling sway of the palms in the sweet night breeze, and the distant, yet insistent, sounds from the square.

The Assembly of the Dead. I had a sudden dark

premonition, and shivered in the warmth of the air.

And then I hurried back through the paths towards the hotel, wanting to return to the safety of my room.

CHAPTER THIRTEEN

I T WAS IN EARLY FEBRUARY, eleven months after my
father died, that I realised what had happened. By then,
Etienne and I had been lovers for five months.

I waited an extra week to make certain before I shared
the news with Etienne. I didn't know how he'd react;
he had made a point of assuring me that I wasn't to
worry about any consequences of our lovemaking. I
understood. He was a doctor; he knew how to prevent it.
But somehow, in spite of his reassurances, his precautions
had failed.

I was excited and nervous, wanting to find the right
moment to tell him this unexpected news. We lay facing
each other in my bed, our bodies still heated, although our
breathing had resumed the normal rhythm. It was the
perfect time, I knew then, a moment of openness and
emotion. I smiled, running my hand up and down
Etienne's bare chest, and said, 'Etienne. I have something to
tell you.'

He leaned over and kissed my forehead, murmuring
sleepily, 'What is it, Sido?'

I licked my lips, and perhaps my hesitation made him
lean up on one elbow and study my face. 'What do you

have to tell me, with this expression? You look pleased, and yet shy.'

I nodded, taking his hand. 'It's unexpected, I know, Etienne, but . . .' I could barely say it, such was my joy and wonder. 'It's a baby, Etienne. I'm expecting a baby.'

I held my breath, waiting for his reaction. But it was not as I expected. In the pale shafts traced on his face by the cold winter moon through the windowpane, he lost all expression. His skin took on the texture and colour of a bleached fossil. He pulled his hand from mine and sat straight up, looking down at me with his mouth slightly open.

'Etienne?' I said, sitting up to face him.

'You're certain?' he asked. Cinnabar, still surprisingly nimble in spite of her age, jumped on to the bed beside Etienne; he pushed her off with an uncharacteristically brusque sweep of his arm. I heard the soft thump as she landed on the carpet, and knew she would twitch her tail in indignation and slink under the bed.

I nodded.

'But I use the . . . what . . . *la capote*, the rubber, prophylactic,' he said. 'Always I use it.' He was still frightfully pale, and, for a completely unknown reason, had switched to English.

I was stunned. 'Etienne?' I finally said, a terrible sensation growing in me. 'Etienne? Aren't you . . . don't you . . .' I stopped, not knowing how to continue.

Now he stared over my head at the window and the darkness beyond, as if he couldn't bear to look into my face. 'You see a doctor?' Without waiting for an answer he turned in the other direction, reaching for the pill bottle on the bedside table; he said he suffered headaches, and he also had difficulties sleeping. I hated when he took pills to make him sleep. Only the first two times he spent the night with me did he not take them, and although neither of us fell into a deep sleep, I thought this was only because we weren't used to sleeping together. I was so aware of his touch and was so full of awe at having him beside me that I revelled in the feel of his body pressing against mine when he shifted and turned in my narrow bed. After the second time, he took his pills, and slept a hard, empty sleep, with no movement except for the slight muscling of his jaw, the tiny rasp as he ground his back teeth. Those drug-induced sleeps left me feeling alone, even when lying beside him.

He opened one of the bottles and dumped three capsules into his hand. They would be for a headache; he wouldn't take a sleeping tablet now, surely, not with what I had just told him. He tossed them in his mouth and washed them down with the remains of the bourbon still in his glass.

I didn't know whether it was worse having him look at me or busy himself with his pills and drink.

'I ask you, you have see the doctor?' he repeated, turning back to me but again looking over my head at the window, still speaking that stilted English.

'No. But I know it's true, Etienne. I know my body, and the signs are unmistakable.'

Finally he looked at me, and there was a heavy, dull thud in my stomach. 'No. *C'est impossible*. Perhaps there is other reason for the symptoms. On Thursday – one day behind the next day – I have the late . . . what is it . . . the shift. I

179

take you, in the morning, to the clinic I know, in the next . . . next place, county . . . and you will be examine,' he said, his tongue tripping on every word. It was as though he had forgotten how to speak the proper and rather formal English diction he had used until he'd switched to speaking French with me. 'Not at my hospital.'

His strange way of speaking, combined with his almost blank stare, made me feel that I might be sick. This wasn't what I had envisioned, the hundreds of times over the last few weeks I'd imagined myself telling him this remarkable news.

He was the man – the only man – I had ever shared myself with. My life was entwined with his. Until Etienne had come into my life, I had assumed and accepted that I would live out my days alone. Of course my adolescent promise to God and the Virgin Mary about keeping myself pure was just that – a youthful, naïve promise, made out of desperation. And in the life I had carved out for myself there were few opportunities to meet a man I might look at with a certain curiosity, and I had never before sensed that a man might be attracted to me.

Not until Etienne.

He added a dimension to my life I didn't know I was missing. I now saw it – that former life – as a grey twilight, empty and colourless.

And when I realised there would be a child . . . there was no choice but for us to marry. He was a man of sub-stance, of integrity. I hadn't doubted, for even a moment, that he would immediately propose, and we would marry without delay. I had mapped it all out in my head over the last few weeks, with an ecstasy I could barely contain: he would leave his rooms and move in with me. We would buy a new, bigger bed and move into the larger bedroom. My old bedroom would become a nursery; I could set up my paints in a corner of the kitchen. But now . . . I swallowed, and knew that even though it was close to midnight, I would be sick, as I was most mornings now. I rushed from the room, retching over and over in the bathroom.

When I had finished, I shakily washed my face and rinsed my mouth, and then returned to the bedroom. Etienne was already dressed, sitting on the bed tying his shoes. He looked up at me with such an unreadable expression that something like fear came over me. Again my stomach heaved, although it was empty now.

I put my hand over my mouth.

He stood. 'I'm sorry, Sidonie,' he said in French. 'It's . . . it's just the shock. I need to think. Don't be hurt.'

Don't be hurt? How could I not be hurt by his reaction? 'Won't you stay with me tonight? Please?' I said. I needed him to put his arms around me. I shivered, partly from chill, in my light nightgown, and partly from my anxiety. But he didn't. I stood in the doorway, and he near the bed. Only a few yards separated us, but it felt like a mile.

'I'll come on Thursday morning then, at nine, and take you to the clinic. For a professional opinion,' he said.

'But . . . but you're a professional.'

'It's different,' he said. 'A doctor doesn't treat his . . . shouldn't diagnose those he's close to.' He came to me; he couldn't leave the bedroom with me in the doorway. I didn't step aside to let him pass.

'Etienne,' I said, putting my hands on his arms. I tried not to dig my fingers into his sleeves. I needed to hold on to him, to keep him with me.

He did pull me to him then, pressing my head against his chest. I heard his heartbeat, too fast, as though he'd been running. And after too brief a time he gently moved away, stroked my hair once, and then was gone.

The rest of that long night, and all of Wednesday, had been endless and confusing and filled with distress. I wouldn't let myself think that I had been wrong about Etienne's feelings for me. I couldn't. I couldn't have been so wrong.

The almost silent ride to the clinic – where my pregnancy was confirmed – had been bad enough, but as we approached the outskirts of Albany I could bear it no longer.

'And so, Etienne?' I waited, desperate to have him say something to comfort me. 'I know it's a surprise. For both of us. But perhaps we should view it as fate.'

Staring straight ahead, his hands gripping the steering wheel so intensely that his knuckles were white, he said, 'Are you saying you believe in fate, Sidonie?'

'I'm not sure, Etienne. But . . . in spite of it being a surprise . . . Etienne, these things happen. They happen.' I didn't know what else to say. Of course I knew how I wanted him to react, what I wanted to hear. I wanted him to smile at me, to say that we would share the joy of this child. I wanted him to say, right now, *Marry me, Sidonie, marry me and we will spend our lives together. With our child. With our children.* Over the last few weeks, when I knew with certainty I carried a baby, I had created scenes that I had never imagined could be a part of my life. Etienne and I, playing with our child on a grassy knoll on a summer day. Christmas, with a decorated tree and gaily wrapped gifts: painted dolls or hobby horses, pretty smocked dresses or little vests and trousers. Tottering, tiny steps, birthday parties, the first day of school.

I had created a portrait of myself as a traditional woman, with a husband and children. Me, a doctor's wife, a mother. And that vision looked huge, and within my reach.

In the silent car I saw, with something close to desperation, how I did want it – this gift – more than I had wanted anything in my life. Unexpectedly I thought of the Karner Blue butterfly, its wings quivering as it landed lightly on the wild lupin.

Now Etienne pulled the car to the side of the road and stared through the windshield. Snow came down, gently, and the edges of the road ahead and the dark, bare branches of the trees on either side grew soft, blurred. 'I'm sorry, Sidonie,' he said, his tone unreadable. 'I know I'm not behaving in the way you hoped.'

I looked out the side window, seeing how the long dead grass at the side of the road poked, brittle and yellow, through the snow. I was so confused. Did he not wish to have a family? I wanted to say it, to ask, *Don't you want a child, Etienne? A child with me? Don't you want to marry me and be a husband and father?* So many emotions: shock, and sadness and disappointment, and also, yes, also anger, all combined in a swirling fusion of dark colours.

I looked at him again. 'So what will we do, Etienne?' I spoke slowly, clearly, my voice low and controlled. 'I know it's not what we planned. But . . . but I want this baby. I want it more than anything,' I repeated, more loudly, and then closed my lips before I could say anything further, because I wanted to say, *And I want you more than anything. I want you to want me in the same way*.

I wouldn't allow myself to beg.

He looked at me then, for the first time since we'd left the clinic, and for an unknown reason, I felt something like sympathy. I suddenly knew how he would have looked when he was a boy, unsure and frightened.

I thought it was how he would have looked upon hearing of his brother's shocking death. And because of this look I was able to speak more rationally than I had felt only seconds earlier.

'You owe me nothing, Etienne,' I said, quietly. 'You didn't seduce me. I knew what I was doing.' My heart was thudding as I spoke the next words. 'You are free to go, if you wish.' They were brave, false words. Not about the seduction – that part was true. What was bluff was my dismissal of him, telling him he didn't have to stay with me. Didn't have to marry me.

And the bluff was taking a huge chance. What if he said *yes, yes, you're right, Sidonie, we shall part company. Surely it is for the best*.

What would I do? I knew absolutely nothing about children. I had never even held a baby. And what of my dwindling bank account? How would I support this child? I saw myself bent over a sewing machine, like my mother. I thought of not being able to give my child the things it needed. I tried, in those few moments of silence, to imagine my life in the house on Juniper Road with an illegitimate child. And I saw myself, an ageing recluse, a dark stain on the righteous community because of my fatherless child. Could I bear to watch that child be treated with disdain because of my sins?

Finally he spoke. 'Do you really believe me to have such a low character, Sidonie?' He picked up my hand from where it lay between us on the seat. His fingers were cold as they closed loosely around my own.

I looked down at his hand, holding mine in that unnatural, stiff way.

'Of course we will marry,' he said, his voice hoarse, as if his throat was too tight, and then his face softened, and, using his other hand, he cupped my chin. 'Of course, *ma chère* Sido,' and at that a sob caught in my throat. Tears came to my eyes, tears of relief, and he pulled me to him.

I cried against his lapel.

He did love me. He would marry me. It was not the proposal I had hoped for, but it would be all right.

When he walked me to my door he said he would come by in three days – his next day off – so that we could discuss our plans. We would marry at the City Hall in a few weeks, he said, as it would take too long to arrange a marriage in the church and wait for the banns – we were both Catholic.

He smiled; it was a tentative smile, but suddenly all my fears blew away. 'Would you like an engagement ring, Sidonie?' he asked. 'Shall I surprise you and choose?'

It was him, the old Etienne, my Etienne. It had simply been shock, as he'd said.

'No. A wedding band is all I need.' I smiled back at him.

He put his hand against my abdomen, through my thick coat. 'You will sing to it. *Dodo, l'enfant, do.* I can see you as a mother. I can hear you sing a lullaby to our child.'

I put my arms around him and again pressed my head against his chest, my eyes filling with tears for the second time. *Our child*, he had said. Our child.

Etienne didn't come three days later. I had expected him to be at the door just after breakfast. I waited until early afternoon, then went next door and asked Mrs Barlow if Dr Duverger had called for me.

He hadn't. I told myself he'd had an emergency at the hospital. Of course, for what else could keep him from coming? I waited through the evening, every hour carrying a heavier dread. Finally I undressed and went to bed, but couldn't sleep. What if he'd had an accident on the road, coming to my house? I remembered the steering wheel wrenching in my hands, the sensation of rising into the air. I saw my father lying in the cold field, and then the image of his body turned into Etienne's.

Would anyone from the hospital come to tell me if he'd been hurt? Or was ill? Had he spoken of me to anyone at the hospital?

I tossed and turned, too hot, then too cold. Cinnabar refused to stay on the bed, and finally I rose as well, and walked around and around the house. I was sick, a number of times, although whether it was from the baby or worry I don't know.

The morning was dark and snowy. By eight o'clock I was next door again.

'I'm sorry, Sidonie,' Mrs Barlow told me, 'but the line is dead. It went down early in the evening. It's the heavy snow.'

I nodded with relief. Here it was, then, the explanation. Etienne had been trying to phone all evening to explain what had kept him from coming to take me into Albany to set up our marriage, but couldn't get through.

'Why don't you stay and have a cup of coffee?' Mrs Barlow asked. 'You're looking drawn, dear. Are you feeling all right?'

My stomach churned. 'Thank you, but I'll go back home. I . . . I'm expecting to hear from Dr Duverger. Once the telephone is working, and he calls, would you mind coming to get me?'

I sat at the living-room window, unable to read, unable to paint. I watched the street, in case Etienne drove up. The snow stopped and the sun came out. A few cars toiled through the snowy street; each time I saw one I rushed to the front door and stepped out on the icy porch, willing it to be Etienne. But he would be at the hospital today, I told myself. Yesterday was his day off. He wouldn't be able to come today.

Finally, just after two o'clock, Mr Barlow came to my door, telling me that the telephone lines were finally working.

'And . . . has there been a call for me?'

He shook his head, and, without bothering to take my coat, I followed him to his house, across our back yards and through his kitchen door. Mrs Barlow was at the table, pushing back a strand of heavy grey hair from her forehead with her wrist. Her hands were covered in flour.

'Mr Barlow said the telephone is working,' I said.

She nodded. 'We're not sure when it started; Mike just picked it up a few minutes ago,' she said, nodding at Mr Barlow as he took off his boots.

They weren't sure when it started working? Didn't they understand how important it was to me? I tried to hide my anger; I knew it wasn't their fault, but I was so distraught.

'Do you mind if I use it – the telephone?'

'Of course not,' Mrs Barlow said. The kitchen was warm and fragrant. There was a bowl covered with a tea towel sitting on the back of the stove, and another round of dough on a floury board on the table. 'I'm making raisin bread. There are some loaves already baked. You take one, dear,' she said, kneading the dough.

'Thank you,' I said, taking the receiver from its hook and pulling the hospital phone number from my dress pocket. When I was put through to the hospital operator I asked for Dr Duverger. There was a moment's silence, and then the woman said, 'Dr Duverger is no longer at the hospital. Can I give you another doctor?'

'No longer . . . What do you mean?' I turned so that my back was to Mrs Barlow. There was a dull thump as she slapped the dough on the board. My ears were humming, and I cleared my throat.

'We're referring his patients to Dr Hilroy or Dr Lane, ma'am. Would you care to make an appointment with one of them?'

I stood there, the heavy black receiver pressed to my ear, my lips touching the fluted mouthpiece.

'Ma'am?'

I hung up the receiver, but didn't turn around. I was vaguely aware of Mrs Barlow's endless thumping.

'Sidonie? Make sure you take one of the—'

I left the kitchen, quietly closing the door behind me.

CHAPTER FOURTEEN

I ALREADY HAD ON MY coat and boots when Mrs Barlow came to the back door with the bread a few moments later. The loaf was wrapped in a clean tea towel, and gave off a yeasty, fruity smell. 'I wanted you to have it while it was still warm. Oh,' she said, as she held it out to me, 'you're going somewhere?'

I nodded, but Mrs Barlow asked, 'Is everything all right, Sidonie?'

'Yes,' I said, and then shook my head. 'Not really. Etienne – Dr Duverger – was supposed to be here yesterday.'

'Well,' she said. 'Doctors are busy men. Surely he had a reason.'

I shook my head. 'I'm worried that something has happened to him.'

'Why would you think that? Because he didn't come round when he said he would? There's no reason to worry yourself, dear. Give it another day or so.'

I didn't want to tell her what I'd just heard on the telephone. I stood in front of her, now looking at the bread she still held towards me.

She set it on the table and patted my hand. 'Give him time, Sidonie. He'll most likely be along as soon as he can,' she said, turning to leave, and then added, 'My. You look more like your mother every day now.'

I was ashamed to ask Mr Barlow to drive me to the hospital, knowing Mrs Barlow thought I was irrational for worrying because Etienne hadn't come when he said he would. But of course she didn't know the whole story. Something had happened to him. He wouldn't promise to come and then not show up. Especially not for something as important as arranging our marriage.

I walked to the hospital; it was a good hour and a half, but after the heavy snow the weather was surprisingly warm for mid-February, and by the time I reached the hospital I was too warm.

At the front counter I asked for Dr Duverger. Somehow I hoped that my physical presence in the hospital would actually produce him. When I was given the same answer, that he was no longer in the hospital's employ, I asked to speak to one of his colleagues. I tried to remember the names of the two doctors he worked with.

'Dr Hilroy or Dr Lane,' the woman said.

'Yes. Yes, either of them. Could I speak to one of them?'

The woman consulted a series of papers in front of her. 'Do you need an appointment? There will be a week wait. I can book you for next Monday, at noon.'

'No, I don't need an appointment. I simply have a question. It's not anything medical.'

The woman looked up from her appointment book, frowning.

'I just have a question,' I repeated, annoyed that I was forced to explain myself.

'Have a seat then, please. Dr Hilroy is almost done with his shift. When he's finished I'll have him speak to you.'

I sat down, taking off my coat and dabbing my forehead with my gloves. I felt truly ill; clammy and nauseous. I waited for what felt like a long time, and finally a tall, white-haired man came from behind swinging double doors.

'I'm Dr Hilroy,' he said, after speaking to the woman at the desk. 'May I help you?'

I stood, explaining that I had expected to hear from Dr Duverger.

'I assume you're a patient of his. But you mustn't worry. Dr Lane or I will take over your records.'

I shook my head and cleared my throat. 'Actually . . .' I licked my lips, 'although I was a patient once, now . . . I'm a friend of Dr Duverger's. A good friend,' I stressed. 'I'm concerned for his well-being. As I said, I expected to hear from him, and now I'm afraid something must have happened to him.' I hoped I didn't appear as shocked and confused as I felt. 'Naturally I'm very worried.'

The doctor frowned. 'I'm sure he's all right.'

'You don't think that something may have happened to him? Has anyone checked on him?'

'Well, I don't know, but there was no reason to suspect . . . Look, he did leave a month early, but it was quite straightforward.'

'A month early? What do you mean?'

Dr Hilroy looked as if he'd said too much, and shook his head.

'Did he . . . when do you expect him to return?' I asked.

'Would you care to sit down, Mrs . . . ?'

'No. But it's quite out of character for Etienne – for Dr Duverger – to act in such a spontaneous manner, you must agree. Leaving. So suddenly,' I added. 'Surely there's something more.'

Dr Hilroy looked even more uncomfortable. I told myself I sometimes had that effect on people even under normal circumstances. 'As I've just said, it was only a month less than the year contract. As a visiting surgeon.'

I blinked. 'He was leaving next month? For where?'

'I really don't know of his plans once his term contract was up. But frankly, none of us got to know Dr Duverger very well. He never spoke of his family before this, although I assume they're in France.'

I nodded, vacantly, trying to take in everything Dr Hilroy was saying. Etienne's family? But . . . they were all dead. 'He's gone to France?'

Now Dr Hilroy looked vaguely displeased, shifting and glancing at his watch. 'I really can't help you any further. He simply said it was impossible for him to stay on, due to family circumstances, and that he had to return home.'

Return home. Family circumstances. I thought I only repeated it in my head, but I must have spoken aloud, for the doctor said, 'Yes. Good day, then, Mrs . . . ma'am.'

'So . . . you have no way of reaching him? He must have . . . did he leave an address? Some way to contact him?' I asked, no longer caring if I appeared desperate. It didn't matter what this man thought of me.

Dr Hilroy suddenly looked down, and I followed his gaze. I saw my own hands, gripping his. I let go and took a step back. Now he rocked, ever so slightly, on his toes.

'I'm afraid not,' he said, and I must have made a sound,

perhaps a small cry, or a sudden intake of breath, and stared into Dr Hilroy's eyes. I saw my tiny reflection there.

I'd thrown on the first dress my hand touched in the wardrobe, and my hair ... had I brushed my hair? I remembered how colourless and hollow my face had been in the mirror last night. Surely I appeared a madwoman.

'I'm sorry,' he said.

'Is there anything, anything more at all, you can tell me?' I heard the beseeching tone of my voice. 'What about ... can you tell me the address where he lived? A rooming house nearby. I know that much.'

I know that much. The words only emphasised how little I did know.

Dr Hilroy frowned. 'I don't believe I should be giving out that information.'

'I'm Miss O'Shea,' I said, forcing myself to stand straighter. I knew I couldn't carry on in this manner; it was obvious Dr Hilroy was unsettled by me. I spoke more calmly. 'Miss Sidonie O'Shea. You can check the hospital records. You'll see I was a patient of Dr Duverger's last year. And I don't see how it could hurt to give me the address now. If Dr Duverger has truly left Albany, it won't matter, will it?'

He studied me for a moment longer.

'Please,' I said, in little more than a whisper, and he shook his head, as if to himself, and then walked away from me, speaking to the woman at the front counter in a low tone, glancing towards me. Then he motioned me towards the desk, leaving before I stepped up to the high counter, and the woman handed me a slip of paper.

★

The rooms Etienne had rented were ten long blocks from the hospital. I told myself he was actually still there; that he hadn't left Albany. He wouldn't leave me like this, especially not now. He had said we would marry. He had said *our child*.

He wouldn't possibly have gone to France without talking to me, without telling me what had happened – what family circumstances he had spoken of. And when he would return to me.

The house was tall and narrow, the red brick well maintained and the creamy paint around the windows and door obviously fresh. In one of the front windows there was a hand-printed sign: *Furnished Rooms for Rent*. I told myself there were many rooms in the house; the sign didn't have to refer to Etienne's rooms.

I knocked on the door, and it was opened by an elderly lady in a neatly pressed brown housedress with a white lace collar.

'I'm sorry,' she said, immediately. 'The rooms haven't been properly cleaned yet. If you would care to come back in a few days, I can show—'

'No,' I said, interrupting her and taking a deep breath. 'Actually, I'm a friend of Dr Duverger's.'

'He doesn't live here any more,' she said, starting to close the door, but I put my hand on it, pushing against it.

'I know,' I said, panic filling me even more than it had at the hospital. 'I know,' I repeated, 'but . . .' I stared at her face. 'But he asked that I come and see if he left a black leather case behind.' I didn't know where that sentence came from, but I wanted – needed – to go to Etienne's rooms. I needed, for myself, to see that he was gone.

'A leather case?'

'Yes. Black. With a brass clasp. He's quite fond of it; he asked me . . . as I've told you, to come by and look for it here.' As I spoke, I pushed harder on the door, and then stepped into the hall. There was the faint smell of boiled beef. Etienne did indeed possess such a case; I had seen it lying in the back seat of his car when he drove me to the clinic. At least that was the truth.

'Well, it wouldn't surprise me if the doctor forgot something. He certainly left in a hurry.'

'I'll only take a moment, if you'll point out his rooms,' I said, staring into the woman's eyes.

'I suppose it won't hurt.' She turned and pulled out the drawer of a cabinet in the hall, handing me a key. 'Upstairs, first door on the left. There are two connecting rooms.'

'Thank you,' I said, and went up the stairs. 'Oh,' I said, turning to look back at the woman. 'Did Dr Duverger remember to leave you his forwarding address, so that any mail might be sent on?' I struggled to keep my voice deceptively casual, but I heard the beat of my heart in my ears.

'No. Although he only got one or two letters the whole time he was here. Foreign, there were.'

I nodded, but just as I put my foot on the next step she added, 'He got one just days before he left, too.' I looked back at her. She nodded. 'The same foreign stamps.'

Without answering I climbed to the top of the stairs. I had to stop there, out of view of the woman, and lean heavily against the first door, trying to breathe. Finally I straightened and unlocked the door.

The shade of the wide window in the first room was

drawn, and the room had a musty, stuffy air. The room was simply furnished with a tufted couch and small table with two straight-backed chairs, as well as a sturdy desk with a swivelling wooden chair. There were a few papers in a pile on the desk. I shut the door and crossed the room, giving the tassel of the shade a quick tug. Pale light flooded the room, and dust motes scattered through the dull rays. I struggled to raise the sash, managing to lift it enough for cool air to rush in, riffling the papers on the desk and bringing in a fresh scent.

Through the open door into the next room I saw a neatly made bed with a candlewick bedspread.

I sat in the chair in front of the desk, my fingers shaking as I scrabbled through the papers. But they were only printed pages of a study on throat ailments. I opened the drawer on the right of the desk. It was empty but for a pair of spectacles. I picked them up and ran my fingers over the thin frame. I pictured Etienne sitting here, one finger absently tapping the bridge of his spectacles as he read.

'Etienne,' I whispered into the empty room. 'Where are you? What's happened to you?'

I set the spectacles on the desk and slowly pulled out the other drawers. They were empty apart from the usual desk items: a few paperclips, a half-empty bottle of ink, some pencils with chewed ends.

I looked under the desk; there was a trash container. It held a crumpled paper and a small pill bottle. I smoothed out the paper, but it was only the wrapper from a packet of mints. The pill bottle was for a drug with the long and unpronounceable name of oxazolidinedione, and was prescribed for Etienne. I knew the bottles that held the pills for his headaches – a simple painkiller, he had said – and the ones to help him sleep. There was another he sometimes took before he left my house in the morning. *To help keep me alert through the long day ahead*, he had said, in an offhand way. But this was one I hadn't before seen.

I put the spectacles and empty pill bottle into my handbag. I needed something – anything – of Etienne to hold on to. Then I leaned back in the chair, closing my eyes in sudden exhaustion and despair.

I wanted to go home, but first I knew I had to go into the next room. Here a sliver of cool wind blew with a tiny, persistent whistle through a crack in the sash of the window. The room contained only the bed, a dresser and a wardrobe. Again I pulled out each of the dresser drawers. There was nothing. Like the drawers, the wardrobe was empty, but as I turned to leave, I noticed a book on its floor. It was the one on famous American watercolourists I had given to Etienne for Christmas. He had, more than once, said he knew he was lacking in knowledge about the other side of life, the one opposite science, and wished to know more.

For some reason, seeing this book left behind – abandoned – filled me with overwhelming grief, and I sank to my knees, staring at it. I picked it up, running my hand over its cover. A small edge of paper, a bookmark, I assumed, emerged from the top, only a few pages in. I opened the book at the folded piece of paper, so thin that I could see writing through it.

Still on my knees, I pushed the book from my lap on to the floor and unfolded the paper; it was etched with creases, as if it had been crumpled and then flattened again.

The spidery writing, from a fine nib, was in French, and the delicacy of the script indicated a woman's hand.

My eyes darted to the signature – the single name – at the bottom.

I held the paper in both hands. As on the stairs, blood pounded in my ears. Staring at the letter, I was aware of my breathing, shallow, as if coming from my throat only. There was dampness under my arms and down my back, the wool of my dress sticking to my flesh in spite of the coolness of the room.

> *3 November 1929*
> *Marrakesh*

My dearest Etienne,

  I write to you yet again. Although you haven't replied to my former letters, I once more, with even more desperation, beseech you to not abandon us. I have never given up the hope that after all this time – it is now more than seven years since you have been home – you would find it in your heart – oh, your kind and loving heart – to forgive me.

  I shall not give up, my dear brother. Please, Etienne. Come home, to me, and to Marrakesh.
Manon

The onion-skin paper in my hand trembled violently. *Manon.*

Come home, she had said, to Marrakesh.

I looked down at the letter again. *My dear brother*, she had written. *It is now more than seven years*. Manon was his sister . . . but when I'd asked about his family, he had said

199

there was only Guillaume, hadn't he? *There is nothing and no one*, he'd said, *in Marrakesh*.

Too many secrets. There was too much I didn't understand. Was this what he'd meant when he'd told the hospital he was going home because of family circumstances? Had he left me without a word – abandoned me, like the book – because of his sister?

'Did you find the case?' a voice asked, and I turned my head to see a pair of sturdy laced shoes. I looked up.

The woman in the brown dress was staring down at me.

Clutching the letter, I managed to get to my feet. 'No,' I said, and pushed past her.

As I limped heavily down the stairs, holding the railing to steady myself, she called after me, 'Who did you say you were?'

I didn't answer, leaving the front door open behind me.

I don't understand, even now, my desperation to reach home. I fled as if hounds were at my heels. I only knew I wanted to be within the safety of my own walls, where I would take out the letter, and read it, over and over, trying to make some sense of it all.

The letter was the only link I had to Etienne.

Etienne. More and more, I felt as though I had never truly known him.

CHAPTER FIFTEEN

L OSING SOMEONE IS NEVER what one expects.
  When my mother died I had mourned, a quiet, sad
sorrow that was steady but understandable. While I missed
her presence, I knew I would carry on as before, tending to
the house and looking after my father. It was an inevitable
death, and I knew, instinctively, that the sadness would
lessen over time, would stretch and fade.

When my father died I had felt something else, a frenzy
of guilt and despair, of endlessly reliving the moments
when I argued that I would drive, when I looked away
from the road for that instant too long, when I turned the
wheel a few inches too many. It was the grief of regret, of
not having a chance to hear his forgiveness, to say goodbye.
It was followed by sheer loneliness because of the tragic
unexpectedness of his absence.

But now . . . what I felt when I returned to Juniper
Road late that afternoon was shockingly raw in its power.
It came over me in waves, a rolling weight that made me
weak. My legs wouldn't support me, and I had had to hire
a taxi to bring me home.

I was filled with a roaring confusion. I lay on my bed,
staring at the lengthening shadows.

I knew Etienne loved me. He wanted to be with me, and with our child. I played and replayed so many of our moments together, trying to see something, something I may have missed. I clearly could see, in my mind, the way he looked at me, the way he spoke to me, how he had laughed at something I'd said. How he had touched me. I thought of the last time I'd seen him, and the way he had put his hand on my waist and had spoken of me singing to our child.

No. I sat up in the near darkness. He would never treat me so poorly. He would never leave me in such a way. Something had happened to him, something out of his control. It had to do with a secret, or maybe more than one.

Nothing he had done, or hadn't done, was unforgivable. I would forgive him anything. He needed to know that.

When I rose the next morning I was stiff and cold, and my head was heavy, as though I couldn't quite awaken from a disturbing nightmare.

I was anxious, restless, as I had been when my father died. All day I wandered through my small rooms, possessing a strange and twitching energy, knowing I had to do something, but unable to figure out exactly what path to take.

My studio was damp and chilled, with an unused air about it. I hadn't painted in the last month; I had been too caught up in my new life and the thoughts of my future with Etienne.

There was a stealthy movement behind me, and Cinnabar forced her way through my ankles, and then jumped on to the table holding my supplies. She lowered herself, tucking her front paws under her chest and staring at me with wide topaz eyes. I saw how old she had become, her haunches withering and her small spine a line of bumpy vertebrae. She had lost the rich copper hue of her fur; now she was a dull brown.

The last paintings I had done were pinned up on the walls. They were careful and polite, executed with – as Etienne had once pointed out – a precise, unwavering hand, each small stroke thoughtful and certain.

Suddenly I was impatient with the work, impatient with myself for being that woman, a woman who simply allowed life to happen to her. Who thought that such a tiny piece of land, less than a mere pinpoint on the earth's surface, was enough to sustain her for a lifetime.

Cinnabar was falling asleep, her eyes half closed, her chin on her paws.

And so here I am, I thought, watching the old cat. I was neither formally educated nor worldly. Although Etienne had called me beautiful, I had no misconceptions about my appearance. My face and body were lean, my eyes wide and curious under thick arched brows. My hair was curly and difficult to hold in place; impossible to attain the cultured, sophisticated look I saw on other women. Stubbornly, I had refused to bob it in the latest style.

At thirty, I was no longer young. In fact, in some societies I would be considered old. In all probability those who knew me in Albany already viewed me as a spinster.

I left my paintings and went into the bathroom, studying myself in the spotted mirror over the sink. My normally dark complexion had an ashy sheen, and my lips were an odd mauve hue, matching the half-moons under my eyes. There were a few strands of paler hair along my temples. Not as dramatic as grey or white, but it was as if the normally rich black gloss of my hair had faded. Had this been there before, or had I simply been unable to see it? As to what I saw in my own eyes: nothing. Their colour had faded to something wholly unremarkable. Mysterious, Etienne had once called them. *Your eyes are mysterious, Sidonie*, he had said. *Mysterious, and, like you, elusive as the early fog.*

Did I only imagine that he had once spoken to me so?

'And now what?' I said, aloud, and behind me there was a sound. I turned; Cinnabar had followed me, and was standing in the doorway. She looked at me as if to ask, *Will you not sit still? Will you not settle in one place so that I can rest?*

I went to the living-room window. There was only darkness beyond the pane, and the quiet, persistent tapping of the linden branch. Tonight the tapping was nothing like dancing, as I had once thought; tonight it was the ticking of time, a bony finger on the shoulder. I was sick of my own predictability, and of my own small compass.

Again I saw my reflection, this time in the glass of the window, shadowy and vague, as if I were a ghost of myself.

I picked up my handbag from the sofa, where I'd dropped it the day before, and carried it into the kitchen. I took out everything I'd brought home from Etienne's rooms: his eyeglasses, the pill bottle, and the letter. I spread them out in front of me on the table and sat down, staring at them. I read the letter three more times; there was no reason to read it again, as by then I knew the words by heart.

Now I looked at the pill bottle, then rose and went to the bookcase in the living room, pulling out a thick medical journal from beside the dictionary and atlas. I took it back to the kitchen and turned to the index. There it was, this oxazolidinedione.

It was a medication for neurological pathologies, I read, prescribed to help deter both epileptic conditions and palsy.

But surely Etienne was not epileptic. He had never experienced a seizure in the times I was with him. And he didn't have any signs of palsy. He was occasionally slightly clumsy, stumbling against a piece of furniture or tripping on the edge of a rug. I remembered watching him carving a chicken I had cooked for our dinner, and how suddenly the knife appeared to jerk to one side. Etienne had dropped it, staring at it as if it were an unknown object, then turned from me, going to the sink and washing his hands, over and over. I hadn't thought anything of it at the time, but now I also remembered how these seemingly inconsequential acts upset him, and how he reacted with uncharacteristic anger, muttering under his breath and tersely brushing off my enquiries or concerns.

I didn't know what to make of the prescription. If Etienne had an illness, I would have known. Wouldn't I? I picked up the eyeglasses and again ran my fingers over and over them. I put them down and picked up the letter again.

This woman, his sister Manon, was related to the secret: the secret Etienne felt he was unable to tell me. This was why he had left. But he didn't realise that I could accept anything he told me. He had to know that. He had to know that I loved him enough to not care what his past held. That it was our future that would cleanse him of what plagued him.

But to find him . . . the only clues I had were the Christian name of his sister – a woman he had never mentioned – and the city where she lived. Where Etienne had grown up. I would go there. I would find him, in Marrakesh, and tell him this.

Would this be a spontaneous and foolish act? Yes. Had I ever before acted on such an impulse? Yes, when I had allowed Etienne into my home, and my bed. Into my life.

I had been a woman who previously had reacted with her head, with caution. My own past felt strangely distant, as if I were a character in a novel, a book I had put aside, half read, because that character held little interest for me.

But perhaps it was more important to think about the woman I thought I was now: a woman who acted on an urge, listening to her heart. I thought of my heart, seeing it, formerly, as a lumpy, liver-coloured affair, beating dully. But then Etienne had come, and in a short while it had changed into a rich bowl of scarlet blossoms, pumping with bright heat.

I feared that without some understanding of what had happened to Etienne, my heart was in danger of returning to what it had been, of withering back to that organ, as calm and undemanding as the subjects in my watercolours.

And, more importantly, now there was another beating heart – so tiny – to consider.

'I'm going abroad, Mrs Barlow,' I told her, standing in her kitchen. 'I'm going to . . .' I stopped. I didn't want to say *look for Dr Duverger*, or *try to find him*. It would be too difficult to explain to her that I knew with certainty he wanted to be with me. It was up to me to tell him it was all right. I would love him, no matter what. 'I'm going abroad,' I repeated, rather lamely.

'Abroad?' Mrs Barlow said, her eyebrows lifting. 'How will you do that?'

I swallowed. It had been over a week since I had made my decision, and in that time I had been planning and acting. I had already done what was necessary to obtain a passport. I had taken the stack of money from the sale of the Silver Ghost to the bank, changing most of it into francs. I had also withdrawn almost everything but a few dollars from my bank account, and had gone into the travel offices on Drake Street and purchased a ticket for a ship leaving from New York to Marseilles in two weeks. By that time I would have my passport. I had bought two suitcases. 'It's all organised,' I said now.

'And when will you return?'

'I don't know yet,' I told her. 'But could you and Mr Barlow watch the house while I'm gone? And Cinnabar. Could you keep Cinnabar for me?'

Mrs Barlow's mouth closed in on itself. 'Now, Sidonie. You're not the type to go off and spend all your money on a hare-brained holiday. Correct me if I'm wrong, but I get the sense this is something to do with that missing doctor of yours.'

I didn't answer. I studied the painting of three snipes on the wall behind her head. I had given it to her and Mr Barlow last year.

'Because if you're off to try and convince that man to come back . . . well, you can't make a man do what he doesn't want to do, Sidonie. If he doesn't want to be here with you, then going to the other side of the world to persuade him to come back won't make it right.' Her voice was unfamiliar: disapproving, and a tone louder than usual. 'Wouldn't it be easier to just let it be, and go on with your life? There's really no arguing with a man once he's got his mind set. I know.'

'But something's happened to him, Mrs Barlow. I need to tell him . . . I need . . .' I stopped, unsure of how to go on. 'I just need to go and speak to him, Mrs Barlow.'

'What's happened to him?'

I smoothed my hair back. 'There's been an emergency, of sorts. With his family.'

'But . . . why didn't you just speak to him while he was still here? Or can you not phone him? They have telephones wherever he is, don't they? I don't understand, Sidonie.'

Of course she didn't understand. I couldn't imagine Mrs Barlow ever feeling about Mr Barlow the way I felt about Etienne. Or if she once had, she wouldn't remember it after all these years.

'Mrs Barlow, please. I just have to go.'

'Is it France you're off to, then?'

I nodded. It wasn't entirely a lie; I was first going to Marseilles. And I felt an overwhelming need to not talk about it too much. If I said I was travelling on to Morocco, she'd question why I was going there. Then I'd have to tell her about the letter from the woman named Manon.

Suddenly my lips and chin trembled. I put my hand over my mouth and turned aside.

'Besides. There's your . . . state to consider.'

I looked back at her.

She nodded, her eyes dropping to my middle.

I took my hand from my mouth. 'How do you know?'

She cocked her head to one side. 'A woman can see the signs, if she's looking. And I imagine that it won't be too long until you're showing. So how will you travel about, a woman alone, with no ring on her finger and her belly a flag for all to see? For all to know what kind of woman she is?'

Mrs Barlow had never before spoken to me like this. I cleared my throat. 'I don't care what anyone thinks of me. You know that. I've never cared.'

Her eyelids lowered, just the slightest. 'Perhaps it would have been a better thing if you had cared, Sidonie. Perhaps then you wouldn't find yourself in the condition you do. Why, if your mother could see you, bringing a man into the house, carrying on—'

'Berating me now will do no good, Mrs Barlow,' I said, my tone as hard and loud as hers. 'My mother is long dead. And it's not your business.'

Mrs Barlow drew back as if I'd slapped her face, and I knew I'd hurt her. But I was angry with her because what she said was true.

'I'm sorry, Mrs Barlow,' I said quickly. 'You've always been so good to us. To me.' I didn't want to think about the fact that I hadn't paid Mr Barlow any rent for months, as he'd told me after my father died. I didn't know whether Mrs Barlow knew this fact. 'It's just that I . . . I love him, Mrs Barlow. And he loves me too. I know he does.'

At that Mrs Barlow put her arms around me. 'They always act like they care when they want something,

Sidonie.' She sighed, and I leaned against her. 'You know so little about the world, my girl,' she said. 'And about men,' she added. 'I saw this trouble coming from the first. I saw it, Sidonie, but you were still sorrowing over your dad, and I thought, now, Nora, let the girl have a little pleasure.'

She pulled away from me. 'But there's no pleasure without pain, Sidonie. No pleasure without pain,' she repeated. 'And you can count on that, as surely as you can count on the first frost each year.'

The day before I left my home, I went to the shed. The old Model T was still there, covered with a thick tarpaulin. I pulled it off and ran my hands over the car's hood, but didn't get inside. I thought about my father, sitting in it and smoking his pipe. I thought about my mother, sitting at the kitchen table in front of the sewing machine. I thought about the way Etienne had said *our child*.

I re-covered the car.

I walked all the way down to the pond for one last look. It was the first week of March, and a warm day, the sound of water dripping everywhere in a steady syncopation. The ice in the middle of the pond was softening, and had opened around its edges. A small wind ruffled the water into pretty little ridges that slid, like thin tongues, up on to the hard edges of earth. The late afternoon light flashed on the water, and the smell was spring, fresh, with the promise of new beginnings.

I put my hands on my belly, just the tiniest rise now.

CHAPTER SIXTEEN

I HAD TO STOP OVERNIGHT at Marseilles; the ship for Tangier sailed late the next afternoon. I was strangely weary after the week of sailing from New York, even though I had done little but lie on my narrow bed and, twice a day, walk the deck alone. I looked at the port with little interest as my cases were loaded into a taxi, and we drove through the streets to the hotel recommended on board.

At the hotel, the concierge asked my name, and I hesitated, and then said, 'Madame Duverger.' I hadn't intended on saying this, and had no reason to lie.

'How many days?'

'Only tonight. I'm taking another ship to Tangier late tomorrow.' I was also not sure why I felt I had to divulge my business to this unsmiling, severe-looking woman. The name tag on her blouse said Madame Buisson. She held out her hand.

'Do you wish me to pay in advance?'

She shook her head. 'Your passport, madame. We keep the passport until you leave.'

I swallowed. 'Surely it's not necessary,' I said.

'It is necessary,' she told me, her hand still waiting. 'Your passport,' she repeated.

I reached into my bag and handed the stiff, red-covered little book to her. She opened it and looked at my photograph, and her expression changed, subtly, as her eyes went over the page containing my name and date of birth and marital status: *Sidonie O'Shea. 1 January 1900. Albany, New York. Single.*

Even if she couldn't read English, Madame Buisson could see that the name I had given her differed from what was in my passport. I was not a madame.

She said nothing, but turned and went into a small room behind the desk with my passport. When she came back, she handed me a large metal key on a leather strap. 'Room 267, madame,' she said, and I was grateful that she said the last word with no sarcasm. 'The boy will soon bring up your bags.'

'*Merci,*' I said, and taking a deep breath, slowly climbed the wooden steps to the second floor.

The room was small but clean, with the luxury of an attached *salle de bains*. I sat on the edge of the bed, waiting for my bags so I could undress and ready myself for sleep.

I had no desire to see more of Marseilles. The docks had been filthy, piled with boxes and shipments, and dark-skinned men lounged everywhere, watching with veiled expressions. On the ride to the hotel I had seen too many wasted children and crumbling, decaying ruins of tall buildings.

My mother's family had, at some point in history, come from France; French blood ran within my veins. My baby's father was from this country. Our child would be three-quarters French.

As soon as my bags were deposited on the floor near the wardrobe, I took out my nightdress. It was only seven in the evening, but I had an unfamiliar, persistent pain in my back. I longed for a hot-water bottle. I fell into the single, hard bed with a sigh of relief, and in spite of the discomfort in my back, fell asleep almost immediately.

My body woke me in the night. The pain had moved into my abdomen, more painful now, and I curled tighter into myself, wanting it to stop. I thought a warm bath might help. I slowly put back the covers, and as I stood, there was a rush of fluid down my legs. Horrified, I looked at the wet darkness on my ankles. My hands over my belly, I made my way to the bathroom and switched on the light. The brilliance of the blood made me weak – not because of the sight of it, but because I knew what it signified.

'No!' I cried out into the empty bathroom, my voice echoing. I couldn't leave my room and make my way downstairs to find the concierge; the cramping and blood flow were overwhelming. Who could I call? 'Etienne,' I said, aloud, for there was no other name. 'Etienne,' I repeated, quietly now, but of course there was only my own voice bouncing off the walls and ceiling.

And there appeared nothing for me to do, no way to stop the life rushing from me.

Afterwards, I lay on my side on a towel on the hard tiles of the bathroom floor, my knees drawn up. I had wept so much that my head throbbed; I was so thirsty, and yet I didn't have enough energy to even pull myself up to drink from the bathroom faucet.

I stayed that way, on the floor, until a thin morning light

came through the window and on to my face through the open bathroom door. I stared at the light as it moved across the bed and wall. There was a light tapping on the locked door, but I didn't call out. I couldn't get up, and I couldn't close my eyes. It was as though my body was an unco-operative, flimsy shell, but my mind was a tight, rigid fist, with only one pulsing, hard sentence that kept running through it. *Your baby is dead. Your baby is dead.*

Shouts came through the partly opened window, then children's voices, the ceaseless barking of a dog.

Someone knocked, more heavily, and a girl's voice said, 'Madame! Madame, I will clean the room.' The handle rattled. At that I drew a deep, shaky breath, and managed to lift my hands to my face. My cheeks were wet. The rattling on the handle stopped.

It hurt to move; my joints ached as though I were in the grip of influenza. Shakily, I managed to sit up, looking at the bloodied towels on the floor around me.

'Etienne,' I whispered. *What do I do now? What do I do now?*

I pulled myself upright, holding on to the sink, and ran water into the bathtub and slowly bathed. I put on a fresh nightgown, bundling the soiled one into the waste can. I was too weak to attempt to rinse the blood and tissue from the towels, and left them in a pool of murky pink in the bathtub before going back to bed. I lay there, finally unable to cry any more.

I kept touching my abdomen; it was difficult to comprehend that the tiny thing Etienne and I had created was gone.

★

214

I believe I was in a state of shock; I was unable to think of anything more than the death of that little being. I know that at some point I clasped my hands and prayed for its soul.

I don't know how much time passed, but the next time there was the clanging of a pail in the hall, and then knocking at my door, I called out.

'Please,' I said, as loudly as I could. 'Ask Madame Buisson to come to my room. Tell her to come in. I'm ill.'

When she arrived, unlocking the door and standing in the doorway, looking at me across the room, I told her, flatly, that I had been sick during the night, and wished to have a doctor visit me. I had pulled myself into a sitting position in the narrow bed, the blankets piled haphazardly over my legs.

She nodded, her face unreadable as it had been the day before, but when her eyes flickered to the open bathroom door I saw her chest rise. I followed her gaze. I'd left one of the bloody towels on the floor. She went to the bathroom and glanced in, then closed the door with a firm thud, bordering on a slam. She stared back at me, her head giving an almost imperceptible shake, and left.

I think I slept, for within what felt like a very short time she returned, this time with a middle-aged man with a thick moustache and too much hair cream. He carried a black bag, and his fingers were chapped.

'Mademoiselle O'Shea,' Madame Buisson said, adding, 'American, just arrived', as if she smelled something unpleasant. The doctor nodded at me. So the concierge was now calling me by the name in my passport, with special emphasis on the Mademoiselle. She stayed in the room, by the door, her hands clasped in front of her.

The doctor asked her – I wondered why he didn't speak to me – the nature of the visit. The woman said, in a very low voice, that I had suffered a loss of blood in the night. She said the phrase, *pertes de sang*, in little more than a whisper, as if it were highly shameful to utter the words. And then she raised her eyebrows in a knowing gesture.

'Ah,' the doctor said, glancing at me. '*Une fausse couche?*'

'Most certainly. There is every indication it was a miscarriage, Doctor,' the woman said, seeming to take a strangely bitter pleasure in answering his questions.

Glancing back at me, the doctor spoke quickly. 'She's alone?' he said, turning to the woman, and by his tone it was clear he already knew the answer.

Then he asked the concierge what I was doing in Marseilles, and she told him I was going on to Tangier.

He looked back at me and shook his head. '*C'est impossible.* Oh, but it's not possible, mademoiselle,' he said in tortured English, his words loud and slow, as if I were very deaf or very unintelligent. 'You must not make the travel,' he said, and then I knew why he had been ignoring me and speaking only to the concierge about my situation. Because she had emphasised that I was an American, he didn't realise I spoke French, and she hadn't told him. He switched back to French as he again faced the concierge. 'She'll never make it there alone, having just gone through a miscarriage.'

'And she's a cripple,' the woman said, looking over the doctor's shoulder at me. I was too weak, too distraught to care about her callousness.

The doctor shook his head. 'Well. It's all the more

obvious that she's not the sort to travel to such a dangerous location. And it will most likely take her some time to recover. Tell her to return to America as soon as she's able.'

'*Monsieur le Docteur*,' I said, in French, 'I understand. Please speak to me directly.'

His cheeks stained, but he quickly regained his composure, clearing his throat and straightening his already impeccable lapels. 'I apologise.' He glanced at Madame Buisson. 'I wasn't aware you spoke French.'

I pushed back my tangled hair. 'I must go on. To North Africa,' I said. 'I must get to Tangier, as quickly as possible. When do you think it will be safe for me to travel again?'

'Oh, mademoiselle,' he said. 'I really cannot recommend that you take on a journey just now. Do you have friends in Marseilles? Or perhaps elsewhere in France, with whom you can stay for a while? Until your body recovers.'

I shook my head. 'No. I need to go,' I said, trying to make my voice firm, but it refused to cooperate. It was weak, my lips trembling.

'If you're so insistent, I can only say that you should then find someone to accompany you. To . . . perhaps protect you, once you're there. I meant this, when I spoke earlier, in no disrespectful way. It will require physical stamina as well as the ability to adjust to new surroundings. Surroundings that may be offensive to a lady such as yourself, obviously one of a well-bred and delicate nature. And one who has just suffered such a loss.'

My eyes burned, but I blinked rapidly. 'There's no reason I shouldn't recover quickly, is there?' I asked.

'Mademoiselle. As I've said, you must rest and let your body grow stronger. How many months were you?'

'Three,' I said.

He smoothed his moustache with his thumb and index finger, then picked up his bag and opened it, looking through it and pulling out a thin green bottle and setting it on the chair beside the bed. 'Has the bleeding stopped?'

'Almost.'

'And the miscarriage was complete?'

I didn't understand. 'I . . . I don't know.'

'Do you think your body has rid itself of everything?'

I swallowed. 'I think so.'

'Do you feel you should go to the hospital? There is a small one nearby that caters to foreigners. I could arrange a car—'

'I don't think that's necessary.'

'All right. But if there are further symptoms, you must go to the hospital. Otherwise, stay in bed for the next few days, and don't exert yourself in any way. I'm leaving you something,' he gestured at the bottle, 'that helps in these situations. Take two spoonfuls morning, midday, and evening for the next two days. You will experience some cramping. If the miscarriage wasn't complete, this will help to dispel everything from the womb.'

At those last words, the enormity of what had occurred came over me again with a pain so deep that I had to put my hand over my eyes. My body trembled, my teeth chattering the slightest. I knew I had to ask the question looming so huge in my head. I didn't know how I would deal with the answer. I took my hand from my eyes and looked into the doctor's face.

'Could it have been my fault?' I asked. 'Was it the travel, on the ship from America for the last week? Or . . . I've had a great deal of worry lately.' I let my breath out in a long, shaky exhalation. 'Perhaps I haven't eaten well enough. I've had trouble sleeping. Did I cause it? Is it my fault I lost my baby?'

'Mademoiselle,' the doctor said, more kindly now. He came closer to the bed. 'Sometimes this is just the way of nature. We can never be sure.' He patted my hand. 'You mustn't blame yourself. Try to rest. Madame Buisson, have another blanket brought up for her, and some soup. You will have to regain your strength. And please, as I've said, if you have more pain, or other difficulties, you must go to the hospital. Do you promise you will do this, mademoiselle?'

His unexpected gentleness with me was more than I could take. I covered my face with both hands, weeping, rocking back and forth, while the doctor and the concierge silently left the room.

For the next few hours I tried to sleep, but was unable. The bowl of steaming soup set on the dresser by a stout, red-haired girl, who glanced at me and then quickly away, grew cold. I pulled the extra blanket over me and lay on my back, staring at the ceiling.

I put my hands on my belly again, then looked at the limp white curtain lightly dancing in the early afternoon breeze.

I thought of what the child might have grown to be, and imagined him – or her – with gleaming dark hair, thick and straight, like Etienne's. With his same high, intelligent forehead, and slightly worried look between the brows. With my mother's full lips. If it had been a girl I would have called her Camille or Emmanuelle. A boy, Jean-Luc. I would have curled the small fingers around a paintbrush, I would have bought a kitten to love. We would have whispered bedtime prayers in French together.

I watched the curtain, mesmerised by its lift and fall. I told myself that perhaps the doctor was right. Perhaps I should return to Juniper Road – return home, where I would be safe. Would I stay there for ever? I envisioned myself standing in front of my easel, stooped, my hair white. My hands, clutching the paintbrush, were spotted with age marks, my fingers either fleshless digits or puffy with retained water. And I was alone.

That was all I could see: the child who no longer existed, and the bleakness of the rest of my days without Etienne. Without a child.

I wiped my nightgown sleeve over my face and got up, slowly walking to the window, holding back the curtain so that I could look over the rooftops of Marseilles. The shouts of playing children still rang out, and somewhere the same dog still barked. I had begun this journey to find Etienne, and now – even though our baby was no more – I needed him more than I ever had.

I stared at the rooftops, then lower, at the lines of drying clothes strung between the tall, narrow buildings. I knew that if I decided to go on to Marrakesh, there was no guarantee I'd find Etienne, or even his sister.

And yet I could not turn back now. As the room darkened, I knew I could not return to my former life until I completed what I had started, no matter the final outcome.

CHAPTER SEVENTEEN

Aᶠᵗᵉʳ ᴍʸ ꜰɪʀꜱᵗ ɴɪɢʜᵗ in Marrakesh, where I slept restlessly in spite of the wide, soft bed smelling of rose petals, I dressed in a swift, distracted manner and went immediately to the front desk.

I asked Monsieur Henri if Dr Etienne Duverger was – or had been – a guest at Hôtel de la Palmeraie. I realised I was twisting my fingers painfully, and when Monsieur Henri shook his head, I dropped my shoulders and unclasped my hands. 'You're certain?' I asked, and Monsieur Henri stared at me for a second too long.

'I assure you, mademoiselle, I have been here since the opening of the hotel over five years ago, and have an excellent memory.'

I looked down at the thick registry book. 'It would have been in the last while. Could you please check? Maybe someone else was working the front desk when – if – he checked in, or—'

Monsieur Henri closed the large book with a slow, deliberate movement, just hard enough that a puff of warm air blew into my face. 'That is not necessary. I do know our clientele, as I have told you, Mademoiselle O'Shea. Some have actually lived here for the last few years, preferring the ease and luxury of the hotel to the complex bureaucracy of purchasing a home in the French Quarter.'

I didn't respond.

'The requirements for buying land or a house in Morocco are quite antiquated and ridiculous,' he added, and then, looking at me more closely, said, 'I do hope you are assured, mademoiselle, that Dr Etienne Duverger was never a guest here.'

'Thank you,' I said quietly, turning to leave, then looked back at Monsieur Henri. 'What of a Manon Duverger?' I asked. 'I believe she lives in Marrakesh, surely here, in La Ville Nouvelle. Do you know her?'

Again he shook his head. 'I know of no Duvergers. But . . .'

'Yes?' I said, perhaps a bit too eagerly, approaching the desk again.

'Try the Bureau of Statistics on Rue Arles. They have a list of homeowners in Marrakesh.' He pulled a small folded pamphlet from under the high desk. I wasn't sure why he was suddenly being more helpful. 'Here is a map of the French Quarter; it will help you find your way about.'

'Thank you, Monsieur Henri,' I said. 'I appreciate your assistance.'

He gave a tiny, imperious nod, and busied himself refilling his fountain pen.

On the way out, I noticed a series of watercolours on one wall of the lobby. I was anxious to start my search, but glanced at them as I passed. They were by various French artists, none of whom I recognised. But some had managed to capture a particular essence of light in the renditions of what appeared to be the daily nuances of life in Morocco.

There were a number of paintings of the Berber people, in their villages of clay and in their nomadic tents.

I thought of the Blue Man on the *piste*.

I walked along the street so quickly that in moments my leg ached, and I had to slow down. But the sense of urgency was intense, and it was difficult for me to remain calm and walk with my usual gait.

My mind was racing, yet I still noticed what was around me. All the store fronts and street signs were written in French, occasionally with smaller Arabic print underneath. Most of the non-Arabs on the streets were the French who lived and worked in La Ville Nouvelle. The men, dressed in suits and hats, carried cases under their arms, and hurried along purposefully. French women, strolling arm in arm, some with shopping bags, were in pretty summer dresses and high-heeled shoes, complete with hats and gloves. It took me only a few moments to notice that when an occasional Moroccan man passed one of the French men or women, he stopped momentarily and saluted.

More than once, a Moroccan man looked into my face as if unsure, and then passed by.

There were no Arab women on the streets of the French Quarter; I hadn't seen one since I'd arrived in Marrakesh.

I easily found Rue Arles and waited while a clerk looked up the Duverger name. 'Yes,' he said, and I leaned closer. 'The Duvergers owned a home on Rue des Chevaux. But . . .' He hesitated, squinting as he followed a line with his finger. 'No,' he said. 'It was sold some years ago. Now it is owned by a family named Mauchamp.' He looked up at me. 'That's all I have here. Now there is no indication of any Duvergers owning a home in the French Quarter.'

I thanked him and went out into the street. Now what were my options? I couldn't have reached a dead end so quickly. Somebody must know of Etienne Duverger. He had lived here; his parents had died and were buried here, as was his younger brother Guillaume. And somebody must know of Manon Duverger.

I studied the small map Monsieur Henri had given me as I wandered through winding streets, noticing, as I walked deeper through the French Quarter, the red ramparts that surrounded the medina. They were solid, unbroken walls, apart from strange round holes along the top, and although I heard shouts and calls from the other side, I didn't know how one entered the old city.

Towering over all the other buildings was a huge red mosque. It was four-square and untapering, with a triple tier of openings. I went towards it as though it were a beacon; surely something of this dominance played an important role in this rather flat city. But before I reached it, I came upon a set of wide-open gates with high portals over them. The portals were decorated with Arabic script.

I knew it was the main entrance to the old city, the medina of Marrakesh.

I stopped outside the gates and looked through. Everywhere were African men and boys, some leading donkeys and small horses pulling carts piled with all manner of produce. The men's faces fascinated me because of their diversity. Here the combination of races was even more prevalent than I had witnessed in Tangier or Sale or as we passed villages in the *bled*. In Marrakesh there were those so fair-skinned as to look European or Semitic, with long, narrow faces and light brown or reddish beards, their heads covered by their turbans. There were the Berbers of the desert, often high-cheekboned, their faces chiselled and dark from the sun. And there were those with skin so black it shone ebony, their heads covered with tight curls. Slaves, or the descendants of slaves.

I thought about my reaction when Etienne had told me about the slaves in Morocco.

'As soon as the Protectorate was in place, the French government abolished the purchasing of new slaves,' he had said, 'but the Moroccans still own them. Many are descendants of the Africans from the sub-Sahara, brought up on the caravan routes from west Africa for centuries. Marrakesh is full of them.'

'Did you have slaves?' I asked, hoping he would say no.

'We had servants. Arabs,' he said, shortly, and then spoke of something else. It was another case of him making it clear he didn't wish to discuss certain aspects of his past with me.

Thinking of that conversation made me realise that there was no reason to search for Etienne in the medina; it was all Moroccans. As I stood under the portal before turning to leave, there was a sudden call of *Madame!*

I turned towards the voice, seeing a number of horse-drawn buggies lined up along the *allée* leading to the medina. I'd noticed these throughout the French Quarter, the Moroccan driver urging on the set of clopping horses as French men or women sat in the back seat.

Now one of the drivers hurried towards me. 'Madame!

Madame, *un tour de calèche*. Please, come and ride in my *calèche*; I show you Marrakesh. I take you all Marrakesh.' He was extending his hand as he came towards me, grinning in an overly friendly and familiar way, and I shook my head, backing away.

Without warning a Moroccan boy, perhaps fifteen, banged into my shoulder brusquely, nearly knocking me over, and I dropped my handbag. The man from the *calèche* shouted at him, and as I stooped to retrieve my bag and then stood again, the boy was staring at me, and the venom in his eyes frightened me. He didn't speak, but slowly his mouth worked, and like the man in the market in Sale, he spat at me. It hit the toe of my shoe.

I remembered the covered woman, hissing at me through the open window of the car as I crossed the river with Mustapha and Aziz.

The *calèche* driver ran at the boy, slapping him across the side of the head, then bowed to me, again urging me to come to his *calèche*. In spite of the hard blow to his head, the boy stood his ground. I was caught between the two men, the younger one looking at me with surprising hatred, the other with a cagey expectation.

The woman on the ferry had despised me because she thought me a promiscuous and immoral woman. But did she, as the man in Sale, the boy here, hate me also because she saw me as one of the French who had come into her country and forced her subjugation?

I shook my head again, opening my mouth to speak, but nothing came out. Then I walked away as quickly as possible.

★

I searched La Ville Nouvelle for three full days, but every time I said the name Duverger I was met with blank stares. I had wandered through all of its wide boulevards, looking at the villas behind gates in gardens of palm and orange trees for hours and hours each day, my leg and hip throbbing from endless walking. I had looked into all the cafés, had asked about Etienne at the Polyclinique du Sud, the small French medical clinic, and had sat in the main square, studying each European man who passed.

I saw a few men who, from the back, resembled Etienne: wide, straight shoulders, dark hair curling over the collar, confidence in the step. Each time I felt faint for a moment, and then hurried after the man, realising, when I was a few feet from him, that it was not Etienne. Only once was I so sure that I touched the man's sleeve, and when he turned to me he frowned in a concerned way.

'Yes, madame?' he had said. 'How can I help you?'

Such was my disappointment that I simply shook my head, backing away.

My hope – and corresponding anxiety – over finding Etienne had now been replaced with a dull ache of despair. But he must be here, in Marrakesh. The letter . . . I had so frequently taken the folded paper from my handbag and reread it that it was dirty and tearing in the creases.

It was the same when I enquired about Manon Duverger, but I reasoned that I had no idea what she looked like, and that she might have married and now had a different surname.

Staying at the luxurious Hôtel de la Palmeraie, my money was depleting at an alarming rate, and I knew I must find less expensive lodging. And yet, at the end of each of those first three days, when I returned to the hotel hot and exhausted, I no longer had the energy to begin the process of searching out a different hotel and moving.

That fourth day of my search was like the first, and the second and third. At noon, thinking about the time difference between Morocco and Albany, I went to the postal station, and had an operator put in a call to Albany. After half an hour's wait I was summoned to the telephone, and heard Mr Barlow's voice.

'Mr Barlow,' I said, loudly. The line was crackly. 'Mr Barlow, it's Sidonie.'

'Sidonie,' he said. 'Where are you calling from?'

'I'm in Morocco.'

There was silence. 'Where's that?'

'North Africa.'

Another silence.

'And you're all right?'

'Yes. I'm fine. I wondered . . . has there been any mail for me?'

'Mail? Well, I'll have to go and get Nora for you. Just a minute.'

I heard Mr Barlow calling Nora's name, then the murmur of voices. I clicked my fingernails on the counter. *Hurry, hurry up, Mrs Barlow.* I was so afraid the line would go dead.

'Sidonie? Is that you? Why are you in Africa? You said you were going to France. When are you coming home?'

'Mrs Barlow,' I said, not answering any of her questions, aware of the growing crackle of the line. 'How are you?'

'I'm fine. There's been too much rain, though, and the—'

I cut her off. 'Did any mail come for me since I've been away? Did any letters come?'

'Letters?'

I fought to stay patient. 'From Dr Duverger. Or . . . anything with a foreign stamp. Did anything come?'

'No. But . . . you haven't found him? Why haven't you come home, then? And . . . the other. You know. How's that going?'

I didn't answer for a second, and the static on the line increased.

'Sidonie? Are you there?' Mrs Barlow's voice was thin and distant.

'Yes. Is Cinnabar all right?' I was almost shouting.

'Well, she's—' she started, and then the line went dead.

'Mrs Barlow?' I called into the receiver, but there was silence, and then nothing but a rapid, repetitive clicking.

I went to the counter and paid for the call, and then, weary and despondent, returned to the hotel and sat, rather numbly, in the lobby.

Mr Russell stopped in front of me.

'We haven't seen you about, Miss O'Shea,' he said. 'Not even in the dining room.'

I smiled wanly. 'Yes. I've been . . . busy. And taking my meals either in my room, or . . .' I realised then that I'd been eating little.

'Mrs Russell and I are leaving for Essouria tomorrow, but we thought that this afternoon we'd visit the Majorelle Garden,' he told me. 'It's a bit further north-west in the city. Do you know of it?'

I shook my head.

'Have you looked at these paintings?' he asked, gesturing at the watercolours on the wall. 'They're for sale; a lot of people who stay here like to take home images of Morocco. *Une passion Marocaine*, as they say. They go for a pretty price. Some of them are by Jacques Majorelle,' he said.

I didn't comment, not interested in having a discussion on painting with Mr Russell.

But he liked to talk. 'He's a passable artist; manages some quite gentlemanly orientalist watercolours. And as I said, a lot of tourists to Morocco seem to go in for that sort of thing. But Majorelle had this idea, supposedly a few years back, to build a magnificent public garden. He bought a few acres of land in the date palm groves on what was then the outskirts of the city. He's planted an impressive array of cacti, succulents, bamboos, bananas, tree ferns and so on. I believe he's importing dozens of varieties of palms. Parts of it are still being worked on; he's trying to bring in every tree and plant imaginable that will survive this climate.'

In the sudden silence I felt I couldn't be rude as Mr Russell stood over me as though waiting for something. 'Does Monsieur Majorelle no longer paint, then?'

Mr Russell waved one hand airily, as if the answer to my question was not worth much concern. 'I'm led to believe he's an artist of little importance. Nobody outside of Marrakesh seems to know much about him. But please, Miss O'Shea, do feel free to come along with us. It will be quite relaxing.'

'Oh, no. I shouldn't . . .' I began, and then stopped. The thought of spending time in a beautiful garden away from walking the busy streets in the oppressive heat was appealing, and I knew I didn't have the energy to search any further this day. Perhaps it would be a relief to think of something other than Etienne for a few hours. 'Well, yes. Thank you. I'd like to join you.'

We rode to the gardens in the horse-drawn *calèche* Mr Russell had hired. He pulled a cigar from his breast pocket as we drove through the verdant streets of La Ville Nouvelle, rich with green spaces of trees and flowering beds. Mrs Russell said little, and almost immediately, once we were settled in the facing leather seats of the open-topped buggy, Mr Russell continued on about Jacques Majorelle as if our earlier conversation was still in progress. 'The word is that he has a studio, as well as a notable variety of birds. Majorelle decided his garden will be an oasis of quiet, fragrant beauty in the centre of a noisy, busy city.' He clipped the end of his cigar with a small metal implement, and then lit a match, puffing on the cigar with long, satisfied pulls. The smoke rose above his head, and he spoke again, but this time I was able to tune out his words.

As we turned north-west, the *calèche* driver brandished his whip above his head in twisting arabesques, snapping the thin leather back and forth over the backs of the two horses pulling the *calèche*, but never touching them.

I watched the twirling smoke of Mr Russell's cigar and the curl of the whip over our heads as they intersected in the blue sky.

Most striking about Le Jardin Majorelle was the sensation of shade and filtered sunlight, and the colour of many of the arches and huge terracotta vessels containing plants.

They were painted green and yellow and blue. The blue was a vivid and almost electric colour. I tried to find a name for it: perhaps cobalt, perhaps a shade of azurite or lapis lazuli, maybe Prussian or cerulean. But nothing was exactly right. This blue seemed to have its own distinct properties.

And the colours of the garden matched Marrakesh's brilliant hues.

Almost immediately Mr Russell introduced me to a man in a white panama hat – it was Monsieur Majorelle – and he welcomed us graciously. 'I'm happy to show my vision to visitors,' he said in French. Mr Russell could speak a little French, and he translated for Mrs Russell. Monsieur Majorelle led us down a shady path of beaten red earth. Other paths crossed it. Sunlight dappling through the tall, swaying foliage created a rhythmic pattern on our faces. There were a number of young Moroccan men, dressed in white, digging and planting.

'The garden is my expression; for me it has a mystical force. I'm attempting to create a design – one I see here,' said Monsieur Majorelle, tapping his temple, 'with vegetal shapes and forms. I have a love of plants,' he finished.

It was clear that the design of the garden had a certain composition and placement of colour in both its structures and its plant life that immediately brought to mind a painting. I looked at the shallow tiled pool nearest; carp and goldfish wove through the clear water, turned aquamarine by the tiles. I recognised water lilies and lotus, but there were other aquatic plants unfamiliar to me. 'What is that, Monsieur Majorelle?' I asked, pointing to tall stalks topped with a large, tassel-like head.

'Papyrus,' he said. 'I wish to bring in forms representing the continents that sustain life. Please. Enjoy yourselves. Stroll about.'

We said goodbye. Mr Russell wanted to shoot photographs with the Brownie camera he wore around his neck.

'I'll go off on my own,' I told him and Mrs Russell. 'I'd love to explore some of the plantings.'

We parted, agreeing to meet back at the entrance in an hour. I wandered down the pleasant paths, touching the profusion of vermilion bougainvillea twining over trellises. I passed the men in white, the thudding and scraping of their shovels in the red earth a solid, heavy sound in comparison to the high and glorious bird calls from above.

Although the garden was beautiful, it hadn't lifted my despondency. There were few other people, apart from the Arab workers, but I noticed a frail, very elderly woman sitting on a bench under a banana tree. She held a tiny dog with feathery gold fur, a stiff pink bow around its fluffy neck. The old woman stroked the dog with gnarled fingers, each one decorated with a ring bearing a different gem. I thought of Cinnabar, and the soothing feel of her fur.

The shaded bench was inviting. '*Bonjour*, madame,' I said. 'Your dog is very sweet. May I pet her?'

'*Bonjour*,' she answered in delicate French, her voice tremulous with age as she peered up at me. 'Do I know you? My eyes . . . I don't see well any longer.'

'No, madame. You don't know me. I'm Mademoiselle O'Shea,' I said, sitting beside her.

'I am Madame Odette. This is Loulou,' she added, and the little dog looked up at her, its mouth slightly open, its pink tongue curled up on the end, vibrating as it panted in the heat.

'Are you enjoying the gardens?' I asked.

She smiled, almost merrily. 'Oh yes, my dear. I come every day. My son brings me after our noon meal, and picks me up at five. Is it nearly five?'

'I believe so, madame. Do you live nearby?' I reached towards Loulou, but one corner of her tiny lip lifted in warning, and I withdrew my hand.

'Yes. I have lived in Marrakesh for a number of years. Now I stay with my son and daughter-in-law. My husband was in the Foreign Legion, you know. He died many years ago.'

She stopped, looking into the distance. Loulou yawned, shifting in the old woman's lap.

Madame Odette refocused on me. 'But she is unpleasant, my daughter-in-law. Every day some difficulty. I grow weary, listening to her tell my son what to do, and complain about this and that. So I come here, and enjoy the garden.' She looked towards a stand of bamboo. 'My son brings me here,' she repeated. 'Nobody bothers me, and I do not have to hear my daughter-in-law's voice. Loulou and I spend many hours amidst the trees and flowers.'

I nodded, leaning down to pick up a fallen bougainvillea blossom and looking into its deep red centre.

'And you, mademoiselle? You live in Marrakesh as well?' Madame Odette asked.

I looked up, shaking my head. 'No.'

'You're visiting family?'

I touched the velvet of the bloom to my chin. 'I'm here to find someone, but . . .' I again reached towards Loulou.

This time she allowed me to stroke one ear. I moved my hand to her back. 'It's proving very difficult, I'm afraid.'

'I have lived in Marrakesh many years,' she repeated. 'The heat of Africa is good for my bones, although my daughter-in-law's chill is not good for my heart. But I have known many French families. My husband was in the Foreign Legion. Very handsome in his uniform.'

She was watching my fingers running up and down the little dog's back. 'What day is it?' she asked, suddenly looking at me.

'It's Tuesday,' I said.

'Will it rain tomorrow?' Her eyes were milky blue, clouded with cataracts.

I shook my head. 'I don't believe so, madame. It's summer. There is little rain in summer in Marrakesh. Isn't this so?'

'I have lived here many years. I am old,' she said. 'I forget.'

I patted Loulou's head and then stood. 'I'm sure your son will come for you soon, Madame Odette.'

'What time is it?'

'Almost five,' I told her again.

'He comes at five. He will come here, for me. Wait under the banana tree, Maman, he tells me. I always wait for him.'

'All right, then. Goodbye, madame. And Loulou,' I added, touching the dog's silky ear a final time. She twitched, annoyed, as if a fly had lit on it.

'Who is it you seek, mademoiselle?' Madame Odette asked then, looking up at me. Her face was shadowed by the leaves.

'The Duvergers, madame,' I said, without expecting her to answer logically.

'Marcel and Adelaide?' she said, unexpectedly, and I opened my mouth, then closed it and sat down beside her again.

'Yes, yes, Madame Odette. The family of Marcel Duverger. You knew them?' I said, still refusing to grow hopeful.

She nodded. 'Marcel and Adelaide, oh yes. And the son . . . I remember some tragedy. I remember the past, mademoiselle. I remember past days, but often not this day. They had a son. It was a tragedy,' she repeated. 'I have a son.'

'Guillaume was their son. Yes, he drowned.'

She studied me, her head on one side, her eyes suddenly more alive, even though the irises were ghostly because of her cataracts. 'And there was an older one.'

'Etienne. You know Etienne?' My voice was quick, loud now.

'I remember something about him. Clever young man. He went off to Paris.'

'Yes, yes, that's him, Madame Odette. Have . . . have you seen him? Recently?'

She stroked the dog's chest. 'No. But I don't go out, except to come here. My son doesn't allow me to go out now,' she said. 'I am old. I forget things,' she repeated, shaking her head. 'They died some years ago. First Adelaide, and then poor Marcel. There are no longer any Duvergers in La Ville Nouvelle. He was a doctor.'

'Yes. Yes, Etienne is a doctor,' I said, nodding, encouraging her.

'No. Marcel. Many of the doctors worked for the

intelligence service,' she said. 'Once we took over Morocco, the French medical doctors proved especially effective as agents of imperial penetration of Morocco,' she said, her voice dropping to a harsh whisper, as though enemy ears hid in the trees and bushes around us. 'My husband told me many tales of the espionage. Oh yes,' she said, 'they were not always just doctors.'

I sat back; I had been leaning so close I had smelled both the odour of her dentures and a powdery lilac fragrance, although I couldn't be certain whether it arose from her bodice or the dog in her lap. Disappointment flooded through me, and I closed my eyes for a moment. I didn't care about what Etienne's father had or hadn't done decades earlier.

'The person you search for, my dear,' she said, and I opened my eyes.

'Yes?'

'It is a man or a woman?'

'A man. It's Etienne Duverger I'm trying to find.'

'And he is willing to be found?'

I let her words sink in for a moment. 'Willing?'

The old woman smiled, a strange smile. 'Sometimes . . . well, if one can't be found, it is because one is hiding. My husband told me many stories of those unwilling to be found.'

I knew I had refused to think of this, although I had, since arriving, held this very thought like a tiny, hard knot at the back of my mind: that Etienne was indeed in Marrakesh, and had seen me, but had not approached me because he was, as Madame Odette had just said, unwilling to be found.

'Madame Odette,' I said then, not wanting to think about Etienne hiding from me. 'What of the daughter? She's gone as well?'

Now Madame Odette frowned. 'Daughter?'

'Manon. Manon Duverger,' I said, but the old woman shook her head.

'I don't recall a daughter.'

'She may have a married name now.'

'And her name is Marie?'

'Manon.'

Madame Odette nodded. 'I know a Manon Albemarle,' she said, and my mouth opened and I leaned in again, nodding. 'She's quite young. Perhaps fifty-five. My son's age.'

I let my shoulders drop. 'That won't be her. Manon Duverger is much, much younger than that. I was sure she lived here, in La Ville Nouvelle.'

'I forget many things,' Madame Odette said. 'Many things.' The little dog yawned again, this time snapping its tiny teeth as it closed its jaws. '*Ma chérie*,' Madame Odette murmured, stroking the dog with more force. 'I don't remember this Manon. You believe she lives here, in Marrakesh?'

'She did a few months ago,' I said, thinking of the folded letter I carried in my bag at all times.

'And it's with certainty that she lives in La Ville Nouvelle?'

'I . . . I assume so. She's French, after all.'

'There is more than one kind of French woman in Marrakesh, mademoiselle.'

I didn't understand. Madame Odette's gaze was

suddenly coy. 'Perhaps she's gone Arab. She may have moved into the medina to live with the Moors.' She leaned in to my face. 'Some do, you know. There's been more than one French woman who has lost her sense, lured in by a man.'

'You think it's possible that she lives in the medina? I don't . . .' I stopped. I knew nothing about Manon.

'You should try there, among the Moroccans. Outside the walls live the émigrés. The native people of Marrakesh do not live in La Ville Nouvelle. Poor, rich, they all live in the old city; even the sultans and nobles have their fine homes and their harems, their *riads* with their glorious gardens, all within the medina walls.'

Within the medina walls. I thought of D'jemma el Fna. 'The medina is large, Madame Odette. How could I even begin to look there?'

'Yes. It's large, the medina, and you must venture through the souks to the little *rues*, which run in every direction. Very confusing streets – more like alleys, narrow and dark. The homes are windowless on the outside walls. The people believe that conspicuous exteriors are a very poor show. Like their women, the men keep their riches hidden.' She drew a deep breath. 'Always look for the minaret of La Koutoubia. The highest mosque, just outside the medina gates. Koutoubia means bookseller. Once booksellers set up their wares at the base of the mosque.'

She stopped speaking and stroking Loulou, closing her eyes as though her explanation had exhausted her. I knew she was talking about the imposing red mosque I had seen. 'But when La Koutoubia is out of sight, one can easily get lost. It is almost impossible to find the way out when you are buried deep within the medina. I was lost there, once.' She opened her eyes. 'What day is it?'

I put my hand on the old woman's arm. 'It is Tuesday, Madame Odette.'

'I myself have not gone into the medina for many years. My son does not like me to go out. I am old,' she said, yet again.

'Thank you, Madame Odette,' I said, standing. 'Thank you for your help.'

The woman looked at the sky. 'Oh, you mustn't go to the medina now; it's growing too late. It's not a good idea to walk about in the medina by yourself after daylight.'

'Yes, all right. Thank you, madame,' I said again.

'You know I have a son, mademoiselle,' Madame Odette said. 'He comes for me at five. Do you have a son?' she called after me, and those last five words travelled into me like five sharp jabs.

CHAPTER EIGHTEEN

T HE FOLLOWING MORNING I stood, for the second time, and looked through the tall gates at the sun filtering through the medina. I told myself that the old city didn't appear so menacing a place. With one last glance over my shoulder at the streets of the French Quarter, I clutched my handbag more tightly and walked under the high portals, hoping I looked purposeful, with a destination in mind, and not like a woman only pretending to be unafraid.

Finally I saw Moroccan women, although as elsewhere throughout the country, nothing was visible but their eyes above their veils. Their bodies were also made completely indistinguishable by a white cloth – I knew it was called a *haik* – draped over their heads and completely covering them to the ground. Under the *haik* they would wear their daily dress, a flowing gown called a kaftan. I had seen striped silk kaftans, tightly cinched at the waist with wide belts, in a few shop windows in the French Quarter. I assumed some French women bought them on a whim, or perhaps because they were cool and comfortable to wear within their homes.

Most of the Moroccan women in the medina carried

large woven bags over their shoulders, and some had babies swaddled on their backs with slings of cloth, while others had small children clinging to their robes, toddling quickly to keep up. I then noticed that with every woman was a man or older boy, walking closely in front or behind. No woman was without a male accompanying her.

I was immediately aware of the stares of the men, and how the women gave me a wide berth.

Of course I again thought of Mr Russell's warnings, about not coming here alone, and yet he and Mrs Russell had left for Essouria early this morning. But even if they hadn't, I wouldn't have wanted him to accompany me. That would have required me to explain why I was looking for a woman named Manon Duverger in the old city.

I didn't wish to discuss my situation with anyone.

I looked straight ahead, pushing through the throngs in the crowded, narrow street. I didn't know where I was going, but I had told myself that once I was inside the medina I would figure out my next move.

On this first street, every square inch under the tattered straw or cloth awnings, so faded as to be colourless, was crammed with tables or simple threadbare strips of carpets on the ground holding everything imaginable – as well as some things which were, to me, quite unimagined.

There were women's kaftans and endless djellabas of every colour and every fabric. Other stalls held hundreds of *babouches* – the backless leather slippers dyed bright shades of yellow and orange and red – dangling overhead from hooks. There were camel-bone teapots and red felt fezzes and arrays of perfumes: jasmine and musk and sandalwood.

I passed trays of sweetmeats and juicy dates and figs and live chickens and pigeons in crates. Thick swarms of flies buzzed and settled, lifted and settled over everything.

And then suddenly I came into a huge open square with stalls and kiosks lining its edges. It had to be at least three city blocks square. People milled about, and as I watched displays being set up in the centre, I knew I had come to D'jemma el Fna. Men were unrolling rugs and lifting covered baskets out of the back of carts pulled by donkeys. Others were setting up pyramids of oranges on wooden trays or dumping mounds of steaming snails out of pots and into woven baskets.

I didn't dare walk through the open centre; already I felt too conspicuous and uneasy. Instead, I edged along the perimeter of the square. I had to walk around a man hunched over a board on his lap, writing on a thin sheet of paper as a tearful young man crouched in front of him, speaking in a low voice. Beside the man writing was a small square of cotton, and on it a few coins. The young man dried his face with the sleeve of his djellaba and put a coin on to the cloth; the other man handed him the sheet of paper. A scribe, I thought, surely, writing out a letter for the young man.

Even at the perimeter of the square, the crowd was thickening. I was pushed and jostled, usually simply caught up in the bustle, but on occasion I suspected I was knocked into intentionally. I refused to listen to the voice in my head telling me that these were portents, that I was not wanted here, and should leave.

And yet I had no choice. I had run out of options in the French Quarter. I would stay in the medina, and try, somehow, to find out if Manon lived here. I had no plan other than asking about the Duvergers.

I heard a running string of Arabic in a loud, authoritative voice, and looked over the heads of others to see a man on a box, waving his arms, his eyes wild and his face stubbled. He wore a magnificent robe of brown and blue velvet, so different from the other men in the square in their drab djellabas. Around him some men squatted in a circle, many watching his face with their mouths open. Others stood, but all were mesmerised and silent. The man on the box went on and on, his words hammered out as he gestured and shook his head or nodded, and I began to realise, by his pauses and the fire of his words, that he was telling a story. In front of him lay a square of dark cotton, and on it glinted coins, as I had seen beside the scribe. A professional storyteller.

Further on I came across a man sitting on the ground with a cloth filled with pulled teeth in front of him. They were of all sizes, some rotted and some whole, the roots long and pointed. He held up a pair of rusted pliers when he saw me looking at his collection. He tapped his front tooth with the pliers, opening and closing the metal instrument. His own teeth were grotesque, and I hurried away. I had seen enough of D'jemma el Fna.

I walked down one of the alleys that led from the square like spokes of a wheel. I was now in the souks, and looked ahead and behind, trying to find clues to remind myself of the way back to the square. Here were endless stalls and tiny shops, with a man standing in front of each. It took me only a few moments to see that the souks were organised by trade, with the cloth-sellers in one alley, and the silversmiths in another. There were rug merchants and perfume dealers. I saw conical piles of spices of every shade of red and yellow and orange and green and brown, their smells mingling. The men visited back and forth, calling to each other, and sometimes to me, with murmurs of 'Madame, *venez*, madame.' Come, madame.

My vague intention had been to stop women and ask them if they knew Manon Duverger, but it had been obvious from my first moments in the medina that this wouldn't be possible. The women hurried past me, sometimes talking to an accompanying woman beneath their veils, their dark eyes glancing at me in a somehow accusing way, making it clear I was an outsider.

I stopped, looking backwards and then ahead; had I turned left or right at the last corner? I looked up, hoping to see the tower of La Koutoubia, but all that was visible was the slash of azure sky through tattered reed awnings.

Would I be able to retrace my steps? I turned in all directions. Suddenly every man's eyes were on me; every woman pushed past me, banging my shoulders or hips as though in warning.

I edged closer to the stalls, away from the middle of the crowded, narrow streets. Occasionally the owner would spring to life, chattering in Arabic or French, trying to sell me a scarf or a decorated hand mirror or a bag of dried rosebuds or a sack of mint for tea. Each time I asked about the Duvergers. Some of the men shrugged, either because they didn't know the Duvergers, or perhaps because they didn't speak French, or simply didn't care to answer me if I wasn't purchasing something from them. Some shook their heads. Most simply ignored my question, urging me to buy.

I was too hot, hot and thirsty; it was making me light-headed. It had been a mistake to come here, blindly looking for an unknown woman. The thought of my quiet room at the hotel was a vision now; I needed to return to the safety of the French Quarter.

Every man and woman appeared to be staring at me, and I stopped again, turning in a circle, trying to get my bearings.

Suddenly my skirt was yanked, almost violently, and I gasped. Three small children – no older than four or five – stood around me, pointing small, dirty fingers into their open mouths, screeching *Manger! Manger, madame!*

I opened my purse to give them a few small coins, and at that gesture the smallest of the children leapt as if to take it. I held my purse against my chest, and the child cried, piteously, *Bonbon, madame, bonbon!*

'Wait, wait,' I said. 'I have no candy.' I dropped a few sous on to the ground, because the children made it impossible to put them into their hands, clinging to my skirt and jumping up and down. As they stooped to gather the coins, I pulled free and hurried away, but suddenly there were more children running after me, again grabbing at my skirt. I tried to ignore them, because I had only two sous left in my bag – I hadn't thought to bring much money with me.

'*Non, non,*' I said, trying to free myself from their hands, and suddenly, as I reached the end of the alley, I was back in D'jemma el Fna. But the children persisted, and as I pushed their little hands from my skirt, there was a flurry near my ear, and a weight on my shoulder. Shocked,

I turned my head and stared into a tiny scowling face next to mine. I shrieked involuntarily, and the little thing also screeched in response, so loudly that I was momentarily deafened. It was a monkey, I told myself, only a monkey.

And yet the children still beseeched, still clustered around me, jerking my skirt. The monkey was pulling at my hair. I couldn't catch my breath, couldn't call out.

A voice shouted in Arabic, and the children scattered. I stood, trembling, my face wet with perspiration, the monkey still perched on my shoulder.

'Madame, oh madame, this is truly good luck,' said the man who had run off the children. He held a long chain, and the chain led to a leather band around the monkey's neck. 'I am Mohammed, and my monkey, Hasi, has chosen you,' he told me. 'If you give a sou, only one sou, madame, your luck will be threefold. Oh, it is a blessed day that Hasi has chosen you. He has chosen you because he knows you are the possessor of a good soul. This Hasi knows. He goes only to the good.'

I knew the monkey would jump on anyone Mohammed directed him to. Hasi now slid down my arm, looking up at me. I saw how the band bit into his little neck, the fur worn away there and the skin raw. He bared his pointed teeth in a smiling grimace, putting his tiny hand out, palm up.

'Madame,' Mohammed entreated. His eyes were small and oily. 'You must wish for this good luck. Only a fool would turn down such an opportunity. Tell the good lady, Hasi, tell her she must not let this opportunity pass.'

Hasi made a sad chuckling in his throat, his fingers – no

bigger than wooden matchsticks – now plucking at my sleeve.

I reached into my bag and put a sou into that minute, almost human hand, and was rewarded with an ear-splitting screech. Hasi clambered back up my arm and on to my shoulder, jumping in one long leap on to Mohammed's chest. One of his toenails scratched my neck. In a practised routine, he tucked the coin into the pocket of the vest Mohammed wore over his robe. Then he pressed his teeth against Mohammed's ear, grimacing again and making his chuckling sound. Mohammed nodded seriously.

'Madame, Hasi has informed me that a change will now take place in your life. An important change. You will find it here, in Morocco.'

I knew it was nonsense. And yet I couldn't help myself. My neck stung from Hasi's toenail. 'What kind of change?'

Mohammed rubbed his thumb and forefinger together. 'Hasi needs another sou to divulge what he knows,' he said, and I dug in my bag, handing over my last coin to those tiny black fingers. Quick as a flash it was deposited in Mohammed's pocket, and again the chattering into Mohammed's ear.

'Ah. This is a story I have not heard from Hasi before, madame. A significant tale. You have come to Marrakesh to find something. You have lost something, something of importance. Am I not right? I see from your face that you know Hasi speaks the truth.'

I didn't respond for a moment, then shook my head, sure that Mohammed told every foreigner this story, and not wanting him to know that, with me, he had actually hit upon a truth.

'*Vraiment?* Truly, madame? You deny this? Because Hasi tells me that you are sad, but this will soon change. Very soon. Under the Southern Cross you will understand that what you look for may take a different shape. You may not recognise it.'

'The Southern Cross?'

Mohammed squinted at the sky. 'The constellation, madame. Here, in Africa. The Southern Cross. You look for it in the night sky. And under it you will find what you search for. But remember, madame, remember, here are the Others, the *djinns*. They masquerade in human form. Be careful. Be very careful you do not choose unwisely.'

Hasi screamed, jumping up and down.

The sound pierced my ears. I closed my eyes, images coming unbidden: Hasi's cheerless little grimace, his open mouth and tiny pointed teeth, then the open mouths of the beggar children. The pulled teeth and the grinning tooth-puller with his pliers.

I opened my eyes and saw a row of skinned heads; for one horrible instant I thought of the decapitated heads Mr Russell had mentioned. My stomach cramped as though I might be sick, and I instinctively crossed myself. In the next instant I saw they were not human, but goat heads, blue and buzzing with flies, their eyeballs still intact and protruding. They sat in a row on a low table. A man in a torn djellaba motioned me towards them, nodding.

Shakily I walked away. I couldn't faint here, fall to the filthy ground. What would happen to me if I did?

'Come back, madame,' Mohammed called after me. 'For only one more sou, Hasi will tell you more; he will tell you something of the utmost importance, something you need to protect yourself from the Others. Only one sou, madame.'

I kept walking, stumbling now and then. I touched the smarting slash on my neck and stared at the smear of blood on my fingers. When I saw the tall minaret of the mosque of La Koutoubia, I kept my eyes fixed on it, knowing it would lead me to the gates and out of the medina. I walked as quickly as I could, my bag clutched against my chest, my hair falling from its pins, the back of my dress wet from the heat and my own sudden and unexplained fear. I dragged my uncooperative foot; if it had been possible, I would have run.

CHAPTER NINETEEN

I SPENT THE EVENING TELLING myself that I would return to the medina, and not be driven out by unfriendly stares or unwelcome touches or sights and sounds that shocked me. I was strong, I told myself.

And besides, I had no choice.

The next morning I once again set out for the gates that led into the medina. I looked up at La Koutoubia, and then, taking a deep breath, walked under the portals for the second time.

This time I didn't stop, ignoring the cries of the begging children and the clanging bells of the water-carriers, with their high domed hats and their brass cups and goatskins of water. I walked past the tooth-puller, and pushed through a crowd of young men gathered around a snake-charmer with his flute and baskets of writhing, rising snakes, jerking away when I felt a hand stroke my upper arm, not looking back to see who had touched me.

I hurried from the square and into the souks, moving from stall to stall, saying *Duverger, Duverger, do you know the Duvergers?* Finally one man unfolded his arms and picked up a pair of bright orange *babouches*, studying me. 'These shoes will fit you, madame,' he said in French. 'Good shoes; I sell only the best shoes in Marrakesh. I know French, and Spanish, and English,' he said. 'I have travelled many places. Where are you from? England?'

'America,' I said, and he nodded.

'Ah, America. I once had a beautiful American bride. She was my third wife. But she returned to her home.'

I nodded, although I didn't know if I believed his story. The whites of his eyes were yellow, and he smelled strongly of garlic. 'Good, good,' I said. 'But the Duvergers . . . do you know of them?'

'I knew Monsieur le Docteur,' he said.

'Yes? You knew him? Dr Etienne Duverger?' I said it calmly. Instinctively, I didn't want this man to know the importance of his words.

'What about the *babouches*, madame? You will buy them?'

I took the orange slippers from his hands. 'Yes, yes, I'll buy them. But please, what do you know of Dr Duverger?'

He shrugged. 'First we must discuss what price you will offer. We will have tea, and discuss,' he said, waving his hand in the air. I shook my head, but a boy of about ten appeared beside me. The man spoke in Arabic, and the boy ran off. 'He will bring tea. Sit, sit, madame,' he said, lifting a pile of brightly dyed *babouches* off a low bench. 'Here. Sit, and we will drink tea and discuss the price.'

All I wanted was for him to answer my questions, but I realised I must play the game first. I sat down. The shop was only about ten feet long and three feet wide; the smell of the dyed leather was strong. 'Please, monsieur. About Dr Duverger.'

'I knew Monsieur le Docteur Duverger,' he repeated. 'He came to the souks to buy *kif*, and leather goods. He came to my stall because I speak French. Of course, that was before. Afterwards . . .' he threw up his hands, 'nobody saw him.'

'What do you mean, afterwards?'

'His illness. He did not leave his house.'

'What illness?'

'Madame, that is all I know. You asked if I knew the Duvergers. I told you yes, I knew the old man Duverger, who had the sickness.'

Disappointment rose in my throat, sour as the garlic on the man's breath.

'The old man?' I said. 'Not the son? Not Etienne?'

'I found for him the *kif* he wanted, when he could still walk in the souks. We drank tea. Now you and I will drink tea. Soon my nephew will return with it. Maybe you will buy two pairs of *babouches*. One for your husband. Maybe three pairs. For three pairs I make you a good price. Best *babouches* in Marrakesh; best prices. And my cousin sells kaftans, best kaftans in Marrakesh. You wish to buy kaftan? Silk? Velvet? What kaftan you like? I call my cousin after tea; he show you beautiful kaftan. You buy from him; he has the best. Don't listen to other men. Their kaftans are not like my cousin's.'

There was no air in the tiny shop; my hair was plastered against my wet forehead. The smell of the dye and the wafting garlic from the man's breath were making my stomach roil.

The slippers were soft in my hands. 'Perhaps . . . the daughter?' I said.

'Daughter? What daughter?'

'Manon.'

He pushed out his lips. 'Who do you speak of? Who is Manon?'

'Manon Duverger. Or maybe that's not her last name any more. Perhaps she's married, with a different surname. But the elder Duverger's daughter, Manon. I believe she still lives here, in Marrakesh. Maybe within the medina.'

'Manon?' he repeated, as if to make certain. 'You ask about the daughter of Marcel Duverger? That Manon?'

'Yes, yes.' I nodded, my voice again rising in hope, but the shop owner suddenly looked secretive, or disgruntled. He looked over my head, and then reached up and straightened the *babouches* on the shelf.

'That's what I've said, monsieur. Manon Duverger.'

'You are mistaken, madame. The Manon you ask about is not Duverger. She is Manon Maliki.'

'That's her married name?'

Now the man made a face of disgust. 'Hah!' he said.

I ignored his critical tone, fighting to keep my voice even, my face expressionless. 'But . . . you are certain she's Monsieur Duverger's daughter?'

Now he shifted his tangle of a turban to one side, wiping his shaven head. 'I am certain.'

'Can you tell me where she lives, then?' I licked my lips. I was so close.

He was still staring at me. 'Sharia Zitoun.'

'How do I find it? Is it nearby? Please, monsieur.'

'It is past the dyers' alley. *C'est tout*,' he said, slapping his palms together as if to rid them of dust. 'There's nothing more I can tell you. You have taken me from my duties for too long.' He had abruptly lost his earlier friendliness. From the moment I made it clear I looked for Manon Duverger, his attitude had changed.

'I'm sorry to have troubled you, monsieur,' I said. 'I . . . what price do you wish for these?' I held up the orange *babouches*. 'Whatever you ask, monsieur. You have been very helpful. And I . . . I'll take a second pair, as you suggested.'

But he rather brusquely took them from my hands. 'You do not need to purchase anything from me. It will not be a good sale; now there is no *baraka*. Instead, I will give you something. I give it freely. It is this: do not seek out Manon Maliki. No good will come of it. Good day, madame.' He turned then, putting the *babouches* on another shelf. It was clear he would speak no more to me.

'*Merci*, monsieur,' I said to his back, and left the stall. I passed the boy – the man's nephew – hurrying up the alley, a tin tray with two glasses of steaming tea on it. He stopped, staring at me, but I ignored him.

Now I asked anyone who looked at me for directions to the dyers' alley, or to Sharia Zitoun. Occasionally a man would point behind me or in front of me. I had no idea if they understood my question, and, if so, if they actually were giving me the correct information.

The streets twisted like streams beneath my feet; at times I stumbled in the depression that had been worn into the centre. And then, with a turn, there were no more stalls, and I was out of the souks. I was in an alley lined with the windowless house fronts Madame Odette had described. Straight walls and gates, and behind the locked gates lived the people of Marrakesh. There were many small children, appearing from shadowed alleys that led off the one I was in, scampering around me as they had in D'jemma el Fna, pulling on my skirt and chattering in Arabic. And like the children in the square, the only French words they called were *bonjour, madame, bonjour*, and *bonbon*, they begged, but I could only shake my head. *Sharia Zitoun*, I repeated to them, but they just giggled, running ahead or beside me.

There seemed an inordinate number of famished cats; they sat on walls and slunk in and out of the shadows, their ribs protruding, their ears torn and their fur greasy or mangy. Every once in a while I passed two of them, spitting and hissing as they fought over a scrap of food, with the triumphant one dragging its win into a dark corner.

As I wandered deeper, it grew quieter; the noises of the souks had long died away. And then there was solitude. Not a child, not a cat. Nothing. The cooler peacefulness of this alley was a relief after the continuous noise and array of colour and wares and milling humanity. I stopped, leaning against a wall, wiping my forehead and upper lip with my sleeve. The cobbled alley stretched ahead, shaded and dim, with only the gates and the continuous walls. I couldn't tell where one house began and one ended except by the different gates. The alley was so narrow that should I meet a donkey pulling a cart I would have to flatten myself against the wall.

I told myself I should return the way I came – if I could find my way back – and be in the busyness of the souks, or even the frenetic, untamed atmosphere of the square, and find definite directions to Sharia Zitoun.

I should be where there were people; although I didn't feel particularly safe in the crowds, here, completely alone, a sense of panic nudged. I was hopelessly confused, entwined in the labyrinth of the medina. I thought of Madame Odette's words about being lost, and how it was impossible to find one's way out. I saw that the medina was not only a serpentine maze of alleys, but also a network of arteries leading into dead ends and cul-de-sacs.

A gate opened and a man emerged. He stopped when he saw me, and then walked towards me, staring at me as if I were something unpredictable and dangerous.

Instinctively I lowered my gaze, and he passed.

I went to the end of the alley, looking left and right. Three women approached; no man was with them. 'Mesdames?' I said, seeing that the hands clutching the folds of their white *haiks* across their faces were black. They might be slaves, then, I thought, and that was why they were out without a man to accompany them. 'Mesdames,' I repeated, but they passed me as though I were invisible.

I lost track of time. Occasionally I met another figure, and would speak the words Sharia Zitoun. Some turned their faces from me, unwilling to speak to an uncovered foreigner; others stared but didn't respond. I wandered deeper and deeper through the tunnelled streets; it felt as though I had walked for hours in the hot alleyways. My leg ached, and occasionally I leaned against a wall to rest it. I realised that the last strip of sky above me was closing over because of the narrowness of the passageways. I fought to hold down the panic that stayed with me now, just under the surface. I heard the slight splashing of fountains in the courtyards behind the high walls, or the slow clopping of hoofs on stones, echoing from another alley. I stepped around the deposits left by horses and donkeys and goats, as well as over trickling gutters. On the top of a pile of rotting vegetable peelings was the body of a dead cat, sprawled as though unceremoniously tossed there. It was even cooler here, with the high stone walls and the sun unable to reach its long fingers into such narrow passages, and I understood why the streets were built in this fashion.

I turned down another street, and suddenly heard, from nearby, continual mechanical humming. I went towards the sound and walked into an alley lined with tiny niches. In every one an old man hunched over an antiquated sewing machine, working the needle with the hand wheel. I thought of my mother. The tailors' alley, then.

In the next alley were men working wood in their own alcoves. These men weren't as old as the tailors, and used an assortment of tools, some with their bare feet. The smell was aromatic and clean.

When I next turned I found myself in a small square. Over the entire square, from crossed ropes strung between the roofs, hung huge skeins of wool: a ceiling of colour. The dyers' alley. The skeins were scarlet and tangerine and sunflower yellow, greens deep as the ocean and pale as the newest leaves, purples and blues both brilliant and muted. I stood in awe for a moment, looking up. Then I saw that the dyers were all boys, some as young as twelve or thirteen, also in tiny recesses, sitting cross-legged on raised platforms as they stirred vats of dye into which they were immersing the rough grey-white wool. Their hands, on their wooden paddles, were completely stained to the wrists in a muddy, unnameable colour. They looked at me as I passed, but didn't stop their endless stirring. Steam rose from the vats, and I could imagine the intense heat in the tiny domed spaces.

Sharia Zitoun was just past the dyers' alley, the *babouche* dealer in the souk had told me. I stopped at the wall at the end of the alley; I could only go left or right. There was a tiny sign on one wall, but it was in Arabic. Choosing left, I started down the alley, and almost immediately three small children ran towards me. 'Madame,' they shouted, and at their cries a gate opened and a heavyset woman stuck her head out of the doorway, holding a calico kerchief in front of her face. She shouted at the group of children, and they dispersed. '*Pardon*, madame,' I said to her.

She looked over the kerchief at me with a decidedly unfriendly stare.

'*Je cherche* Sharia Zitoun,' I said.

Her stare altered slightly. '*Parlez-vous français*, madame?' I asked. 'Sharia Zitoun,' I repeated, slowly.

The woman nodded, pointing at the ground. I looked down, not understanding until she said, 'Sharia Zitoun.'

'Ah. *Ici*? Here is Sharia Zitoun?'

The woman nodded again.

'Please, madame,' I said, 'I am trying to find Madame Maliki.'

At that the woman took a step back.

'Manon Maliki,' I said, again, nodding encouragingly.

Then the woman did an odd thing. She reached down inside her kaftan and pulled out a small leather pouch, clutching it. I knew it to be an amulet to ward off the *djinns*; Aziz had worn one. What I didn't know was whether she held it to protect herself from me, or because I had said Manon's name.

But then she raised her other hand and flung it in the air, pointing over my left shoulder. I turned and looked at the gate she indicated.

'*C'est là?*' I asked. 'That's where she lives?'

Now the woman simply tucked her amulet into her kaftan and stepped back inside, slamming the gate.

I went to the gate she'd indicated. It was a brilliant yellow-gold, in the way of many of the gates: the colour of saffron. There was a heavy, tarnished brass knocker in the shape of a hand: the *hamsa*. Again, it was a familiar sight. I had seen many of these knockers on other doors, to afford protection from the supernatural.

I stood in front of the gate, breathing heavily. Had I actually found Manon? I lifted my hand to grasp the knocker, then dropped it to my side.

What if I knocked and it was Etienne who opened the door? Wasn't that what I had hoped would happen? Hadn't I made this terribly difficult journey, all the way to Marrakesh, for this very reason, this very moment? Hadn't I been so afraid, and felt so alone? Hadn't I, more than once, wondered if I would ever reach Marrakesh, and, if I did, actually find Etienne?

Here was the moment.

And I was terrified.

What if he simply looked at me, frowning, shaking his head, telling me to go, that I had no right to come here? To leave, that he didn't want me? What if – when I tried to talk to him, to tell him it didn't matter that he'd left me, that I could forgive him, that whatever he was hiding from me couldn't be so terrible – he simply closed the door in my face?

No. Etienne wouldn't do that to me. He wouldn't.

And what if it was Manon who opened the door? What if what she had to tell me about her brother was unbearable?

I couldn't catch my breath. There was a loud buzzing in my ears, and the saffon gate grew brighter and brighter, until it was a shimmering brilliant light. I put one hand on it to brace myself, but I was trembling too violently, and had to lean my shoulder against it, closing my eyes. I didn't want to be here, not now. I needed more time. I would come tomorrow, when I was more in control. This was enough for one day – to find where Manon lived. I needed another day, one more, before I confronted her. Or Etienne.

Finally I could open my eyes, and my ears cleared. I straightened, and with one last look at the gate, turned from it and walked away.

Part-way down the alley I stopped. I had left Albany well over a month ago. I had had enough time. I was not a coward; I had proved that many times over to myself since I'd left Juniper Road.

I retraced my steps and again stood in front of the gate. Instinctively I put my ear against it, but could hear nothing.

Then I lifted the heavy *hamsa*, raised it, and brought it down, once, twice, three times, with firm, heavy thuds.

CHAPTER TWENTY

T HERE WAS NO SOUND from the other side of the
door. I knocked again, harder this time, hitting the
hamsa against the wood with more force. Finally I heard
footsteps, and the door creaked open.

A woman, holding her *haik* to cover her face in the way
I was now accustomed to, peered through the narrow
opening. Her eyes were long and dark, and she blinked
rapidly, as though surprised, as she looked at me. She
carried a metal bucket in one hand. In it was a stick
wrapped round with a rag. Splashes of white dripped from
the rag on to the ground. I assumed her to be a servant.

'*Bonjour*, madame,' I said, hoping she spoke French. 'I'm
looking for Madame Maliki.' I smelled the fresh scent of
the whitewash.

When she didn't answer, I assumed she didn't understand. I used the Arabic greeting – *assalaam alykum*, peace
be upon you – and then slowly repeated Manon's name.

Still she studied me, her eyes now strangely flat, the
earlier light gone from them. I was thankful she didn't
reach for an amulet as the woman in the street had.
Perhaps, I wondered for a moment, she was simple-
minded. But although she was silent, there was intelligence

in her eyes as she studied my face. She shifted, setting down the bucket. At this point she could have been any of the covered women I had passed in the alleys of Marrakesh since I had arrived.

'Madame Maliki,' I said, for the third time, trying to keep the exasperation out of my voice.

'Why do you seek her?' she asked, in perfect French, her voice slightly muffled by the *haik*.

I immediately straightened my shoulders. 'Oh,' I said, somehow surprised by the firm and almost melodic tone of her voice. How could I have thought, only seconds ago, that she might have been simple-minded? 'I . . . I have come to speak with her,' I said, not wanting to divulge the complicated reason as I stood in this dim alley.

'Is there some trouble?' she asked, and again I was encouraged by the modulated tone of her voice, and yet also annoyed by a Moroccan servant expecting me to speak on a personal note.

'There is no trouble for Madame Maliki,' I said. 'Pardon me, madame, but I have gone to great lengths to find her. If she is at home, I should very much like to speak to her. Would you fetch her, please?'

The woman wiped her hand down the front of her *haik*. Her fingers were long, and the half-moons on her oval nails very white.

'Come,' she said, pulling the gate open further, and I caught my breath as I stepped over the pail of whitewash and into the courtyard. My eyes darted over every surface, into every corner. What did I expect? To see Etienne sitting there? Or perhaps a sign of him: a familiar jacket, a book with a pair of spectacles on it?

But there was no such indication. Some sort of house-cleaning was under way, as there was furniture sitting about the tiled courtyard – stuffed ottomans and stools and long, narrow mattresses covered in multicoloured fabric, which I knew were used for both sitting during the day and sleeping at night. There was a fountain in the centre of the courtyard, but instead of water it contained only dead, dry leaves and the small, stiff body of a yellow bird, its tiny black feet curled against its torso. A few large earthenware pots held bedraggled geraniums. There was a set of steep, narrow tiled steps leading to an upper floor with shuttered windows that looked into the courtyard.

The woman still studied me. 'Latch the gate,' she said, and watched me as I did. Then she turned and walked across the courtyard slowly, her body swaying under the *haik*. I was uncertain whether to follow her or remain at the gate. A child, perhaps four or five, ran into the courtyard from the house. *Maman*, it said, but the woman ignored it, sitting on one of the mattresses. And then a girl appeared in the doorway. She was ten or eleven, her skin the colour of milky coffee. She was painfully thin in her simple muslin shift. Her knees and elbows looked too large for her legs and arms, her jaw too narrow. Her right arm was covered in bruises, and one of her eyes was bloodshot, the eyelid puffy. A flowered kerchief was tied around her head, and her hair – the same colour as her skin – hung in long, tangled tight curls. She also held a whitewashing stick, and stared openly at me.

I couldn't tell if the younger child was a boy or girl; the thick black hair was cut in a straight line across the nape of the neck as well as the forehead, almost hiding large eyes that were as black as its hair. The child's skin was pale. It wore a little draped garment too long to be a shirt and too short to be a dress, and cotton trousers, torn off at the knees, with dangling threads. Its feet were bare. 'Who is the lady, Maman?' the child cried. 'Who is she?'

Like its mother, the child's French was impeccable. It came to stand in front of me, its little neck, long and delicate, tilted back to look at my face.

'Please, madame,' I called to the woman. 'Please. Would you ask Madame Maliki to come to the courtyard?' My heart was thumping. I realised, as I spoke, that if Etienne was inside the house he might have heard my voice. I looked at the upper-floor windows, but the shutters remained closed.

'What's your name, madame?' the child asked me, with no hint of shyness.

'Mademoiselle O'Shea,' I said, in a distracted way, still watching the woman. Why did she not do as I asked?

'I am Badou.' Like the child's appearance, the name didn't specify gender; it was a French name used for a boy or a girl. 'We're whitewashing the walls inside. I'm helping,' Badou said proudly. 'I moved the furniture with Falida.'

The woman spoke in Arabic, and Badou and the girl – who put down her stick – pushed, in a slow and painstaking manner, a heavy cork stool until it was across from the woman. I briefly thought that Etienne's sister must be kind to allow the servant to keep her children with her. Or perhaps it was a Moroccan custom, mother and children working together. I didn't know.

'Sit,' the woman said to me, languidly pointing to the cork stool. Badou climbed into her lap, leaning against her, but she paid no attention. The girl — I assumed this was Falida — had gone back to the doorway and picked up her stick, but still stared at me.

My anxiety was growing by the minute, and I was losing patience with this woman. I had asked her repeatedly to fetch her mistress, and yet it was obvious she was in no hurry to do as I wished. I made a small clicking sound with my tongue. 'Madame, please. I would like you to fetch Madame Maliki for me. Is she at home?' I asked, sitting stiffly on the stool. 'Or . . . or is anyone else here? Is . . .' I stopped.

The woman was looking at me sharply now, although still she held her *haik* over the lower half of her face.

'Madame Maliki,' the child repeated in a reedy voice, lacing a bit of string over and around its fingers, creating a small webbed pattern. 'Badou Maliki,' it said, more of a whisper, as if to itself.

'Why do you seek her?' the woman asked again, as she had in the doorway.

'It's a private affair, for Madame Maliki only,' I said, slowly. Suddenly I was very tired, and very thirsty.

At that the woman dropped the hand holding her *haik*, and it fell open. She had a straight nose and well-formed mouth. Her eyes were as dark as mine, but her skin tone was paler. There were a number of fine lines emanating from the corners of her eyes, and something about her expression was infinitely weary. She was definitely older than I. Hers was a sad and delicate face. It was obvious that she had, at some point, been quite beautiful. Although now she looked drawn, she still had a certain sensuousness to her. I realised that while I had seen a few uncovered

Berber women in the square, I hadn't seen behind the face coverings of any other woman since I'd arrived in this country.

When she still didn't speak, I said, 'Please, madame. It's Madame Maliki I must see. As I keep saying.' The courtyard was so hot. A cicada screamed, and the sound pierced my ears.

'I am she,' the woman said, calmly. I had to shake my head the slightest. The cicada's shriek had partly obscured the woman's voice. Surely I had misunderstood.

'I'm sorry,' I said, 'but . . . perhaps I didn't hear you. You didn't say *you* are Manon Maliki?'

She nodded, and at that I stood. 'No.' I said. 'Oh, no.' The back of my dress was wet with perspiration. 'I'm sorry, madame. I have made a mistake. I was looking for someone else.'

I let out a long sigh of frustration, of more disappointment. After such hope, and such anxiety, my search through the medina had been for nothing. The *babouche* seller in the souk had given me the wrong information. He had told me with such surety that Manon Maliki was Marcel Duverger's daughter. But this was not Etienne's sister. This was a Moroccan servant. What now? What more could I do to find Etienne?

'You're looking for someone else?' the woman asked. 'But you came looking for Manon Maliki. I am she.'

'No. The woman I'm trying to find is . . .' I stopped, careful of my wording. 'I have been given the wrong information.' I looked at the saffron gate, and then took a step towards it. 'I'm sorry to have disturbed you.'

'Why do you seek this woman?' The woman's hands,

long and elegant, lay upturned on either side of the child, as if not wanting to touch the little body.

'She's the sister of . . . of a friend.'

'The sister of whom?'

I was annoyed by her direct questions. I simply wanted to leave, and yet this woman had let me into the courtyard. I couldn't ignore her. 'The Manon I'm looking for is the daughter of Marcel Duverger,' I said. 'Someone in the souk told me that Manon Maliki was this woman.'

She sat without moving. The child still played with the bit of string, its large dark eyes on me. The girl's mouth was open as she now crouched, motionless, in the doorway, watching. The cicada screamed again.

'It is correct. I am the daughter of Marcel Duverger.'

'But . . . if you are Manon . . . I'm sorry, madame,' I said. 'It's just that I . . . I . . .' Was this not a Moroccan woman sitting in front of me? 'The Manon I seek is Dr Duverger's sister,' I finally said.

The woman didn't speak for a moment, then she said, 'How do you know Etienne?'

The way she said *Etienne*, with such familiarity, made me catch my breath. I hadn't said his name. 'You are his sister?' I repeated, sitting heavily on the stool again.

She nodded.

The courtyard was far too hot, even though I was in the shade. The cicada's screams went on and on. Now I tried to open my mouth to speak further, but my lips stuck together. I tried to lick them, but had so little saliva. 'Is . . . is he here? With you?' I finally managed to say. 'Is Etienne here?' I stared at her, willing her to nod her head, to say *yes, yes, he's here*.

The woman lifted her hands and pulled the *haik* completely off her head, so that I saw her hair, long and heavy, falling about her face and to her shoulders. Dark and wavy, as was mine, but with a few threads of white. She wore a dark purple kaftan under the *haik*.

'You are from England? Or America? I cannot tell from your accent,' she said.

I again struggled to lick my lips. 'America,' I said.

'Bring our guest water, *mon cher garçon*,' Manon said to the child – so it was a boy – and he slid off her lap and ran lightly through the doorway of the house, putting his hand on the girl's shoulder as he passed her. 'Falida. Go and help him,' Manon said, and the girl leapt to her feet and disappeared.

I studied my hands, clenched in my lap, hearing clinking and splashing. Within a moment the boy returned, crossing the courtyard slowly and very carefully, holding a tin cup in front of him with both hands. He didn't spill a drop, and proudly offered it to me. I drank; it was cool and refreshing, with a hint of lemon.

Badou waited in front of me; I handed him the empty cup and he took it and went back into the house. As I watched him go, I thought to myself that Manon Maliki appeared old to have so young a child; surely he was no more than five years old. And then I thought of how old I would have looked when my child was . . . I stopped my thoughts.

'You have searched for Etienne for some time?'

I nodded, closing my eyes for a moment. 'I have looked for him in Marrakesh – in the French Quarter – for a number of days.'

'And before that?'

I frowned, glancing once more at the house. Why was she holding back? I stood again, unable to sit still. 'Madame. Is Etienne here, in Marrakesh? Please. I must know. I must, Madame Maliki,' I said, my voice louder, an edge of sharpness creeping into it. There was something about this woman that troubled me. I didn't like her, I realised, even though I'd known her only a few moments. 'I keep telling you, I have come from America to find him. I have been travelling and searching for over a month now.'

Manon sat very still. Falida and Badou came back from the house, and again Badou climbed into his mother's lap. He leaned against her chest, and as before, his mother didn't touch him. His little face had a calm, accepting demeanour. I sensed he was unlike his mother; in spite of her stillness at this moment, I felt that beneath her calm exterior was a great deal of fire.

'Why do you appear so distressed?' she asked me, her head at a slight angle, giving her an inquisitive look. 'You look hot, and perhaps a bit ill. Are you not well, Mademoiselle . . . what did you say your name was?' Her eyes suddenly left my face, running down my body.

I took a deep breath. 'O'Shea. Sidonie O'Shea,' I said, something painful in my chest, for at that moment I realised she didn't know who I was. That meant that either Etienne truly wasn't here, or, if he was, he hadn't mentioned me. 'I'm very anxious to find Etienne,' I said. 'That's what you see – my anxiety.' Had I assumed that Etienne had come to her, to his sister, and told her about the woman in America he . . . he what? Loved? Had created a child with? 'You don't know who I am,' I said, stating what was now obvious.

'How could I? You are a stranger, from America, arriving at my door, unexpected and unannounced, speaking of my brother.'

I swallowed. 'I am Etienne's . . .' What to call myself? 'I am his fiancée,' I said then. 'We were to be married,' I added, unnecessarily.

At that, Manon's expression changed. She no longer looked curious. Something dark came over her face, and her hands clenched once, and then loosened. Now it was she who took a deep breath. When she exhaled, the child twisted his head to look up at her.

She spoke to Falida in Arabic. Badou rose without question, and Falida took his hand. They went through the gate, shutting it behind them with a clang.

'So you are Etienne's lover?' Manon asked, her voice toneless.

'I . . . I said I was his fiancée.'

Her lips tightened, and the same strange look as moments earlier passed over her face. Although I didn't know her, it looked like anger. I thought of her fists, clenching for that split second.

'And why have you come to me, Sidonie O'Shea?'

I pulled the single page, now tearing slightly along the delicate creases, from my handbag. 'Your letter to Etienne.'

She glanced at the paper in my hands, then back to my face. 'Written when?'

'Six months ago.'

'A man leaves you, and you find an old letter, and you travel so far to find him?'

I hadn't said, specifically, that he'd left me, although it was an evident observation. Suddenly I knew how ridiculous I must appear. I felt as though Manon must view me as had the others in the hotel in Tangier. *The tragic heroine of her own story.* I was shamed, sitting in front of this rather imposing woman. I looked down at the thin sheet of paper. 'There is . . . there was more to it.'

'Mademoiselle. There is always more to it for the woman.'

We sat in silence. The heat was intense; it was almost as though I could hear it fluttering, like a flock of tiny birds, or perhaps butterflies, around my ears. Finally I looked back at Manon. 'He isn't here?'

She shook her head.

'Do you know where he is?'

At that, she studied me for so long – the silence stretching and stretching – that I felt one bead of sweat run down my temple and along my jaw. Finally she nodded.

I took a deep, shaky breath. 'Is he here, in Marrakesh?'

Again the wait, and then she shrugged. 'Perhaps.'

What was wrong with her? Why was she playing this silly game with me? I stood and walked the few steps to where she sat. I looked down at her. 'Madame Maliki,' I said, my voice hard. 'Do you not understand how important it is that I find Etienne?'

Now she rose as well. 'It's impossible for me to say, right now, where he is. Impossible,' she said.

I shook my head. 'But . . . you just said you knew where he was.' My voice had grown louder. 'Why is it impossible? Why can't you simply—'

'I said perhaps. Perhaps I know. And it's not a good day

for me,' she interrupted. 'The fates are not correct. I can't speak to you any further right now.'

I stared at her.

'You will have to leave,' she said.

'But . . . no. I can't leave until you tell me about Etienne. I have come so far to . . .'

At that she moved right in front of me. I stood with my lips parted, unable to finish the sentence. We were the same height. Her face was close enough for me to see her pupils, dilating and then drawing in until they were two hard, dark points. I smelled the slight scent of some spice, perhaps cumin, perhaps coriander, on her breath. 'You will leave. This is my home, and you will leave when I tell you to leave. You have no right to be here.'

I felt her foot touch mine, and instinctively took a step back, but she put her hand on my arm. Immediately the skin under my sleeve burned.

'Madame Maliki,' I said, quietly now, pulling back from her touch. It was clear she wished to antagonise me, to challenge or frighten me. It was also clear she would tell me nothing at this moment. 'Perhaps tomorrow will be a better day to speak of this. I'll come again tomorrow. Is the morning a good time for you? Tell me when you wish me to come.'

I had been right. Her expression changed the slightest, and I knew it was because my tone was imploring. I had deliberately become submissive, acquiescing, and this pleased her.

'Tomorrow may not be convenient,' she said. 'Let me think.'

We stood there. She looked over my head as if

consulting an unseen calendar, and I fought not to scream, not to strike her. She was enjoying this. At this moment, everything rested upon her. I knew it, and I saw in her face that she knew it as well. For an unknown reason she needed to wield some power over me, and I had no alternative but to bow to her wishes.

Finally she met my eyes. 'All right. You may come at two o'clock. Not before. Do you understand? Not before two.'

I moved my head in one slow nod, then went through the gate and down the alley. When I got to the end of it a small voice said, 'Mademoiselle.' I peered into a dark recess in the long wall and saw Badou and Falida, sitting on the ground in a niche. Each of them held a kitten. I would have passed by them if Badou hadn't spoken.

I stopped, and they both looked up at me, unblinking. 'Yes?'

But he didn't seem to have anything to say. He held up the kitten.

I nodded, turned and took a few steps away. But something made me look back at him. 'How old are you?'

'*Six ans*,' he said.

I had thought him to be five at the oldest; he was small-boned and delicate. 'And your sister?' I asked, looking at her. 'How old are you, Falida?'

She didn't answer, but Badou said, 'She's not my sister.'

'Oh,' I said.

'She's our maid.'

I looked at the girl's bruised arm and bloodshot, swollen eye.

'There are always kittens here,' Badou said. 'The mother cats live in there.' He pointed to a low hole in the wall. 'We play with them when they come out.' He stroked the kitten's back gently.

He was Etienne's nephew. Did I see something of Etienne in him? Maybe the long neck, the serious expression.

I thought of my child, and wondered if he or she would have looked like this little boy.

'Do you like kittens?' he asked, and I nodded again. Then I drew in a deep breath, and walked away from Sharia Zitoun.

CHAPTER TWENTY-ONE

Perhaps, Manon had said, perhaps Etienne was here, in Marrakesh.

I passed through the dyers' square, then the wood-workers' and tailors' alleys. I understood now that while searching for Sharia Zitoun I had walked in endless circles, and this time recognised a few corners, painted gates and round, arched stone openings. There was a wall with the imprint of a blue hand. A sign in canary yellow. I heard the sound of the souks, making mental notes of my route, so that I could find my way back to Sharia Zitoun tomorrow. Eventually I saw the imposing spire of La Koutoubia, and went toward it, through D'jemma el Fna.

I moved in a slow daze; I had found Manon. I still knew little more about Etienne's whereabouts, but I would go back to her tomorrow. I would not allow her to avoid answering my questions any longer.

I left the medina and started towards the hotel, studying every European man. Of course I'd done this since arriving in Marrakesh, thinking I might see Etienne on the street, but now, after meeting Manon, the sensation was enhanced. I watched for a familiar gait, a certain set of the shoulders. By the time I reached Hôtel de la Palmeraie, I was shaking. I went to my room and ordered a light dinner, but couldn't eat. I got into bed early, hoping I would immediately fall asleep and not waken until the next morning. But of course I didn't sleep well, tossing in the hot room all night.

The morning was interminable. I left the hotel too early, and was in D'jemma el Fna by noon.

As I skirted the edges of the square to avoid the crowds in the centre, the chanting of men's voices rose and fell, growing steadily louder. And suddenly I came upon them – a row of at least twelve men. They sat on the hard ground in the bright sunshine, shoulders touching as they swayed back and forth as one. They were all old and ragged, mostly toothless and all blind. Some had empty eye sockets, and some had damaged eyeballs fixed or rolling. They sang together, some stamping their walking sticks to keep the beat. I watched these blind men singing for their living as I had witnessed the scribe writing for those who were unable, and the story-teller enriching the lives of others with his knowledge.

When the song was finished, a Moroccan man standing in front of them picked up the hand of the first blind man in the row and pressed a coin into it. The blind man put the coin to his mouth and bit it, and then spoke – surely some benediction, as I heard the name Allah – to the man who had given it to him. Then he passed the coin to the second blind man, who also bit it, and in this way it was passed down the line, until the final man, after biting it, put it into a pouch tied around his neck.

The men sang another song, and at its completion more Moroccan men gave coins and were blessed. The blind men's faces were lined and scarred, and even their loose robes couldn't hide their painfully thin limbs. I thought of the beautiful Hôtel de la Palmeraie where I was staying, and then these blind men in their poverty. I thought of Etienne living here. How had he treated the Moroccans? He was, after all, an interloper in the country, and in the party of power.

As was I. Suddenly shamed, I took a sou from my bag and put it into the first man's hand. While his fingers closed round the coin, his other hand gripped mine, and he felt it – my palm, and fingers, and then the nails, nodding. His own fingers were hard, the nails yellow and long and ridged. When he let go of my hand he uttered the same line in Arabic as he had to the Moroccans who gave him a coin.

I didn't respond. Then he said, '*Merci*, madame', and I answered *de rien*, it's nothing.

'The women of Morocco would be defiled by touching us,' he said in surprisingly correct French. 'And yet your hand is not the French woman's hand. It is a hand that has known work. You are neither Moroccan nor, I think, French, but I bless you, madame. The poor enter paradise before the rich. When you give to the poor, you buy, from us, a small piece of paradise.'

'*Merci*,' I said, because I didn't know how else to respond. I watched as he bit the coin I'd given him, and passed it down the line.

Manon had told me I shouldn't come to the house on Sharia Zitoun until two o'clock, but I could wait no longer. It was ten minutes to one when I knocked with the *hamsa*.

The heavy door was pulled back by Falida. I nodded at her, and she lowered her head in a submissive reflex. Now that I knew she wasn't Manon's daughter I was surprised I had thought so yesterday; it was quite obvious that she was a descendant of the slaves Etienne had spoken of. But of course yesterday I had been filled with uncertainty and dismay; nothing had seemed clear.

Today the courtyard wasn't jumbled with furniture, but held a long daybed with a thick, bright cover, an assortment of cork stools, and a low round table, all arranged in an orderly manner. Badou was walking around the edge of the empty fountain, balancing with outstretched arms. He jumped down and came to me as Falida shut the heavy gate.

'*Bonjour*, Badou,' I said, and he nodded with a solemnity that suddenly made him seem much older than six.

'*Bonjour*, mademoiselle,' he said, holding out his little hand. '*Venez*. Come. Maman is inside.'

I looked down at his hand, surprised by the unexpected gesture. I took it, and together we crossed the courtyard. His fingers were so small but sturdy, and dry and warm.

We stood in the doorway, and the first thing I was aware of was a strong, sweet, smoky odour. I blinked, trying to focus in the dimness after the brilliance of the sunshine in the courtyard.

'Mademoiselle O'Shea.' Manon's voice was sharp. 'I specified you were not to come until two o'clock. You are too early. It is not a convenient time.'

I couldn't see her in the darkened room.

'Madame Maliki. Please. I won't stay long; all I wish is for you—'

279

'Badou. Open the shutters,' she interrupted, and Badou took his hand from mine and ran to open one of the tall wooden shutters that faced the courtyard. Louvred lines of light illuminated a long, narrow room furnished with daybeds, several camel-hide ottomans and a low table of intricately carved wood. There was a thick, rich-looking rug of red and blue and black, and tall mirrors leaning against two walls. The ceiling was high, and of polished wood. A fireplace, cold and dead in the summer heat, was in one corner. A room opened from this one; I could see blackened pots and a low brazier, and a sink with a single tap over it. The fresh smell of whitewash was still prevalent.

And then I saw them: the paintings on one wall. There were at least ten of them, unframed oils of various sizes. All the paintings were in violent colours, with disregard to smaller details, as though the images had come straight from the palette to the canvas with no structure or careful reflection. And yet there was a raw beauty that could only be created by one with a natural talent.

'I did not expect such inconsideration,' Manon said, her words followed by a deep inhalation. She was underneath the paintings on a green velvet daybed, a long curling tube in one hand. It was attached to a container like the *sheeshas* I had seen in Tangier. She exhaled, and a long, straight line of smoke came from her mouth.

Badou left the windows and sat beside her.

'I apologise, Madame Maliki,' I said. 'But certainly you can understand my need to find out about Etienne. Certainly,' I repeated. My heart was thudding, and I rubbed my hands together, unable to hide my impatience. I scanned the room, as I had the courtyard yesterday, hoping to see something, some sign of Etienne's presence. But there was nothing of a man in this room: no *babouches* near the door, no djellaba tossed on to a mattress. What of Manon's husband? I tried to imagine what kind of man she was married to. 'It was difficult to wait, as you asked, but now I'm here. Tell me where I can find him. Or . . .' I stopped. 'Or anything that you know of his whereabouts.'

She put down the tube with its moulded mouthpiece, and I approached her.

There was a faint ashen gleam to her face, which was paler than I remembered. She wore a kaftan of green and orange silk, and another type of Moroccan overdress – a *dfina*. It was soft green, and had slits in the sides that allowed the skirt of the kaftan to be exhibited. Without the drape of her *haik* it was clear that she was willowy beneath the thin layered dresses. I had never seen a Moroccan woman without her *haik*; although I had seen kaftans in shops in the French Quarter and swinging from hooks in the souk, I didn't realise how beautiful they were on the female form.

Since it was obvious she wouldn't rise, I lowered myself to the daybed across from her. Falida appeared silently – I hadn't heard her come in – and propped hard, stuffed round pillows between the wall and my back. But I wasn't there to relax; I leaned forward, staring at Manon. The paintings over her head – the wild and swirling images – made the room pulse, growing brighter and warmer.

'Please make your way out, Mademoiselle O'Shea,' Manon said now. 'And fetch my bag, Badou.'

I stayed where I was while the child ran to a chest against the wall and returned with a decorated cloth bag.

He gave it to his mother and then sat cross-legged on the floor at her feet.

Manon stared at me, but I didn't move. She raised one shoulder in a nonchalant shrug, and I knew I had won this very small battle. She drew a comb, a mirror and some vials from the bag. In silence, she slowly combed through her long, shining hair, but left it hanging loose. She applied rouge to her cheeks and lips. Then she took a small piece of wood from the bag and rubbed it over her gums, staining them with something on the wood. Her pale pink gums turned reddish brown, setting off the whiteness of her teeth. She dug once more into the bag, taking out what I knew, from seeing them in the shops in the French Quarter, to be a wood *merroud* containing kohl.

The inside of one of my cheeks was raw from chewing on it. I wanted to shout at Manon, to shake her, to somehow force her to tell me about Etienne. But I knew it would do no good. In fact, it might make her refuse to answer.

She would tell me what she wanted, when she wanted.

'My kohl is special,' Manon said, the *merroud* in one hand and the mirror in the other. She outlined her eyes. 'I only make it on nights with a new moon. I use charcoal from burned oleander roots. Some ground nutmeg and aloe. And also – most importantly – a bit of camel bile. But without the moon's effect it won't work.'

I refused to ask her what she meant.

Manon, staring at herself in the mirror as she worked, now sang, her voice low and rich, '*I will make my eyes the moons in a dark sky. I will madden men with desire; one man or many. All will desire me.*' She looked away from her reflection, and straight into my eyes.

In spite of the warm room, the skin on the back of my neck tightened as though I were in a draught, and I fought not to shiver. I thought of Etienne's talk of the women of Marrakesh and their magic practices, and his dismissal of them as nonsense. Manon was still staring at me, and my uneasiness continued. It was eerie; with a few applications of colour to her face, she had transformed herself from a pretty, although ageing woman, into an earthy beauty. There was a lushness about her now, as of a rose slightly past its bloom, and yet still highly seductive. She was an exotic creature of this country. There was nothing about her that indicated she was Etienne's sister. The only thing French about her was her perfect speech.

'Has any man ever been mad with desire for you, Mademoiselle O'Shea?' she asked then. Her voice held a sarcastic tone.

I didn't reply. I had told her I was Etienne's fiancée. Was it so impossible for her to believe he desired me? 'And your husband, Madame Maliki? He's at work?' I asked, partly because she angered me, and also because somehow I knew – some instinct – that she wouldn't like me questioning her.

I was correct. Her face changed again, her eyes narrowing.

'Your husband?' I repeated, but now Manon ignored me, returning her toiletries to the bag and then lifting her chin and raising her eyebrows at Badou.

'Well?' she asked him.

'You are so pretty, Maman,' he said, in a practised way.

Falida, still standing beside my daybed, bowed her head. '*Très belle*, my lady.'

283

Then Manon looked at me with the same expression. I knew she was waiting for me to compliment her. It was obvious that Manon Maliki was a woman used to being complimented.

I said nothing.

Manon pulled the drawstrings of her bag with one quick, angry jerk, and tossed it on to the cushion beside her. Falida picked it up, returning it to the chest. Then she sat cross-legged on the floor beside Badou. Manon looked down at them, then back to me. I was reminded of a queen with her subjects.

'I will not ask – demand – again that you leave,' she told me. 'You may return in an hour. And consider yourself lucky that I will see you at all, in spite of how you have angered me.'

'Madame Maliki,' I said, exasperated. 'What difference does one hour make? Can't you simply—'

'Manon?'

We all turned to the doorway. A man stood there; he was so tall that his turban brushed the lintel. He wore a dark blue cotton djellaba with yellow embroidery at the neck. The deep purple-blue turban was wrapped around his head and neck, one end of it tucked over his nose and mouth. Because of the light behind him I couldn't see his eyes. He carried a basket under one arm.

I immediately remembered the man on the *piste*. L'Homme Bleu.

Badou ran to him, first kissing the man's hand in the Arabic gesture of respect for an elder, and then winding his arms around the man's leg. 'Onçle Aszulay,' he said.

Uncle, I thought. But Etienne was his uncle. Why did he

call this man uncle as well? He must be Manon's husband's brother.

I glanced at Manon; she was smiling at the man in a coquettish way. Suddenly I knew that Manon didn't want me here because she was waiting for this man.

Was it her husband? No, because Badou called him uncle, but more because of the way she was looking at him: not as one would greet a husband, but . . . I thought of Etienne arriving at my door on Juniper Road. Manon was looking at him as if he were her lover.

'*Assalaam alykum*, Badou,' the man said, greeting Badou in Arabic, smiling warmly at him and smoothing his hair. He set down the basket and looked at us.

Manon, no long smiling, said, off-handedly, 'This is Mademoiselle O'Shea. But she is leaving now.'

I stayed where I was, seated.

The tall man studied me for a moment, then solemnly bowed his head. 'Good afternoon, Mademoiselle O'Shea,' he said, his French quite clear, but with a strong accent of his mother tongue – Arabic, I assumed.

'Good afternoon, Monsieur . . .' I hesitated.

'I am Aszulay, mademoiselle,' he said simply. He stepped out of his *babouches* before entering the room, and once across the threshold pulled down the end of his turban, uncovering his face. Then he unwrapped it from his head, pushing it down so that it encircled his neck. His head wasn't shaved in the way of the Arab men I'd seen throughout the souks, but was thick and wavy, very black. Now he was standing in a beam of light from the open louvres. His eyes were a surprising blue.

Badou clung to the edge of the man's robe, and in a

swift and obviously routine move Aszulay swooped him into the crook of one arm. Badou wrapped his arms around the man's neck.

'Falida,' Aszulay said, 'take the food into the kitchen and set it out for the meal.'

The girl took the heavy basket and lugged it across the room.

'You join us to eat, mademoiselle?' Aszulay asked.

'No,' Manon said, 'she will not stay. She is going now. You may return later, as we discussed,' she told me, standing.

I stood as well, facing her. 'But madame—'

'We will talk later. At two o'clock.'

'Please. Just tell me where—'

'No!' Manon's voice was loud, forceful. 'I tell you two o'clock, I mean two o'clock.' She came around the table, pulling on my sleeve. 'Go, mademoiselle. I'm ordering you out of my home. Do you not understand?'

'Manon,' Aszulay said, in a firm voice. I looked at him, hoping, somehow, that he would intervene. But I couldn't read what was in his face, and he said nothing more.

I had no choice but to leave. As I did, I heard his voice, low, questioning, and Manon's answers, high and argumentative. They spoke Arabic. I understood nothing.

I hung about the nearby alley, walking up and down a few streets, until an hour had passed. At exactly two o'clock I went back to Sharia Zitoun and knocked on the gate. Nobody came. I called out, first Manon's name, then Badou's. I called for Falida.

But there was only silence behind the saffron gate.

★

What choice did I have? I waited by the gate for another hour, leaning against the wall, shifting constantly to take the weight off my leg. There wasn't a sound from within. I told myself I would wait until they returned, even if it was late, the medina dark. I would wait.

But as the light filtering down into the narrow street took on a shadowed appearance, and I smelled the odours of cooking meat wafting through the street, I knew I couldn't stand any longer.

Limping heavily, I went back to the hotel for yet another restless night, another night when I was still no closer to finding Etienne than I had been twenty-four hours earlier.

CHAPTER TWENTY-TWO

MY FIRST INSTINCT, UPON ARISING the next morning, was to rush back to Sharia Zitoun. But I was disheartened after yesterday, and also afraid that when I got there I would be met with the same silence. What if Manon had gone somewhere, somewhere I couldn't find her, to avoid speaking to me of Etienne? What if I had missed my chance with her?

What was she hiding?

To distract myself for a few hours, I wandered for a while in the French Quarter. I went into a store selling art supplies, hoping the smell of paint, the feel of a brush, would take my mind from waiting. I thought of the paintings on the walls of the hotel lobby, and remembered the sketch of Mustapha and Aziz I'd done on the *piste*. By the time I walked down Sharia Zitoun it was noon.

Again I steeled myself for silence, but as I came closer I heard Badou's voice from the other side of the gate. Putting my hand on my chest and taking a deep, relieved breath, I knocked, calling his name. He opened it. 'Hello, Mademoiselle O'Shea,' he said, smiling up at me as if pleased to see me. I tried to smile back at him, but my mouth wouldn't do as I bid.

Aszulay was there — again, or still. He came to the doorway. 'Mademoiselle O'Shea. You have returned.' He smiled, much as Badou had.

'Yes. When I came back yesterday, no one answered my knocking or calls.'

He frowned. 'But when I left, shortly before two, Manon said she was expecting you.'

'She wasn't here. I waited a long time.'

'Please. Sit. Manon is resting,' he said. 'Soon we will eat. I wish you to join us.'

I closed my eyes for a moment, not wanting to carry out this social charade. And what if, when Manon saw me, she treated me as she had yesterday?

'I apologise for Manon's behaviour yesterday. Sometimes she has headaches.'

I thought of Etienne.

'She suffers, and this makes her . . . the way you saw her. Today you must stay. Hospitality is the Moroccan way, mademoiselle. It is an insult not to accept it.'

I nodded, sitting on one of the low cork stools, which was not comfortable for my leg. I stretched it straight out in front of me. Once I was seated, Aszulay sat cross-legged on the daybed, with the round table between us. Badou climbed on to his lap and, unlike Manon, who never touched her son, Aszulay wrapped his arms around the little boy.

L'Homme Bleu. Again I thought of the man in blue robes on the *piste*, appearing out of nowhere and trading the tile for bread. How he had intrigued me, with his height and his direct stare, his slow walk of dignity and grace, disappearing down the dusty track as mysteriously as he had appeared.

'I will ask Falida to bring tea,' Aszulay said, and I jumped slightly, realising I had been staring at him. 'We will eat here, where it's cooler.' He set Badou down and stood. 'Badou, go and tell Maman to come downstairs and eat. Please, be comfortable,' he said to me. 'I will return shortly.'

Badou scampered up the courtyard stairs, and in a moment I heard the faint sound of his voice from above. I wanted so badly to see Manon, to hear what she would tell me, yet at the same time I dreaded having to deal with her. There was something cruel and twisted about her; the enjoyment on her face was obvious as she made me beg and wait. She made no attempt to hide her lack of interest in her own son, and I knew how cruelly she treated the little servant girl.

How could this woman be so different from Etienne?

Aszulay returned with Falida; he carried a tagine – the large round earthenware plate with its high, cone-shaped cover to trap the steam. Falida balanced a circular brass tray that held a heaping platter of flat round bread, a teapot, three painted glasses in tin holders and four small porcelain bowls of water with a slice of lemon floating in each.

She set everything on the round table, then filled the three glasses with tea. She handed the first one to Aszulay, then one to me, backing away from the table to run into the house. She had left the third glass for, I assumed, Manon.

'Please. Drink,' Aszulay said.

I nodded, taking a cautious mouthful – the familiar mint and so much sugar, as always – and set it down. The weather was far too hot for such a drink. I longed for a glass of cool water.

Aszulay didn't speak, but appeared relaxed as he sipped his tea. For me, the silence was too large; I tried to think of something to say. What does one say to a Blue Man? I was acutely uncomfortable, and cleared my throat twice before speaking. 'What is it you do in Marrakesh?' I finally asked.

He swallowed his mouthful of tea and said, 'I dig.'

'Dig?' I repeated, not sure if I had understood the word.

Aszulay nodded. 'I dig, and plant trees, and flowers.' He took another sip of tea, and I watched his lips on the rim.

'Oh. A gardener. Do you have a specific family you work for?' I asked, not caring at all, and yet unable to bear the silence.

'I have worked in the gardens of many of the larger *riads* in the medina, and in some of the gardens and parks in La Ville Nouvelle. I'm working there now.'

I nodded. 'I'm staying at Hôtel de la Palmeraie. In La Ville Nouvelle,' I added, unnecessarily. Again, I had no interest in this idle conversation.

'*Bien entendu*,' Aszulay said. 'Naturally. It is very . . . it is luxurious.'

I nodded.

'I'm working in the garden of Monsieur Majorelle,' he said. 'But many days I bring the midday meal for Manon and Badou.'

'I went there once, to Le Jardin Majorelle.'

Aszulay had put down his glass. 'Yes. I saw you.'

'You've seen me?' I felt a tiny nudge of curiosity.

'It was last week. I was working as you walked through. I saw you speaking with Madame Odette. She comes every day; she is a rather sad woman,' he said, and now I felt a

291

small stab of shame. I'd paid no attention to the men working under the hot sun.

'Not so many foreigners are here now. They come in the cooler months,' he said, by way of explanation, I suppose, for having noticed me.

Had I appeared imperious, or dismissive, as I walked slowly along the paths? 'It will be lovely when it's done,' I said, too quickly. 'Certainly the peaceful oasis Monsieur Majorelle is hoping for. I've always liked gardens,' I said.

Aszulay was watching me, still relaxed, his hands loose on his thighs. His eyes were so blue; how did this come about? For some reason his direct gaze, unthreatening and also unguarded, made me more ill at ease than the earlier silence.

'I have a garden at home. In America,' I added. 'I always look for a balance – order, and yet with a certain untamed influence – in my plantings. As for flowers, well, I also . . .' I stopped. I was droning on in a silly and inconsequential way. I had been about to say that I painted botanical images. Why would I tell this man more about myself than I'd disclosed to anyone since I'd left Albany? 'I'm interested in plants,' I finished.

Aszulay nodded. 'You must visit Majorelle's garden again,' he said, with complete confidence. He suddenly turned from me. 'Oh, here you are.' He stood, looking at the steps.

'Why is she here?' Manon said, frowning. Badou peeked from behind her.

Aszulay went to Manon, climbing the steps and extending his hand. 'Come. We are hospitable, Manon. When a guest arrives we offer tea and food.' He said this patiently, as he might to Badou. 'Come,' he urged again, and took her hand.

At that she smiled, although very slightly. I saw she had once again made up her face, and this time wore a different outfit, beautiful purple and mauve silk. On her feet were burgundy satin slippers embroidered with cream-coloured vines. Her hair flowed, thick and luxurious, over her shoulders. As she came down the steps, perfume wafted towards me.

She was like a glorious flower, inviting all to come closer, to gaze and breathe deeply, to wonder at her beauty.

I sat with my hands in my lap, in my simple blue organdy dress and heavy black shoes. As usual, my hair trailed from its pins in the heat and humidity. One thick strand had fallen over my cheek, perhaps hiding my scar.

'Sit here,' Aszulay said, holding Manon's hand until she was seated where he had been, on the daybed. 'Badou, take a stool and sit beside Mademoiselle O'Shea,' he added, as if he were indeed the master of the house. I saw how completely at ease he was with Manon, putting a cushion behind her to make her comfortable, gently pushing back on her shoulder to settle her against it, tousling Badou's hair and stroking his little cheek for an instant.

Aszulay was unlike any of the other Moroccan men I had seen in Marrakesh. In fact, I had never seen any form of contact between Moroccan men and women. I realised that the men and women I saw in the souks and alleys were those of the working class. The men sold their goods; they pushed or pulled carts through the streets; they carried heavy sacks on their backs; they drove the taxis and the *calèches*, they drank tea with each other at small tables throughout the alleys. They were not the nobles and sultans of Morocco. And the covered women shopping for their daily needs were either the wives of these men, accompanied by a father or son, or servants for the ladies of the harems, those of the higher realms of Moroccan society who rarely left the seclusion of their homes and courtyards.

I didn't know how Aszulay and Manon fitted into this world. Aszulay had the vibrant and open gaze of a man in his prime, an attractiveness that was due not only to his features, but from within. And from the moment he had met me he didn't treat me with anything like the curious or disapproving attitude of the other men of Morocco, who either leered at me or ignored me. He treated me and, I saw, Manon, with a distinctly European air. And his French was formal, the grammar close to perfect.

Manon was watching Aszulay with what I could only interpret as a sultry look. Although he didn't respond, I knew this man was Manon's lover. Certainly. There was no doubt.

She didn't have a husband any longer, then. I thought of the words she had sung as she outlined her eyes the day before, of men maddened with desire for her.

I felt, for one tiny instant, disappointment. Disappointment that a man like Aszulay could be so taken with a woman like Manon. But, I also reasoned with myself, in a strange way he also reminded me of Manon, as though caught somewhere between two worlds. She appeared completely Moroccan, and yet she was French by birth. He was a Blue Man of the Sahara, working as a gardener, and yet spoke and carried himself with a sophisticated air.

I shook my head the slightest, annoyed that I was even

entertaining these thoughts. I was also annoyed at having to sit here, to actually attempt to eat and drink and act as a polite guest. To wait for Manon to bestow me with information when and if she felt the time was right.

In spite of the shade in the courtyard, it was still very hot, and my stomach was upset by nerves. I knew I wouldn't be able to eat. All I needed was Manon to tell me about Etienne.

But now I would have to wait. She was paying me no attention, apart from obvious but suppressed anger.

Aszulay held Manon's glass of tea towards her. She didn't reach for it, but shook her head, sighing lightly.

'It's your head again?' he asked, and she made a small, sad sound in her throat.

At that Aszulay held the glass to her lips, and she sipped, her eyes closed.

I didn't believe her; surely she was putting on this air of helplessness for his attention.

He took the lid off the tagine and gestured at it, looking at me now. It was a pyramid of couscous with long slices of carrots and a green vegetable – zucchini? – arranged up its sides. Bubbling pieces of chicken poked from within the couscous. I knew that even if I forced myself, I would only be able to eat a few bites, simply to be polite. But I also knew that the sooner I ate, the sooner the meal would be over. Then Aszulay would leave to return to work, and I would get the truth from Manon.

This time I would not allow her to ignore my questions. Today I would find out about Etienne.

'Please,' Aszulay said to me. 'As the honoured guest. Begin.'

There was no cutlery, no plates to put the food upon.

'May I eat, Oncle Aszulay?' Badou said. 'I am very hungry.'

Aszulay looked at me; surely my face portrayed my confusion. 'No, Badou. You know we must wait for our guest.'

'Please, Badou,' I said, 'please eat.'

Aszulay looked at me again. Then Badou glanced at him, and he nodded. The little boy scooped up some of the couscous with the fingers of his right hand, kneading it until it was a small ball, and then put it in his mouth. Aszulay tore a thin round of bread in half and, folding it, used it to spoon the couscous into his mouth.

I suspected he had seen that I didn't know how to eat in the Moroccan way, and so was showing me. I was thankful to him for not embarrassing me further, and took a piece of bread and used it as he did. In spite of not believing I could eat, the couscous was delicious, and I realised I had eaten nothing today, and little the day before. Suddenly I was very hungry, and scooped up more of the couscous. When Aszulay picked up a chicken leg with his fingers, I reached into the hot couscous and extracted a thigh. But I dug too far into the steaming mass, and burned my fingers. I dropped the thigh, embarrassed, then picked it up with the tips of my fingers and set it at the edge of the tagine.

'For the Moroccan, the fork is unnecessary,' Aszulay said, and I looked at him, still thankful for his understanding, and saw that Manon was staring at me with open antagonism. She didn't like him paying any attention to me. She was jealous.

'Manon,' Aszulay said, turning to her. 'Come. Eat. You love *les courgettes*.'

Manon looked at the long slices of zucchini, but shook her head weakly. 'I cannot,' she whispered, closing her eyes as she'd done earlier. 'I'm not well today. It's not a good day for me.' She sighed again, an overdone sigh.

'Do you promise to eat later?'

How could he not see her transparency?

'Yes, Aszulay,' she said, demurely, so changed from the forward and volatile woman who had held me in the palm of her hand the day before and the one before that.

I picked up the cooling chicken and bit into it. The skin was crackly and tasted of tumeric. When we were done, we rinsed our fingers in the cool lemon water, and then Badou went back to the fountain and once more walked carefully around its narrow edge, his arms out for balance.

Aszulay looked at my glass, still full, and poured himself another. I drank my tea, no longer hot.

'So,' Manon said, finally looking at me. 'What do you think of my Tuareg?'

I ran my finger around the rim of my glass. Aszulay said nothing.

'You know of the Tuaregs? The Abandoned of God, the Arabs call them, because no one can impose a will on them. They obey no laws in the desert. Aszulay obeys no laws anywhere, do you?' she asked him now.

Again, he didn't answer, nor did his face show any expression.

'His name is a Berber Amazigh name. It means *man with blue eyes*. Quite unusual, aren't they?' she went on, still staring at me.

How was I to respond? There was more silence except for the buzzing of flies and the soft breathing of Falida, who again crouched in the doorway, watching us.

'And unlike so many of this country and those beyond, they honour their women,' she said. 'Don't you, Aszulay? The Tuareg women have respect, and freedom. They go about uncovered, and the men are proud of them. They don't hide their beauty away. Descent – and inheritance – comes through the women. Why don't you tell our guest about your women, Aszulay?'

I didn't understand why she was badgering him. But he ignored her.

'Manon has avoided telling me the reason you've come to Marrakesh,' he said. 'How do you know Manon, mademoiselle?'

I licked my lips, glancing at her, and set my empty glass on the table. 'I've come in search of Manon's brother,' I said.

Aszulay's face became very still. 'Manon?' he said, and something about the way he said her name filled me with foreboding. He looked back at me. 'You're . . . you are looking for Etienne?'

I stood so quickly the edge of my skirt knocked my glass to the tiles of the courtyard. It shattered. 'You know him?' I asked, moving around the table. He stood; I had to look up to study his face. 'You know Etienne? Is he here? Where is he? Please, where is Etienne?'

'Mademoiselle O'Shea,' he said. 'Are you—'

Now Manon stood as well. 'Leave us, Aszulay,' she said, her voice loud and firm, suddenly changed from the weak, clinging woman she had appeared throughout the meal. 'I want you to go. I will speak to her about it now.'

About it, she said. Not *him*.

'Mademoiselle O'Shea,' Aszulay said again. 'Etienne—'

Again Manon stopped him. 'Aszulay!' she said, her voice harsh. 'This is my home. You will do as I say.'

So. She spoke to him the same way she had spoken to me.

He opened his mouth as if to argue, then closed it. He grabbed up the long expanse of indigo cloth from the end of the daybed – his turban – and strode across the court-yard, his blue robe flashing behind him as he went through the gate. It closed behind him with a bang.

'Falida. Take the dishes and wash them. Badou, help her,' Manon ordered.

I stayed where I was. When the children had carried away the dishes and glasses, Manon patted the daybed. 'Come. Sit beside me,' she said, suddenly friendly, and that alarmed me more than all of her rude behaviour. I didn't move.

'Come,' she said again, smiling. 'Sit here with me,' she said, 'so I can tell you where you will find Etienne.'

Swallowing, I did as she asked, and as soon as I was beside her she picked up my hand. 'So small,' she said, stroking the back of it. 'Your hands tell me you have worked, but not so hard, eh, Sidonie?' I noticed her use of my Christian name. She said it with complete familiarity, as if she had a right. And then she gripped my hand with both of hers, squeezing my fingers painfully. I tried to pull away, but she wouldn't release me. I was shocked at her strength, and so wary of her.

'I have always worked,' I said, distractedly thinking of the laundry, the housework, the cooking and gardening.

'You haven't worked like me. Not like the work I have done, to survive,' she said, and in another instance I might have used the word coy to describe her voice.

I thought of what Etienne had told me of his upbringing. 'But . . . when you were young, with your brothers . . . Etienne always said his life was one of privilege.'

When she didn't respond, I said, 'And you have this house. To live like this . . . surely your life can't have been so difficult—'

She made a sound with her tongue against the roof of her mouth, shushing me, and I fell silent. 'I have not always had the luxury of this kind of home,' she said, confusing me. Now she ran her own fingers over the raised bump on my middle finger, and the callus on my palm where my paintbrush had rubbed for so many years. Even though the callus had softened and almost disappeared, she kept stroking the bump.

'What is this from?' she asked.

'A paintbrush,' I said.

She shook her head, still smiling that awful smile. 'It grows ever more interesting.'

'What? What do you mean?'

After another endless moment she said, 'But you saw my paintings.'

It took a moment for her meaning to register. 'In the house? Those . . . you painted those?' My voice rose a half-tone.

'You don't believe me?' she said, lazily, the smile never leaving.

'No. I mean yes, of course I believe you. It's just that . . .' My voice trailed off.

Another mystery. Etienne had grown up with a sister who painted, and yet had never mentioned this fact to me when he looked at my paintings, when he spoke about knowing so little about art.

'How did you learn to paint like this? Was it in France? Did you study under someone?'

'In France, Sidonie?' Manon gave a croak that was perhaps meant to be a laugh. 'In France?' she repeated, as though amused. 'You think I have studied in France?'

'But Etienne – his schooling in medicine. And Guillaume . . . Yes, I assumed you had, as well . . .' Again my voice faded as I saw the expression on Manon's face. She was no longer amused, but now angry.

'Of course I didn't study in France.' Her tone implied I was an idiot. And then she suddenly smiled again. I shivered. 'Now tell me about your paintings.'

'Please. Can we not—'

'But I insist. We are having a nice friendly chat. You tell me what I want to know, and then I'll tell you what you want to know.'

I gnawed, for a moment, on the sore on the inside of my cheek. 'I don't paint like you. I use watercolours. I paint plants. Birds.'

Manon stared at me for a moment with a look I couldn't interpret it. 'So Etienne liked his little American *souris* to make pretty pictures?' There was a mocking tone in her voice.

I wanted to shout at her, *I am not a mouse! How dare you?* Instead I said, with as much calmness as possible under the circumstances, 'Yes. Etienne liked my paintings.' I could not anger her further. I knew how quickly she could shut down, and send me away with no answers.

'He told you this? That he *liked* your paintings? You think he liked such tame subjects? What do you think he thought of my work?'

I shook my head. 'I don't know. And I don't know why you're so angry with me. I made your brother happy, madame. Don't you want him to be happy?'

Still holding my hand, still staring into my face with a frightening intensity, Manon opened her lips, bringing her face so close to mine that for one fleeting moment I thought she would kiss me. I instinctively turned my head, to escape her mouth, and Manon put her lips to my ear. 'Etienne is no more,' she whispered. Or perhaps it wasn't a whisper, but I found it difficult to understand her.

I pulled away from her breath on my cheek. 'What? What did you just say? What do you mean?'

Now Manon sat back, her grip on my hand lessening but not releasing, and her voice returned to normal. 'I said that Etienne is no more, Sidonie. He does not live. He is buried in the cemetery behind Eglise des Saints Martyrs.' In spite of the space between us, I smelled something sour and acidic on her breath, something that came from deep within her. It made my stomach sick. I swallowed.

'You can't mean this, Manon.' I used her first name without thinking. My head moved swiftly from side to side, as if by its motion I could erase her words. I violently yanked my hand from hers. 'It's not true. It's not true,' I repeated, shaking her. 'Tell me Etienne isn't dead!'

She nodded, no longer smiling, but staring at me, her eyes, ringed with kohl, huge. I couldn't look away from them. I couldn't catch my breath; it came in great rolling heaves, and Manon's form thinned and wavered. I stared at her, choking now, while she simply sat, nodding, holding me with her eyes.

CHAPTER TWENTY-THREE

I DON'T REMEMBER HOW I found my way back to Hôtel de la Palmeraie. My senses weren't working properly, and the alleys and souks and square were seen and heard through an opaque haze of colour and sound. I held my handkerchief over my nose and mouth as I rushed through the confusing streets of the medina – how long did it take me? Did I get lost? I know there was a jolting ride in a taxi, and finally I was safely hidden in my room.

I lay on my bed but continued to press the handkerchief against my face. *He's dead*, I thought, over and over. *Etienne is dead. He's dead.*

I remembered the exact scene after the miscarriage, the words echoing inside my head.

My eyes and throat and head ached in an almost debilitating way as I thought of my lost baby, and of never again seeing Etienne. A strong part of me believed that if I found Etienne, he would still want me. But even if he hadn't . . . I would have known he was in the world. And that in itself would have been a small, strange comfort. Maybe I had dared to think that even if he turned me away in Marrakesh, some day I might open the door of my home in Albany – as I had the first time he had come to Juniper

Road – and he would be sitting outside in his car.

I saw his smile, saw his fingers closing around mine. Never again. Never . . .

Flat on my back, rocking with my arms around myself, a low keening came, unbidden, from my mouth. The room was dark, and so hot. I heard the distant roar of D'jemma el Fna.

Now my chest hurt as well as my head, and I found it difficult to breathe. How had Etienne died? Had he called out for me as he lay dying, or had he died so quickly that there was no time for even a word to pass his lips?

Now I would never know why he had left me. I relived the hours I had wrestled with my choices in Marseilles that day as I lay in bed after the doctor's visit: whether I would travel on to Marrakesh or return home. But I had made the decision to come, to try to find some answers.

And now I had. I had an answer. It wasn't why he had left me. But it was an answer, a terrible, and totally unexpected answer.

It wasn't right: first my baby, and now Etienne.

I tried to slow my breathing, tried to will away the frightening sensation. But a huge and swooping panic filled me, and my heart beat so violently that I thought it would burst, frightening me further. I sat up in the heat, gasping. Was I having some sort of attack? Would I die here, like Etienne?

You are not dying, Sidonie. You are not dying. Stop it.

I wanted to go to the open window, to lean out and try to catch my breath; there was no air in here. But the very small task of walking across the room was too great. I lay down again, pressing my hands over the pain in my chest.

I again thought of my unborn child, and what he or she would have looked like, would have felt like in my arms. Unexpectedly the image of Badou's face came to me. I saw it, so accepting of the cruel mother that fate had presented him with; felt the way his warm little hand took mine, so trustingly. I kept my eyes closed, drawing in short breaths until at long last I again sat up. I ripped open my dress, shrugging out of it and my slip and underpants. I undid my shoes, tossing them on to the floor with loud thuds, and then pulled off my stockings. I drew in my breath at a new pain, and saw that my knees were torn, the drying blood sticking to my ripped stockings. I had no idea what had happened to them.

Naked, I fell back on to the soft bed, and again I wept, not caring if anyone passing in the wide, opulent hall heard me.

I didn't think I would possibly sleep, but the morning sun on my face woke me. I lay still for mere seconds, blinking in the light, before the memory of what had happened the day before came back with a hard rush.

'Etienne is dead,' I said, aloud. 'Etienne is dead.' *Dead*.

My head pounded. I pushed back the coverlet, and saw my body. I had never before slept without a nightdress, even with Etienne.

I thought of my hysterical behaviour the evening before. Had I really had such pain in my chest that I thought my heart would burst open, the chambers and aorta spilling blood, killing me instantly? How foolish Etienne would have thought me.

Etienne, always so calm and in control. I couldn't

imagine him any other way. Even when we had that first conversation when I told him about the baby, and he had stumbled with his English, and seemed a stranger, he hadn't completely lost his focus. But then I remembered that one moment, the instant in the car when his face had betrayed him, where I had seen him uncertain, and fearful.

Behind his almost infallible veneer, something fragile and secretive had lurked. What had he been hiding? What part of him was unprotected, and why had he worked at covering it with theory and distance?

I lay on the bed all day, watching the sun move across the room. I stayed there, not bathing, not drinking or eating. Once someone tapped on my door and I called out for them to go away. I watched the shadows lengthen and turn to darkness.

When the sun again shone through the windows, I was suddenly immensely thirsty. I wanted fresh orange juice. Taking my white slip from where it lay beside me on the bed, I pulled it over my head. As I rose, my knees shot through with pain; I looked at them, remembering, vaguely, that they had been bloody when I undressed. Now they were freshly scabbed, the bruises around the scabs dark and spreading. I tugged the bell cord to call one of the staff.

Within a few moments there was a quiet knock on the door. Wrapping the bedcover around my shoulders, I opened the door to instruct the boy to bring me a pitcher of orange juice. But it wasn't one of the boys who worked in the hotel. It was Monsieur Henri.

'Mademoiselle,' he said, looking, for the first time since

I'd seen him, flustered. 'There appears to be a very uncomfortable situation.'

'What is it?'

'Downstairs. In the lobby,' he said, as if unsure of how to continue.

'Yes, yes, Monsieur Henri. Please. I'm very tired, and wish to return to my bed.'

'There is a man,' he said. 'A man who says he knows you.'

My legs suddenly felt as though they might give way. It had all been a mistake, or a terrible, macabre prank. Etienne was not dead. He was alive, and waiting for me in the lobby.

'Monsieur Duverger?' I cried out, putting one hand on Monsieur Henri's shoulder. He turned his cheek, the slightest, and I realised I had offended him by grabbing at him. I took my hand away. 'I'm sorry,' I said, 'but is it he? Is it Etienne Duverger?'

Now Monsieur Henri raised his chin, just the slightest. It gave the impression that the end of his nose lifted as well. 'I assure you, Mademoiselle O'Shea, that it is not this Monsieur Duverger you speak of. It is a man . . . an Arab, mademoiselle. An Arab with his child.'

I blinked. 'An Arab?'

'Yes. With some name of the Sahara. I don't remember. And really, mademoiselle, I assured him that we, at Hôtel de la Palmeraie, are not in the habit of allowing non-European men into the hotel, let alone upstairs to the rooms. He insisted I come to speak to you. He was . . .' He stopped. 'He was rather menacing in his insistence. It appears, mademoiselle,' he leaned closer, and I smelled a flowery scent, perhaps jasmine, 'that he has brought you something. Food.' He drew back. 'It's quite unacceptable. I told him that if you were hungry you would order from our extensive menu. But he stood there – and is standing there, I'm sure, as we speak – with a tagine and the child. The child is holding greasy fritters strung on a piece of grass. The food is, I'm afraid, creating a disagreeable oily smell in the lobby. And although fortunately, at this time of day, not many of our guests are about, I truly wish this man and child to be gone before—'

'You may send them up, Monsieur Henri,' I said, and his eyes widened, then he took in my hair, and the coverlet draped around me. I knew one bare, scabbed knee was visible where the coverlet didn't meet, but I didn't care.

'Are you certain, mademoiselle? The safety of our guests is of the highest—'

Again I interrupted. 'Yes. I am a guest as well. And I can assure you that there is absolutely no reason for your concern. Please allow them up to my room. And also have a pitcher of orange juice sent up.' It wasn't my voice speaking. It was someone else's, someone who wouldn't be trifled with.

Monsieur Henri's nostrils tightened. 'As you wish, mademoiselle,' he said, and then, without the courtesy of a goodbye, turned and walked down the hallway, his back as stiff as if he had a steel rod inserted into his spine.

I picked up my dress from the floor, where it lay in a crumpled heap, and put it on. I jammed my bare feet into my shoes, leaving them undone, but had no energy to attempt to comb through my hair.

Within moments there was another knock on the door.

I opened it to Aszulay and Badou. As Monsieur Henri had told me, Aszulay carried a tagine, while Badou held a long and tough green twine, strung with a half-dozen fragrant, sugar-coated *beignets*.

'Aszulay. And Badou,' I said, as if they didn't know their own names. 'What . . . why have you come?'

Aszulay studied me, balancing the tagine with one hand. I was aware of how I looked, my eyes red and swollen, my hair a disgusting tangle. I pulled a strand of hair away from my cheek, where it was stuck with perspiration.

'We brought you some *beignets*, Sidonie,' Badou said. 'But what's wrong with your eyes? They—' Aszulay put his free hand on the boy's head, and the child was immediately quiet.

'I thought perhaps . . .' Aszulay said, and then stopped, as if unsure how to continue. 'Yesterday Badou told me . . . he said that the day before you had cried out, and fallen to the ground. He came to you, but you only stared at him, without speaking. Then you got up and . . . he said you were unable to walk properly, and fell again, but left the courtyard. I knew then that Manon had deeply upset you. I'm sorry for what she had to tell you. About Etienne,' he added. 'As I have said, Manon does not always speak or act in the most suitable way.'

There was silence. I had cried out, fallen? Now I knew what had happened to my knees. Finally I looked at the tagine and said, 'Thank you. But . . . I think it's better if I'm alone at this time. But thank you, Aszulay,' I repeated. 'And thank you, Badou.'

Aszulay nodded. He still had his hand on Badou's head. He took it off and set the tagine on the floor just inside the door. A lovely smell rose from it – lamb and apricots. Rosemary. 'Come, Badou, give Mademoiselle O'Shea the *beignets*, and we will leave her.'

I took the ring of little doughnuts Badou silently handed me. By the lingering way his small hand remained on the length of grass, I knew he had expected to share the meal – and this treat – with me. Even in the short time I had been in Morocco, I understood its hospitality, and how utterly rude – no matter what my mood, and even to a small child – I appeared.

I thought of returning to the bed, wrapping myself in the coverlet, alone with my thoughts.

'Wait,' I said, as Badou let go of the doughnuts, and they both turned. 'No, no. Of course, you must come in and eat with me.' At that moment a boy appeared behind them with a carafe of orange juice and a glass on a silver tray. He looked at Aszulay for a moment too long.

'You may put the juice on the table, and fetch two more glasses, for my guests,' I told him.

He nodded, putting down the tray and leaving.

'Come in,' I said to Aszulay and Badou, 'come in, and sit.' I picked up the tagine and set it on the table beside the juice. Through the open window came the faint, insistent bray of a donkey. Aszulay and I sat on the two chairs, Badou on Aszulay's lap.

I took the lid from the tagine. Steam and the fragrant aroma rose into the air. 'Please, eat. I . . . I don't know if I can,' I said, and Aszulay and Badou put their fingers into the dish and ate.

I simply sat there, knowing that if I put food in my mouth it would not stay down. Once again, to me the silence, as Aszulay and Badou ate, was uncomfortable, but they didn't seem aware of it.

The boy returned and set down two more glasses. He again glanced at Aszulay, and Aszulay nodded at him. The boy lowered his head in a respectful manner.

When at last Badou had had his fill of couscous and lamb and apricots, he ate two of the small *beignets*. As he reached for a third, Aszulay took the boy's hand in his. 'That's enough, Badou,' he said. 'Your stomach will hurt. Remember the last time.'

Badou obediently nodded, but his eyes were still on the remaining *beignets*.

'I have only a few hours – simple work – at the gardens today. I will take Badou with me,' Aszulay said.

I nodded, distractedly.

'Perhaps you would like to join us.'

'No,' I answered immediately. I couldn't imagine going out into the noisy street, fighting my way through the cars and horses and donkeys and crowds of people. Did Aszulay not realise what I was going through?

'Monsieur Majorelle has brought in some new birds. I thought you might be interested in seeing them.' He was speaking to me as if I were Badou, cajoling me as he would a child, and this annoyed me. I remembered how he'd spoken to Manon like this, calming her.

'I said no, Aszulay. I don't . . . I . . .' Tears came to my eyes, and I turned my head so that he wouldn't see them.

'It's a difficult time. I understand,' he said, standing. 'I'm sorry you have come all this way only to be disappointed. Come, Badou.' He held out his hand to the child.

'His death is far more than a disappointment,' I said, quietly.

At this Aszulay turned his head sharply. 'His death?' he repeated.

I looked up at him, and something in his expression made me catch my breath. 'Yes,' I said, still staring at him.

'But . . . Mademoiselle O'Shea,' he said. 'Etienne . . . he's not dead. Why do you say this?'

I couldn't breathe, couldn't look at him. I fixed my gaze on the tagine, the orange juice, the glasses. They pulsed as if beating with life. 'But . . .' I covered my mouth with my hand, then took it away and looked back at Aszulay. 'Manon . . . she said . . .' I stopped. 'She said Etienne was dead. Buried, in the cemetery. She told me he was dead,' I repeated.

In the silence, Aszulay and I stared at each other.

'It's not true?' I finally whispered, and when Aszulay shook his head, a sound burst from me, a sound unlike anything I'd ever made. I had to cover my mouth again, this time with both hands, to stop it.

'She really told you this?' Aszulay said. His lips straightened, but he said nothing more.

'Tell me the truth, Aszulay. Just tell me what's happened to Etienne. If he's not dead, where is he?'

Aszulay didn't speak for a long moment. 'It's not my business,' he finally said. 'It's between you and Etienne, you and Manon. Between Manon and Etienne. It's not my business,' he repeated. 'But for Manon to . . .' He didn't finish the sentence.

I reached across the table and put my hand on his forearm. It was hard and warm under his blue sleeve. 'But

313

why? Why would Manon do this to me, lie like this? Why does she hate me enough to drive me away from Marrakesh in such a terrible way? I haven't done anything to her. Why does she not want me to be with Etienne? Why would she go to this length – to announce him dead? Why is she so full of hatred towards me?' I was repeating myself, speaking too quickly. It was too confusing, too unbelievable.

Aszulay looked at Badou then, and I looked as well. The little boy's face was watchful, his eyes intelligent. Full of life. But also too full of something else. He had seen and heard far too much, I knew. Not just today, but all his short life.

'She has deep unhappiness within her,' Aszulay said. 'The reasons are hers alone. I don't know why she told you this.'

'And what is the truth, then? Where is Etienne? You can see she won't tell me. I understand . . . we are in similar positions, aren't we?' *I am – was, am, I no longer know – Etienne's lover; you are Manon's lover.*

'Positions? I don't know what you mean. But Etienne was here, in Marrakesh. He stayed with Manon for perhaps two weeks. Then he left. Left Manon, and left Marrakesh.'

'Did he go back to America?' *Could I have passed him, missed him as he journeyed one way and I the other? Was he looking for me in Albany?* This was the stuff of Shakespearean drama, of Greek tragedy.

'No. He said he would remain in Morocco, now that . . .' He stopped, looking at Badou again

'Is that all? Can you tell me nothing more?'

'Perhaps we can speak of this another time.'

'When?'

314

'Another time,' he repeated. He took Badou's hand and left.

The rest of the day passed in a strange twilight. I alternately lay on the bed or sat at the table, looking out the window. I wanted to rush back to Manon's house, to confront her, to demand that she tell me the truth. And yet I was filled with an odd exhaustion, an inability to move more than a few steps. I was confused by my feelings. Only a few days ago, upon meeting Manon, I had been filled with hope at finding Etienne. Then Manon had told me he was dead, and I keened and despaired. And now . . . according to what Aszulay had told me – and of course I believed him over Manon – Etienne wasn't dead, but alive, somewhere in Morocco . . .

I was no closer to finding him, no closer to understanding why he had done what he'd done – abandon me, without telling me why. But something had shifted. Something very small. I had grieved for Etienne, convinced he was dead. Something in me had gone cold. Was missing. And finding out he was still alive hadn't brought it back.

I thought of all of this, trying to understand. I put shreds of cold lamb into my mouth, licking the grease from my fingers. I drank the rest of the orange juice. I bathed my knees, inspecting the abrasions and bruises.

And then it was dark, and again I took off my clothes and once more lay naked on the soft bed, the night air hot on my body.

In the morning, flies were crusted on the remains of the tagine. I drew a bath and pinned up my hair. I put on a clean dress and threw out the remains of the food, then went out into the street and hailed a taxi to take me to the gates of the medina.

It was time to confront Manon. Although I never wanted to see her again, I would not let it end like this.

I would not let her think she had driven me away. And I would stay until I made her tell me where I could find Etienne.

CHAPTER TWENTY-FOUR

WHEN I ARRIVED AT Manon's just after nine o'clock, Badou was in the courtyard, playing with a yellow pup with white paws and one ragged ear.

'*Bonjour*, Badou,' I said, after Falida let me in and went back to listlessly sweeping the courtyard with a short-handled broom made of dried brush. 'Where is your mother?' I asked him.

'She's sleeping,' he said, cradling the little dog against his chest. It gnawed, lightly, on his knuckle, and he smiled down at it, then up at me. 'Look at my dog.'

I sat down on the wide edge of the fountain. 'Is he yours, really?' I asked, and Badou shook his head.

'*Non*,' he admitted, sadly. 'He belongs to Ali, across the lane. Sometimes Ali lets me play with him. But I would like him to be mine. I want a dog.'

I thought of Cinnabar, and the comfort she had brought me, even though I had been ten years older than Badou when she came into my life. 'I know,' I said. 'Maybe one day your *maman* will get you a dog.'

But Badou shook his head again. He put down the dog and came to stand in front of me. 'Maman said no. She said a dog is trouble. She said I can never have one, and not to ask any more.' He spoke without the expected childlike disappointment, but again, with a mature stoicism that touched me.

'But it's good that you can play with this little dog,' I said.

The dog danced around him, jumping up to pull on Badou's sleeve. 'Sidonie, I do not like your *dar*,' he said, ignoring the dog.

'You don't like my house?' I said. Basic Arabic words were becoming familiar to me now.

'Yes. I do not like it,' he repeated. 'It's too big, with too many people. And they do not love you,' he added, gravely.

'Love me? Who, Badou?' I asked, confused by his statements, his morose expression.

'Your family. All the people in your big house,' he insisted, and then I understood. 'They do not love you,' he said, again.

'Oh, Badou, that's not my house. It's a hotel,' I said, realising, as I spoke, that he didn't understand the word. 'A . . . yes, a big house. But not my house. I'm only staying there for a short while. And the people aren't my family.'

'Who are they?'

I shrugged. 'I don't know them. Strangers.'

'You live with strangers?' His eyes grew even wider. 'But Sidonie, how can you live without your family? Aren't you lonely?'

I looked at him. When I didn't respond – because I wasn't sure what to say – he went on.

'But . . . where are they? Where is your mother, and your father? Where are your children?' Badou already understood the Moroccan importance of family. In spite of the coldness of his mother, he spoke of love.

Perhaps he read something, some small and subtle thing, in my expression. He then added, so casually and yet with such weight, in the way of a child who knows too much of the world, too early, 'Dead?'

There was only one way to respond to a child like Badou. I nodded, slowly. 'Yes. They are all dead.'

Badou came to me then, climbing on to my lap as I had seen him do with his mother and with Aszulay. On his knees, he laid his cheek against mine. I felt the heat of his skin, smelled the dust in his thick hair. I absently thought that he needed a bath.

I couldn't speak, but simply put my arms around his small back. I moved my fingers to feel his ribs, and then the faint bumps of his vertebrae. At my touch he relaxed into my lap, so easily. The yellow pup settled at my feet, lying on its side on the smooth, warm stones. Its pink tongue protruded slightly, and its one visible eye twitched to repel the flies. Falida continued her languid sweeping, the sound of the soft broom a rhythmic lull. We sat in the dappled light of the courtyard, Badou's head under my chin, and waited for Manon to awaken.

Eventually Manon called for Falida, her voice hoarse and querulous through an open upstairs window. Falida went up the stairs, but returned in a moment, going into the house. Badou stayed on my lap.

In another few moments footsteps came down the courtyard steps; I braced myself, ready to face Manon.

But it wasn't Manon. A man, his dark blond hair roughly smoothed across his forehead and his face shadowed by the night's whiskers, looked as surprised to see me as I was to see him. He was quite handsome, and wore a well-cut, although rumpled suit of cream linen, and carried his wide-brimmed hat.

'Oh. Madame,' he said, stopping halfway down the stairs. 'Good day.'

'Good day,' I responded.

'Manon is waiting for her morning tea. I don't think she's aware she has a visitor,' he said. 'Shall I tell—'

'No,' I interrupted. Too many things were swirling through my head. This man had obviously spent the night here. Was he her husband, then? No. He couldn't be, could he? I glanced at Badou; as the man had come down the stairs, Badou had jumped off my lap and was now pointedly petting the dog, his back to the man. And what of Aszulay? 'I'll wait here for her,' I said.

'As you wish,' he said, bowing slightly at the waist, and then left the courtyard. He had completely ignored Badou.

As the gate closed behind him, I wondered where Badou and Falida slept at night, wondered what they were subjected to.

Badou ran upstairs. I heard his high, clear little voice telling his mother I was in the courtyard.

'What does she want?' Manon responded, her voice cranky.

'I don't know, Maman,' he said. 'Maman, her papa and mama, her children, they're all dead.'

There was rustling. 'She doesn't deserve a family,' Manon said, shocking me, not only because of her open resentment towards me, but because it was a terrible thing to say to a child.

I thought of the sweet curve of Badou's head as he leaned against me. 'Manon!' I called, rising from the edge of the fountain before she could say anything more to him. 'I must speak to you.'

'You will wait until I'm ready,' she said, in the same irritable voice she had used with both Falida and Badou. Again, I had no choice but to sit down again, and wait until she appeared at the top of the stairs.

Finally she descended slowly, as if she had all the time in the world. She wore only a loose, almost diaphanous kaftan; I could clearly see the slender and yet curvaceous outline of her body through it as the light touched her. Her breasts were still high and firm. Her hair was uncombed, and her kohl smeared around her eyes. Her lips were puffy, as though slightly bruised.

As I watched her come down the stairs in such an imperious manner, with such studied nonchalance, I wanted to rush at her, to push her, hard, so that she fell down the steps, to pull her hair, to slap her. I wanted to shout at her that she was a liar, and a deceitful person not worthy of her beautiful little son, her gracious home. Not worthy of her lover – her other lover – Aszulay, who had such a presence, who treated her and Badou with such consideration and loyalty. Did he know she deceived him as well as me, although in a different way?

But I didn't do or say anything. I stayed on the edge of the fountain, my hands gripping each other, my mouth a tight line.

She seated herself on the daybed, and once more called, sharply, to Falida, and the girl hurried out, carrying a tray with a teapot and one glass, rounds of bread and a bowl of something that looked like dark jam. She set it on the low table. Badou, moving almost stealthily, had come down the steps and now sat beside his mother.

'Did you see my man, Sidonie? The charming Olivier? Quite something, isn't he?'

I didn't respond, staring at her. What did she want of me? To agree with her on the qualities of yet another lover?

'You look poorly, Sidonie,' Manon said now, as if it pleased her. 'Pale, and shaken. Not well at all.' There was the hint of a smile on her lips. She first took a sip of tea, then spread a spoonful of the fruity substance on the bread and bit into it.

I had absolutely no expectation that she would offer me anything. But she didn't offer anything to her son, either. He watched as his mother ate and drank.

'How do you expect me to appear, after what you told me?' I didn't attempt to keep the anger from my voice. 'Manon. Did you think I wouldn't find out about your lie? That I would simply believe you, and quietly pack my bags and leave Marrakesh, like a beaten dog?' Of course that was what I would have done, had Aszulay not told me the truth. 'What kind of cruel game were you playing with me? And why?'

Manon's mouth worked at the bread and jam. She swallowed. 'I have had many things to survive in my life. Many things,' she repeated. 'My level of unhappiness far surpasses anything you might ever feel.' She lifted her chin as if daring me to argue, then glanced at Badou. 'Go away,' she told him.

I shook my head impatiently, still gripping my hands so I wouldn't rush at her and strike her across the face. I had never hit anyone in my life. But I wanted to, so badly, at that moment. Badou crossed the courtyard and went out the gate, making kissing sounds to call the pup.

'Whatever you've had to deal with, Manon, has nothing to do with this. There is no reason imaginable for you to lie in such a terrible way. Why couldn't you have simply told me he wasn't here, when I first came to you asking about him? What twisted pleasure did you get from seeing me so . . .' I stopped. I didn't want to think of her expression as she watched me cry out, fall, when she told me Etienne was dead.

Manon lazily lifted one shoulder. 'Etienne would not have married you, you know,' she said. 'He would never have married you,' she repeated. 'So I thought it easier that you believed him dead. Then you would have no reason to hope any further. You would go home and put your silly dreams out of your head.'

She didn't fool me. She would never have thought of making it easier for me, of doing what she did out of perverted kindness.

'How do you know he wouldn't marry me? How do you know what your brother felt for me, or what he would have done?' I knew he hadn't discussed me with her, or she would have known who I was when I first came to her door.

I thought, for one moment, that I would tell her about the child, then dismissed the idea.

'Etienne is too selfish to marry anyone,' she said.

'You don't know that. You didn't see him with me.'

'I didn't have to. I know him all too well, Sidonie.'

'You only know him as a brother. You can't see some

things when you're tied by blood to a person. Brother and sister is not the same as the relationship between man and woman,' I countered, and as I spoke something shifted in Manon's face, something very small and slippery.

'Plus he would not marry because he would not wish to father a child,' she said, and I saw it again, that distinctly goading look.

I swallowed, glad I hadn't mentioned my pregnancy. 'Why do you say that?'

Now she sat back and smiled. There was a tiny blob of the red jam in the corner of her mouth; she licked it off. Her tongue was very pink, and pointed. '*Majoun*,' she said, leaning forward again and taking another spoonful from the bowl. 'Do you like *majoun*, Sidonie?' she asked, the spoon in mid-air.

'I don't know what it is, and I don't care,' I said.

'Sometimes the smoke from *kif* hurts my throat. This is better, the cannabis cooked with fruit and sugar and spices,' she said, eating the spoonful without even bothering to put it on bread. 'I give it to Badou, to make him sleep. When I need him to sleep,' she added, and I thought of her entertaining the man the night before.

I was so sickened by her that I stood. 'I came here today hoping, in some small way, that you would give me the truth about how to find Etienne. And that perhaps I would also uncover the reason for your behaviour towards me,' I said. 'I should have known there's no explanation. You're simply a malicious and spiteful woman.'

'You think I care about your opinion?' She made a sound like a laugh. 'You don't know what life has given me, you with your easy existence, your house and garden, painting as a hobby to pass the time, playing with your old cat. All your life you've done only what you wanted.' The *majoun* was gone. Manon lifted the bowl and, looking at me over its rim, delicately licked out the last traces of the hashish jam with that small, pointed tongue.

I stared at her. She didn't know I had a garden, or a cat. I hadn't told her those things. I had briefly spoken to Aszulay about my garden, but Cinnabar . . . I had never mentioned her.

'When you know what life is really about – when you have actually lived outside of your small, safe circle – then you may question my behaviour.' She rose, facing me. 'I lied to you because I can. Because it gave me pleasure to see you cry out, to see you so weak. You and Etienne made a good pair. He's weak, like you. He didn't even tell you, did he, about his illness.' It was a statement, not a question.

'His illness?' *But it had been his father who had been so ill.*

She laughed, a loud, merry laugh. 'Etienne was too weak to tell you the truth, and also too shamed to let you see him as he really is. Only I know the depth of his faults. I am the only one who has seen him at his lowest.'

'What illness?' I repeated.

Manon sat again, pouring herself another glass of tea and then leaning back and languidly crossing one leg over the other. She drank her tea in one long, fluid swallow, and then called out in Arabic. Falida appeared with the *sheesha* and set it on the floor in front of Manon. She fussed with it, opening it, pulling out a flint and lighting a plug of tobacco, then fitting the *sheesha* together and handing the mouthpiece to Manon.

'You didn't see the evidence?' she asked, the mouthpiece just touching her lips.

I blinked, trying to find answers in her face.

'He had only the earliest signs, but can you really tell yourself you didn't see it? The moment I saw him, when he arrived here, I knew. He was possessed in the same manner as our father. Are you really so thick-headed? So blind?'

I envisioned Etienne at the hospital, and then at my home. When we were out for dinner, when he drove his car, in my bed. Small, unimportant images flashed through my mind: the way he sometimes dropped his fork or knife with an unexpected clatter on to the table, his occasional tripping over the edges of carpets. A sudden lurch and stumble as he walked across the bedroom to me one night, when I assumed he was simply exhausted from a long day at the hospital, or that the continual glasses of bourbon he took after dinner might have affected him more strongly that particular evening.

I thought of the empty pill bottle I'd found in his room, the medication that could be taken for palsy.

'Etienne inherited everything from our father,' she said. 'I was left nothing. But now I'm glad, for along with his wealth, Marcel Duverger left his son something else.'

I felt behind me for the stool, and lowered myself to it.

'Our father also left Etienne the *djinns* he carried in his body,' she said. 'The disease that killed him will now kill Etienne. But not for a long time. First he will suffer, as our father suffered.' She smiled, a calm, slow smile, tilting her head the slightest, as though hearing music from afar, music she recognised and loved. 'Am I sorry for my father's suffering? No. My father paid for his behaviour towards me.' Her smile suddenly turned to a grimace, and her voice was bitter. 'This house,' she waved one arm in front of her, 'was bought for me by Etienne, before he left for America. But it wasn't enough. There will never be enough to even the score. I was glad when my father died, and now I'm glad Etienne will suffer in the same way. He's welcome to the inheritance, and now he will live with it until it kills him, crying and soiling himself like a baby.'

What was it? What did she mean, the *djinns* in their bodies?

'The *djinns* travel from parent to child,' she added, then repeated, 'Parent to child. Father to son.'

The disease was genetic. She was talking about genetics. I remembered Etienne's interest in genetics.

Badou came back into the courtyard with the dog. He again sat beside his mother, holding the dog around the middle. The little creature's short legs stuck straight out. Badou reached, tentatively, towards the round of bread still sitting on the plate, glancing at Manon. When she didn't react, he took the bread and broke off a small piece and fed it to the dog. Then he stuffed the rest into his own mouth.

'But . . . if Etienne is in Morocco,' I said to Manon, 'surely he'll come back to Marrakesh. To see you, and Badou,' I stated, my eyes darting from her to the child. These two people were his only family. 'When will he come again, Manon? If what you say is true . . . I need to see him even more now.'

She shrugged again, drawing in a deep breath from the mouthpiece, and then parted her lips, very slightly, letting a thin waft of smoke drift upwards into the still, warm air.

CHAPTER TWENTY-FIVE

I WALKED FOR A NUMBER of hours. If this time Manon told the truth – that Etienne had a disease that would eventually take his life in a gruesome way – perhaps I had found the answer I wanted.

Etienne had left me because he didn't want me to have to marry a man who would walk through what remained of his life with a noose around his neck, a noose that would grow tighter and tighter with each month, each year.

He had left me because he loved me too much to do that to me. But he didn't realise the depth of my feelings. I couldn't envision him any other way than as I had last seen him, strong and loving. Whatever form the disease took – whatever *djinns* Manon spoke of – I could cope: I could care for Etienne when he eventually grew weak, as I'd cared for my mother.

I went back to Sharia Zitoun and pounded on the gate; it was mid-afternoon.

There was no sound from within. I knocked again, trying the handle, but the gate was locked. I hit the flat of my hand against the gold paint. 'Manon!' I called. 'Badou. Badou, are you there?'

There was a tiny sound; bare feet against tile. 'Badou?' I said again, my mouth against the minuscule line of light where the gate met the jamb. 'It's me, Sidonie. Mademoiselle O'Shea. Can you open the gate, please?'

After a complicated scraping of the inside lock the gate swung inward. Badou looked up at me. 'Maman said nobody can enter,' he said.

'But it's me, Badou. Can I come in for only a moment?'

He studied my face, and then nodded solemnly, stepping back. In the courtyard was a tub of water, sticks floating on the surface.

Badou went to the tub and pushed one of the sticks around as though it was a boat.

'Maman is sleeping?' I asked him.

He shook his head. 'She went to the *hammam* to bathe,' he said, not looking at me.

'And Falida? Where is Falida?'

'In the souks, buying food.'

I looked at the house. 'You're here alone?' I asked.

'Yes. I am a big boy,' he said, busily taking the sticks from the water and setting them in lines on the courtyard floor, kneeling and arranging them in different patterns. 'Maman says I am a big boy, and can look after myself.'

I was quiet for a moment, and then said, 'Yes, yes, you are a big boy, Badou.'

I studied his features as he concentrated on his sticks. I saw Etienne again: this look, right now, of intensity. The intelligent forehead under the thick hair. The long, slender neck.

I thought, again, of what our child might have looked like.

'Are you sad, Sidonie?' Badou asked, and I realised he had stopped arranging his sticks and was looking up at me. He hadn't called me mademoiselle, as usual.

My initial response was to say *oh no, of course I'm not sad*, and try to smile. But as before, I couldn't bring myself to be dishonest with this serious child. 'Yes. Today I'm a little sad.'

He nodded. 'Sometimes I'm sad too, Sidonie. But then I think for a while, and become happy again.' He was so earnest.

'And what is it that you think of, Badou, when you are feeling sad? What do you think about to make yourself happy again?'

'Once, a long time ago, my mother made a lemon cake,' he said, his lips turning up in the beginning of a smile. 'Oh, it was so sweet, and so yellow. When I think of that cake, I'm happy. Inside my head I make a picture. I put the cake in the blue sky, beside the sun. The sun and the lemon cake. Like two suns, or two cakes. Two are always better than one.' He stood. 'Maman used to paint me pictures. I asked her to paint this picture for me, of the two cakes, but she didn't. I wanted to put it on the wall beside my bed. Then I would always be happy, because I could look at it whenever I liked.'

Unexpectedly, tears came to my eyes. Was it normal for a six year old to speak like this? I didn't know.

'Sidonie? Now you must think about what makes you happy, to make the sad things go away.'

I kneeled, wincing at the pressure on my sore knees, and put my arms around him. I pressed his head against my shoulder.

'What are you thinking about?' he asked, his voice muffled against me. He pulled his head back and looked at me again. 'Is it happy?'

I couldn't answer. His soft cheek, his thick hair. I looked into his huge eyes. He was so still, as always, watching me. And oh, so clever.

'You can think of the lemon cakes, Sidonie,' he finally said, easing out of my arms and again picking up the little sticks, smiling at me.

Half an hour later Manon returned, carrying two buckets filled with various implements. When she saw me she glared at Badou, and he stared back at her with a stricken look.

'Don't be angry at him,' I told her. 'I made him let me in.'

Manon set down her pails.

I licked my lips. 'What about you, Manon? Do you have the disease as well?'

'No,' she said, and I wanted it to be true, looking at Badou. I couldn't bear to think of something dangerous and harmful within his small, perfect body. 'But how touching,' Manon went on, her voice laced with sarcasm, 'that you care about my health.'

I didn't answer for a moment. 'I just want to know either where Etienne is, or when he'll come back to Marrakesh. It's even more important, now, that I tell him that . . .' I stopped, suddenly knowing it would be unwise to divulge anything more to this woman.

'As well as not discussing his weaknesses, Etienne obviously didn't share his dreams with you, either. As he did with me,' Manon said, not answering my question. 'He had a dream of fame and glory for his work. He wanted to discover a way to prevent the passing of the *djinns*.' She was still staring at me. 'And he did,' she added, then fell silent.

'And so?' I finally prompted. 'What did he uncover?'

'That there would be no glory. That there is only one way to prevent the disease. Only one. He was very despondent, Sidonie, when he came here.'

'Of course,' I stated. 'He realised his future.'

'Yes. But also something else. He told me he had failed.'

'Failed?'

'He told me about you. I know everything, Sidonie.'

I blinked, remembering how she'd mentioned my life in Albany, facts she couldn't have known. So Etienne *had* spoken of me, had told her about me, and she had known who I was from the first time I came to her door. But why had she toyed with me? Why had she pretended she knew nothing about me? She had put on such an air of innocence when I introduced myself. Manon Maliki was an actress extraordinaire. Every time I saw her, this became more clear.

'He told me about the child.'

I instinctively put my hands to my abdomen, and her eyes followed.

'Obviously you lied, to try to force him to marry you. Such an old and tiresome trick, Sidonie. But then I would expect something like this from a woman like you.' Again she smiled, that slow smile I hated. 'I saw with the first glance there was no child. Foolish woman. How did you think you would explain this to him if you caught

332

up to him? Another lie, this one about losing it?'

I couldn't let her see how her words were affecting me. I looked into her eyes, keeping my face still.

'You wanted Etienne to marry you, and so you lied to trap him. But the trap caught you. Because of your lie, you lost him. He came here because I wanted him to. Unlike you, I could get Etienne to do my bidding. But you had driven him away anyway. The only sure way for the *djinns* to die, he told me when he came,' she stopped again, delicately stroking one eyebrow with her middle finger before continuing, 'was for those possessing them to never procreate. Within a generation it would have disappeared. *Just one generation, Manon*, he told me. That's all it would take.'

Light fell in soft shafts through the leaves, shimmering across Manon's face, making it look as though waves passed over it. Her pupils were huge, perhaps an effect of *kif* or *majoun*.

Suddenly the gate banged open, and Falida came through, carrying a woven bag in each hand, the handle of a third bag looped around her neck so it hung on her back. Its weight caused her to walk bent almost in two.

Manon went to her and grabbed one of the bags. She looked inside, scrabbling through it, questioning Falida in Arabic. Falida's voice was weak, fearful, and then Manon struck her on the side of the head. Falida fell. I heard the heavy thump of her elbow and hip hitting the tiles. Oranges spilled from the bag on her back, olives from another. Badou ran to pick up the oranges, cupping them in the bottom of his djellaba.

Falida didn't cry. She took the bag from around her neck

and then gathered the olives, wrapping them back in their paper. An orange rolled towards my foot. I picked it up.

Manon returned to me as if the small, miserable scene hadn't occurred. 'So, Sidonie, in essence . . .' I looked away from the children, and back at her, 'it is you who pushed Etienne away when he thought you would produce a child who might carry the *djinns*. Because he realised he was a hypocrite.'

I pressed the dimpled skin of the orange over and over, thinking about Etienne's face when he learned I was pregnant. About his expression, which I had presumed to be simply shock, but now, with Manon's confident words, thought, suddenly, could have been panic.

I thought of the child we had created, half me and half him. I tried to swallow, but my mouth and throat now felt cloaked in wool. Etienne knew there was a chance that he had passed on the gene, as his father had to him. He had seen the child we had created as possibly one of nature's aberrations, a mistake.

'You were just a diversion, a plaything for a short time,' Manon said now. 'He had no intentions of anything serious. He told me this himself.'

I had to compose myself for a moment. I looked again at Badou, still helping Falida gather the spilled food. He glanced back at me and then came and took the orange from my hand.

'Etienne made a choice to be with me,' I said, 'and the . . . result was unforeseen by both of us. There *was* a baby, Manon. And I lost it – before arriving in Tangier.' I didn't care if she believed me or not. 'If he had felt so strongly about this, about not procreating, he wouldn't have been with me. Nobody forced him.' I hated the way my voice faltered on the last sentence.

She waved one hand dismissively in the air. 'He was a man, Sidonie. He grew lonely for a woman, and acted on impulse. He had planned to have the procedure he said was the answer – the sterilisation – when he finished his year at the hospital in America. But he grew impatient. And he knew you were a safe bet, naïve and inexperienced. You wouldn't cause trouble.'

But Etienne was not the kind of man she described. He had loved me, and wanted me. 'I don't believe you. You can't say this kind of thing to me.'

Manon watched me, her face now blank. 'I can say whatever I wish, Sidonie. I can say whatever I wish,' she repeated.

We stood, facing each other. The children took the bags and disappeared into the house. There seemed nothing more to say.

I returned to Hôtel de la Palmeraie. I stood at my window, looking at the High Atlas mountains against the blue sky. I heard the noon call from the minarets in the medina, and smelled the fragrance of the jacaranda, the lilacs.

I tried to remember the smell of Etienne's skin, his rare, slow smile. I tried to bring back memories, memories of us talking, eating, falling asleep, waking up together. But I could only think of the look on his face as I'd told him about the baby, and how he'd suddenly become a stranger.

I knew I couldn't count on Manon for any truths. Etienne was protecting me. I needed to tell him I was strong enough; I could live with his disease. I would marry him, and stay at his side. He could put his fears to rest.

There was no reason to return to Sharia Zitoun. I was done with Manon. She would only continue to lie and confuse me. She wouldn't tell me anything about Etienne's return. There was only one other person in Marrakesh who could help me now.

I took a *calèche* to Le Jardin Majorelle. I hoped I would find Aszulay working there. If not, I could ask Monsieur Majorelle when he would come next. I saw three men in white clothing, digging in one of the flowerbeds close to the entrance.

'*Pardonnez-moi*,' I called, hearing desperation in my own voice. All three men straightened. The middle one was Aszulay.

'Aszulay,' I said with relief, as though I had been searching for him for years. 'Aszulay,' I repeated, going closer. I knew my voice was too loud, but I seemed unable to speak quietly. 'Please. May I talk to you? It's about Etienne. I . . . I need . . .' I stopped, closing my mouth. What did I need?

The other two men watched as Aszulay stepped over the piles of red earth and came towards me. 'Please, Mademoiselle O'Shea,' he said, 'go and sit there, in the shade. I'll finish here soon. Wait for me,' he repeated.

After some time, he left his shovel standing in a pile of earth, and came to me.

I stood. 'I need to ask you—'

But he interrupted by raising one hand. 'Please. We won't talk here.'

I realised I had acted inappropriately, coming to his place of work.

'I can leave, but I must return before too long. Come. We'll go to my house.'

I nodded numbly, following him through the garden and into the street. I didn't question going to his home.

'You can't walk far in the heat,' he said to me, looking at my face.

Again I simply nodded. He hailed a *calèche* and we climbed in. I stared at my shoes as we rocked and swayed, only looking up when I felt the *calèche* stop. Aszulay climbed down and took my hand to help me step out.

We walked into the medina, but didn't pass through D'jemma el Fna; obviously there were other entrances to the old city. I didn't know where we went, or how far through the narrow alleys. Finally Aszulay pulled a large key from within his robe and opened a blue gate. His hands were covered in red mud. I looked at his face; there were streaks of mud along his neck and jaw. His white clothing – the robe and loose cotton pants and turban Monsieur Majorelle must have insisted all his gardeners wore in the garden – was also covered in a fine dusting of the red earth.

'I'm sorry for taking you from your work,' I said. 'But Aszulay . . . Aszulay, I need to talk to somebody about Etienne. I need you to tell me what you know. Manon says . . .' I stopped. I didn't want to talk about my baby. Did he already know?

A man passed the gate, staring openly at me. Aszulay motioned with his head. 'Come inside.'

Again I followed him; I noticed only that we walked through a courtyard. When he stopped, I stopped. He stepped out of his *babouches* and gestured at an open doorway. I hesitated, now knowing it was ill-mannered to leave one's shoes on when inside someone's home. And yet . . . I glanced down at my shoes, thinking of the time it would take to undo them, of hobbling across the room without my built-up sole.

'Please,' he said, and by the way he put out his hand, indicating I was to enter, I knew he didn't expect me to remove my shoes. Once inside, he gestured at a daybed, and I sat on its edge. He disappeared, and I closed my eyes and put my face into my hands.

After a few moments I heard the whisper of fabric, and looked up to see an elderly woman carrying a tray with a teapot and two glasses. She set down the tray and poured one glass, handing it to me.

I took it, saying *shukran*, then set it on the table. The woman poured another glass and put it on the table beside mine, and left.

I stared at the two glasses of tea for an unidentifiable length of time. And then Aszulay appeared; he still wore his work clothes, but he had washed his hands and face and taken off his turban. One bead of water clung to his left earlobe like a diamond; his hair was damp and curling along his collar.

'What is it you need to know about Etienne?' he asked, picking up his tea.

'When you came to the hotel, when I thought . . . when Manon lied to me . . . you said we would talk about him again. I must have some answers now.'

Aszulay looked into my face, his long fingers wrapped around the glass.

'I was his . . . we were to be married.' It was suddenly difficult to say this with Aszulay's intense blue eyes looking into mine. 'He left America so unexpectedly.' I didn't say *he left me*, and yet I imagined Aszulay would hear the unspoken words, and I fought not to lower my gaze. 'His abrupt departure . . . we didn't have a chance to speak of . . . of important things. I came here to find him, to try and understand . . .' My voice kept faltering. Why, in front of this man, was I feeling humiliated? It was nothing he did; he simply watched me, letting me take my time to tell the part of the story I needed him to know. I took a deep breath to calm myself. 'I have just spoken to Manon again,' I went on. I watched for his face to change as I said his lover's name. But still he didn't react. 'I know more. I know about his illness. Now I believe I know why he left. But I must find him, and tell him . . . it's imperative that I see him again. It's imperative for his future. For our future. I need to know where he is.' Still Aszulay studied me. I couldn't read his expression, but it was slightly distant, as if he was debating with himself.

'I know you can tell me more than Manon will. It's clear she's keeping things from me.'

Aszulay hadn't taken a drink, but he still held his glass, small in his large hand. 'Manon's secrets are hers,' he said. 'I have little more to tell you, apart from Etienne's behaviour when he was here. The behaviour I witnessed.'

I nodded, leaning forward. 'Yes, yes, all right. Tell me about that, then.'

Aszulay looked over my head, as if he didn't want to look at me as he spoke. 'He mentioned that he couldn't sleep, that he hadn't slept in many nights. He suffered from

339

anxiety; I saw him take tablets from a bottle.'

'He always took them,' I said, encouraging Aszulay.

'The last evening I saw him,' Aszulay said, 'he drank a bottle of absinthe, all of it, one glass after another. He smoked *kif*, more *kif* than is good. He took even more tablets. Yet he couldn't find peace. He walked and sat, walked and sat. His hands trembled.'

'But I understand. The thought of the disease . . . not knowing how long it would be before . . .' I stopped. I didn't want to tell Aszulay that I knew Etienne's distress was also over leaving me. 'So he simply left? He must have said something about where he was going. Or when he'd return.'

We sat in silence. Finally Aszulay said, 'He mentioned both Casablanca and Rabat.'

I thought of those teeming cities, and remembered the drive, with Mustapha and Aziz, through Sale. I thought of the difficulty I'd had in finding Manon here, in a smaller city, with a French Quarter where I was in a large community of Europeans, where I could speak a familiar language and have secure lodging. I tried to imagine how I would make my way around Casablanca or Rabat, looking for a man nobody knew, who might not even be there.

I put my hand over my eyes at the sheer impossibility of it, and Aszulay said, as if reading my mind, 'They are not good cities for a woman to be alone, Mademoiselle O'Shea. Foreign or native, women do not go about alone.' He stopped, and I took my hand away. 'He will return to Marrakesh.'

'Yes?' I said, too eagerly. 'What would be better? To wait?

But when?' I sat straighter. 'When, Aszulay? When will he come back?'

'Perhaps he will return next month. Because of Badou. To see Badou.'

'Next month,' I repeated.

'He asked that I care for him – for Badou – in any way I could, while he wasn't here. But then . . . I have always cared for Badou.'

'Because Manon can't be trusted to look after him properly,' I stated, waiting for him to defend her. As his lover, he would defend her, wouldn't he?

The late afternoon call for prayer came, but Aszulay didn't kneel and press his forehead to the floor. He simply rose, saying, 'Now I must go back to the garden, to my work. I have been gone too long.'

'Of course. I'm sorry. Thank you, Aszulay, for . . . for speaking to me about Etienne. Now that I know with certainty he'll return to Marrakesh, I'll wait.'

At this he shook his head, very slightly. 'I'll accompany you out of the medina,' he said, and stepped into his *babouches*.

As we walked through the courtyard and into the street, I was aware of how self-absorbed I had been, how forward, going to Aszulay's job and taking him from it. And he had acted with the utmost consideration, bringing me to his home.

We emerged from the medina into the French Quarter, and Aszulay touched my shoulder, very lightly. 'I think it's better if you go home, mademoiselle,' he said.

'Yes. I'll take a taxi back to the—'

'No. I mean home, to America.'

I frowned. 'As I've told you, I'll wait here until Etienne returns. It's even more important now. I . . . I want to help him.'

Aszulay closed his eyes for just slightly longer than a blink. 'Mademoiselle O'Shea. I see you are a woman of determination. But . . .'

'But what?'

He looked down at me, as if wanting to say more, but then raised his arm, and a taxi stopped in front of us.

Aszulay turned and disappeared into the crowds.

On the ride back to the hotel, I thought about the look on his face as he told me I should go back to America.

I couldn't read what I saw there.

CHAPTER TWENTY-SIX

I TOOK THE SMALLER OF my cases from the top of the wardrobe shelf and, from behind the lining, removed my passport and open return ship tickets and envelope of what money remained. I counted the dwindling bills, and knew they couldn't last long in the style I was living.

I sat at the table with the money and passport and tickets, thinking about Aszulay's eyes, so intent, as he looked into mine, as if trying to convince me of something with that blue gaze.

As the night softly unfolded, the sweet fragrance of the rose bushes and the orange trees wafted through the open window. It was April, and summer in Marrakesh. In Albany the trees would only be in bud, the soil still too cold for planting the garden. There would be rain, and grey skies, but also warming spring breezes.

I thought of Aszulay's advice. Of going home.

I envisioned unlocking the front door of my house, and the musty smell that would greet me, the smell of rooms closed for too long. I thought of walking next door to the Barlows' and picking up Cinnabar. I knew the clean smell of her fur, the softness of her paws.

I saw myself back in my house, putting on the kettle

while Cinnabar wove between my legs, purring. I thought of going into my studio and looking at my paintings, still tacked up on the walls. I remembered Manon's paintings, and the wild freedom they possessed.

Then I saw myself alone in my bed that first night home, looking up at the shape of the old woman on my ceiling. I saw myself the next morning, walking to the sewing factory and applying for a job, and then buying a few items to cook for my simple dinner. After I'd eaten, I would put on a heavy sweater and sit on the porch and try to read, looking up as the occasional car passed on the road, churning the dust behind it, or, if there had been rain, making ruts through the mud. Perhaps I would go inside and take up my paintbrush and stand before my easel.

What would I paint?

I thought of the summer unfolding, of getting up early for my job, and coming home weary from repetitive, tedious work that demanded nothing of me. I'd tend to my garden. Maybe, once or twice through that summer, I'd ask Mr Barlow if he would drive me out to Pine Bush, so I could walk through the marsh and look for the Blue Karner and watch the wildlife.

And then there would be the first signs of fall, the geese flying overhead, the tomato plants in the garden curling and blackening with frost. I heard the strong, cold nor'easters wailing around the windows, heralding the long and bitter winter, followed by another spring of rain so powerful it bent the trees. And then another humid summer. Of course they were simply the seasons, the turning of the year, no better or worse than so many places. But it wasn't only the thought of the seasons that made my chest tighten as I sat at the table in my hotel room in Marrakesh.

It was beginning that life over again, the one I had known before Etienne came into it, before I had travelled across the ocean and arrived in this confusing, intriguing and often frightening country. Before my eyes had seen colours and heard sounds I had never even imagined. Before I breathed in the scent of unknown foliage and winds, before new tastes exploded on my tongue.

Before I had known the wrenching grief of losing a child, and, for the first time in my life, also holding a child, of smelling his hair and feeling his body rest against mine.

I knew exactly what shape my life would have when I returned to Albany, not only for the next months and the next year, but for the rest of my life. I was thirty years old. Could I continue that life for another thirty years, or more?

I picked up my passport; it was hard, unyielding, against my palm. There would be no sacrifice in returning home. But also no reward.

I didn't want that life, alone. I thought again of the odd look on Aszulay's face when I told him I wanted to stay and find Etienne, and help him through his illness.

How could he understand?

I went to the window and looked at the palm garden, with the outline of its rows of trees. The stars pulsed overhead, vivid, and the darkness beyond the lights of the hotel was filled with noise: the shouts of Arabic and other unknown tongues, the drumming from the square, the noises of domestic animals. But nearer was the sudden whoosh of the wings of a night bird, the quick, rubbery flap of a bat, the tiny humming and buzzing of insects.

Would I listen to Aszulay, and go home? Or would I listen to my heart, and stay here, waiting for Etienne? It would only be a month. A month, if Etienne returned when Aszulay expected.

As I had so often, I tried to bring back the warmth of Etienne's smile, the depth in his dark eyes. But it was difficult; he was fading, as if the brilliant sunlight of Marrakesh was washing through him, making his image thin and somehow less significant.

It frightened me. I didn't want to think that Manon's words, about how weak Etienne was, and how he'd simply used me, were influencing me.

I didn't want to think of Aszulay, concern in his blue eyes, when he told me to go home.

Neither of them – Manon and Aszulay – although, surely, for different reasons, wanted me to wait for Etienne. But I had to, didn't I? I would prove them both wrong. I would prove to them that Etienne loved and needed me in the same way I loved and needed him.

I would stay. I would find a way.

'*Inshallah*,' I whispered, into the soft night air.

The next morning I told Monsieur Henri I would no longer be staying at Hôtel de la Palmeraie. He had the good grace not to look relieved, although since I'd allowed Aszulay and Badou into my room, he'd treated me with even more coolness. 'You're leaving Marrakesh, Mademoiselle O'Shea?'

'No,' I said. 'But I'll return in a few hours, and settle my bill.'

'As you wish, mademoiselle,' he said.

I hadn't slept, tossing in my soft bed until just before sunrise. And then, as the first pale rays of light came through the window, I looked around the opulent room, envisioning a few more weeks of afternoons sitting politely under the palms in the courtyard with the other foreigners, who drank too many cocktails and spoke of nothing of real importance. Apart from Mr and Mrs Russell, who had now left Marrakesh, nobody had made an offer of friendship.

I thought of the way Aszulay and Badou had been treated when they came here to bring me comfort, and the whispered gossip that had followed me when I came downstairs after their visit.

Not only could I not afford to stay at such a sumptuous place, I also didn't fit at Hôtel de la Palmeraie.

If I was to bide my time in Marrakesh, it could not be in this hotel.

I went into the street and booked a room at a small, inexpensive hotel far off the main street of La Ville Nouvelle. The place was shabby and less than clean. I would have to share a bathroom with other guests, but there was also a small communal kitchen, so I could cook for myself and wouldn't have to pay for all of my meals. There was no garden. But it would do while I waited for Etienne to return.

Two days after I had settled into the small hotel, I went back to Le Jardin Majorelle. I was embarrassed to seek out Aszulay again, and yet I had to tell him that I was no longer at Hôtel de la Palmeraie. Then, when Etienne returned, Aszulay would tell him where I could be found; I knew with certainty that Manon would not pass on my information to her brother.

This time Aszulay, obviously finished for the day, was walking towards the entrance as I was coming in.

'Mademoiselle O'Shea,' he said, looking . . . what? What was his expression? I couldn't decipher what I saw, but somehow it warmed me. Did he look almost pleased at my unexpected appearance? If so, his voice didn't indicate it. 'So you are still in Marrakesh.'

'Yes.' I moved into the shade of thick overhanging branches, and he stepped under the tree as well. 'I have moved hotels, and came to tell you. I know you will tell Etienne where he can find me when he returns. I'm at Hôtel Nord-Africain, on Rue—'

'I know of it,' Aszulay interrupted.

'Oh. Well. You'll tell him, then, when he comes?' I asked.

'Yes.'

'And . . . what of Badou? Is he well?' I asked. I had been surprised by how many times I'd thought of the little boy since I'd seen him last.

'Badou is fine,' he stated. 'I passed by Sharia Zitoun yesterday.' His voice was more clipped than usual.

I wondered how Manon kept her lovers from running into each other. For all I knew, she had more men than Aszulay and the Frenchman. Olivier, she had called him.

'And Badou's father, Monsieur Maliki,' I suddenly said, not knowing I was going to say the words until they were out of my mouth. 'Where is he? Does he ever see his son, or help with his needs?'

Again Aszulay's expression changed. 'There is no Monsieur Maliki.'

'But . . . Manon is Madame Maliki,' I argued.

'She is Mademoiselle Maliki.'

'Mademoiselle?' I realised no one else had ever called her Madame. Only I, because I had assumed it was her married name. 'How is this? If she isn't married . . . why isn't she Mademoiselle Duverger?'

Aszulay ran his sleeve across his face. Again, I saw the dirt of the garden on his hands and wrists, a fine red dusting on his dark skin.

'Aszulay. I'm not asking you to disclose secrets. I'm trying to understand Manon so I can understand Etienne. Manon is Etienne's sister, but . . . it's puzzling. More and more things don't make sense. Her hatred for her father; even her anger towards Etienne. Is it only over the fact that she wasn't left what she thought her fair share when their father died? Is it this that's made her so bitter and full of rage?'

'How do you not see it, Mademoiselle O'Shea?' Aszulay said then, frowning down at me. He seemed, somehow, upset with me. I knew I shouldn't question him further, should just leave. But I didn't want to. I wanted to keep talking to him. 'How do you have to ask me this?' he continued.

I frowned back at him. 'What do you—'

He shook his head. 'Surely it's the same in your country. It's the same everywhere. The man has a wife. And the man has another woman. There are children.'

I waited.

'Manon's mother – Rachida Maliki – was a servant in the house of Marcel Duverger. Monsieur Duverger and she . . .' He stopped. 'They were together for a long time.

Manon told me that Monsieur Duverger came to Marrakesh and went back to France for some years before the French began to rule, and she was born during that time. But after the French took over Morocco, Monsieur Duverger brought Madame and Etienne and Guillaume from Paris, and they made their lives in Marrakesh. Still Rachida Maliki worked in the Duverger house.'

He stopped. It was the most I had heard Aszulay say at one time. I realised I was staring at him, watching his lips. He had a sensitive mouth, I suddenly thought. His mastery of French, with the Arabic influence, had an undercurrent of rhythm that was almost a melody.

He tapped his temple. 'Often the wife suspects. But if Madame Duverger had known about Rachida, she wouldn't have allowed her to remain a servant in her house. And she was kind to Rachida, and even to Manon.'

'She knew Manon?'

'When Manon was small, her grandmother took care of her, but when she was older, her mother often took her to the big house, to the Duverger house, to help with the work. And Manon told me that Madame Duverger gave her little gifts and some of her clothes she no longer wanted. Manon knew who her father was. In Marrakesh, in the medina, all the families know the father of the child. It's not a secret in the medina. In the French Quarter, yes, but in the medina, no.

'When Manon was helping her mother, she sometimes played with Etienne and Guillaume. But she knew she couldn't speak of the secret – that Etienne and Guillaume's father was also her father – because then it would go badly for her mother. She would lose her job and the extra luxuries Monsieur Duverger gave her.'

'So Etienne . . . he didn't know, then?'

Aszulay's face changed slightly. 'He didn't know for many years. Manon was simply a servant's daughter. But Manon has great strength, great determination. She educated herself. She learned to speak French as if born to it. She was – is, as you can see – very beautiful. Very . . .' He shook his head in frustration, saying an Arabic word. 'I can't think of the right word. But she could always make men come to her, and want her. From the time she was fifteen years old, Manon always had men to look after her.'

I knew the word he was searching for. Sensuous. Desirable. I had seen it in her flirtatious behaviour with Aszulay. I also saw how much power she knew she possessed. Had Aszulay known Manon for this long, then? Since she was fifteen years old? Had he loved her all these years?

'Manon would never be a subservient Moroccan wife, confined to the house and courtyard and roof,' Aszulay continued. 'She wanted a French husband, a man who would treat her as she saw the French women treated. And she had French men, many of them.' Again I thought of Olivier, leaving her bedroom. 'But none would marry her; they saw her for what she was.' Aszulay stopped for a moment. 'Manon is not wholly an Arab, nor is she a European. She is not alone in this; many women like her live throughout Morocco. But they find ways to make decent lives for themselves. Manon's downfall was that she was also a woman who at one time gave herself too freely. She wouldn't be a Moroccan wife, and yet she wouldn't be a *chikha* – a concubine. It's a legal profession here.'

So many questions, questions I found difficult to have answered. It was a complicated web: Manon, Aszulay, Olivier. Etienne.

'Instead,' Aszulay said, 'she looked for love. Always looking for love, Manon, clutching at it with her fingertips, and yet, sadly, unable to understand why what she thought was love was always taken away.'

I watched his face; had he once begged Manon to marry him? Had she spurned him because he was a Tuareg, and yet he loved her still?

'But . . . when did Etienne find out Manon was his sister?' I asked.

At that, Aszulay stepped out of the shade and looked at the sun. 'I must go,' he said.

I stayed where I was, not wanting him to leave. The story, and his voice, had mesmerised me.

He looked back at me. 'I have your information to pass on to Etienne, Mademoiselle O'Shea,' he said.

'My name is Sidonie,' I said, not sure why.

He nodded once. I wanted him to say it. I wanted to hear how he would say my name. But he turned and strode away.

While biding my time at Hôtel Nord-Africain, there were still times when I'd see a man from afar at one of the outside cafés in the French Quarter and think it was Etienne. At other times, as I caught a glimpse of a tall Tuareg swathed in blue walking regally down a street, I thought it might be Aszulay.

Sometimes I dreamed of Etienne: troubling, anxious

dreams where he was lost, or I was lost. Dreams of finding him, but he didn't recognise me. Dreams where I saw him in the distance, but as I came closer he grew smaller, and finally disappeared.

Dreams where I looked in the mirror and didn't recognise myself, my features moving, changing.

When I awoke from these nightmares, I tried to calm myself by remembering the times of love we had shared in Albany. But it was harder and harder to recall tender moments, to think of his expression as he watched me walk towards him.

One morning, lying in bed and listening to the morning call to prayer, I reached to my bedside table and picked up the tile from the Blue Man on the *piste*. I traced the bold blue and green design; the tile was smooth and cool under my fingertips. How had the tile-maker created this depth of colour?

I thought of the wildness of Manon's oils, then compared them to the painful attention I had always taken with my genteel renderings, my careful, perfect blooms of delicate hues. The cautious, minute brushstrokes that went into a bird's crest, a butterfly's wing. Yes, they were pretty flowers, pretty birds and butterflies, true replicas, but what did they make me feel? What part of myself had I put into those re-creations?

I again saw myself in my old room in Albany, holding a brush, trying to capture a small, quiet image. But I knew that those paintings were not part of my world any more – not this world, this new world.

I thought again of the journey with Mustapha and Aziz,

of the bright moored boats along the Atlantic, the sky yellow at the end of the day, alight with wheeling gulls. I thought of the alert and hungry dogs under the tables of the meat merchants in the villages, waiting for the daily slithering mess of goat and sheep and lamb entrails the men threw down.

I thought of the palms lining the main street of La Ville Nouvelle, and the richness of the flowers growing in tangled profusion in gardens. I closed my eyes, seeing, on my lids, the vibrancy of Moroccan colours everywhere: the fabrics, the clothing, the tiles, the walls and shutters and doors and gates. Colour so bright it almost pained my eyes, colour so soft, so subtle and ethereal I wanted to reach out and close my hand on it, the way one wants to capture a cloud.

I sat up.

Suddenly I wanted to paint it all: the boats, the sky and birds – both the free gulls and the imprisoned beauties in cages in the markets. I wanted to paint Marrakesh's scrawny cats, even, perhaps, the gruesome decapitated goat heads, or the lonely solitude of a Muslim cemetery. I wanted to capture the serpentine labyrinths of the souks, overflowing with intricately woven baskets and the awe-inspiring designs of the carpets, the winking gems in the jewellery, the glint of silver teapots and the rainbows of *babouches*. I wanted to duplicate the chilling bone white – produced by lye – of whitewashed walls; I wanted to create the rich and riotous panoply of the mounds of spices in D'jemma el Fna; I wanted to copy Majorelle's glorious blue.

I had no idea if I could produce any of the images with even the slightest sense of authenticity. But I had to try.

I went back to the art shop I had often passed and purchased watercolours and paper and an easel and brushes of various sizes. The purchases took more of my hoarded bills and coins, and yet I felt the need to paint so strongly that I knew I must.

I came back to the hotel and set up the easel near the window, and spent the rest of the day experimenting. The brushes felt so right in my hand. My strokes were sure and strong.

When I realised the light was failing, and my neck and shoulders were stiff, I stopped, studying what I had done.

I thought of the watercolours in the lobby of the grand Hotel de la Palmeraie, comparing mine to them.

A thought came to me. Preposterous, perhaps.

CHAPTER TWENTY-SEVEN

A FEW DAYS LATER, AS I tried to capture the look of a Moroccan woman on paper, I stopped, going to the mirror. I tied one of my white linen handkerchiefs around the bottom of my face. With a *haik* draped over me and only my dark eyes and eyebrows visible, I would be indistinguishable from the other women in the souks.

Although D'jemma el Fna and some of the markets were, by now, more familiar, I was still uncomfortable going into the medina. The few times I ventured in I cringed at being stared at, at being set upon by small bands of demanding children, at being shouted at by all the vendors to buy their wares, at being surreptitiously touched.

I went out, stopping to look at the expensive silk kaftans in the windows in the French Quarter, and then went into the medina and found a souk selling them for a fraction of the price. I fingered the simplest of the kaftans, and finally bought one, after a great deal of bargaining. It was calico, small red flowers on a yellow background. I bought a long, wide piece of coarse white fabric – the *haik* – and a veil. I took it all back to my room at the hotel and put it on.

I stared at myself for a long time, then took it off and finished my painting. The next day, dressed as a Moroccan woman, I left the hotel and went to D'jemma el Fna, walking slowly through the square, looking around me. I had always hurried through, making sure I didn't meet the eyes of any of the men, making sure I didn't attract attention. This time was so different. I had become invisible. And with the invisibility came a freedom. Nobody looked at me – not French men or women, not Moroccan men or women. I could move about as I chose. I could watch and listen. It was so much easier to learn things, to understand, when one didn't have to be aware of oneself.

I saw Mohammed with the little monkey crouched on his shoulder; he didn't glance at me. I stopped to watch the snake-charmers, seeing that when the sun was at its brightest, the snakes reacted in the liveliest fashion. I saw children swarming a European couple trying to escape as I once had. One of the smaller boys in the little group reminded me of Badou, and I was overcome with a rush of wanting to see him again. I hoped that when Etienne returned I would have the chance; when Manon saw that Etienne welcomed me, she would have no choice but to accept me. She might not like it, but she would have to accept it.

At the end of my first week in the small hotel, I took two of my watercolours and, putting on my green silk, went back to Hôtel de la Palmeraie. When Monsieur Henri saw me approach the desk, his features tightened.

'*Bonjour*, monsieur,' I said. 'How are you?'

'Fine. Fine, mademoiselle. How can I help you?' He glanced to see if I had my suitcases.

'I wish to discuss something.'

'You don't wish to stay with us?'

'No,' I said, smiling, trying not to show my nervousness. This moment was so important. 'No, I will not be staying here again.' I took out the watercolours. 'But I have completed these recently, and wondered if you would be interested in placing them with the others, to be sold on commission.'

He studied them, then looked up at me. 'You say you have done these, mademoiselle?'

I nodded. 'Do you not agree they would fit with the others you have displayed?' I repeated, the same tight smile on my face, willing myself to appear businesslike, and not show too much hope. Not to let him see my desperation. If I was to stay on in Marrakesh, waiting for Etienne to return, I needed money. This was my only option.

He didn't say no, but he tilted his head to one side. 'Of course it is not my decision. We have a buyer for the goods – the artwork and jewellery – sold in the hotel.'

'I'm sure you could use your influence,' I said. 'A man such as yourself, with such good taste.' I swallowed.

He liked the compliment, his face loosening, and then he actually smiled. 'I'll see what I can do,' he said. 'We've sold a number recently, and perhaps a new artist would be of interest.'

My relief was so great that it took me a moment to answer. Nothing was certain, but at least he hadn't rejected them. 'Fine,' I said. 'Yes, fine. I'll leave them with you, and come back in a few days to find out if the hotel wishes to take them. I have more, as well,' I said. I had completed two more, with another started only that morning.

'Thank you, mademoiselle,' Monsieur Henri said,

bowing slightly, and I raised my chin and smiled at him, an open, thankful smile.

As I walked out of the hotel, I thought of his words, *a new artist*, and walked more briskly, swinging my arms. When an elderly man looked at me, lifting his hat as I passed, I realised I was still smiling.

A few days later I was in the silver souk, looking at a square-cut topaz ring in a delicate silver setting. I had returned to Hôtel de la Palmeraie only that morning, and Monsieur Henri had told me that the man responsible for the decision-making on what the hotel would accept had been pleased with my work. He would take the two. If there was interest shown, he would take more.

I held the ring out at shoulder height, admiring the way the light caught in its facets, trying to think of how I could mix colours to create this hue. As I returned the ring to the stall owner, I heard a familiar voice and turned. It was Falida, a large, threadbare cotton handkerchief draped on her head and a woven basket looped over her shoulder. She held Badou's hand.

My heart leapt. 'Badou,' I called, and he looked around. I realised he didn't recognise me. I let go of the edges of my *haik* and said his name again, and this time he stared for a moment, then dropped Falida's hand and ran to me, throwing his arms around my legs as I'd seen him do with Aszulay. I knelt and enclosed him in my arms. He felt very thin. His hair was too long, hanging over his eyes, and he had to continually toss his head so he could see properly.

'I haven't seen you for a long time, Mademoiselle

Sidonie,' he said to me, pulling back and studying me. 'You are a different lady now.'

'I missed you,' I told him.

Falida came to us. She had a dark purple bruise, its edges yellowing, on her cheekbone. My heart went out to her. Although Badou appeared undernourished and dirty, at least there was no evidence that Manon beat him. Not yet, I thought. 'Are you shopping, Falida?' I asked her.

She shook her head, frowning.

'Where are you going?'

She didn't answer, but took Badou's hand.

'Wait,' I said, as they started to walk away, Badou looking over his shoulder at me. I followed them. 'I'll come with you.' They were going in the opposite direction to Sharia Zitoun.

In this city of strangers I was surprised to realise how good it felt to see someone – even these two children – whom I knew.

Falida shrugged one shoulder as if it didn't matter whether I followed them or not. We went down narrow passages I hadn't yet discovered, and then Falida opened an unlocked gate. I had to duck my head to pass under its stone lintel, and when I straightened up, I saw that we were outside the medina. A Moroccan graveyard lay behind a low crumbling wall. Atop the wall was a tattered sign, written in both Arabic and French: *Interdit Aux Non Muslemans*. Forbidden to Non-Muslims. I stopped.

But Falida climbed on the wall, reaching down to pull Badou over. They walked among the scattered mounds. There were no trees, no flowers, no headstones apart from a few tilting, broken tiles at the head and foot of some of the newer graves. Garbage was littered about. It was a bleak and desolate place.

'Wait,' I called again, and scrambled over the wall after them. I didn't like the idea of Badou being taken into such place.

Falida was looking for something, stopping by mounds and peering closely at them. I stayed with them, not understanding what she was doing. Badou said nothing, but tightly clutched the girl's hand.

And then, at one of the shallower graves, she set down her basket and prised Badou's hand from hers, squatting. Badou moved closer to me. Instinctively I reached out from the folds of my *haik*, and Badou gripped my hand, watching Falida as I did.

When I realised what she was doing, I was horrified. This grave had loose soil tossed haphazardly over it, and she was digging in it with both hands. 'Falida,' I said, but she ignored me. As she pulled away more rough earth, I saw the edges of a rotting muslin shroud. I turned Badou so that his face was against me, and pressed my hands on his shoulders.

'Falida,' I said, more sternly, and she stopped digging, looking up at me. 'What are you doing?'

'I fetch for my lady,' she said.

'Fetch what?'

'She needs,' she said.

'What does she need from here?' I asked.

But now Falida stuck her hands down, feeling around. As the soil moved, I saw the shape of a skull, covered in the muslin, wedged into the narrow opening. It was on its side. I swallowed, keeping Badou's face against my *haik*. I wanted to stop Falida, but she moved about gingerly, although with purpose and familiarity, tearing at the aged shroud, which fell apart at her touch. And then, to my shock, she pulled out a bleached, brittle bone. 'Only from old grave,' she said, smiling, holding it up. 'Heat bake bones.' The bone was roundish. She put it in her basket. 'One more,' she said, putting her hands back into the soil.

'Will Aisha-Quandisha get us?' Badou asked, his voice muffled against me. He was trembling. Why had Falida brought him to this terrible place, to watch her grisly behaviour? Had Manon sanctioned this?

'Not if you are good boy,' Falida said, but looked around, her head jerking on her neck, her eyes wide.

I thought the person Badou named might be a watchman for the cemetery. 'Where is he?' I asked Falida.

'She. Is woman, but legs from camel. Bad demon. Eyes like . . .' She stopped. 'Fire. Comes to graves at night, catch mans. She likes mans.'

'I'm taking Badou home,' I said, unable to bear his trembling. I took his hand, and as I started to step over the narrow grave, Falida shrieked. I stopped, my foot in the air.

'No, no, madame,' the girl said, her voice incredulous. 'No step.'

I put down my foot.

'Step over grave, no baby grows for you,' she said, patting her own stomach.

I looked at her narrow, bruised face, her worried expression.

With Etienne, I suddenly thought, there would be no more chances for another child. He wouldn't allow that to happen.

Why hadn't this come to me before? I had only been thinking of looking after Etienne, loving him, as he grew more ill. But now, in this bleak place, Falida had just reminded me that I would never be a mother. I would never hold my own child, watch it grow. Before I met Etienne and became pregnant, I had accepted life without a husband and children as a part of my legacy, and had never succumbed to any deep yearning or desire. But once I had experienced such a brief, tiny taste of the dream of motherhood, it was much more difficult to go back, to repress the longing.

Standing rigidly in the dismal graveyard, I stared at Falida as she returned to her digging. Badou's small fingers curled tightly over mine, his palm damp.

I walked with him around the end of the grave.

At that moment Falida let out a small cry of joy. 'I have!' she said, this time holding up a tooth with long, pointed double roots.

Bile rose in my throat.

'Tooth most best,' Falida said, grinning. 'Now my lady happy with me.'

We went back to Sharia Zitoun together. I stopped in the woodworkers' alley to buy Badou a small carved boat, trying to take his mind away from what he had just seen. It had been frightening and distressing for me; what was he feeling?

When I came through the saffron gate with Falida and Badou, Manon jumped up, her mouth open. In the court-yard with her was the Frenchman, Olivier, in linen trousers but without a jacket, his white shirtsleeves rolled up to the elbow. They were smoking from Manon's *sheesha*, and an open bottle of cognac and two glasses were on the low table. As usual, Manon was dressed in a glorious kaftan with a diaphanous *dfina* overtop it, her hair arranged elaborately, her make-up perfect.

She frowned, studying my *haik* as I stood with one hand on the open gate.

'Why are you still here?' she asked brusquely. 'What are you doing in Marrakesh?'

I didn't answer.

Falida handed her the basket. 'Kneecap and tooth, lady,' she said. 'Good?' she asked, hopefully.

'Take it into the house,' Manon said, too quickly, glancing at the man. He stood, picking up his jacket. 'You don't have to leave already, do you, Olivier?' she said, laying her slender hand on his arm.

He rolled down his sleeves. 'The children are back. And besides, you have company,' he said, raising his chin at me.

'She's not welcome,' Manon said. 'And I can send the children out again. Say you'll stay for just a while longer, Olivier,' she said, her voice cloying.

But the Frenchman shook his head. 'I should get back to work anyway.'

'When will you come again, *mon cher*?'

'The same time next week,' he said. As he walked towards me, I stepped out of the way to let him pass. Manon followed him, slipping her hand into his. 'We will carry our discussion further the next time, *oui*?' she asked, and he stopped, looking at her, running the back of his hand down her cheek.

'Yes,' he said, nodding, the hint of a smile on his mouth. 'Yes.'

As the gate closed behind him, Manon whirled to face me. 'Why have you come? You interrupted an important conversation,' she said. 'There's no reason for you to be here – here, at my home, or in Marrakesh. You're wasting your time,' she said, spitting out the words. '*Allez*. Go. I don't want you here. We have no more business.'

Badou was running his new boat around the edge of the fountain, but watching us. I could see that the dead bird was still there. It was almost completely rotted now, its eyes eaten out, its body flat and feathers sparse.

Manon turned and went into the house, her kaftan and *dfina* floating behind her.

I left. What had I expected when I came back to Sharia Zitoun with Badou and Falida?

There were shouts down the alley; four boys were kicking a ball against the walls.

Badou followed me, clutching his boat as he stood beside me and stared at the boys. Two were bigger than him, one about the same size, and one slightly smaller. The smaller one hung back, only occasionally aiming his foot at the ball if it came towards him.

'Are they your friends?' I asked Badou.

He looked up at me, then shook his head. 'I know Ali. He is six, like me. He lives there.' He pointed at the gate across from his.

'Why don't you go and play with them?'

'Maman says I mustn't, because they're only Arabs,' he said, watching the boys again, and I bit my bottom lip.

'She says it's better if I help her. She says a son must always help his mother.'

I thought of him spending his days in the house and courtyard, helping Falida and fetching things for his mother. I had never seen him with another child on Sharia Zitoun, had never seen him play with anything except his bits of string and wood, the borrowed puppy one day, and now, with the boat I'd bought him.

'I am the son,' he repeated. 'Will you come to our house again, mademoiselle?' he asked.

'I don't know, Badou. Maybe . . . maybe when Oncle Etienne comes back. Do you know . . . is he coming soon? Or has he already come to see Maman?' I asked, lightly, but deeply ashamed of my own behaviour. Asking a small child for information. Perhaps Etienne was already here but Aszulay wasn't aware of it, I told myself.

'No,' Badou said. 'Now I have to go inside, or Maman will be angry.'

'All right, Badou.' On instinct, I leaned down and hugged him. He hugged me back, quickly and easily, his small arms tight around my neck.

Now I wore kaftans and a *haik* and a veil at all times, quietly going about my daily shopping with my woven bag. I watched, with new eyes, the foreign women in the French Quarter, those who sat indulgently with their drinks and their cigarettes. I watched them in D'jemma el Fna or in the souks, haggling over carpets and teapots, ignoring the beggars with outstretched hands and cries of *baksheesh, baksheesh*: please, give.

I realised how vulnerable these women appeared, everybody able to read their expressions, their bodies defined by their fitted clothing, the skin of their arms and legs uncovered so that, I suddenly thought, they almost appeared naked.

Although in reality it was only weeks, it felt that it was long ago that I had been one of these women, exposed and susceptible away from the safety and familiarity of the European enclave. And suddenly it was surprisingly important that I not think of myself as such a woman, engrossed only in her own petty desires.

On the morning that marked a month since Aszulay had said Etienne might return, I counted my money again. If I ate barely anything, I could stay perhaps two more weeks. That was all. Neither of my paintings had sold; I checked every few days. I had painted three more, but had run out of paper and some paint colours, and couldn't afford to buy any more.

But Etienne was expected any day. And then everything would be all right.

As usual, on this morning I went down to the splintered hotel counter and asked if there were any messages for me. The man who was most often behind the counter – there were three or four who worked there – glanced at the boxes behind him, then shook his head. 'Not today,' he said, as he or the others always said, and I nodded.

'Thank you,' I said, but before I could leave he said, 'Mademoiselle,' and his cheeks slightly reddened. 'I know you are American. But the other guests . . .' He stopped. 'Some have mentioned to me that they stay here because it is a hotel for visitors to Marrakesh. Visitors from France, from Germany, from Spain and Britain. Also from America, like you.'

I waited.

Perspiration gleamed on the man's forehead. 'I'm sorry, mademoiselle. It's not suitable that you dress as a Muslim woman while staying here. It is unsettling for the others. There have been complaints, you understand. If you insist on dressing in this way, I will have to ask you to leave the hotel.'

'I understand,' I said, blinking, then turned and went out into the hot sunshine.

Aszulay was there, standing on the street in front of the hotel, in his blue robes, the bottom of his face covered by the end of his turban. He was looking down the street, so I saw his partly obscured profile, and I caught my breath.

CHAPTER TWENTY-EIGHT

I APPROACHED HIM. MY BREATHLESSNESS was, surely, because seeing him meant he had news of Etienne.

At the sound of my footsteps, he glanced at me, then turned away.

I said his name, and he looked at me again, then said something in Arabic, his tone questioning.

I pulled my veil from my nose and mouth, and he drew back, just the slightest. 'Mademoiselle O'Shea,' he said, his voice muffled. Then he said, 'But why are you—'

'Have you news, then? News of Etienne? Has he arrived?'

'Manon has had a letter,' he said, pushing down the bottom of his turban, uncovering his lower face as I had. I'd forgotten how white his teeth were. His skin had grown darker from working in the intense summer sun, making his eyes appear even bluer.

I stepped closer. 'A letter from Etienne?'

He nodded. 'It arrived yesterday.'

I waited, but by his expression I knew, before he said it, what he would tell me. 'I'm sorry. He wrote to say he couldn't come this week. Perhaps in a few weeks, another month, the letter said.'

I swallowed. Another few weeks, a month. I couldn't stay that long; I didn't have enough money. 'But then . . .' I said, the thought swooping in quickly. 'The postmark . . . it will tell the city, or surely . . . surely he told Manon his address, so she could get in touch with him. It makes sense, Aszulay,' I said, looking up at him. 'It makes sense. I could go to him, then, wherever he is in Morocco. I don't have to wait for him here.'

Aszulay was watching me without speaking.

'Did he say where he was?' I asked. 'Did the envelope—'

'She didn't show it to me, Sidonie,' he said. 'She only told me he wasn't coming yet, not for a few more weeks or a month.'

'But I'll go to her and ask her. Or no, you go, she'll tell you if you ask. She won't tell me, Aszulay, but she'll tell you.'

He shook his head. 'She's not here right now,' he said, and suddenly the air was too hot, the sun a white, burning disc on my face.

'She's not here?' I repeated. 'What do you mean?'

'She's gone on a holiday. For a week, maybe two, with . . .' he stopped, then continued, 'a friend.'

I knew that Manon had gone off with the Frenchman. Olivier. Surely Aszulay knew as well.

'Did she take Badou?' I couldn't look at him, but stared at a tile on the wall behind him.

'No. She left him with Falida.'

'She's only a girl,' I said. 'They're just children.'

'She's eleven. She could marry in two or three years,' he said. 'I'll go to Sharia Zitoun every few days, to bring them

370

food and make sure they're all right,' he added.

I nodded, pulling my *haik* around my face to block out the sun's rays. Not only had Manon gone off with another man, but she expected Aszulay to check on her child. Had she no conscience at all? And did Aszulay have no backbone?

I looked at him now. I knew he was a man of dignity, of honesty. How could he allow Manon to use him like this? How could he continue to be with her when she showed him so little respect? He didn't deserve to be treated in this way.

'So you will continue to wait?' Aszulay said, something odd in his voice. 'You'll stay in Marrakesh and wait for him – for Etienne – no matter how long it takes?'

I licked my lips. 'I . . .' I stopped, embarrassed to say I didn't know how I would manage it. 'Yes.'

'Sidonie, I think . . . maybe you shouldn't wait any longer. Maybe you should return to your life.'

'My life?' He still didn't understand. But how could he? How could he understand there was nothing for me in Albany? Suddenly I was angry at him, at Aszulay, for telling me I shouldn't wait. I was angry with Manon, for thwarting my efforts to find Etienne. And perhaps I was the most angry with Etienne.

I was so hot, and I was hungry; I hadn't eaten anything since the day before. 'As you'll wait?' I said to him, my voice louder, stronger. I stared into his eyes.

He shook his head the slightest. 'Wait for what?'

'For her. For Manon.' I couldn't keep the venom out of my voice as I spoke her name. 'You'll wait for her, doing her bidding, while she's off with another man?'

He shrugged. 'It's for the child,' he said, as if surprised, but this didn't satisfy me.

'I can tell you think I'm a fool to wait for Etienne to come back to me,' I said. 'Go ahead. Tell me you think I'm a fool. And then I'll tell you that I think you're a fool to wait for Manon. She's only using you to look after her son. How can you allow her to do that to you?' I didn't want to say these things; Aszulay had been nothing but kind to me. What was wrong with me? Why did I care how Manon treated him? Why was I annoyed that he cared so much for her?

His nostrils tightened. 'Perhaps the same way you allow Etienne to do what he does to you.'

We stared at each other. His words stung me. *What Etienne was doing to me.* And then suddenly I couldn't look at him any longer, and put my head down, as if shielding my face from the sun. Instead of shaming him, as I tried to do, he'd shamed me. Suddenly I realised how he must see me, waiting endlessly for a man who . . . I was dizzy. The sun was too bright; it was making everything too clear, too transparent.

Still looking down, I said, 'I'm sorry, Aszulay. I don't have a right to tell you what to do. I'm sorry,' I repeated. 'I'm . . . I'm upset. All this waiting. And now . . .'

'I understand,' he said, and I looked at him again. Did he? His voice was a little stiff, as was his expression.

'There's something else,' I said then, because I knew that once he walked away from me I didn't know when I'd see him again. Now I knew I would have to make another change in order to stay in Marrakesh.

'Yes?'

'I need to find a place to stay. I . . . I will no longer stay at the hotel. I wonder . . . could you help me?'

'But the hotels in La Ville Nouvelle are for foreigners. For people like you. Why don't you continue to stay there?'

'It doesn't suit me any longer,' I told him.

'Doesn't suit you?'

'I can't wear these clothes. They don't like it.' I didn't want to have to tell him I had so little money left.

'But then . . . wear your American clothes. Why do you even wear these?'

'In this way,' I gestured down my body, and at my *haik*, 'I can move about the city more freely.'

He shook his head. 'I don't understand. How do you wish me to help with this?'

I found it so difficult to not be completely honest with him. 'The truth, Aszulay, is that I can no longer afford to stay in any of the hotels in the French Quarter. Perhaps there's someplace, someplace you know, that's very inexpensive. In the medina.'

He looked startled. 'But the medina isn't good for you. It's only Moroccans. You should be with your people.'

Without thinking, I said, 'I like the medina.' Yes, I realised, I did like it. Since I'd begun dressing in a way that allowed me to blend in, when I was there I felt alive in a way I'd never known before.

'There are no hotels in the medina,' he said now. 'When Moroccans from other cities come, they stay with relatives, or with friends.'

'All I need is a room. One room, Aszulay.'

'It's impossible,' he said, again shaking his head.

373

'Impossible? For one room? I would keep to myself. I won't—'

'You must understand the country,' he said. 'A woman, a Nasarini, alone, in a Muslim house. It's not proper.'

Nasarini. A Nazarene, a Christian, the name foreigners were called by the Moroccans. I had heard it before, in the souks, as I understood more and more Arabic.

I hadn't thought of how my presence might cause difficulties in a house in the medina. 'But otherwise I can't stay in Morocco any longer. All of this – my coming here, everything – will be for nothing. I'm so close, Aszulay,' I said. 'I know you don't think I should wait, but . . .'

We stood there, people moving around us on the street in front of the hotel.

'Please,' I finally said. 'I can't go home. Not yet. Please understand how important this is to me. Haven't you ever . . .' I stopped. I wanted to say *haven't you ever loved someone so much you would do anything for her,* but it was too intimate a question. What did I know of this man, and his feelings?

'I'll see what I can do, Sidonie,' he said, but he looked troubled now.

'Thank you,' I said, and, relieved, and on impulse, I touched the back of his hand to show my gratitude.

He looked down, and I looked as well; my fingers were small on his hand. I pulled my fingers back, and he looked at me then.

I was sorry I'd been so forward. Obviously I'd made him very uncomfortable. It was only later that I remembered he'd called me Sidonie.

★

The man with the withered arm, his djellaba sleeve rolled up over it, didn't appear pleased when Aszulay brought me to the house on Sharia Soura two days later. Aszulay said it wasn't yet a sure thing, but this man – his friend – might allow me to stay there for a short while.

It was early evening, and as we stood in the courtyard – my face covered but for my eyes – the man stared at me. I immediately looked at the ground, knowing I couldn't appear bold. When I glanced up, the man was shaking his head.

Aszulay spoke to him. They argued back and forth, quietly, in Arabic. I realised it was simply the usual market haggling over price. Except this time it was over me.

Aszulay's tone remained the same, calm and firm, and finally the man threw up his hand in what appeared resignation. Aszulay quoted me the price of the room as well as my meals for a week; it was a tiny fraction of what I had paid for one night at the cheaper hotel. I nodded, and Aszulay took my cases and went inside the house. I was carrying my painting supplies in my woven basket, and my easel in the other hand.

I followed him; after the bright courtyard, the narrow passage we walked through was almost dark, and for a moment I felt as though I were one of the blind men in D'jemma el Fna. I climbed the stairs after Aszulay, fixing my eyes on his heels in his yellow *babouches*. The stairs were narrow and steep, and my right leg ached with the effort of lifting it so high on each tiled step. As we reached the top, a cat noiselessly came from nowhere and bounded down the stairs beside me.

Aszulay opened a door and set my cases in the middle

of the room. He turned to look at me.

'It's all right?' he asked, and I nodded, not even having time to take in my surroundings, but knowing I had no choice. There was a pleasant smell in the room, something woody and fresh.

'Yes. Yes, it's very good, Aszulay. Thank you.'

'There are two wives. They will give you tea and bread in the mornings, and a meal midday and evening. Downstairs, off the kitchen, is the lavatory.'

I nodded.

'But you must understand that you can't move about as you do in a hotel; you can't leave the house without a male escort. Although my friend understands you are not Muslim, if you wish to stay here you must act in the way of a Muslim woman, or he will be shamed. He has two sons, and one will accompany you when you want to go out. And if they will allow it, you can help the wives with the work of the house, although I believe they'll resent you.'

'Why? I'm not—'

'They'll see you as a rival, perhaps to be a new wife. It doesn't matter what their husband tells them, they won't believe him. His second wife died a few months ago; this was her room. They know he's looking for another. Stay out of their way, unless they invite you to join them. *Darra marra kif defla*,' he said. 'The saying for the wives is that another woman coming into the home is bitter like the oleander. They devise many ways to try and prevent the taking of an additional wife. If the husband enters when you're with the wives, turn your face to the wall so he can't look at you. He's doing this because he owes me a favour, but he isn't happy. So you must do all you can to stay out of the way and not create any upset.' He stopped. 'It helped to convince him to let you stay because he said that you don't appear to be a foreigner. This way, he said, he could tell neighbours you were the distant cousin of his youngest wife.'

'Thank you,' I said. 'For getting me this room. And for . . .' I wanted to say more. 'Thank you,' I repeated.

Standing alone with him in the small, dim room was different from standing outside in the sunshine with him. 'Will I see you again?' I asked, feeling even more connected to him now because of this room. His friend.

He looked into my face, opened his mouth as if to speak further, then nodded, tucking the end of his turban over his nose and mouth. He left, shutting the door firmly behind him.

The room had such a low ceiling that if I reached my arm over my head I could lay my palm flat on it. The walls were of a cool, hard substance. Looking closer at the spot where a small piece of the plaster had fallen off, I saw that they were simply some form of mud. It had to be Marrakesh earth, for it was red, and looked as though it had been pounded until it was hard and flat and then plastered over. On the floor were a number of small fringed carpets. They were of mismatched patterns and faded colours, and yet beautiful. I picked up a corner of one and saw that the floor underneath was smooth wooden planks. I dropped the carpet back down, and on instinct took off my shoes, and then my stockings. I pushed my toes into the carpets. In spite of being old, they were still thick and yielding as I dug my toes deeper. Beside the sleeping mattress was a small ornamental stool, and on the wall opposite, a carved wooden table of light wood. The table emitted the woody scent in the room, and I wondered if it was the *thuya* Mrs Russell had mentioned that was abundant around Essouria. Leaning on the wall beside the table was a long mirror with a frame made of brilliantly coloured glass chips.

I looked out the tall, narrow window to the courtyard below. Not a whisper of air came through the window into the room. I took off my *haik* and kaftan and pulled a simple cotton slip over my head.

It was my first night in the medina, in my tiny room of earth, with its glorious carpets and its smell of the forest. The sleeping mattress was covered with a soft cotton coverlet of blue and white stripes. I looked at it. I tried not to think of the unfortunate wife; had she died in the bed?

I unpacked the other kaftans I'd purchased recently, and the few toiletries I needed. I left all my dresses folded in the cases. I hung my kaftans and *haik* on the nails on the back of the door, put my toiletries on the table, and the tile from the Blue Man on the *piste* – what had the Arabic word been? *Zellij*? – on the stool beside my bed. I left my easel folded beside the mirror.

I sat on the deeply recessed windowsill then, my back against one wall – it must have been one and a half to two feet thick – and my feet on the other. The day was losing its heat, dropping quickly, and finally the air grew soft and still, cooler.

I looked down at the dimming courtyard, at the potted trees and large earthenware containers of plants and the geometric design of the tiles that covered the floor. Apart from the distant thrum of the square, there was no other sound. The cat – now I could see that it was reddish brown – crept stealthily through the courtyard, pausing, alert, in front of one of the pots. I thought of Cinnabar.

I was awakened by the street outside the courtyard coming to life. I squinted at my watch; it was only just after seven, but already very noisy. I got out of bed and looked out the window; the courtyard was still empty. But hoofs tapped on the narrow cobbled streets outside the gate, and men's voices urged on their donkeys. A bicycle bell tinkled, and I smelled fresh bread. Then there was a rhythmic hand-clapping, and children's voices singing. The voices and clapping grew louder and then faded; the children must come down this street on the way to school. Babies cried. From beneath me in the house there was the unmistakable sound of throat-clearing and hacking, followed by a great deal of spitting. I went back to my bed and tried to sleep, but it was impossible. As I lay there, I realised my sleep had been deep and dreamless. I hadn't thought of Etienne since I'd arrived yesterday.

I heard a man's voice and got up to look into the courtyard again. It was the husband; he spoke to someone I couldn't see and then went out the gate. Knowing he was gone, I covered my face and went downstairs. I found the kitchen and entered. There were three women preparing food; one middle-aged and one younger, as well as a very old and wrinkled black woman. They all wore plain kaftans with more colourful *dfinas* over them. Their faces were uncovered; they stopped what they were doing and looked at me.

'*Assalaam alykum,*' I said. The servant pushed out her lips and went back to stirring a pot. The older woman turned her back and chopped at a slab of meat with great resounding hacks. Only the third woman – she was younger than I – looked at my eyes, and said, '*Slema.*' I didn't know this word, but it sounded like a greeting, and so I nodded and smiled. I knew she couldn't see my smile under my veil, and yet hoped my eyes let her know I appreciated her attempt at friendliness. She had a pattern of tiny dots tattooed on her forehead.

I used the lavatory and passed through the kitchen again; none of the women glanced at me this time. I went out to the courtyard and sat on a wooden bench there. The cat appeared. I snapped my fingers at it and made a whispering sound. It crept towards me and sniffed my fingers, but then darted away.

Eventually the younger wife brought me out a plate of thick unleavened bread and honey and soft white cheese and a slice of pale green melon; she went back into the house and brought mint tea. When she left me again, I removed my face covering. As I raised a piece of cheese to my mouth, I thought of what Aszulay had told me: that the wives would do what they could to deter another woman. I thought of Falida, digging up bones and teeth from the graveyard for Manon, and then of Manon telling me how she made her own kohl with ingredients that would make men mad with desire. Surely she would use the bone and tooth for some of the magic Etienne had told me about.

That memory of Etienne felt so old now: sitting in my house in Albany, listening to his tales of witchcraft and demons in a country splashed with endless sun while a cold winter wind howled around my windows. It was as if it was a scene from a book I had read.

And now here I was, in a steamy courtyard, looking at a piece of cheese and wondering if powdered bone or a sliver of tooth or some other spell had been cast upon the food that was served to me.

Then, telling myself I was becoming as superstitious as a true Moroccan woman, I took a deep breath and bit into it, chewing and swallowing carefully. It was smooth and creamy and delicious. I finished all the food on the plate and drank my tea. Then I sat in the courtyard, unsure of what to do next. Knowing that I couldn't rise and leave the house when I wished was a strange feeling. I wondered if it felt claustrophobic to women who had lived this way all their lives.

Eventually I heard female voices from above, and looked up. I could see nothing, but could discern at least three separate voices, surely from the roof.

I covered my face again, climbing back up the stairs past my own room, then up the next flight of stairs, the women's voices growing louder. After the darkness of the stairway, when I emerged on to the roof the morning brightness was sharp. The voices stopped. It was the two wives and the servant; they sat cross-legged around a pile of golden grain.

Aszulay had told me not to join them unless I was invited, but when they all looked away from me and continued sorting through the grain, tossing out bits of dirt and spreading the cleaned grains on a long strip of jute, I sat on the far edge of the roof.

I kept my face covered; somehow I felt more

comfortable if they couldn't study me, and perhaps see the insecurity I felt. What had their husband told them about me? What did they think of me, a woman alone in a country where a woman without a man was nothing? Surely pity. Perhaps disgust. I couldn't tell.

I stayed on the far edge of the roof, apart from them, and they resumed speaking to each other, but quieter now, occasionally glancing at me. I alternated between watching them and looking out over the city. Swallows swooped overhead. I wished I could understand what the women were saying. All around me were the flat roofs of other homes, some a bit higher and some lower than this one. The flatness was punctuated, further out, by minarets. They rose, square and solid and yet slender, like displaced lighthouses.

The Atlas mountains gleamed; if I squinted, it seemed I could reach out and touch them.

I thought of standing on the rooftop of the hotel in Tangier, and how I had felt, like a woman caught between two worlds. And yet here, in my kaftan and face-covering, my few belongings in the room below, I felt some line had been crossed. This world, at this moment, was the one I inhabited.

Many of the neighbouring roofs held women and children; there were no men anywhere, and it was clear that the roofs were the women's freedom. Here they were all unveiled, and could be themselves. They were not the shadowy, silent figures gliding past me in the medina alleys and lanes. They laughed and chattered as they spread wet clothes flat to dry and nursed their babies and sewed. One woman argued loudly with a younger one; I sensed they were mother and daughter by their familiarity. An old woman slept on her back in the sun, her mouth open. Small children played about, climbing over their mothers or chewing on fistfuls of bread.

After some time it appeared the women on my roof had forgotten about me. They laughed and nodded, their strong hands quick and confident as they sorted through the grain with effortless speed, and suddenly I envied their closeness, their friendship.

I had avoided any offers of friendship on Juniper Road, but now, for reasons unknown even to myself, I wanted to be part of this small group. I wanted to let handfuls of golden grain fall through my fingers, and even if I couldn't understand the conversation, I wanted the foreign words to flow around me, to settle on my shoulders like a light mantle.

CHAPTER TWENTY-NINE

I HAD BEEN LIVING IN the house on Sharia Soura for three days. I was never confronted by the husband, although in the morning and evening I heard his voice, and saw him in the courtyard when I looked down from my window. He was often with two boys of perhaps fourteen or fifteen; they must be the sons Aszulay had mentioned, and were surely twins – both the same height and size; tall and gangly, yet with broad shoulders.

The older wife and servant ignored me, but it was clear the younger wife was curious and interested in me. There was little we could do to communicate, but I appreciated her smiles, which came more frequently after the first day. She told me her name was Mena, and laughed as she tried to pronounce Sidonie. She had a high, sweet voice and a round, pale face, which I knew was a look favoured by Moroccan men. She was probably no more than twenty years old.

When I pointed to objects, Mena said their names in Arabic. In a short time I had learned many words and simple phrases. She was eager to try and speak with me; she seemed lonely, in spite of the constant companionship of the two other women.

She chattered constantly, showing me how to make couscous – rolling and shaping the moistened Seminole wheat, coating it with finely ground wheat flour before steaming it. I watched as she made *harira*, the lentil and chickpea and lamb soup. When I demonstrated that I wanted to help with other dishes, she gestured how thick to cut meat and vegetables and how long to cook them, sometimes rather impatiently taking my hand and stirring a pot with more strength or quickness. She ignored the disapproving glances of the ancient servant, but when the older wife – Nawar – entered the kitchen, Mena would fall silent.

By the fourth day I grew restless and anxious, and could no longer stay within the house, on the roof or in the courtyard. I expressed to Mena that I wished to go out. She consulted Nawar, who looked a bit sour, but called out a name – Najeeb – and one of the boys materialised from a back room. She spoke a few lines to him, raising her chin at me, and Najeeb went to the gate and stood, waiting. I covered myself and followed him through the twisting lanes. I watched his bare heels as he moved ahead of me; they were like horn. I recognised some of the streets, and realised that we passed Sharia Zitoun on the way to the souks. I saw the niche in the wall – with the kittens – where Badou and Falida went when they were sent out by Manon.

Once Najeeb had led me to the souks, where I was sure he expected me to shop, I walked ahead of him, looking back, and he followed.

I went through D'jemma el Fna into the French

Quarter, and all the way to Hôtel de la Palmeraie, glancing back every now and then at Najeeb. I gestured for him to wait while I went into the hotel, pulling off my *haik* and veil as I did so. He immediately turned from me.

In the lobby, Monsieur Henri saw me coming, frowning at my kaftan, but then nodded. 'Ah, mademoiselle. Yes. Splendid news. Both your paintings have sold, and the buyers are interested in more. They are a young couple decorating their home in Antibes, and wish at least four additional paintings in the same vein.'

A strange heat filled me. I had no idea it would feel this way to be told such news: that my paintings were sought after.

'Mademoiselle? You said you have more paintings. The couple leave next week, and would like the opportunity to look at them before then.'

I nodded. 'Yes. Yes,' I repeated. 'I'll bring them. Tomorrow.'

'Fine. Now, let me see,' he said, turning to open a drawer in the cupboard behind the desk. 'Yes. Here you are. The hotel has taken the fifty per cent commission, as usual. The details of the sale are written out.'

I took the envelope from him, still nodding. 'Thank you, Monsieur Henri,' I said. 'Thank you,' I repeated.

'I shall see you tomorrow, then,' he said, and turned, making it clear our business was over.

I went out to Najeeb, covering myself before embarrassing him again. I couldn't wait, and ripped open the envelope. Along with the typed receipt, there was a cheque, with an amount I hadn't expected. I stared at it, thinking that perhaps I was reading it incorrectly. But I wasn't. The sum I'd received for my two paintings filled me with euphoria.

It was the first time in my life I had received payment. For anything.

Once I'd stuffed the cheque back into the envelope, Najeeb started down the street towards the medina, but I said his name, gesturing for him to again follow me. I went into a bank, saying I wished to open an account.

The teller looked at me. 'You must have a form of identification, mademoiselle,' he said, and I nodded.

'I'll return with my passport, tomorrow,' I said, and then let Najeeb lead me back to Sharia Soura.

The next day I again expressed that I must go out, and Nawar looked just as annoyed, but again called Najeeb.

First I went to Hôtel de la Palmeraie, leaving Monsieur Henri the other four paintings I had completed. Then I went back to the bank and opened an account, withdrawing the money I needed, and after that to the art store. I purchased more paper and paint. On a whim, I bought a wooden box containing tubes of oil paint and a few canvases and different brushes. I thought of how much more depth I could achieve by painting with oils. It would be a completely new technique, and yet I was eager to try.

On the way back, I wandered through the noise and colour of souk after souk, stopping here and there, fingering cloth and wooden carvings and silver goods. Najeeb stood just behind me at all times, holding my purchases. I bought a large bag of cashews for him.

I was excited to try the oils immediately; I had painted

in my room, but this time of day there wasn't enough light. I brought my easel down to the courtyard, set up the canvas and squeezed paint on to my palette.

Mena came out, pulling up a stool and watching, her eyes bright and a flush in her normally pale cheeks as she watched the courtyard slowly emerge from my brushes.

I turned to her, pointing at her face and then putting my brush back to the canvas. But as I started to create her image, she cried out, putting her hand on mine and shaking her head, saying *la, la*. No.

'What's wrong?' I asked her, and she went to great lengths with words and gestures, and I understood enough to know she was telling me I couldn't paint her. I would capture her soul on the canvas.

I nodded, asking in my simple Arabic if I could paint a man.

She thought for a moment, and then nodded. A man was all right. A man's spirit was strong enough not to be taken, I understood from her words and gestures. But I couldn't paint a woman or a child.

We were sitting in companionable silence, Mena watching as I worked, when Nawar came into the courtyard. She stopped, then came and looked at the picture. She shook her head, her lips tight, and spoke in a torrent of words to Mena, leaving with a great flurry of her kaftan.

I looked at Nawar disappearing into the house, and then at Mena. Mena shook her head slowly, and with a few sentences I knew I was not allowed to paint in the courtyard. Nawar felt it would draw in evil spirits.

★

The next day I was on the roof with Mena and Nawar when the old servant shouted something from the courtyard. Mena leaned over the edge and called back, then looked at me.

'Aszulay is here,' she said, in Arabic; I jumped up, perhaps a little too quickly, and went towards the stairs.

'Sidonie,' Mena called after me, and when I looked back at her, she put her hand over her nose and mouth, as if to remind me to cover my face.

I nodded, but couldn't explain this wasn't necessary, and went down the stairs.

Aszulay stood in the courtyard, holding Badou's hand.

'Hello,' I said, a little breathless from hurrying, looking from Aszulay to Badou. 'Is Etienne in Marrakesh?' I asked.

Aszulay lifted one shoulder; the small movement gave me the impression he was annoyed with my question. 'No.'

'Is it . . . is it that I'm no longer allowed to stay here?' I asked, swallowing. 'Is that what you've come to tell me?'

'No. I have spoken to my friend. You may stay on.'

I nodded, relieved that I would be here a bit longer, and yet disturbed that time was stretching out with no more word from Etienne.

I let out a long breath. 'Thank you. How are you, Badou?' I asked, looking at the child.

He smiled, and it pleased me to see that his hair was trimmed, and shone, and his little djellaba and cotton trousers were clean. 'We're going to see the turtles,' he said.

'At the garden,' Aszulay explained. 'I finished early today, so I'm taking Badou there. We were passing near to here, and I thought perhaps you would care to join us.'

He said it in a casual tone, but also with a slight hesitation.

'Oh,' I said, surprised.

'You will come, Sidonie?' Badou asked.

I realised how much I wanted to go out again. I had thought so often in this one week how restricted Nawar and Mena's lives were. 'Yes,' I said. 'I'll get my veil and *haik*.' As I went up to my room I met Mena, standing hidden on the stairs. She was obviously listening, although she wasn't able to understand our French. She lifted her eyebrows, as if to ask what was happening.

I fumbled for the Arabic words for going out, followed by Aszulay's name.

Her lips tightened in the same way Nawar's did when she was displeased with me. Without another word she turned and went back to the roof.

In my room I took up my veil, but before I adjusted it over my lower face, I stared at myself, then smoothed my eyebrows with my middle finger, as I had seen Manon do.

Before leaving the medina, we stopped to buy some sweets for Badou, Aszulay putting a few centimes into the boy's hand.

Badou scampered to a seller in front of a table stacked with piles of powdered jelly squares in gem tones.

'I'm going to look at the knives,' Aszulay said, and went to a nearby stall.

I watched Badou make the small purchase on his own, seeing the proud lift of his chin as he spoke to the man in Arabic, holding the centimes out to him on the palm of his hand. The man took the coins and measured the sweets into a paper cone and handed it to him, saying something to him and nodding.

Badou came back to me, looking from me to Aszulay, who was feeling the blade of a knife with his thumb. He took a square of candy from the cone and popped it into his mouth. Then he extended the cone to me. 'The man told me I must share my sweets with my father and mother,' he said, then smiled. 'He's so funny, isn't he?'

'Yes,' I said, smiling back at him, and took one of the powdered squares.

Once we emerged from the medina, we rode to Le Jardin Majorelle in the back of a cart pulled by a donkey.

'We'll go to one of the bigger ponds,' Aszulay said, when we were in the garden. 'The turtles there are the largest.'

We went to a reflecting pool, and while Badou ran to its edge, I set my *haik* on a stone bench and untied the veil from my face.

Monsieur Majorelle passed us, greeting Aszulay, then stopped, looking at me.

'*Bonjour*, Monsieur Majorelle,' I said. 'It's Mademoiselle O'Shea. I met you with Monsieur and Madame Russell, some time back.'

He looked surprised. 'Ah, yes. You are blending into the life of Marrakesh, it appears.' He glanced at Aszulay in an enquiring way, but Aszulay simply stood there. 'I shall see you tomorrow, Aszulay. Some new pots have arrived.'

Badou crouched beside the motionless water, which mirrored the sky, his little shoulders tense, staring into the smooth surface dotted with lily pads. Aszulay spoke to him in Arabic, and Badou put his fingers into the water and wiggled them, breaking the glass-like surface. Almost immediately a turtle popped its head up, only inches from Badou's fingers. Badou jumped back, gasping, and then turned and looked at us, and laughed.

'Une *tortue*,' he said, still smiling. 'He scared me.' He again crouched and splashed his fingers in the water. 'I want him to do it again.'

The turtle came nearer, possibly hoping for food, and again lifted its round head, this time opening its toothless mouth, and then quickly plopped back under the water.

Again Badou laughed, delighted. He was a different little boy like this, the usual serious expression gone.

'This is the first time I have heard your laughter,' Aszulay said.

I covered my mouth with my hand, unaware that I had laughed along with Badou.

Aszulay studied me. 'Why do you look as though you regret laughing?'

I blinked. 'I'm not sure.' I thought about the baby, about Etienne, about all that had happened in the last number of months. I realised I hadn't laughed since Etienne had left me. Did I feel I had no right to laugh? To happiness?

I looked down at Badou, flicking his fingers in the water. He had made me, for this brief moment in the sun, forget about the heaviness of my recent life. I glanced back at Aszulay. He wasn't looking at me, but I had the distinct impression he pitied me.

I didn't want this man to feel sorry for me. I left the bench to kneel beside Badou. 'Let's make the turtle come out again,' I said, and lightly splashed the surface of the water with my fingers.

As we left the gardens, Aszulay spoke to Badou in Arabic. Badou's mouth opened and his eyes shone. 'Yes, Oncle Aszulay, yes, when will we go?'

'In one week. Seven days,' he said, lifting Badou into the cart, which had waited for us. Badou looked at his fingers, his lips moving as he counted. 'Every few months I visit my family,' Aszulay added, turning to me. 'Badou likes to come with me. He likes to play with the children there.'

His family.

'Oh. You have children?' I asked, somehow startled. Somehow . . . disturbed. Why? I realised I presumed he had no wife, no children, mainly because when I'd gone to his home I'd seen no one but the older woman who served me tea. Was it also because of his association with Manon? Because I thought him above having a lover outside of marriage?

'No,' he said, then pointedly turned to Badou and spoke to him about the turtles.

Once we had left the cart, Aszulay and Badou walked me back to Sharia Soura. Badou asked, 'Sidonie, are you coming with us to the *bled*?'

'No, Badou,' I answered, stopping at my gate. 'But I hope you have a good time.' I turned, knocking on the gate.

We waited, and then Aszulay said, 'Do you wish to come?'

I thought he was just being polite. But that was my assumption: an American assumption. It was not Aszulay's way.

He added, 'We will be gone two days.'

The gate was opened by Najeeb.

Two days meant we would stay overnight. As if reading my mind, Aszulay said, 'There are women's quarters.'

I thought about my night in the *bled* with Mustapha and Aziz: the stars, the silence, the wild camel. Again I thought of the word *family*. Aszulay had said he didn't have children, but did he have a wife there? Two, or even three?

'I have *une camionnette*,' he said. 'We will go in it.'

'A truck? You own a truck?'

He nodded. Somehow I was surprised. I had only imagined him walking down the dusty *piste*, like the first Blue Man I had seen. Or perched upon a camel.

'You find it odd?'

I smiled. 'No. Not really.'

'And so? Do you wish to come?'

'Yes,' I said. 'I'll come. Unless . . .' I stopped. Unless Etienne had arrived by then.

'Unless . . .?' he asked.

'Nothing,' I said.

'I will come for you in seven days, after breakfast,' he said.

'Will you bring us food tomorrow, Oncle Aszulay?' Badou asked, looking up at him.

Aszulay put his hand on the boy's head. 'Tomorrow I must work too many hours. But I have left food. Falida will cook it for you,' he said.

'Will Maman come home soon?' Badou then asked.

Aszulay nodded. 'Soon.'

I looked from Badou to Aszulay. 'I could go to Sharia Zitoun and check on Badou and Falida,' I said.

'Yes. Come to my house, Sidonie,' Badou said.

'As you wish,' Aszulay said.

'I'll see you tomorrow, then, Badou,' I told him, and he nodded.

Aszulay took Badou's hand, and I went inside my gate.

CHAPTER THIRTY

THE NEXT MORNING, CARRYING a basket of bread and a pot of *kefta* – minced, spiced lamb I'd made – I had Najeeb accompany me to Sharia Zitoun. It was just before eleven when I knocked on the gate.

Najeeb leaned against the outside wall, and I knew he would wait for me no matter how long I stayed.

I had to knock twice before Falida called out, cautiously, to ask who it was. When I told her, she pulled the gate open slowly.

'My lady is not here,' she said, her eyes wide.

'I know. But I've brought some food, and came to see Badou.'

She nodded, and let me into the courtyard.

Badou came down the stairs; again, I could see that his hair had been brushed and his face washed. 'Sidonie,' he said, looking at the pot, then back to me. 'Look,' he said, pushing his tongue behind his front tooth. 'My tooth is funny.'

I smiled, looking closer. 'It will come out in a little while,' I said. 'And another tooth will grow.'

'Will it hurt?'

'No. Or only a tiny bit.'

'Good,' he said, so trusting, again looking at the pot.

'Do you like *kefta*?' I asked, and he nodded, running ahead of me into the house. I followed him into the kitchen, and Falida followed me. The kitchen was spotless. 'You are looking after everything so well, Falida,' I said, and her mouth opened, as though surprised. Then she smiled. The smile transformed her face; although she was so thin, and had dark circles under her eyes, she would soon be very pretty.

'Falida gives me a bath every day when Maman is not here,' Badou said.

'I can see that,' I said, and smiled at Falida. She ducked her head as though embarrassed.

I dished out the food and we each carried a plate to the courtyard. I sat on the daybed while Badou chose the ground, setting his plate on the table in front of him. But Falida hung by the door. 'Come,' I said to her. 'Eat with us.'

She shook her head. 'I am not allowed,' she said.

I looked at her. 'Today you are,' I said, and she shyly came forward and sat on the ground beside Badou.

Before I left, I promised Badou and Falida that I would come the next day.

When I got back to Sharia Soura, Mena was in the courtyard. She had been quiet with me the evening before, after I'd returned from the gardens with Aszulay and Badou, and I wondered if she was feeling ill.

I hadn't seen her this morning, before I left for Sharia Zitoun, but now, as soon as I came in, she took a pair of her husband's shoes from where they sat near the gate. She pointed at them, then at me. I didn't understand at first, but she kept gesturing at the *babouches*, holding them to her chest, then pointing them at my chest. Finally she said *rajul*, the Arabic word for man.

She was asking where my husband was.

I struggled for a way to make her understand, gesturing towards the gate. Out there, I wanted to tell her. The man who will be my husband is out there, somewhere in Morocco.

Then she said Aszulay's name in a questioning tone.

I shook my head. 'Aszulay, *sadeeq*.' Aszulay, friend.

But Mena frowned, shaking her head. '*La, la*,' she said. No, no. She pointed at herself, and said *imra'a*, woman, followed by *rajul*. Then *sadeeq, la*.

I knew exactly what she was saying: *woman and man, friends, no*. I understood that this wasn't possible in her world. Of course I understood. And yet . . . how else could I describe Aszulay?

'*Sadeeq*, Mena, *na'am*. Friend, Mena, yes,' I said, looking at the gate again, thinking of Aszulay.

I wondered what he was doing, imagining him in Le Jardin Majorelle, lifting a huge earthenware urn with little effort.

But I reminded myself it was Etienne I should be thinking of.

When I went to Sharia Zitoun mid-morning the next day, I had Najeeb bring my new oils and easel and a canvas. I stopped first in one of the souks and bought a simple French children's book for Badou.

Falida had made a goat stew, and again we all ate together. Once more I realised how capable she was, and how different she seemed – both in appearance and temperament – without Manon's menacing presence.

As she and Badou looked through the book, she laughed aloud at one of the pictures, and poked Badou with her elbow. He poked her back, and laughed with her.

Manon would surely return any day. I couldn't bear to think of her continuing to mistreat this girl. But what could I do, other than tell her what I thought of her behaviour towards Falida. Although I knew it would do no good.

I read the book to them with Badou on my lap and Falida sitting beside me. Then I set up my easel and canvas under the shade of the jacaranda in the courtyard. I asked Badou to open my box of paints. He set the box on the ground and, with a look of concentration, snapped it open, reverently laying back the lid as if opening a sacred container. He watched as I took out tubes and squeezed them on to my palette. After a while he sat at my feet, again turning the pages of the book. He put his finger under each simple word, waiting until I glanced down and said the word, and he repeated it.

After three times through the little book he knew all the words.

The paint was brilliant on the canvas. There was a freedom with oils. Watercolours required much more delicacy, each fine line precise. But with the oils I could attempt bolder, freer strokes. I could cover my mistakes with ease. My arm was looser; I painted more from the shoulder than the hand.

And then there was a knock on the locked gate, and I jumped. 'Badou, it's Aszulay.'

Badou rose and ran to open the gate. When Aszulay came in, carrying a sack, he looked at me standing at my easel.

'I knew you were here when I saw Najeeb,' he said. 'I came on my midday break and brought more food.' He handed the sack to Falida.

I nodded. 'Falida made a goat stew, and we've eaten. Are you hungry?'

He nodded, and I looked at Falida. She went into the house. Aszulay came and stood beside me.

I was suddenly self-conscious; I had been trying to paint the way the rays of the sun shone through the leaves of the jacaranda, and now, to my own eyes, the work looked amateurish.

'You paint,' he stated.

'Yes. I brought my supplies here because the first wife at Sharia Soura doesn't want me to paint in the courtyard, and the light in my room is only right for a few hours. But I'm not used to painting in this heat.' I was babbling. 'Or using oils. I usually paint with watercolours; I always painted with watercolours in Albany,' I said, glancing sideways at him. 'My home. But the colours here – they're so brilliant and vibrant, and the subjects require more depth, more strength. I can't capture them the way I want to with watercolours. And of course there's an entirely different technique needed, and I haven't mastered it at all. It will take some time.' I put down the brush, wiping my hands on my kaftan. 'My hands are damp, and the paintbrush slips.'

'Is it ever hot like this in your part of America?' he asked. 'Albany. Where is this?'

'It's near New York City. In the state of New York.'

Aszulay nodded. 'Statue of Liberty,' he said, and I smiled.

'The summers there can be very hot, and humid. But nothing like this. And the winters are long and bitter. There's snow. Too much snow. It's cold. All white, and somehow untouchable,' I said, looking at my own rendition of the Moroccan sun. 'I just mean it's not . . . it's not like here. Warm and bright.'

'Do you miss it? Your home in New York?' Aszulay asked, not looking at me, but at the canvas.

I didn't answer. Did I miss it?

'I'm curious about places,' he added.

I thought that Aszulay was more than curious. He was inquisitive. Curious denoted a passiveness, a wondering. But nothing about Aszulay was passive. I thought, then, that he would not simply look at the world, but watch it. Also such a subtle difference, and yet it carried a loud implication.

'I have always been amazed that . . .' Aszulay stopped speaking. I waited. Was he searching for the proper French word? He looked intense, staring at the canvas as if mesmerised.

And then I heard it, and realised why he had so abruptly gone quiet. Birdsong, a soft trilling from the thick branches of the tree that spread its shade over us. Aszulay didn't look above, searching for the small creature responsible for the beautiful melody, but kept his gaze fixed on the canvas, almost, I think, unconsciously, for it appeared he was using all his concentration on the song.

I opened my mouth – should I say something, some non sequitur about the sound; ask what bird created this lovely trill?

The sound ceased, and I closed my lips. Aszulay blinked,

and then continued, as if that tiny lapse in his speech had not occurred. 'That there are animals in America who make their home in the snow.'

And I believe it was at that moment – watching this tall Blue Man, his face glistening in the sun, his forearms corded from recent digging, stopping his conversation to listen, somehow respectfully, to birdsong – that something inside me tore. Not a painful tearing, but a slow, careful breaking apart.

Falida brought a dish of stew to Aszulay. He sat on the stool nearby, eating and watching me paint.

When I returned to Sharia Soura a few hours later, I went to the roof. Mena was there with another woman. In Mena's lap sat a toddler; a baby nursed at the other woman's breast. They stopped talking when I arrived, both saying *slema* to me, which I now knew was the greeting used for non-Muslims, meaning a wish for welfare on this earth. I greeted them and then went to the other side of the roof. I looked out over the roofs of the medina, as always, but listened to Mena and her friend. I could make out a few of their phrases, and knew they were talking about the other woman's husband's mother, and then something about a dish containing eggplants, then talk of a sick donkey. The toddler wailed, suddenly, and I looked over. Mena laughed and held him, rocking him back and forth, putting a piece of bread into his mouth, her face soft and warm. I didn't know how long she'd been married, and wondered why she didn't yet have children. The other woman spoke, nodding at the child, whose cries were lessening, and Mena answered.

This was their lives. Caring for their families. And this was why I wasn't part of their world, maybe more so than the fact that I was a foreigner. They could never see me as a woman like them.

A crashing wave of grief came over me, new and powerful, unexpected. I remembered the loneliness after my father died. And then Etienne had come, and while we had shared the most intimate act of man and woman, perhaps, I suddenly saw, there was always an emptiness. He would never fully give himself to me. I knew now of the secret – his illness – he had kept from me.

Watching the baby at the woman's breast, I remembered the inexplicable joy I had felt at the knowledge of my own baby.

The wave threatened to overtake me, but this time it was for another reason. By choice, I had been insulated, protected, self-absorbed. Apart from my polio, I was the creator of my own life. And now I saw all that I had passed up: further schooling, friendships, being part of the church and the life of the community, helping others. Taking my painting further, perhaps with instruction. Meeting a man to share my life.

I was ashamed that I could have been so convinced by what I considered pride: pride at my acceptance of what boiled down to a lonely, rather meaningless life.

As the toddler wandered from Mena's lap, looking at me, I smiled at him, thinking of Badou. He had no hand in the fate that had given him a mother without the natural instinct to care for him. I thought of Manon's careless dismissal of him and his small concerns over having friends, or a puppy – small because he was a small child. But those concerns would grow, as he did. And when he was ever more capable of taking care of himself, Manon, caught up in her lovers and her indulgent habits, would give even less of herself than the tiny bits – a thoughtless smile, a rough caress – she now parcelled out to him.

As for Aszulay – it was obvious he was kind and caring to Badou, but how long would he continue to put up with Manon? What would happen to Badou if Aszulay was no longer involved with her?

I pictured Badou, with the smell of bread on his sweet breath, the way his loose tooth wiggled. After Aszulay had gone back to work and I had put away my paints, I reminded Badou that we would go with Aszulay to the *bled* before too long.

'What about Falida?' he asked, looking at her. 'Will you be lonely when we go, Falida?'

'Falida?' I asked, turning to face her. 'Where is your family?'

She shook her head. 'My mother is servant for lady. When I have nine years, my mother die, I go on street.'

I thought of the children begging in the square.

'Lady see me, say I stay Sharia Zitoun, work for her, she give me food.'

'You have nobody?'

She shook her head.

'Ali's *maman* is nice to her,' Badou said.

Falida nodded. 'Most nice lady. One time give me food.'

I picked up my bag. 'Come, both of you. Let's go with Najeeb to the souks. We'll buy a treat,' I said. 'Maybe some sweets. Would you like a new headscarf, Falida?'

She looked at me for a moment, and then put her head down. 'Yes,' she whispered.

'You are very good, Sidonie. Like Ali's *maman*,' Badou said, solemnly, and I put my arms around him and held him tightly.

At that moment I felt he needed me. Falida needed me.

I lay on my back on the roof. The air was luminous, the sky a clear blue. The sun on my face filled me with a strange, slow heat that was clean. I thought of Badou and Falida again, and something stirred in me. I didn't recognise it at first.

It was purpose. I was filled with purpose.

CHAPTER THIRTY-ONE

T HE NEXT DAY, MENA came to me and spoke slowly in Arabic. I understood enough: today, *hammam*, you come with me.

I had been living at Sharia Soura for two weeks, and while I'd been bathing with warm water in a dented tub in my room, I longed for a true bath. I knew the men and women of Marrakesh went to the *hammam*, the public baths, weekly, but I had no idea of the rituals involved.

When I nodded, Mena handed me two tin pails, and she carried two as well. Inside were several rough cloths she called *kese*, indicating that they were for scrubbing ourselves, as well as large rolled sheets of fabric – *fotas* – that she demonstrated wrapping around herself. I knew the Muslims' belief that it was sinful to gaze upon another's naked body, so assumed that even in the baths we would keep these around ourselves, and I was relieved. I knew the baths would be segregated, but I couldn't imagine how I'd feel bathing publicly.

There were more thick cloths, surely for drying.

Mena held a container of a sticky black substance to my nose. I smelled an unlikely combination of olive oil and roses, and Mena mimicked washing her hands: soap.

Carrying our pails and with Najeeb leading the way, Mena and I walked through the medina. Within ten minutes we stopped in front of an unmarked entrance and climbed up stone steps, hollow in the centre from generations of feet. There was a half-hidden door, so narrow that as I followed Mena through it my pails clanged against the frame. It was dim inside, with a strong odour of eucalyptus. The air was hot and steamy. An unveiled woman wearing a plain white kaftan came towards us.

Mena gave her two coins, and the woman called out. Two other women, their *fotas* tied around their chests and falling below their knees, came through a doorway towards us. Their hair was hidden beneath white wraps twisted on top of their heads.

'*Tayebas*,' Mena said, and I thought they must be helpers or assistants of some kind. We followed them through a honeycomb of dark, tiled rooms. There were only a few guttering lamps here and there, giving the whole atmosphere a wavering, netherworld sense. The walls were wet with moisture, and all around was the sound of dripping and splashing, and the humidity made my nose run.

We passed a room and a blast of heat struck me; I peered inside but could only make out shadowy figures stoking fires with dry palm leaves.

We were led into a room filled with wooden cubicles, some empty and some holding women's clothing. Mena immediately began to undress, removing first her *haik*, then her *dfina* and then her kaftan, placing them into one of the empty cubicles. She wore a white cotton petticoat; she pulled it off and stood in a long-sleeved singlet and thick baggy trousers, like pantaloons, with embroidered lace at the edges of the legs. I had no idea Moroccan women wore so many layers; how did they bear the heat? Mena turned from me, holding her *fota* to shield herself while she took off the last of her clothes. I did the same as she, wrapping the *fota* around myself and tying it over my chest in the same fashion as the *tayebas* who waited for us.

Then Mena and I again followed the two women, carrying our pails. We went into a large, misty room with high cisterns at one end. There were many women, mostly sitting on the stone floor, scrubbing themselves or being scrubbed by *tayebas*. Very young naked children crawled or toddled and splashed on the wet floor. I saw a baby of perhaps six months sitting in a bucket, smiling and gurgling as its mother dripped water over it. My *tayeba* urged me to stand near one of the cisterns, and then took one of my pails, filled it with water and poured it over me. I gasped, as it was much hotter than I had expected. She did it again and again, until I was completely wet. Then she filled the pail with hot water once more, and walked to an empty spot far on the opposite wall. The floor sloped down towards the cisterns, and all the water pooled down into a narrow trough at the foot of the cisterns. The *tayeba* indicated that I was to sit on the floor. My skin was slick from the water and steam. As soon as I sat down, the *tayeba* began to scrub me with the rough *kese* she took from my empty pail. I held my breath; it hurt. She scrubbed and scrubbed, holding up my arms as if I were a small child, pushing my head forward so she could get at the back of my neck. She scrubbed until I saw layers of dead skin rolling off my arms and legs, and my skin was reddened.

She kept rinsing me as she worked: scrubbing and rinsing, scrubbing and rinsing, going back to fill the pail when it was empty. Finally she sat down across from me, grabbed my left foot and put it in her lap, and pulled a brick-like stone from somewhere within the folds of her *fota*. She scraped my sole with such intensity that I flinched. When she was done she picked up my right leg, holding it out against my left, examining it. As she started on my right foot with the stone, she worked less briskly, stopping after only a few seconds, glancing at me and saying something in a questioning tone. I could only guess that she was asking if it hurt this shortened leg to work on it. I shook my head, and she bent over it and scraped with more fervour.

The light was so dim – only a few tiny lamps flickering on the walls – that I really couldn't discern the other figures in the room, although I could make out that a woman beside me was applying some sort of mushy substance to her armpits, and then quickly rinsing it off. I realised the substance somehow removed hair.

Finally my *tayeba* scooped out a handful of the black olive oil and rose soap I'd brought, and lathered me with it. It had the texture of oozing warm butter, and I closed my eyes, relaxing and enjoying the feel of her hands rubbing it all over me, reaching under my *fota* to get at my thighs. She lathered and rinsed, again and again, from my head to my feet. When there were no more traces of soap, she moved behind me. I felt her hands on my wet hair, and then she was scrubbing my scalp. I reached up and felt a grainy substance like clay smeared on my head. I smelled the bits on my fingers: lavender and, again, roses. When she'd rinsed it all out, she handed me my pails and led me to a second room and left me there.

This room was as hot as the first, but not as steamy. Here women, still wrapped in their *fotas*, were lounging about on the floor, chatting and laughing quietly. I saw then that the *hammam* was more than a ritual bath; it was, in a way, like the roofs, where women could be themselves. In this culture, where men and women moved in different spheres, and outside their homes women were expected to glide silently about, fading into the background, here there was freedom and camaraderie. I found a spot against the wall and spread a sheet from my pail on the warm stone floor and sat on it, my legs straight out in front of me, pushing my wet hair out of my eyes and looking at the women around me.

Skin tones ranged from pale to tawny to warm brown to rich coffee. I saw deep scars and strange growths and moles and patches of eczema. Every body, it appeared, bore some mark life had left. I looked down at my own body, and suddenly – perhaps for the first time – liked the warm tone of my skin. I also saw that it was rich, and flawless in its texture; I had never seen it as having its own beauty. I had always thought my skin too dark, unattractive in contrast to the pearl and creamy white and alabaster complexions of so many of the Saxons I had always compared myself to in Albany. I ran my hand up and down my own thigh, marvelling at its silky texture after being so intensely scrubbed. Then I rubbed my arms, letting my hands linger on my shoulders.

Nobody paid any attention to me, even with my shortened leg and heavy limp. I was just another woman in a moving sea of females, just another woman whose body demonstrated that she had lived.

Mena appeared and sat beside me. I smiled at her, and she smiled back. She looked at my legs, pointing at the right and talking. I couldn't think how to explain my polio other than the Arabic for *I am a child, very sick*. She nodded, holding up her hair from the back of her neck and showing me a deep, badly healed scar. I understood the word *father*, but she kept saying another word I didn't know, frowning, and I couldn't understand what she was trying to tell me about what had happened to her.

Then she made a sign for rocking a baby, raising her shoulders and nodding at me, and I knew she was asking if I had any children. I looked into her face, and then, for a reason I didn't understand, I nodded, putting my hands on my stomach, and then pointing upwards, hoping she understood what I was demonstrating.

She did. She did the same movement, and held up three fingers.

Three? She'd miscarried three times or had three children die? But she was so young. Instinctively I put my hands on hers, squeezing them. When she squeezed mine back, tears came into my eyes, and then I was crying.

I hadn't shared my loss with anyone – apart from telling Manon, in a cold way, that I'd lost the baby she denied had ever existed. And now, even though I couldn't use words to describe my sadness, it came again, fresh, with Mena. I knew she understood what I felt, and I knew what she must feel. Her eyes filled, and she kept nodding, kept squeezing my hands.

I saw that she cared about me, and suddenly I cared

about her, too. I thought of the middle-aged man with the withered arm, her husband, coming to her in the night. I thought of days spent under the watchful eyes of the stern Nawar, with all the power of the first wife in the house, surely not welcoming to a beautiful younger wife.

Where was Mena's family? Did she love her husband, or had she simply been sold to him in an arranged marriage? What had made the deep scar on the back of her neck? Why had she lost three babies? Would she have more? Eventually she let go of my hands, patting my forearm, and I wiped my face with the edge of my *fota*.

We sat side by side, our shoulders touching. I felt a deep sense of calm, after crying. How odd, I thought, that I would come halfway round the world to find the only friend – a young Moroccan wife – I'd had since I was sixteen years old.

My tranquillity increased; since the day I told Etienne about the baby I had been so overwhelmed, so unsure of everything, on my confusing, frightening and at times dangerous journey. And yet now that uncertainty was lessening.

I thought of how this new feeling, the feeling of something within me letting go, had begun as I watched Aszulay listen to the bird, and then later, as I lay on the roof in the sun, thinking of Badou and Falida and their expressions as I bought each of them a treat – another book for Badou, the wrap for Falida's hair. I thought of Aszulay, watching me as I laughed in Le Jardin Majorelle, and the whiteness of his teeth in his dark face. I again pictured his expression as he listened to the glorious song of the bird overhead in the courtyard at Sharia Zitoun. I grew drowsy, letting the peacefulness wash over me, and brought up my knees and rested my arms on them, putting my head on my arms and closing my eyes. I think I slept. After a while, Mena spoke, and I looked up. She gestured for me to come, and I went with her to a door leading to a passage; I assumed it would take us back to where we had left our clothing. But it was yet another room, and in this one women lay on the floor or sat on it cross-legged while other women rubbed their skin, pushing and kneading it the way I had kneaded dough to make bread.

Mena motioned for me to lie on my stomach, pointing at me, and then herself, and I understood that we were to do this to each other.

My immediate instinct was shyness, to shake my head, and say *la, la, shukran* – no, no, thank you – and yet . . . I didn't. This was the natural order of the *hammam*: the scrubbing and cleaning, the steamy room to relax, and then the massage. I spread my sheet and lay on the warm floor on my stomach, my head on my folded arms in the way of the other women. Mena knelt beside me and immediately began squeezing my shoulders.

I expected to be somehow shocked – or if not shocked, at least uncomfortable – at another woman's hands on my body, but as was becoming so clear to me, in the *hammam* it was all natural.

Again I closed my eyes.

It had been – how long? I mentally calculated – over four months since my body had last been touched: the February morning I had told Etienne about the baby. I tried to remember how Etienne and I had come together, tried to re-create his caresses. With Mena's strong, capable hands massaging my clean, damp back, and then my hips and buttocks through the *fota*, and finally my thighs and calves and feet, I fell into a languorous stupour. I kept thinking of Etienne's hands on me, of his body on mine, letting my imagination create scenes of intimacy.

As Mena touched my shoulder, I knew it was my turn to repay the favour, and opened my eyes, blinking, coming back to the fragrant warmth of the *hammam*.

As I knelt beside Mena and slowly rubbed her shoulders, I realised I hadn't been thinking of Etienne at all. The hands, and the body I imagined on mine, all had the faintest hint of blue.

Finally we went back to the dressing area, drying ourselves and putting on our clothes, and then, carrying the pails with our wet scrubbing cloths and sheets, we made our way back to Sharia Soura with Najeeb, as ever, shadowing us.

As we walked silently through the streets, I was more aware of my body, moist and clean and free under my kaftan, than I could ever remember. It was as if every nerve had been awakened, and although my breathing was slow, my heart felt as though it beat a little faster than usual.

I had a sense of well-being I didn't recognise.

I couldn't stop thinking about my unexpected fantasies about Aszulay, arguing that they had only been a reaction to the situation, and the sensuous nature of the *hammam*. That was all it had been.

Nothing more, I tried to convince myself.

★

I wanted to check on Badou and Falida that afternoon. Taking Najeeb – or perhaps it was the twin brother, as I couldn't tell them apart – I went to Sharia Zitoun. I knocked and called out, smiling, waiting for Falida or Badou.

But it was Manon who pulled open the gate.

I drew in my breath; although I knew she could come back any time, somehow I hadn't expected to see her.

'What do you want?' she asked.

I lifted the basket I carried. 'I brought some food. For Badou,' I said, knowing it was wiser not to mention Falida.

'You don't need to feed my child. I'm quite capable of that,' she said.

'I know. It's only because you were away, and Aszulay . . .' I stopped. I knew I should say as little as possible to Manon about Aszulay. About everything. I couldn't trust what she might say, or do.

'So you and Aszulay are becoming friendly. Is that it?' she asked, staring at me.

I was still standing in the doorway. 'As long as you're home, I won't worry about Badou, then.'

'You have no reason – no right – to worry about my child,' she said. 'Come in. I don't like the neighbours watching everything.'

I glanced around the empty street, then stepped inside. She closed the gate behind me, and slid the bolt. 'Where's Badou?' I asked. The courtyard and house were quiet.

'I have sent him and Falida to the souks,' she said. 'What have you brought?'

She took the basket from my hands and lifted the cloth, then took the lid from the pot of couscous with vegetable stew. 'You cook Moroccan food now?' she asked.

'I'll go then, and, as you say, you don't need the food.' I reached for the basket's handle, but she didn't let go.

'Badou has told me you're going to the country with him and Aszulay,' she said, no expression in her voice now. She still held the basket, her hand a few inches from mine. 'Why would you go? There's nothing to see but Berbers and their camels. Dust and filth. You couldn't drag me there.'

I didn't answer.

'You know he has a wife,' she said, with a wily smile, putting her thumb on top of my fingers, pinning them against the basket handle.

I felt a jolt at her words. I thought I had convinced myself he didn't. I hadn't thought of Aszulay with a wife when I fantasised about him in the *hammam*, only hours before.

Manon was lying, as she had lied about Etienne dying.

'Really?' I said. 'I was in his house. I saw no wife.' Although I'd had no intention of telling her I'd been in Aszulay's home, Manon had angered me with the way she said *you know he has a wife*, waiting to see my reaction. As if it should matter to me whether Aszulay was married or not; as if she knew – or suspected – what pictures had been in my head so recently.

Now her smile again disappeared as quickly as it came, and the pressure of her thumb on my fingers grew more intense. 'You went to his house,' she stated.

I looked at her but didn't attempt to move my fingers. 'I didn't see a wife,' I repeated.

'What were you doing there?'

'That's my business.' Suddenly I stood straighter. I saw that I had caused a reaction in *her*. I could match this woman. She couldn't harm me with her words.

'Of course you didn't see her there. She doesn't live in the city.'

What had Aszulay said, exactly? I tried to remember our conversation, when he had invited me to come with him and Badou. *Every few months I visit my family*. I pulled my fingers from under hers. 'And so? What of it if he has a wife?'

'She's a real country girl. So beneath him,' she said, with contempt. 'A nomad simpleton. She stays where she belongs, surrounded by her goats.'

'Oh?' I said, with feigned lack of interest.

'You still want to go to the *bled*? You want to go and watch Aszulay with his wife?'

'Why should it bother me?' I asked, troubled at this game we were playing. She was trying to make me jealous.

Suddenly I didn't want to continue the conversation. Perhaps I wouldn't go to the country with Aszulay now.

But that would mean Manon had won.

Keeping my voice even, I asked, 'Why do you dislike her so?' Of course I knew why she spoke of her like this. It was she who was jealous – of the wife. And of me, because Aszulay had shown me attention.

But she had Olivier. And she had Aszulay, in spite of his wife. Wasn't that enough? How much of Aszulay did Manon want, and need?

I tugged, slightly, on the handle of the basket, and she finally relinquished it. 'I'm going now,' I said, and turned to the gate.

'Oh, please, Sidonie, please wait,' Manon said, in a polite voice I hadn't heard before. 'I meant to give you something. I'll be right back.'

It was too suspicious; Manon had never treated me with any courtesy. But I was curious. She hurried up the stairs, and within a moment came back down, holding something in her hand.

'It's a pen and inkwell,' she said. 'An antique, used by scribes in the past.' She held it towards me. It was an egg-shaped silver container, the sides etched with designs. 'Look. Here's the pen,' she said, pulling on one end of the container, and a long metal implement slid out. Something dark – ink? – gleamed on its tip. She made as if to lay it in my right palm, but somehow its point jammed into my flesh, making a small nick in my skin. Instinctively I jerked away, and a bead of blood rose up on my palm.

'Oh, I'm so sorry,' she said, licking her fingers and putting them to the blood. With her fingers on the cut she murmured a line, very quietly.

I felt a chill. 'What did you say?' I asked, pulling my hand away and rubbing my palm against my *haik*.

Her look was intense. 'I just said how clumsy I was,' she answered, but I knew she lied. There was something in her look, something that I could almost call pleased.

I looked at the pen and inkwell she still held. 'I don't want it.' I turned and slid back the bolt of the gate and left without closing it or looking back.

I grew ill during dinner. The husband and sons had been served, and now I sat on cushions at the low table in the sitting room with Mena. Nawar was still in the kitchen, and we were waiting for her. But as I stared at the food on the table it blurred. My hand was aching, and I looked at it. My palm was swollen, the small wound puffy and dark red around the edges.

I wanted to lie down. I tried to get to my feet, pushing with my left hand on the table. Mena looked at me quizzically, then asked me something, but her voice came from far away.

'Sick,' I said in Arabic, unnecessarily, and Mena rose and came to me.

My face was wet with perspiration, and I wiped my forehead with the back of my right hand.

Mena put her hand on my wrist, looking at my palm. She held it for an instant too long. I understood her Arabic question: *what is this?*

I was trembling now. What did it matter? I needed to lie down, and tried to pull my hand away, but Mena held it firmly, asking the question again.

How could I explain, with so little Arabic? *Woman,* I said weakly. *Hurt me.*

'*Sikeen?*' she asked, and I shook my head, not understanding. She picked up a knife from the table with her other hand. '*Sikeen,*' she repeated, and gestured at my palm.

I shook my head, making a writing motion with my other hand. What was the Arabic word for pen, and why was Mena making a fuss over something so insignificant when I felt so sick?

'*Qalam?*' she said quickly, and this time I nodded.

'Yes. *Qalam*. Pen. She just poked me with a pen,' I murmured, knowing she couldn't understand my French. Again I tried to pull my hand away, but Mena held it firmly, calling out for Nawar and the servant. They both came from the kitchen, and Mena spoke rapidly, gesturing at my hand.

The old servant let out a wail, throwing her apron over her face. Nawar's eyes widened, and she let out a stream of Arabic, as if praying.

Mena spoke to me again, saying a word over and over, then turned to Nawar, and I heard Aszulay's name.

The room was too hot, too bright. Mena's voice and Nawar's prayers mixed with the old woman's wailing, and the sounds turned into gibberish, demonic shrieks. The room tilted, and the floor rose up to meet my cheek.

CHAPTER THIRTY-TWO

THE SMELL WAS STRONG, burning my nostrils, and I turned my head from it. But my forehead ached at the movement, and when I opened my eyes my sight was blurry. It took me a moment to understand I was lying on the daybed in the main room, and Mena was waving a small, smoking cloth bag in front of my face.

'*Besmellah rahman rahim*,' she kept repeating. She looked into my eyes and spoke again, and this time I understood the word *djinn*.

I wanted to shake my head, to say no, it's not a *djinn*, not an evil spirit. It must be something I had eaten earlier in the day, something that disagreed with me. I wanted her to stop waving the smoking bag over me, but couldn't think of any Arabic words except *la*. No.

And then I saw Aszulay. He came up behind Mena, and spoke to her. She kept her face turned away, pulling her headscarf down so that it completely covered her features, and answered in rapid, short sentences, again picking up my right wrist, her voice rising as she held it tightly.

Aszulay said one sentence, and Mena left.

He crouched beside me. 'Mena says a bad woman performed witchcraft on you.'

I tried to smile at the absurdity of it, but it was as though I was floating, as though I was in a painful dream. Was Aszulay really here, or was I just imagining him, as I had in the *hammam* earlier today? 'No. I'm just . . . sick. Maybe food . . .' My voice faded.

He picked up my hand. His fingers felt so cool around mine. My face was burning, my cheek throbbing, and I pressed the back of his hand to it, closing my eyes at the coolness. Then I put my lips on his skin, breathing, trying to smell indigo.

'What happened to your face, Sidonie?' His voice was soft. He didn't pull his hand away.

I opened my eyes, and suddenly his features stood clearly, so close, and I realised what I was doing. It wasn't a dream. I let go of his hand and ran my fingers over my scar, then saw that he was looking at my other cheek. I moved my fingers to touch it; it felt swollen. 'I fainted. I must have hit my face,' I said, embarrassed. 'I'm sorry they brought you here.' I struggled to sit up, but was too weak. 'I'll be all right tomorrow. After I sleep.'

'Who is the woman you told Mena about?' Aszulay said then, gently pressing on my shoulder, and I lay down again.

'Manon. I went to see if Badou and Falida were all right, earlier today,' I said. 'They weren't there. Manon was.'

'And? What happened to your hand?'

I made a small sound, as if attempting to laugh. 'It's nothing. She wanted to give me a gift. I don't know why; she doesn't like me, does she?'

He sat perfectly still.

'It was an old pen and inkwell. She handed it to me, and the point of the pen stuck me. That's all.'

Something in his face changed. 'Perhaps I should take you to the clinic in the French Quarter,' he said.

'What? No,' I said. 'I have some ointment in my room. Maybe that will help.' My teeth were chattering; no longer did I feel feverish, but now shook with a chill.

Aszulay turned his head and called something, then picked up my hand again, bringing it close to his face and studying it. Now I saw that my palm was even more swollen, the cut already festering. I tried to bend my fingers, but couldn't.

The old servant's face appeared over Aszulay's shoulder; he spoke to her and she left. 'She'll bring you a blanket. And I've told her to send one of the boys to fetch something from my house,' he said. 'You need more than blessings and burning herbs.' His eyes left my face, moving lower, and then he reached out. 'Or amulets.'

I looked at what he held: a circle with an eye on a gold chain. It was Mena's; I'd seen it when she undressed in the *hammam*. She must have put it on me tonight.

Aszulay let go of the amulet and stood as the servant came near, muttering, holding a blanket out at arm's length. Aszulay took it from her and tucked it over me.

I dozed off and on for the next little while, aware of Aszulay sitting on a low stool beside me. Then I felt him pick my hand up again. It was hard to open my eyes, but I did, and saw his head bend over my hand as he held something between his thumb and index finger. There was a sudden deep sting, and I tried to pull away, but he held my hand firmly. I moaned as I felt him prodding and digging in my palm with something hot and sharp.

He murmured something in Arabic, something with a soothing sound, as if telling me it would soon be over, or that he was sorry.

I held my breath.

Finally he lifted his head, and I let out a soft cry of relief as the pain stopped. 'I have it,' he said, but I didn't understand what he meant, nor did I care.

But immediately my hand burned, and I sucked in my breath and lifted my head to see what was happening. Aszulay was pouring something smelling of disinfectant over my palm. 'It hurts,' I said, and he nodded.

'I know. Soon it will stop.' He wrapped clean gauze around my hand. 'Now drink,' he said, and held a glass to my mouth. The drink was syrupy, but couldn't hide a bitterness. 'It will take away the pain and help the fever.'

I drank it all and lay back again, my hand throbbing terribly. Aszulay sat beside me, silent, and at some point – I had no idea of the time that passed – I realised I was no longer in pain, and a sleepy peacefulness came over me. 'It doesn't hurt any more,' I murmured.

'Good,' Aszulay said, stroking my forehead with his hand.

I knew I was falling asleep. 'I thought of your hands today,' I whispered, 'in the *hammam*,' and then I remembered nothing more.

When I awoke the next morning, I lay for a few minutes, blinking in the dimness, wondering why I wasn't upstairs in my own room.

And then I lifted my hand, seeing the neat gauze wrapping.

Mena came in with a glass of tea, and I struggled to sit up. '*Kayf al-haal?*' she asked, handing me the glass.

I accepted it awkwardly with both hands, mindful of my palm. 'I am good,' I said in Arabic, answering her question. I did feel all right; I was no longer feverish, and my hand only felt a little tender and stiff.

I thought of Aszulay bending over me. 'Aszulay?' I said. 'He is here?'

'*La,*' Mena said, shaking her head.

Within an hour I felt well enough to go up to my room and change my clothes and brush my hair, although I was slightly shaky and my movements were clumsy because of my wrapped hand. The bruise on my cheek was a dark bloom, but only hurt if I touched it.

I was sitting in the courtyard shortly after that when Aszulay came in. I was shy as I looked at him; how much of last night had happened, and how much had been in my head? My memories of the night before were mixed in with my thoughts of him in the *hammam*.

But he smiled at me, and I smiled back. 'You look much better,' he said, nodding. 'I stayed until early this morning, but when I saw you no longer had a fever and the swelling was less, I left.' He crouched in front of me and took my hand, gently unwrapping the gauze. 'Yes, look. You will be all right now. The poison is gone.'

'Poison?' I said, looking at my upturned hand, resting lightly in Aszulay's. My palm had returned to its normal size, apart from the small sore in the middle.

I suddenly remembered that I had pressed my lips to his hand the night before. But he knew I had been delirious, and couldn't be responsible for my actions.

Aszulay rewound the gauze. 'Leave the wrapping for today, to keep the hand clean,' he said. 'By tomorrow it will be fine.'

'Poison?' I said again. 'What poison?'

He stood and looked away. 'I took out a small shard of something from the wound. Bone. Some older pens had points made of sharpened bone.'

I thought of Falida in the graveyard. Her ghoulish quest for what Manon wanted. I shuddered as if the chill of last night had returned. 'But why would old bone cause an infection?'

He looked back at me. 'Old bone alone wouldn't. Perhaps . . . if it had been dipped in some substance . . .' He stopped. 'I don't know with certainty.'

'And if you hadn't taken it out? If Mena hadn't sent for you?'

'In two days I'll take Badou to the country,' he said, clearly changing the subject, not wanting to answer my question. 'Do you still wish to go?'

I nodded, understanding that he wouldn't speak any further about what had happened to my hand. I couldn't ask him if he believed – as I did now – that Manon had intentionally tried to harm me. When she knew that I was going off with Aszulay and her son, she wanted to stop me.

Manon had never wished to give me the pen and inkwell as a gift. She had done what she did on purpose, and it was horrible and frightening.

I didn't ever want to see her again.

I also didn't want to think about Badou and Falida, alone with a woman capable of such evil.

Two days later, Aszulay came to Sharia Soura with Badou. Badou waited in the street while Aszulay came into the courtyard. I was draping my *haik* over my head when Aszulay said, 'Sidonie,' in such a way that I stopped, the cloth part-way over my head.

'Yes?' I asked. He looked odd. Perhaps uncomfortable. I had never seen Aszulay uncomfortable.

'You're certain you wish to go?'

I nodded. 'Yes. Why?'

'At Manon's . . .' He stopped, then continued. 'When I went to get Badou—'

'No,' I said, and he fell silent. I imagined the conversation they must have had. Surely Aszulay would have brought up what Manon had done. They must have quarrelled. Now Aszulay would tell me what Manon had said, or try to explain her actions. I knew she would have asked Aszulay if I was going with them. She would have expected him to say no, that I was ill. She didn't want me spending time with Aszulay; of course she was jealous of me. And when she found out that I was still going . . . In the darkest part of me I was pleased to imagine her anger when she thought she had been unable to hurt me. I wanted her to think that I was stronger than she.

'Whatever happened at Manon's, I don't want to know,' I said. 'I want to leave all thoughts of Manon and Sharia Zitoun behind. Just for two days, Aszulay. Please don't tell me anything about her.'

He looked at me for a long moment, as if debating with himself, and then, almost reluctantly, nodded. We went out through the gate, and he and Badou and I walked through narrow medina streets I hadn't yet discovered. I felt completed recovered, and carried a woven bag. Aszulay had two large burlap sacks slung over his shoulder.

As we passed through a covered souk and then under a high arch in the medina wall, there was instantly a subtly different atmosphere. The people's dress was slightly altered, and many of the women, although draped in head shawls, weren't covered. The buildings were higher and narrower, the doors more richly ornamented.

'Where are we, Aszulay?' I asked.

'The Mellah,' he said. 'The Jewish Quarter.' He looked at me. 'You know about Morocco's Jews?'

I shook my head. Etienne had never mentioned them.

'*Melh* means salt. After the battles – in ancient times in Marrakesh – the Jews were given the task of salting the enemies' head. The heads were placed on the city walls, as was the custom.'

I frowned, and thought of the genesis of the name for D'jemma el Fna.

'Now the Jews – especially the Jewesses – are important to the wealthy Moroccan women. They provide many services for those wives unable to leave their homes, bringing them high-quality cloth, making their clothing, showing them samples of jewellery to purchase. They are welcome within the harems.'

I looked around the city within a city, my ear discerning a different language. As we passed an open gateway, a crowd of small boys sat shoulder to shoulder on rough wooden benches in a courtyard. They held little books and rocked back and forth, reciting in a babble of high voices.

'Look, Oncle Azulay, *l'école*,' Badou said, tugging on my hand to make me stop. 'Those boys are at school.'

Aszulay didn't slow down, and as I urged Badou away from the scene, he let go of my hand and ran alongside Aszulay. 'Soon I will go to school, yes, Oncle Aszulay?'

Aszulay said nothing. Badou was still looking up at him as we walked.

'Why doesn't he go to school?' I asked. 'He's old enough, isn't he?' I thought of the boys I had seen, surely no older than Badou, walking together in threes and fours, their hands held by older brothers as they manoeuvred through the twisting alleys of the medina.

Some of the children in the Jewish school had looked even younger than Badou.

But Aszulay shook his head slightly, and I sensed I should say no more. 'Come this way,' he said, turning sharply into a dark, narrow passage. 'I have my truck parked outside the Mellah's walls.'

Finally we went through another series of gateways, and Aszulay unlocked a wide set of double doors. Inside the enclosure was a vehicle with a box-like shape. It was dusty and dented; like all the vehicles I had seen in Morocco, it appeared to have been driven hard.

Aszulay unlocked the doors, putting the sacks into the back, which was covered with canvas. I walked around the truck, running my hand over its bumpers.

'What is this vehicle? I don't recognise it,' I said.

Aszulay looked at me over the hood of the car. 'Fiat la Camionnette, 1925.'

'Ah. A Fiat,' I said, nodding. 'I haven't seen a Fiat truck before, although I've read about them. We had a . . .' I stopped. I was about to tell him about the Silver Ghost. 'I had a car,' I said.

'Does everyone in America have a car?'

'Oh, no,' I said. 'Not everyone.'

'Come, Badou,' he said now, 'climb in.'

Badou clambered in the driver's side, and, on his knees, grabbed the steering wheel and violently twisted it from side to side. 'Look at me, Sidonie, look! I'm driving,' he said, grinning. His left front tooth was hanging by little more than a thread. I smiled back, setting my bag at my feet. Badou slid beside me on the bench seat as Aszulay got in. He wound the end of his turban over his nose and mouth and turned the key. With a great cough and then a roar, the Fiat came to life.

We stopped on the outskirts of Marrakesh; Aszulay went to a stall and came back with a crate holding four live chickens. He put the crate in the back of the truck, which was separated from the seat by a canvas curtain. The chickens clucked and squawked.

When we were outside of Marrakesh, off the road and on to a *piste*, I asked Aszulay how long it would take to get to his family's home.

'Five hours, if there are no problems,' he said, his voice muffled by his turban. 'We're going south-east, into the Ourika valley. It's less than seventy kilometres from Marrakesh, but the *pistes* are very difficult to drive.' I watched him for a moment, enjoying the spectacle of a Blue Man of the Sahara driving the jolting truck instead of leading a camel. 'My family lives in a small village there.'

The afternoon was blue and red and white: the sky so

clear and large overhead, the earth around us its distinctive colour, the snow-capped mountains towering in the distance. Aszulay uncovered his mouth and sang an Arabic song, his voice low and rich, and Badou clapped his hands in time to the rhythm, joining in on the chorus.

What would Etienne think of me if he could see me now? I was no longer the woman he had known in Albany.

Then again, he was not the man I thought I knew, either.

I didn't want to think of Etienne. I joined Badou in the hand-clapping. Jolting along in this truck on the narrow track, I thought I might feel insignificant surrounded by such immenseness. And yet I didn't feel small; instead, the grandness of the sky and mountains filled me with something that was almost, I told myself, the opposite.

The *pistes* were, as Aszulay said, difficult, even more treacherous than those running through the land I had travelled over with Mustapha and Aziz. There were winding hairpin curves and patches where only stony gravel disappeared through the lower foothills of the Atlas. We had to traverse between donkeys, horses and camels. At times we bounced and swayed, Badou sliding back and forth between us, sometimes laughing at the sensation when we hit a particularly large bump and he was thrown up and then back down.

After about three hours we stopped at a group of tall feathery trees. There was a shallow, fast-running spring, which bubbled from a rock formation, and a man and woman – Berbers, for her face was uncovered – crouched at the edge of the water, filling skin bags. Two donkeys, bulging straw panniers on their backs, shifted impatiently on their short, strong legs, braying until they were led to the stream and allowed to drink.

Three small children – a girl and two boys, one little more than a toddler – splashed about in the shallow water, laughing, and as I lifted Badou down I saw him watching them. I left my *haik* and veil in the truck.

I took Badou's hand and went to the stream, crouching and cupping my hands, drinking, and he did the same. I ran my wet hand over his face; it was dusty from the ride. I noticed, then, that Aszulay was striding off. He went over a slight rise and disappeared. Badou and I sat near the water, and I took bread and cheese and walnuts from my woven bag, and while we ate, Badou solemnly watched the other children.

Suddenly one of them, the older boy near Badou's age, ran towards us, and spoke to Badou in Arabic. Badou shook his head. The boy ran back to the donkeys and reached into one of the panniers, pulling out an orange. He came back to Badou, squatting in front of him, and peeled the orange. When he had finished, he broke it in half and handed one of the halves to Badou.

Badou looked at it, and then at me. 'Take it, Badou,' I said, and he took it from the boy's dirty hand. 'Tell him thank you,' I said then, and Badou murmured to the boy. I put a handful of walnuts into Badou's hand, motioning to the boy. Badou gave them to him, and the boy rammed all of them into his mouth at once, then said something, spitting around the nuts; again Badou shook his head, and the boy ran off to join his brother and sister.

'You don't want to play with them?' I asked, knowing

that was what the boy had asked, and Badou shook his head. He didn't eat the half-orange, but held it in his fist. Juice seeped from between his fingers.

The children picked up stones from the edge of the water, tossing them high into the air and watching them land back in the stream, creating tiny splashes. Badou stood, pulling apart sections of the orange and eating them, one by one, and then picked up a stone that lay at his feet. He mimicked the children then, throwing his stone high into the air and watching it hit the water. He did it again, edging closer to the children. My heart beat a little faster; I wanted, so badly, for Badou to be unafraid, to join them, to play like an ordinary boy.

Eventually he waded in up to his knees, standing with the other three, tossing stones as they did.

I rose, pleased, and wandered further along the edge of the stream, stooping to pick up smooth wet stones that gleamed in the sun. I looked back at Badou, and saw him still standing in the water, but now watching the smallest of the children, the toddler. He had left his older brother and sister and was following his mother, holding on to the back of her robe as she moved about. I wondered where Aszulay had gone.

Badou resumed playing; in a few moments the mother called out, and the two children ran out of the water to where she had laid out their food.

Badou looked for me, and then splashed along the edge of the stream, smiling, his tongue pushing on his loose tooth so that it wiggled. When he stopped in front of me, I stooped and hugged him; I felt a surge of pride for Badou, for his small act of bravery. He smelled of orange.

'Help me find some pretty stones,' I told him, but he didn't. Instead, as I slowly moved along the bank of the stream, he stayed behind me, holding the back of my kaftan.

Badou and I sat in the shade under the trees. The family had finished their meal, and the father lay sleeping in the sun. The mother sat with her back against a tree, holding the youngest child; he had fallen asleep on her shoulder. The other two children sat cross-legged, facing each other and piling small stones. The donkeys were grazing at the tough vegetation growing up around the rocks. There was no sound but the slight splashing of the stream, the rustling of the long, slender leaves of the trees in the slight breeze, and the rasping tear of the donkey's teeth.

Badou lay down and put his head in my lap; I saw the shadow of his long eyelashes on his cheeks as his eyes closed.

We were sitting like this when Aszulay returned. 'He's sleeping,' I said, quietly, my hand on Badou's head. 'Would you like some food?'

He shook his head. 'Soon we must go, so we won't arrive too late,' he said, looking up at the sky. He appeared distracted, perhaps a little distant. He splashed water on his face and neck, and then took more handfuls and wet his hair. It shone blue-black in the sun, tiny droplets trembling on the thickness of it. He sat beside us then.

'You asked about Badou going to school,' he said, looking down at the boy. 'But it's not a possibility.'

'Why not?'

'His mother hasn't made him a Muslim. He's a nonbeliever, so he can't enter a mosque, or a madrasa – the school – to learn the Koran,' he said. 'And he isn't allowed into the private French schools in La Ville Nouvelle, because Manon can't claim full French ancestry. There is nowhere Badou will be welcomed to learn.'

'But . . . surely Manon wants him to be educated,' I said. 'Why doesn't she at least teach him herself? She's an intelligent woman, if nothing else.' I didn't mean for the sarcasm to be so apparent, but there it was. I was always, always aware that Aszulay must be in love with her, in spite of her cruelty and devious nature.

Aszulay simply looked at me, then put his hand on Badou's shoulder, shaking him gently.

'Now we'll go on,' he said, and, sleepily, Badou got to his feet and we all went back into the truck.

As we drove away, following the same rise Aszulay had taken, we passed a cemetery. What was it doing here, in the solitude of the *bled*? The small pointed stones that rose on the gently elevated slope reminded me of uneven rows of jagged teeth. I wanted to ask Aszulay about his wife; I realised I grew more and more anxious the further we drove. What would she think of me, arriving with her husband and another woman's child?

Suddenly I wished I hadn't come. I should have listened to that small instinct, at Manon's, when she announced that he had a wife.

'Less than one hour, and we will arrive,' Aszulay said.

I nodded, looking out the side window.

CHAPTER THIRTY-THREE

'OURIKA VALLEY,' ASZULAY SAID, a short time later, as we drove through gardens and plots of cultivated land. There were date groves, and intoxicating scents of mint and oleander. I recognised apricot and pomegranate and fig; it was a verdant valley. The sides towered above the masses of fields on the valley floor, and green crops undulated in the gentle breeze. Also on the sides of the hills running down from the High Atlas were hamlets made of the pounded red clay of the earth, mixed with straw: *pise*, Aszulay called them. Everywhere on the meandering *piste* near these small villages were women, trudging with sacks or bundles of sticks on their backs, often balancing babies in slings on one hip or on their chests. I kept swallowing, and my head ached slightly. I put my hand to my forehead, and Aszulay glanced at me.

'It's the height,' he said. 'Drink water.' I took the goat-skin of water from behind the seat and drank, giving some to Badou and offering it to Aszulay, but he shook his head.

The valley grew narrower but kept rising gently. And then the *piste* came to an end. As we stepped out of the truck, I heard violently rushing water. Aszulay took the sacks from the back of the truck and slung them over one shoulder, balancing the crate of scolding chickens on the other. He motioned for me to bring my bag. 'You don't need your *haik* or veil here,' he said, and so I again left them in the truck, wearing only my kaftan, and followed him, holding Badou's hand, towards the sound of the water. It was a convergence of seven narrow waterfalls flowing down a rocky scree to a village below. We started our way carefully down the path, worn by hoofs and feet.

Within a moment I knew I wouldn't be able to keep my balance, and picked up a long, firm stick from beside the path. Badou's smooth-soled little red *babouches* were slipping on the pebbly slope, and he stopped, clutching my kaftan for support. Aszulay looked back at us; he'd taken off his own *babouches* and thrown them down ahead of him, and was making the descent in bare feet.

'Wait,' he said, and, at a half-run reached the bottom of the slope. He set the sacks and crate on the ground. Then he stooped, taking a small pinch of the earth, and put it on his tongue. I watched, curious. I didn't know why he tasted the dirt, and yet something moved in me; it signified his connection to this red earth. He came back for us, scooping Badou into the crook of one arm. Badou put his arm around Aszulay's neck. Aszulay held out his hand to me, and I put mine into his, although I still used the stick with my other hand. We went slowly down the rough path. Aszulay's hand was able to completely close around mine; it was warm and dry. I knew mine was damp with nervousness, not only about keeping my balance, but about what was to come when we entered the village.

At the bottom of the slope he dropped my hand and set Badou down and again picked up the sacks and crate.

The village, climbing haphazardly up the side of a sloping hill, was one of the terraced settlements of *pise* houses with flat roofs. Because the hill and the houses were the same reddish-brown earth, and the houses clung to it as if dug out of the very hill itself, there was a chameleon sense about it.

At the foot of the hill was a circle of tents of woven animal hair. I hadn't seen them as we approached; like the village, they were indistinguishable from the earth. Camels sat on their knees in the dust, gazing straight ahead with their usual aloofness. Donkeys brayed and roosters crowed.

Footpaths wound up into the terraced village. A few children on their way down greeted Aszulay with shouts of recognition. I watched Badou as the children came towards us, and again, as at the stream, he held back, staying close at my side. We walked upwards, through the village, and people came from their doorways, calling to Aszulay. He continually set down his burdens, greeting the men by kissing three times on the cheeks as they hugged, chest to chest. They all stared at me, and I was uncomfortable. The women here wore long, modest dresses, but they resembled flocks of colourful birds; their dresses were embroidered around the hem and sleeves and neckline, sometimes flashing with small bits of silver jewellery. Some of the dresses were hooked on the shoulders with brass or silver clasps, which I knew, from discovering them in the souks, were called *fibulae*. The women, their faces uncovered, wore shawls draped over their heads, but these, while mostly black, were all embroidered with bright designs and flowers. Elaborate silver and amber jewellery was on their necks and wrists. They were all barefoot, and their feet and hands were decorated with henna.

I tried not to stare at them, but they were wonderful to look at. Some had streaks of saffron painted on their faces, or blue patterns tattooed on their chins or in the middle of their foreheads. I thought of Mena's tattoos, and knew she was from the mountains. Many of the forehead tattoos were two diagonal lines crossing each other at the top. Others had a line running straight from their lower lip to the bottom of their chin, with tree-like branches radiating from it. Most of the tattoos had a geometric design. I could only assume that as well as being a thing of beauty, they designated a tribal identity.

We continued our gentle upward climb along the winding paths. Aszulay finally stopped in front of a house, setting down the crate and sacks and calling out, and an older woman and two younger ones came from inside. While the two younger women wore the same decorated dresses and headscarves and jewellery as the other village women, their faces were not tattooed, and the older woman wore a simple dark blue robe and headscarf. Aszulay put down the sacks and crate and embraced the older one.

He looked at me and said something to her, but he wasn't speaking Arabic; I recognised nothing he said. Then he looked at me and said, '*Ma maman.*'

I nodded, anxious, unsure of whether to smile. His mother looked at me curiously, speaking in a questioning tone to Aszulay.

He answered, briefly, gesturing at Badou, and whatever he said satisfied his mother, for she just murmured something over and over, something I took to mean *yes, I see*.

I reached into my bag and pulled out a small bone teapot. I knew enough about Moroccan customs, by now, to bring a gift when visiting. I gave Aszulay's mother the teapot. She took it, turning it over in her hands and nodding seriously.

'And my sisters,' he said, pointing to the two other women, who looked to be in their mid- to late twenties. 'Rabia, and Zohra.'

I had expected one of them to be his wife.

As his sisters looked at me, I said, '*Ismi* Sidonie,' telling them my name, and then added, respectfully, '*Assalaam alykum*, peace be upon you.' I didn't know whether they would understand the Arabic greeting, but they both replied, in hushed and rather shy tones, *wa alykum assalaam*, and peace be upon you.

I gave each of them a small ceramic painted dish.

Badou stood beside me; the women paid no attention to him.

They all had a similar look: thin, sun-darkened faces with high cheekbones, dark flashing eyes touched with kohl, and strong white teeth. Zohra, the younger sister, had a dimple in her left cheek that gave a certain charm to her smile. In the folds of Rabia's dress a baby with kohl-lined eyes wiggled, peeking its head out. It stared at Badou; its eyes were blue, like Aszulay's.

'A baby, Badou,' I said, as if he didn't recognise what it was. But I was tense, not sure how to behave, and this gave me something to focus on. 'Is it a boy or a girl, do you think?'

He shrugged. I sensed he was experiencing a similar

440

feeling to mine, even though he'd been here before. Aszulay's mother patted his shoulder, saying something to him, and he smiled, a small, tight smile.

'My nephew is Izri,' Aszulay said, answering my question. 'Eight months. Rabia's fourth child. Zohra has two daughters.' He opened the neck of one sack and drew out lengths of cloth and two necklaces of silver and amber, which he handed to his sisters. From the other sack he pulled out a large brass cooking pot for his mother. They all nodded, murmuring and looking at each other's gifts, smiling their thanks at Aszulay.

Then they looked back at me. Aszulay's mother spoke. 'My mother welcomes you,' Aszulay said. 'The village is preparing a special meal in honour of the other guests, those in the tents below. They're from a distant village, but have travelled to visit members of their families living here now. We came at a good time.'

'*Shukran*,' I said, looking at Aszulay's mother. 'Thank you.' Again, I didn't know if she could understand anything I said, but I couldn't remain mute. I also wondered when I would meet Aszulay's wife. These women – his mother and sisters – appeared curiously calm and accepting of my presence.

'The language of the village – the people are Amazigh Berbers – is Tamazight. With my mother I speak our old language of the Sahara, Tamashek, the Tuareg language. The villagers understand only a little Arabic, basic phrases. They're isolated here, not seeing many strangers.'

Standing beside Aszulay, clutching my woven bag, I was very aware that I was not only a stranger, but a foreigner. I shook my head at all he'd just told me.

'It's complicated. But don't worry. I've taught Zohra a small amount of French. She's the scholar of the family.' He smiled at the younger woman and spoke, obviously telling her what he'd said, for she put her hands on her cheeks as if blushing, and then swatted his arm playfully. It was clear that the village people were informal and comfortable with each other in a way I hadn't seen among the people of the cities of Morocco.

Aszulay's mother patted my hand, in much the way she had patted Badou's shoulder, and this time I smiled at her.

A small crowd of children now joined Aszulay and Badou and me as we walked about the village. The houses were all the same, with small attached outbuildings: sheds for animals and storage, and latrines. While the boys ran along beside us, the girls were skittish, stealing glances at me but immediately turning away if I looked back. They eventually left us, scampering off to chase each other, shouting and laughing. Dogs jumped at their knees, barking. A herd of black goats behind a thorny enclosure bleated in a steady accompaniment. At the small river created by the waterfalls, some women washed clothes, pounding them against the rocks, and others filled goatskin water bags.

'Is this where you grew up?' I asked Aszulay, as we stopped to watch a group of playing children.

'No,' he said. 'We didn't live in a village. As Blue Men, we lived on the other side of the High Atlas, across the Tizi-n-Tichka pass, in the south-western Sahara that borders Mauritania. The women lived in tents while the men traded throughout the Sahara.'

'But why is your family here now?'

'When I was twelve, my father died,' he said. 'It's almost impossible for a nomad woman to live without a husband. She's forced to depend on the kindness of other nomads, and in hard times, it's even more challenging. As it is all over Morocco, a woman alone is not looked at with respect.'

I knew he wasn't thinking of me, but still, it made me wonder again how I was viewed here.

'So my mother and I and my sisters – they were very young then, babies, really, and have forgotten the Tuareg language – came here to live. But it was difficult; I was the man of my family, but still young.' He stopped, as if remembering. 'It took some time for us to be accepted.'

He looked around. 'In spite of that, it was a better place for us than the desert,' he said. 'And later, when I left, I always knew where they were, and could bring them what they needed when it was possible. Otherwise I would never know where they were; nomad families can go years without seeing each other, passing maybe a few miles apart, but not knowing. We might have lost each other.'

Suddenly I tried to visualise him as a child. Had he been like the nomad children I saw today, with their matted hair and ragged clothes, their limbs sturdy, their knees and elbows scabby from playing on the rough gravel of the countryside, seeming happy-go-lucky as they chased each other and played with loud voices? How had he moved from living in a goat-hair tent, travelling in a camel caravan, with no schooling, to the man he was now, with his mastery of French and his European mannerisms?

I looked down at Badou, always close at my side. Although in Marrakesh I had thought him to look much the same as the other city children, here he stood out because of his shining hair and his clean djellaba and cotton trousers and bright *babouches*.

But his face did not reflect the light-hearted frolic of these Berber children. He stayed back, obviously wanting to join in, and yet somehow fearful.

Aszulay called out, and one of the older girls – perhaps eight or nine – came to him. She kept her face turned from mine as Aszulay spoke to her. Then she took Badou by the hand and led him towards the other children. Badou walked stiffly at first, as though reluctant to go with the girl, but she chattered to him and he looked up at her, his eyes wide.

'Is your language – Tam . . . I'm sorry, what is it?'

'Tamashek.'

'Yes. And the other one, the Berber language these people speak – are they taught in your schools?'

Aszulay looked down at me, smiling slightly. 'The Berbers have no schools,' he said. 'And the languages are only oral, nothing written.'

'So . . . you had to learn Arabic when you went to Marrakesh?'

'I already knew it, from the caravan routes. We had to be able to trade with many peoples.'

'Can he understand what the other children are saying?' I asked, watching Badou with the girl, and Aszulay shook his head.

'Our visits are too infrequent. But children understand in ways other than language,' he said. 'Children everywhere are children.'

The girl took Badou to the shade of a house where a

dog lay on its side. The dog lifted its head as they approached, and as the girl leaned down, one corner of the animal's lip lifted as if menacing. And yet the girl paid no attention, and I saw, as she straightened, that she cradled a tiny puppy. She carefully put it into Badou's arms as the mother dog sat up and watched, alert.

Badou looked down at the puppy, then lowered his face to rub it against the little dog's tawny fur. He shifted so that he held the pup on its back in the crook of one arm, then stroked it with his other hand, lifting its tiny paws and examining the minuscule flap of an ear. The girl, bossy now, her head waggling as she said something to Badou and pointed at the mother dog, took the pup out of Badou's arms and returned it to the female, who sniffed at her puppy and then, obviously satisfied, lay down again, flopping her head against the soft earth as the puppy nuzzled back in amongst its siblings.

The girl took Badou's hand again, this time leading him to the other children, and, as I watched, Badou's face relaxed and he smiled, a tentative smile, and then joined in the game of tossing pebbles into what looked like concentric circles drawn in the earth.

'He is all right now,' Aszulay said. 'He forgets, between the months we come, how to play with other children.'

I thought of Badou's reticence in joining the nomad children at the stream, and remembered him watching the boys playing ball in the street, forbidden to play with them.

Zohra approached us then, and spoke to Aszulay. He looked at me. 'Zohra will decorate you with henna, if you wish,' he said.

I looked down at my own sun-darkened hands.

'It is a gesture of friendliness. Of acceptance,' Aszulay said, and I was ashamed for my hesitancy.

'*Naam*,' I said, looking at Zohra. Yes.

At the foot of the village, in the middle of the circle of tents was a fire. Over it hung a huge, bubbling black cauldron. A very short old woman, her face a myriad of lines and damp with sweat, stood with one hand on her hip, regularly stirring whatever was in the pot with a stick almost as tall as she.

Other women gathered around us as we sat in the doorway of one of the tents; Aszulay had gone to drink tea with the men. The women all sat gracefully, cross-legged, with their skirts draped over their knees. I couldn't do the same because of the inflexibility of my right leg, and had to sit with it straight out in front of me.

'You take,' Zohra said in French, and I frowned at her, not understanding. She touched the laces of my shoes. 'Take,' she said again, and I realised she meant I should take off my shoes. 'I make feet henna.'

I shook my head. 'I can't walk without my shoe,' I said, and she looked puzzled at my words. I tapped the built-up sole of my right shoe, pulling up my kaftan to the knee and touching my leg, and finally she nodded. 'You can do my hands,' I said, putting them out in front of me.

She smiled, unwrapping a little roll of cloth, and held up a slender pointed stick.

Then she set the stick in her lap and picked up my hands, turning them over, studying them and murmuring to the other women. By the movements of their heads and the tone of their voices, I knew they were discussing what

446

designs would be best. Two little girls watched, crowding against Zohra, and when one tried to climb on her back, another woman took her away. I assumed the little girls were Zohra's daughters.

Finally Zohra held the wooden stick in the air, and they all fell silent. Someone set down a small earthenware container of green paste, and Zohra dipped the end of the stick into it. Holding my right hand firmly in front of her chest, palm up, she bent over it, dipping and drawing, painstakingly but deftly covering my palm with an intricate pattern of geometric swirls. The tip of the wood touched my skin with the lightest sensation, almost like an insect making its way over my palm; the paste was cool. When she had covered the whole palm and fingers she turned my hand over and created a different pattern on the back. My hand grew tired, holding it so still with the fingers spread, and when it trembled, slightly, one of the other women gently held my wrist in support.

Zohra finished the right hand and took up the left. She reversed the pattern, so that the palm of one hand and the back of the other were the same.

When she had finished, she demonstrated that I was to keep my hands very still; another woman brought over a blackened chafing dish, its coals glowing. Zohra made it clear I was to hold my hands over the heat to help dry the paste.

Then she took the hands of the two little girls and left me, still sitting on the ground with a few other women. They stayed there, talking and embroidering. My right leg ached from the unaccustomed position. More and more women came to the centre, taking turns stirring the big pot, and setting other pots on the edges of the fire. My hands were warm over the chafing dish. There was the comforting smell of cooking meat, and I realised I was very hungry. I hoped Badou was all right with the other children.

Eventually Zohra returned with a pot of warm water. She gestured for me to stand, but I was embarrassed; because of my leg I couldn't get up without using my hands to push myself off the ground, and I didn't want to spoil their design. One of the women said something to another, and then came behind me and put her hands under my armpits and rather unceremoniously helped to haul me up. I smiled, in a kind of grimace, at my awkwardness, but the woman smiled openly at me, saying something in a friendly tone.

The paste had turned black, and as Zohra gently washed and peeled it away, the designs, dark reddish-brown and delicate, emerged. I held out my hands, turning them over and admiring them.

'*C'est magnifique*, Zohra,' I said, and she smiled proudly, then gestured again, this time for me to come with her and eat, saying,'*Manger, manger*.'

The whole village and their guests were now gathering around the fire. Badou appeared with the older girl, and sat beside me; Zohra and her two daughters sat on my other side. I didn't see Aszulay; surely he was with his wife, I told myself.

One of the older women briskly stirred the pot, and then, with a huge metal lifter, pulled out a large goat's head. I thought of the heads I had seen in D'jemma el Fna. I didn't think I would be able to eat it.

Bowls of warm water were passed among us by little girls, and we washed our hands, drying them on the strips of cloth tied around the girls' waists.

I watched the spectacle of more heads taken from the water and set on large brass trays, and then the stripping of the soft, meaty skulls. At least there were no eyeballs. As the women pulled off steaming, pale yellow meat, they seasoned it with what looked like salt and crunchy paprika. They passed out smaller, earthen dishes of the meat, accompanied by cooked lentils and rice. I took my plate; I saw that the children ate from their mother's plates, and so I picked up a few shreds of the meat and blew on them, as I noticed the other women doing, and then put them into Badou's mouth. He chewed obediently, then opened his mouth for more, reminding me of a baby bird. I put the plate on my lap and gestured for him to help himself, and then, taking a deep breath, put a small sliver of the meat into my own mouth. It was salty and a bit stringy but surprisingly unobjectionable; I couldn't liken the taste to anything in particular, but it had an interesting flavour. Badou and I ate all the meat and lentils and rice on our plate, and then finished off the meal, as everywhere throughout Morocco, with sweet mint tea. The sun suddenly dropped behind the mountains, and as the sky darkened and the air cooled, the fire grew brighter and higher.

I hadn't noticed when Aszulay returned, but as the women collected the empty plates, I saw him sitting with some other men. Like a few others, he held a long instrument that looked like a flute or fife.

I was glad he was back.

I looked at the women around me. Their thoughts were of the rhythms of the seasons, and how those seasons would affect their lives — if there was drought or too much rain, if their animals were healthy. They carried the fear of whether they could feed their children, or if they would have to hear them crying in hunger, or watch them die from simple illnesses.

I wanted to think I could be like them, strong and capable.

I thought of how far I had come, and the decisions I had made.

Badou got up and ran to Aszulay, settling beside him. One man beat a steady, slow rhythm on an hourglass-shaped clay drum, its top covered with what looked to be stretched and oiled goatskin, which he held between his legs. Others clapped their hands in a variety of syncopations. And then Aszulay and the other men put their flutes to their mouths and played, the melodic notes a sad lament.

I watched my own hands as I joined in the clapping. They looked beautiful, as if I wore rosy lace gloves. I clapped and clapped, moving my shoulders to the beat, wishing I knew the words to the songs the rest of the village sang. Their voices, some harmonious and sure, others wavering and off-key, rose into the sky, slowly filling with stars. The fire sent sparks shooting into the darkness.

Aszulay put the mouthpiece of his flute to Badou's lips, and encouraged him to try. Badou's cheeks puffed up as he blew, and Aszulay held the boy's fingers over two of the holes.

The music stopped, and women served more tea. There

were conversations all around me. Badou left Aszulay and again sat beside me, leaning his head against my arm. Then slowly a drum-beat started, and then another. One man warmed his drum over the fire, testing it, and I realised that the heat on the goatskin would change its pitch. Others took up their flutes again, but this time the music was not the former rather sonorous tunes, but a lively, rhythmic beat. Some of the men rose; Aszulay did as well, his forehead and lower face covered by the folds of his dark blue turban.

They danced to the music then, whirling with each other, their robes flying out like dervishes. The women and children watched, clapping and making sounds with their mouths: a clicking and humming from their throats, and a strange high, continuous vibrating with their tongues. The men danced and danced; the fire grew higher, and above the stars pulsed.

I closed my eyes, letting the sound wash through me. I had the same sensation as walking home from the *hammam*, that my body was somehow not my own, but light and quick, unfettered by my heavy shoes. I wanted to get up and whirl among the Berber men; I felt the rhythm and beat within me, and I moved my upper body back and forth, making my own sounds with my mouth, clapping my hands.

I opened my eyes. Everyone was absorbed in the joy of the night and the music and the dance. As was I.

And suddenly I saw myself, as if from afar, a woman in Moroccan dress, eating the food of the land, sitting around a fire under the North African sky and clapping my hennaed hands. I understood what it was to love, and to grieve over losing those who meant the most. To feel joy and to feel pain.

I understood life, whether it was in Albany or in Africa.

I closed my eyes again, turning my face to the sky and letting joy wash over me.

When I opened my eyes, a woman I hadn't seen before sat beside Aszulay. He was looking at her tattooed face, speaking intently, nodding, and she answered, and whatever she said made him throw back his head and laugh in a way I had never before witnessed: joyful, and full of life.

The woman was young and attractive in the bold, nomad way, her hair loosely braided, with a number of silver necklaces against her dark skin, her slender wrists covered in bangles. She laughed with Aszulay, taking the flute from him and putting it to her lips. I watched them across the fire, the heat casting wavering shadows on their faces.

Here she was then: Aszulay's wife.

And suddenly I was overwhelmed, dismayed and confused by my own feelings. I couldn't bear to watch them together, and yet I couldn't look away.

The sensations of only moments before fled, and somehow, the beautiful evening was now spoiled.

I wanted to be sitting beside Aszulay. I wanted to make him laugh the way his wife did. I had never said anything clever or witty to him. All I had done was force him to be serious, to help me. To look after me, as he looked after Badou.

CHAPTER THIRTY-FOUR

B ADOU, LIKE MOST OF the other younger children, had fallen asleep, curled in the cooling dust at my side. Zohra picked up her own sleeping daughter and motioned to me. I got to my feet and lifted Badou; he was limp and surprisingly heavy. I slowly followed Zohra; it was difficult to walk over the rough ground carrying him. The sky was alight with stars, and a new moon lay on its back.

As we went towards a tent, Zohra stopped, pointing to a small constellation that looked like a kite with a tail. She said something in Tamazight; I shook my head. She closed her eyes, concentrating, then opened them and said, '*La croix.*'

'The cross?'

She nodded, and I remembered the prediction of Mohammed and his monkey, Hasi. Mohammed had spouted clichés about finding something under the Southern Cross, most likely, I had thought at the time, the same story he told every foreign woman foolish enough to part with a sou or two. And yet, standing beneath the pulsing sky, it was suddenly important that I remember his exact words. *Under the Southern Cross you will understand that what you look for may take a different shape. You may not recognise it . . .* and then something about *djinns*.

Badou stirred against me, and, still looking at the Southern Cross, I held him tighter. His little body, even in the cool evening air, was so warm, and he smelled like the earth. I thought of Aszulay eating a pinch of red earth.

I looked away from the sky and down at Badou.

His bare feet were covered in dried mud from the river bank – where were his *babouches*? – and his face was content. He turned his head so that his nose pressed against my shoulder.

Zohra pulled aside a tent flap. Here a number of children lay asleep on piles of rugs and skins. A few coughed; the air in the tent was warm from all the bodies. An older woman sat in a corner, a decorated shawl wrapped around her as she watched over the sleeping children. Zohra laid her daughter down, and motioned for me to put Badou beside her. Then she pulled a rug tightly around them both. Badou murmured something. I leaned closer; again he spoke, in a mixture of French and Arabic. I only understood *le chien*, dog. And then he was silent, his breathing deep and even.

I followed Zohra back to the fire. The air was cold now, and I shivered, crossing my arms over my chest. When I sat down, relishing the heat of the fire, I again saw Aszulay, now speaking earnestly to another man. The woman was no longer beside him, and although I knew he would join her later, the fact that he hadn't rushed off to be with her made me feel better.

What was wrong with me?

He had removed his turban, and in the firelight I saw

that his forehead and the sides of his face were banded in a shadowy hue; his skin, heated from dancing, had pulled the colour from his turban. Suddenly I wanted to breathe in the scent of his face. He would smell of woodsmoke, and indigo.

I understood then that Aszulay would always be thus: a combination of what he had been and who he was now. Whether speaking his lovely, formal French, or Arabic or the complex twist of Tamazight, whether dressed in white, holding a spade in Monsieur Majorelle's garden, or driving a truck along the *piste* in blue, he was both sides of a coin. Distinguishable from each other and yet incapable of splitting.

In a while, Zohra again stood, motioning to me, and I picked up my bag and followed her. She carried a small burning torch, but even with the moon and the carnival of stars above us, it was difficult to see. She stopped, looking back at me and holding out her hand. I took it, gratefully, and we walked around the fire. As we passed the men, Aszulay looked up at me.

I looked back at him, and something in his face made me open my mouth as if I couldn't get enough air. It wasn't a quick glance, and it wasn't with the dancing light as when he laughed with his wife. It was something different, something deep and mesmerising, and it made me dizzy, as if the fever of a few days earlier had returned. I stumbled on a root, and Zohra stopped, holding me upright. As I fell back into step with her, the moment had passed, and I didn't have the nerve to look back at Aszulay again.

★

In a few moments a form loomed in front of me. When Zohra ducked her head, I did the same. We stood inside one of the tents, where what looked, in the wavering light of the torch, like shadowy piles of skins covered with rough blankets were tightly packed together. Some forms lay still, as if deep in sleep. From a corner came girlish whispers and giggles; certainly this was a tent for unmarried women. Zohra led me to one of the piles of skins and left. I clutched my bag, which I'd carefully packed in Marrakesh, but knew it was far too cold to undress and put on my light nightdress. I simply took off my shoes and got under the blanket in my kaftan. The other girls were quiet now, their breathing deep and even. The young woman beside me pushed closer, her back against my chest. I had seen this type of closeness all over Morocco. Men crushed into each other in the square and the souks; Mena and Nawar and the old servant sat closely together on the roof, their shoulders and hips touching as they worked. I thought of the way the women in the *hammam* washed and massaged each other. Perhaps the closeness and bodily warmth produced a sense of belonging. Even little Badou wanted to be close, constantly climbing into his mother's or Aszulay's or my lap.

The Europeans and British and Americans in North Africa were the opposite of this. We each kept our polite space; we apologised over an accidental touch.

Lying there in the utter darkness, I heard the murmur of the men still around the fire, and the far-off bleating of a goat. The girl nestled more tightly against me. She smelled of cooking oil and perspiration and something else, an unidentifiable spice.

I tried to still my mind, but it was alive, whirling with what I had experienced under the night sky. With the way Aszulay had looked at me. I thought of him going up the terraced walk into one of the mud houses, lifting a rug or skin and lying beside his wife. Thoughts of her turning to him, of him wrapping his arms around her, came to me, and I put my own arm over my eyes, not wanting to visualise such things.

But, just as unbidden, now visions of Etienne, beside me in my bed on Juniper Road, flooded my head. I had known one man in my life, for such a brief time. At the memories of what it felt like to have a man's body against mine, I grew too warm, and, at the same time, was overcome with loneliness and yearning.

I turned on to my side, my back against the girl's, trying to find comfort on the hard bed, and wishing for sleep so that I could escape from the unexpected desires of my body.

Etienne. What was I feeling for him now, knowing what I knew? What would my life have been if he'd stayed with me in Albany, and had married me? What would my life have been if I hadn't lost the baby, and had one day been a mother?

What would my life have been if I had never come to Morocco?

But then . . . didn't I still wish that Etienne would marry me? Once he returned to Marrakesh, and I convinced him that his illness wouldn't stop me from loving him, he would surely agree to marry me.

I tried to remember how it felt to make love with Etienne.

But instead, my thoughts went to Aszulay and his wife.

What it would be like to make love with Aszulay. His sensitive mouth. His hands.

I couldn't sleep. I got up and pulled a heavy blanket from the bed. I wrapped it around my shoulders and went out into the night air.

The fire had died down, although it was still glowing. Without its high flames or the flares of torches, it was easier to see in the starlit night. My feet bare, I limped only a few feet from my tent, afraid I would become lost if I went further. The air cooled my body, and I drew deep breaths. And then I realised that there was a single figure still sitting in front of the fire.

Did I simply want it to be Aszulay, or was it really him? He sat in the place I had last seen Aszulay, but that didn't mean anything. Did I only imagine I recognised the set of his shoulders, the length of his hair? As I watched, the man wrapped himself in a blanket, and lay down by the glowing embers.

I returned to my tent, somehow comforted. It was wrong to feel pleasure at thinking that perhaps Aszulay didn't wish to be with his wife. And yet there it was.

I was glad.

I awoke at some point in the night, stiff and cold. I heard snuffling – a camel, a goat, a dog; what was it? – along the outside wall of the tent. Perhaps that was what woke me. I shivered, clenching my teeth to keep them still, and from the cold and the tea my bladder was uncomfortable. But I couldn't bear to get out of bed and leave the tent to crouch in the dust behind it. I pressed closer to the girl beside me for warmth; her slightly huffy breathing halted, and she sat up and coughed. And then, so unexpectedly that I didn't even have time to wonder at it, there was a rush of air and an animal smell and a heavy weight was placed upon me. Immediately I felt warmer. There was more rustling, and the girl snuggled against me, her rhythmic breathing resuming in minutes.

I was awakened, warm and relaxed, by the flap of the rug over the doorway pulled back so that clear morning light flooded into the tent. There was a large goatskin over my blanket, and although the girl beside me was gone, I was grateful to her for covering me when she felt me shivering in the night.

Outside the tent, women sat around a large brass kettle and a tin pan, taking turns pouring fresh water into the pan from the kettle, splashing the water over their faces. I did the same; then one of the women produced a tiny mirror and handed it to me. I thanked her with a smile, holding it up and then frowning and shaking my head at my wild reflection. Rabia came up behind me and, on her knees, combed through my hair, then braided it with fingers swift as swallows. She made one long braid, securing it with something. I reached back to feel it, pulling it over my shoulder and seeing the braid was tied with a twist of goat hair.

Then she came in front of me, again kneeling, and held up a long, thin stick, gesturing towards her eyes, and then mine. Kohl. She wanted to line my eyes with kohl. I had never worn any form of make-up, but I nodded.

She held my chin with her left hand and outlined my

459

eyes with the stick she held in her right. When she was done, she nodded, again smiling.

I followed her up the footpath to the house where she and her mother and sister and their husbands and children lived. When I entered the one windowless room, the only light coming through the open doorway, it was difficult to see. I smelled something meaty, and there was the sizzle from a pan over heat.

I eventually made out piles of carpets with beautiful Berber designs covering the walls and floor; more were stacked in one corner to be used as beds. I recognised the design on my hands in one of the weavings. In the middle of the floor was a fire enclosed by stones, and a chimney made of pipe led out of an opening in the roof. The men must have left; there was only Aszulay's mother and Zohra, and a number of children of different ages. Aszulay's mother squatted on the floor next to a cluster of pots, stirring one of them.

Badou ran to me; I hadn't discerned him immediately in the tangle of children milling about the small room. His hair stood out at wild angles, and his mouth was smeared with what looked like honey. He again had on his red *babouches*. '*Bonjour*, Badou. Did you sleep well?' I asked him, and he didn't respond, but held out his open hand.

On his dirty palm was his tooth.

'Badou,' I said, raising my eyebrows, and he grinned at me, showing me the little empty space in his smile.

'Keep it for me, to show Falida,' he said, giving it to me, and I put it into the bottom of my bag.

One of the girls took his hand, and he left the hut with

her. He seemed a different child today. I watched him go, and then looked at Zohra.

'*Bonjour*,' I said, and she laughed in a delighted way, returning the greeting, gesturing for me to sit down. I sat on one of the beautiful rugs, and she handed me an earthenware plate. I ate a spicy sausage and what appeared to be fried pancakes made from something grainy. It was all delicious.

Just as I had finished, Aszulay spoke my name. I looked behind me, and saw him in the doorway. I was unable to speak. I couldn't let him see, in my face, what I had been thinking about last night. The images of him and me, the things we did . . .

He didn't smile, and I realised he was studying my kohl-lined eyes. Then he said, 'I'm going to look at some of the crops. I'll take Badou. We'll leave later.'

All I could do was nod.

I spent the next few hours with Zohra and her daughters. The little girls were shy at first, but eventually spoke to me in questioning voices. I kept looking at Zohra, but she seemed unable to translate anything for me. We went to the river, Zohra carrying a basket of clothing on her head, and I watched as she and the children pounded the laundry against the rocks. I offered to help, but Zohra shook her head. She chatted with the other women, and I simply sat on a rock, looking around me at the terraced hills.

The light was pure, with the sense of a shimmering mirage as I looked at the waving green of the fields. Here and there men moved about; they were too distant to distinguish, but I knew one was Aszulay. The scene had a

461

magical quality, and I could understand how the village people lived a totally different reality than what I'd always known.

We returned to the house, the wet clothing left behind to dry on the rocks. Aszulay's mother sat in the sun with her back against the wall, sorting olives in a basket. When she saw us she stood and went inside, returning with a beautiful shawl, its edges deeply embroidered with delicate twining vines and multicoloured flowers. She held it out to me.

I looked at it, running my hands over the designs. 'Very beautiful,' I said, knowing she couldn't understand, but, by my smile and gestures, surely understanding.

She pushed it towards me now.

'*Pour vous*,' Zohra said. For you. '*Cadeau*.'

Refusing the gift would be an insult. I accepted it from the older woman's hands, clasping it against me and smiling at her. Then I draped it over my head and around my shoulders, and she nodded, pleased.

Aszulay came from inside the hut. He stopped, studying me, and then nodded in the same way his mother had, with only the beginning of a smile, and that small hint of pleasure playing about his mouth gave me a strange sensation. I immediately told myself I couldn't think of his mouth.

He was married, although he hadn't introduced me to his wife, the young woman with the slender wrists who had sat beside him around the fire. Only the night before I had imagined their heated bodies under their blankets and animal skins, him whispering to her as they moved together.

The way he held me when it was over. No, held her, I thought. Held his wife, not me.

Of course it hadn't been him sleeping by the fire.

I turned from his smile.

'Aszulay?'

We'd left the village and had been driving, silently, for over an hour. Something had shifted between us since we'd come to the village. The way Aszulay had looked at me at the fire, and at my kohl-lined eyes, as I stood wrapped in the shawl his mother had given me . . . I knew, with certainty, that it wasn't just me feeling the change. The easy talk we had shared on the drive here had fled. I wanted to say something, but didn't know what. I wanted him to say something.

Badou had climbed into the back of the truck, separated from us by the opened curtain of canvas. I had brought more French picture books with me, and had handed them back to Badou. He was slowly turning the pages of one of them.

Aszulay looked over at me when I finally said his name.

I couldn't avoid speaking of her any longer. 'Your wife. I saw her sitting with you around the fire. She's very pretty.'

Something flitted across his face, turning into something odd now, some unreadable expression. His jaw clenched, and suddenly I was afraid that I had, unknowingly, made a mistake with my simple statement.

'I'm sorry, Aszulay. Have I . . . did I say something wrong?'

He took his eyes from the *piste* to look at me. 'The woman – she was just one of the village women. I have known her many years.' I saw his throat move as he swallowed. 'I have no wife,' he said.

463

My mouth opened. 'But Manon . . . Manon told me you had a wife. She told me . . . when I saw her last.'

Again he didn't speak for a long time. Then he said, 'Manon was playing with words.' It was an odd statement, and I didn't understand it.

'Oh.' There seemed nothing more to say, and we again drove in silence. Last night, what I had experienced was jealousy. I wasn't proud of it, but I couldn't deny it. So now, when he dismissed the woman as simply one of the villagers, saying he didn't have a wife, shouldn't I feel something like pleasure? But my reaction was the opposite. Aszulay's response troubled me. His face, his voice, his suddenly stiff hold on the steering wheel all told me there was something more. I had somehow upset him.

He pulled to the side of the *piste* and turned off the engine, and then got out of the truck and unstrapped one of the large metal containers of fuel from the roof. Using a funnel, he poured gas into the tank. When he got back into the truck, the smell of the fuel surrounded him.

'We shouldn't have left so late. The light is going early today; it's the dust,' he said.

I nodded.

'I had children,' he said then. 'Two.'

The word *had* made the air in the truck suddenly too oppressive. It was as if there was no oxygen. I looked down at the edge of the blanket I sat on, running a loose thread through my fingers.

'It was a fever. It killed my children, and my wife. Iliana,' he said, simply. 'Many died of this fever. Rabia's first son also died.'

Suddenly I thought of his disappearance at the stream

we'd stopped near just before the Ourika valley, and the cemetery we had passed.

'Your wife and children,' I said. 'They're buried in the cemetery where we stopped, yesterday?'

He nodded, and then tucked the end of his turban over his lower face and started the engine, and we continued along the *piste*.

I thought of Manon, slyly smiling as she told me Aszulay had a wife. I glanced at Aszulay, but he said nothing more.

Within half an hour, the sky had turned a strange pale yellow. There was no more sun, and a wind came up, blowing so strongly that I saw how Aszulay had to grip the steering wheel to keep the truck on the track. Suddenly there was no distinction between earth and sky; it was a solid wall of dust. And yet Aszulay seemed to know where to go. I imagined him in the sandstorms of a desert, and how the knowledge of direction would be part of his nomadic instinct. Perhaps part of his genetic make-up, carried within his ancestors for centuries.

I thought of what Etienne carried from his father.

We had rolled up the windows as soon as the wind started, but still it howled around the cracks, blowing in the sandy dust. Finally Aszulay turned the wheel sharply to one side, and stopped the truck.

Badou kneeled behind us, looking through the windshield. The wind whipped around the vehicle so ferociously that it swayed, just the slightest.

Nothing was visible.

'I don't like it, Oncle Aszulay,' Badou said, and his mouth turned down as his breathing became ragged. 'Is it *djinns*?'

Tears filled his eyes. It was the first time I had seen him cry. 'Will they eat us?' I reached back and stroked his cheeks to dry them.

'Of course not, Badou. It's only wind. Only wind,' Aszulay repeated. 'It can't hurt us. We just have to wait until it stops, so we can see the *piste* again.'

'But . . .' Badou leaned over and whispered into Aszulay's ear.

'He must go outside,' Aszulay said, his hand on the door handle.

'I'll take him,' I said, because I was in the same situation.

'No. The wind is so strong. I'll—'

'Please, Aszulay. Let me take him,' I said, and Aszulay nodded, understanding, while Badou climbed over the seat into my lap.

'Keep one hand on the truck at all times,' Aszulay said, as we pushed open the door and clambered out into the wind.

Badou immediately turned to face the truck, pulling up his djellaba.

'I'm just going around to the back of the truck, Badou,' I said, loudly, into his ear. With one hand on the truck as Aszulay had instructed, I went to the back, where I fought with my kaftan, whipping about me in the wind.

It took only moments, and when I made my way back to the passenger side, Badou wasn't there. I opened the door and climbed in, pushing my hair back and rubbing at my eyes.

'Where is he?' Aszulay said, and I turned to him, blinking.

'What do you mean?' I climbed on my knees, pushing

aside the canvas curtain, but Aszulay had already opened his door. 'I only left him for a second . . . I thought he came back . . .'

'Stay inside,' Aszulay shouted, over the wind.

'No, I'll come—'

'I said stay inside,' he yelled again, and slammed the door. I sat as if frozen, staring through the windshield. Surely Badou was just at the front of the truck. Or maybe I hadn't seen him as I'd felt my way back along the side. He must have been crouching near the tyre. Aszulay would bring him right back.

But Aszulay didn't immediately come back into the truck with Badou. My heart thudded. How could I have left him, even for that moment? I had been so critical of Manon's lack of concern over him, and yet what had I just done? I put my hands over my mouth.

Then I closed my eyes, my fingers laced in front of my face, rocking back and forth, saying, 'Let him find him, let him find him, let him find him.'

But they didn't come back.

The truck grew darker and darker. I wept, I prayed, I banged the side of my head against the window. I was a fool, an idiot. Could Badou survive even for a short time in this dust, or would it choke him? And Aszulay. I saw him wandering, calling for Badou, the wind snatching the name from his mouth. He had just told me he'd lost his own two children. Now . . .

I couldn't bear it. I put my hand on the door. I would get out and find Badou. I was responsible for this, and I would find him. But as I reached for the handle I thought of Aszulay, shouting at me to stay inside, and knew he was right. I would be even more of a fool to leave the truck and wander about on my own.

I held my watch close to my face in the dim light, trying to think what time it had been when we'd left the village, how long we had driven, how long I had waited here. The time didn't make sense. All I knew that it was too long, too long.

Aszulay hadn't found Badou.

CHAPTER THIRTY-FIVE

I HAD STOPPED HOPING. I simply sat there, in the slightly rocking truck, staring at the nothingness beyond the windshield.

I didn't want to look at my watch, but finally I could stand it no more. Almost an hour had passed.

Again I covered my face with my hands; again I wept.

And then the driver's door banged open, and Aszulay pushed Badou in, climbed in behind him, and slammed the door.

I grabbed Badou, pulling away Aszulay's turban. It was wrapped completely around Badou's head and torso. I uncovered his little face; he stared at me. Sand was stuck in dried tracks down his cheeks.

'Sidonie. I was lost. I didn't keep my hand on the truck.'

'I know, Badou,' I said, weeping, rocking him against me.

'I tried to find it,' he said.

'I know. But you're safe now. You're safe,' I repeated, 'you're back in the truck.' And then I looked over his head at Aszulay, afraid of what I would see, knowing what a fool he must think me, how angry he would be.

There was nothing but exhaustion on Aszulay's face. His

eyes were closed as he leaned his head back. His hair and eyebrows and eyelashes were so coated that they were no longer black, but an odd dusty red. His nostrils were filled with the dust as well.

'Are you . . . you're all right, Aszulay?' I asked, my voice stuttering with tears.

'Give him water,' he said, and I moved Badou so I could lean over the back seat and grab the skin of water. I took out the cork and held it to Badou's mouth. He drank and drank, letting it run down his chin and neck. When he had finished, I held the skin to Aszulay, but his eyes were still closed. I moved closer, putting the mouth of the skin to his lips, and as it touched them he drank, still not opening his eyes.

When he put his hand up to push away the skin, I poured water on to the end of his turban and wiped his eyes, trying to clear away as much grit as I could. He took the wet cloth from me and rubbed his face until he at last opened his eyes.

'I'm sorry,' I whispered.

He didn't answer for a moment. 'I found him not far from the truck. But I couldn't take a chance on not getting back, on wandering in the wrong direction. We took shelter in a small shelf of earth driven up by the wind. I waited, and finally the wind changed direction just enough for me to see the truck.' He looked down at Badou. 'I made you a little Blue Man, yes?'

Badou nodded, and left my lap to push against Aszulay's side. Aszulay put his arm around him.

Time passed. At some point Aszulay began to hum, holding Badou against him with one arm. It was a quiet, sad melody, much like the one he had played on the fife — the *rekka*, I knew now that it was called.

I imagined him holding his own children like this, humming to soothe them. I turned my head, staring at the swirling sand and dust, feeling I was witnessing something too personal.

After a while he stopped humming, and I looked back at him. Badou had fallen asleep, his head on Aszulay's chest.

'Will the wind end soon?'

'I don't know. But we'll spend the night here. Even if the wind stops, it's too dark for me to drive the *piste* safely. Much of it will be covered now.'

I nodded. It was almost completely dark in the truck, due to both the dust and the approach of evening. Aszulay reached beneath the seat and pulled out a candle and a box of wooden matches. He lit the candle and wedged it into a small opening on the dashboard.

We sat in the soft light.

'Aszulay,' I said. 'I'm so sorry. I don't know how—'

'It's over,' he interrupted. 'He's all right. He was only frightened.'

'So was I,' I said, my mouth trembling. 'I can't tell you how frightened I was.'

'This country can be a fearsome place,' he said. 'I know all of its tricks, because it's my home. I don't expect those not born here to know it in the same way.'

He was telling me he understood, and I was grateful. I took a breath, and then reached my hand to him. 'Thank you,' I said.

He looked down at my hennaed hand, then took it and looked back at me. I thought of the look we had shared the night before, and had to lower my head, staring at our joined hands, unable to look into his face. His thumb traced my palm, gently touching the healed sore.

Finally I raised my head. He was still looking at me. In the flickering candlelight the curve of his high cheekbone was moulded. I wanted to touch it. He leaned closer to me, then looked down at Badou.

'He's asleep,' I whispered, not wanting him to stop because of the child.

But Aszulay sat back, and I felt a deep stab of disappointment. 'Maybe you will tell me a story to pass the time,' he said, softly. His hand closed more tightly around mine. 'A story about America. About an American woman.'

It was difficult to breathe. I shook my head. 'You,' I said. 'First you tell me about yourself.'

'There's little to tell,' he said.

'Just to pass the time, Aszulay,' I said. 'As you said. Your story, and then mine.'

He stroked Badou's hair with his other hand. 'When I was thirteen years old, Monsieur Duverger bought me, to work for Manon's mother,' he said.

I drew in my breath. 'You were a slave?'

'No. I'm not a slave. I'm a Tuareg. You know this.'

'But . . . bought you?'

He shrugged. 'Children often go from the country to work in the city. Children of the *bled* are hard workers. They don't complain, and don't speak much.'

'I don't see the difference.'

'There have long been slaves brought in from other parts of Africa. With my father, on our caravans, we sometimes transported salt, sometimes gold, sometimes amber and ostrich feathers. Sometimes black slaves, from Mali and Mauritania. But it's not the same with young Moroccans from the country. The family is given a certain agreed-upon amount, and the children act as servants. They're paid a small sum, and a few times a year, if they know where their family is, they can visit them. Or if a member of the family comes into the city, they're allowed to see each other. When the child servant reaches a certain age, he can leave if he wishes. Some do, returning to the *bled*, or taking on other jobs in the city, but some stay on and work for the family for many years. For some, the family they live with and work for become more their own than the one in the *bled* or the village.'

The truck still rocked slightly, back and forth. Back and forth. But now, sitting in the candlelight with Aszulay, my hand in his, Badou asleep between us, it was comforting.

'I told you my father died when we lived as nomads,' he said. 'At twelve I was too young to go on the caravans through the desert by myself, and I didn't wish to join another nomad group. I knew I would find no respect from the other men, as a boy. So it was my choice to sell our camels and tell my mother I would work in Marrakesh. She didn't want me to. But I knew that in this way she would get a price for me, and after that I could help provide for her and my sisters. And they would be safe, in the village.'

'But are children sold to the French, or to Moroccans?'

'Both, although not so often do the French want the nomad children, because of the language and cultural differences. But it wasn't a bad life, Sidonie. We work hard in the desert and in the *bled*; we work hard in the city. Work is work. But in the city we always had food. In my other life it wasn't always so. When the camels died, or the goats didn't give milk, we sometimes didn't have enough to eat.'

I thought of the young boy at Hôtel de la Palmeraie who had brought the orange juice to my room when Aszulay and Badou were there, and how he had looked with familiarity at Aszulay. I thought of so many of the older boys and young men I had seen working in the souks or pulling carts or carrying heavy loads through the crowded streets of the medina or driving taxis and *calèches* about the French Quarter. I had assumed they were sons of the Moroccan men who owned these businesses. Now I knew that perhaps they weren't; perhaps they were young men like Aszulay, sold into the work.

'So, as I said, Monsieur Duverger bought me for Manon's mother, to be the man of the house. He wanted Rachida's life to be better, and so he gave me to her, and I did the heavy work. Manon was a year younger than I, and she became my friend. She was kind to me.'.

'Manon? Manon was kind to you?'

The wind was lessening.

The light from the candle wavered across Aszulay's face. 'She taught me to speak French properly. She showed me how to read and write. I don't know how she learned. She was the daughter of an Arab woman; there was no school for her. But you know how clever she is,' he said, and stopped.

My face must have involuntarily shown my distaste for her. 'Go on,' I said.

'We became friends immediately,' he said. 'And then grew to be more than friends.'

So it had gone on all this time; since they were little

more than children. They had been lovers for how many years . . .

'We became like brother and sister,' Aszulay continued, and I made a sound. He looked at me.

'Brother and sister?'

He nodded. 'We looked out for each other. We were both lonely. I missed my family. She . . . I don't know what she missed. But there was a loneliness about her, always.'

'But . . . you mean . . .' I stopped.

'What?'

I licked my lips. 'All this time, I thought, well, I just assumed, that you and Manon were . . . you were lovers.'

He stared at me. 'Manon? But why did you think this?'

'What else was I to think?' I said. 'How else would I guess at your relationship? And Manon – I saw the way she behaved around you.'

'Manon cannot help herself. If any man is present she acts the same way, out of pure habit. But . . . do you believe Manon is the sort of woman I could be with?' he said, quietly, his eyes still fixed on me, and I had to look down, at Badou.

I didn't answer, although I wanted to say, *no, I didn't want to think you desired her, and needed her. I hated that I thought you took her as a lover, that you were enmeshed with such a calculating, evil woman. You are above her in every way.* But I just continued to look at Badou, trying to keep my breathing under control.

'I helped her in the past because of our shared life, but now . . . it's because of this little one. I am attached to Manon only because of Badou.' Aszulay let go of my hand.

475

He took off Badou's *babouches* and closed his hands around the small bare feet.

'And this is how I knew Etienne and Guillaume,' he continued. 'Sometimes I accompanied Manon to the Duverger house. They didn't notice me, as I was of no importance, just a country boy who did the heavy work for Manon's mother. But I watched them, and knew them through what I observed.'

I tried to imagine the young Aszulay as a servant, seeing how the wealthy French boys lived their indulgent lives. I pictured him like an older Badou, with watchful eyes and a serious expression.

Suddenly I was embarrassed for Etienne, for how he must have treated – or simply ignored – Aszulay. Etienne with everything, and Aszulay with nothing. And yet now . . . who had more?

'Later, when we all grew older,' Aszulay continued, 'Manon couldn't stop talking about Etienne and Guillaume. She was angry with them, no longer liking them, because they had what she didn't. She wanted their lives. When they went to Paris, she begged Monsieur Duverger to send her to a good school too, to study art. She begged, she told me, but he said no. He would give enough money to her mother to pay for a home, and for food, and for me to help with the work, but nothing extra for Manon. He told her her life was good enough, that she was already benefiting. He told her his sons had one place in his heart, and she another. That she must accept this. But Manon would never accept it. It's not Manon's nature to accept what she doesn't like.'

Of course.

'It grew even harder for Manon; her mother died and Monsieur Duverger was being consumed by his illness, growing more and more confused. He gave her no more money, and sold the house he had bought for Rachida. By this time Manon was a young woman; she had to find a job. So she worked as a servant in a French house, like her mother. She was always angry; she was . . . I can't remember the French word . . . she couldn't stop thinking about Etienne and Guillaume, talking about them and how unfair it was. It seemed to take over her mind.'

'Obsessed?'

'Yes. She was obsessed. She talked about wanting Monsieur Duverger's sons to suffer like she suffered. But what could she do? They now lived in Paris most of the time. Then one summer Guillaume came back, but that was when he drowned, in the sea at Essouria. Etienne came to Marrakesh for his brother's funeral, but stayed only few days. The next year he came home again for his mother's funeral; she died suddenly when her heart failed. And the following year Monsieur Duverger died, and that was the last time Etienne came home. Over seven years ago. Manon went to the funeral. She saw Etienne there.'

'And then?'

'The years have made Manon hard, and unkind. Yes, she always was a little unkind, and yes, like now, she always thought of herself first. And she was always beautiful, and she used this beauty with men.'

I nodded, easily able to envision Manon, youthful and striking, knowing the power she wielded over men. But bitter. I knew that the bitterness she exhibited was deep within her.

'She saw Etienne at his father's funeral. And then what?' I repeated.

Aszulay didn't say anything for a few moments. 'Then Etienne went to America,' he said. There was silence but for Badou's soft breathing. '*C'est tout*. That's all,' he said.

But I knew that wasn't all. There was something he wasn't telling me.

'Is that when Manon told him that she was his half-sister? There was no reason not to; her mother was dead, and all of Etienne's family. Did she tell him to hurt him, to make him think less well of his father?' I could envision Manon whispering, angrily and yet triumphantly, to Etienne about their shared blood.

'The rest of that story, the part about Etienne, is Manon's,' Aszulay said. 'I cannot tell it.'

'But you remained friends with Manon all this time,' I said.

'We were apart for some years. When her mother died and Manon went to live with the French family she worked for, I left Morocco.'

'You left? Where did you go?'

'Many places. I was young, and strong. I had saved what I could, and gave it to my mother. I went first to Algeria, later to Mauritania and Mali. When I was younger, I liked moving from place to place. I am a nomad at heart,' he said, and smiled.

I looked at the candle, and its reflection in the windshield.

'And then I went to Spain,' he said.

'Spain?' I turned to him

He nodded. 'I lived first in Malaga, then Seville, and

finally in Barcelona. I learned to speak Spanish easily; it's not so different from French. When I lived in Barcelona, I often crossed the border into France. It was a good time for me. I discovered so much about the world. And about people. I made arrangements with a friend in Marrakesh to give the money I sent him to my mother and sisters. I made more money in Spain than I would have in Morocco in many years. There was much work there.'

He could have passed as a Spaniard, with his thick, wavy black hair, his narrow nose and strong white teeth, his dusky skin. I thought of him in European clothes.

Who he was, as I knew him, became clearer. 'How long did you live there?'

He was silent for a long moment. 'I was there five years,' he said.

'That's a long time. Did you ever think you would stay permanently?'

He reached out and ran his fingers over the tip of the flame. 'I was in the prison in Barcelona for two years.'

I didn't respond.

'I was headstrong. I was in a fight with a group of men. One of the others was hurt very badly,' he said, with no emotion, still watching his hand passing over the flame. 'I don't know who struck the worst blows. None of us knew; it was a terrible and senseless fight, in the way of young men who lose control. But we were all put into prison because of the injury to the victim.'

'For two years,' I repeated.

'Prison gives one time to think. When I was there, I could only imagine returning to Morocco. I thought that if I should live to see my homeland, I would go back to the desert, and go on the caravans again, and live in a tent. Life is simple in the desert, I told myself. I wanted only that simple life after what I experienced in the prison. I knew my mother didn't know what had happened to me; nobody did. I hated thinking of her imagining me dead. I was filled with guilt for my wasted life – those two years.'

'And so when you were released . . . that's what you did?'

He nodded. 'First I went to the village. I saw my mother and my sisters and their families. Then I went back to the Sahara, as I had promised myself.'

'But . . .' I said, because I heard it in his voice.

'I had come back from Spain with no money. I couldn't afford to buy my own caravan of camels, and I found it difficult to work under another caravan leader. Of course it wasn't as it had been when I was a child, with my father. I had changed too much. After one long and unsatisfactory caravan to Timbuktu, I returned to the village. I needed – I wanted – to settle down. I wanted my own family, a permanent home. I married Iliana, and in three years we had two children. A son and a daughter.' He stopped, suddenly, as though his voice had been cut off.

I waited.

He cleared his throat. 'I loved my wife, and my children, but it was the same as when I had tried to make a new life in the desert; I had been away too long. I had known the life of cities, and had seen too much in my travels. I tried hard to accept the village life, working in the fields with the other men, but I didn't belong to this life. It wasn't the work; I'll do any work. It was the isolation. Even though – as you saw – it's beautiful, and the people are friendly, it reminded me, in a strange way, of the prison. I felt as if the mountains were walls. I couldn't see over them, or around them. I spoke to Iliana about moving into Marrakesh, about raising our children there, but she was frightened at the idea; she had always lived in the Ourika valley. So I resigned myself to my choice, and I tried to make a good life for us for those few years. But after . . .' He stopped again, then continued. 'After I lost Iliana and the children, there seemed no point in staying in the village. There was no happiness for me there any longer.'

We sat in silence for a few moments, listening to the wind, now just murmuring.

'I came back to Marrakesh and found work. Of course I saw Manon again, and the life she had chosen. She had left the French family, and lived on the kindness of men.'

I could imagine how he would have viewed Manon at that point. Women became wives, or they became concubines, prostitutes by another name. There was no in-between. There was no name for a woman like Manon.

'But she couldn't find happiness either,' he continued. 'We were both unhappy then, but for me it was the sadness of grief. And I knew that grief would, some day, pass, or at least lessen to where it was not a daily and deep pain.'

It was difficult to watch Aszulay speak; I had never before seen his face like this. It was always honest, but now it was vulnerable, too vulnerable.

'Manon's unhappiness was different from mine; it was caused by her anger. She felt she had been cheated out of a happy life, and didn't know how to find it – or make it – for herself. In this way she has something missing inside her. She held on to an old resentment – that she was not

481

given what she thought she deserved – until it crippled her.'

Aszulay had used the word *crippled* unconsciously; obviously he didn't view me in this way, nor did he know that what he was saying was affecting me, making me think about my own life. My own resentments.

'But when she had Badou – something she hadn't expected or, I believe, ever wanted – I saw her change.'

'And his father? Badou's father?'

He looked away from the flame, and at me. 'What of him?'

'She didn't find any happiness with him?' I asked.

Aszulay shook his head. 'It appeared to me that with Badou's birth Manon became more desperate. She was not young, and had a fatherless child. She has found it difficult to be a mother. She simply tolerates him, but she doesn't harm him.'

Watching Badou's chest rise and fall as he breathed, softly, in sleep, I thought of Falida and her bruises. 'She ignores him. Sometimes he's hungry, and dirty,' I said, not liking that Aszulay was defending Manon and her treatment of Badou.

'I don't think Manon is capable of the kind of love a woman should have – naturally – for a child,' he said. 'As I told you, something is missing inside her. When I think how my . . .' He stopped, and I imagined he was remembering his own wife with their children. He still held the boy's little feet in his large hands, and I watched his hands close, so gently, around them.

Surely Badou filled a tiny bit of the emptiness he had after losing his own children.

The wind changed direction, whispering slyly through the tiny crack at the top of the window, and the candle was extinguished in one sudden whoosh.

'And now you,' Aszulay said.

'Me?' I repeated. I could see nothing in the blackness.

'Your story,' he said. 'I've told you my story. Now you tell yours.'

'But . . . mine has nothing of interest,' I said. 'Nothing at all. Compared to yours . . .'

'What makes you think this?'

'I have lived . . . a small life.'

There was a rustling sound, and the seat between us dipped as he laid Badou down. My hands touched the boy's hair. I gently lifted his head into my lap. I envisioned Aszulay still holding his feet, the child's body a bridge between us. I pulled the blanket on the seat up over Badou.

'No life is small,' Aszulay said, his voice low. 'The life of the bird is as important as the life of the king. Just different.'

And then there was a lift of air, and I felt, rather than saw, Aszulay's face close to mine. I put my hands out, and felt his cheekbones under my fingers, and then his lips were upon mine.

Badou stirred, and we moved apart.

'Tell me your story,' Aszulay whispered in the darkness.

I was silent for a moment, and then began.

CHAPTER THIRTY-SIX

I AWOKE SLOWLY, MY NECK stiff from leaning into the corner. I twisted my head from side to side as I looked through the windshield. The wind had blown itself out, and the morning was still.

Aszulay and Badou crouched around a small fire; a steaming black tin pot sat in a pile of burning twigs.

I got out of the truck, aware of the new intimacy Aszulay and I had shared. It wasn't only our kiss, but even more so the telling each other the details of our lives in the long night.

'We've already had our breakfast,' Aszulay said, watching me as I came to the fire. 'Sit, and eat.' He spoke as always, but the way he looked at me told me something else.

'You had food with you?' I asked, smiling, starting to lower myself to the ground, awkwardly, because of my leg, but Aszulay gestured to a large stone. He'd folded the blanket over it. I went to it, grateful for his thoughtfulness.

'The people of Morocco never trust the weather,' he said, smiling at me as though we shared a joke. I remembered how Mustapha and Aziz had carried supplies in the trunk of the Citroën. Using the end of his turban, Aszulay lifted the pot from the flames and poured it into a tin can that I could see held crushed mint and sugar. Then, still using his turban, he set the can on the ground in front of me. 'Badou, give Sidonie some bread.'

Badou handed me a thick round he held in his lap. I tore a chunk from it and dipped it into the tea to soften it. I ate it all, suddenly ravenous, and by then the tea was cool enough to drink.

Badou was playing with pebbles, stacking them and knocking them over. When he looked up at me I smiled at him, finishing the last of my tea.

'Aren't your feet hot, Sidonie?' he asked, and I thought of Zohra, curious in the same way.

'Sometimes,' I said.

'Why do you always wear such big shoes? Why don't you wear *babouches*?'

'I have to. This leg,' I said, touching my knee, 'doesn't walk right without the shoe.' I pointed to the built-up sole. 'I need that, or my leg is too short.'

He nodded, studying the boot. 'Brahim, the boy down the street, also has a short leg. But he can still run fast, and kick the ball.' He put his head to one side. 'You look like Maman,' he said.

'Really,' I said, trying not to let him see that his statement unnerved me. Manon was earthy, and beautiful.

'*Oui*,' he said, seriously. 'Yes. You look like Maman. Oncle Aszulay!' he called. 'Sidonie looks like Maman now.'

Aszulay had been extinguishing the fire with earth. He glanced at me, but I couldn't tell what he was thinking. 'Come. We're ready to go,' he called back.

As Badou clambered into the cab of the truck, and Aszulay slid in behind the wheel, I stopped, my hand on

485

the passenger door. 'Aszulay,' I said. 'Could I drive the truck back to Marrakesh?'

'But . . . you told me about the accident. With your father. You said . . .'

'I know. But I feel differently today,' I said. 'Today I think it's time for me to drive again.'

'You have forgiven yourself,' he said, and I blinked. Was he right? Did I want to drive – not just myself, like those few reckless moments on the *piste* when I roared off in Mustapha's car, but with Aszulay and Badou – because I no longer felt the unbearable weight of what had happened the last time I drove with someone I loved? I thought of my father, and for the first time there was no deep pain. Perhaps Aszulay was right. Perhaps I had found peace.

'A truck is not like driving a car,' Aszulay said, when I didn't respond. 'And as I said last night, the *pistes* will be covered in places. It won't be easy.'

'Probably not. But I can try. I'm sure you'll help me if I have trouble.' I lifted my chin and smiled at him.

He left the driver's side and came to stand beside me. 'Well. It appears I am to be driven through the *bled* by an American woman. Well,' he repeated, as if a little unsure, or perhaps a little pleased. Then he grinned at me, and ducked his head and looked into the cab. 'I think this will be a good experience. What do you think, eh, Badou? Will you like Sidonie driving us? We can sit back, and let her do the work.'

'*Oui*,' Badou said, seriously. 'Sidonie can do the work.'

I got behind the wheel and placed my feet on the pedals and my hands on the steering wheel. I turned the key, and

486

when the engine roared to life, I looked at Aszulay and smiled. He smiled back.

We were back in Marrakesh just after noon, leaving the truck in the garage on the outskirts of the city. It had definitely been a difficult drive, but I had managed, only once slipping off the *piste*, but immediately redirecting the car and getting back on the narrow track. I let Badou honk the horn in the stillness of the empty *bled*, and he laughed over and over.

We walked in to the medina, but instead of taking me directly back to Sharia Soura, Aszulay took us down another alley, and then another, and I realised, when we stopped and he took a large metal key from inside the folds of his blue robe, that we were at his home.

As he unlocked the gate and pushed it open, the elderly woman who had served me tea the last time rose from the tiled courtyard, a rag in her hand. Her kaftan was looped up over her belt so she could work. Aszulay spoke to her in Arabic, and she nodded and went into the house, pulling down her kaftan, and Aszulay followed her.

Holding Badou's hand, I looked around, realising that when I had come here the first time, questioning Aszulay about Etienne, I hadn't had the presence of mind to clearly see Aszulay's *dar*. But this time was different. I wanted to see everything. The courtyard was lovely, its floor a design of small diamond-shaped tiles in shades of blue and gold. The outside wall of the house was tiled too; here were different designs in gold and green and red. Small niches – also tiled – had candles set into them. The doorway into the house was arched, and a thin white curtain fluttered over it.

Painted pots that reminded me of those in Monsieur Majorelle's garden sat at various angles; some huge ones held small trees, and clusters of smaller ones were planted with flowers and vines.

On one of the walls was a long mirror, and from another hung a rug with a distinct weave and abstract design. Its colours ranged from subtle earth tones to brilliant yellows and golds.

Having just come from the village of earth, clinging to the side of a hill, I saw the difference between Aszulay's life here, in Marrakesh, and what his life would have been in the Ourika valley.

Badou pulled his hand from mine and ran about the courtyard. I took off my *haik* and veil as Aszulay came out with a large tin tub, the kind the servant at Sharia Soura used to wash clothes in the courtyard. He filled the tub with water from a cistern in one corner as he spoke to Badou in Arabic. Suddenly he stopped. 'I'm sorry. Sometimes after I have been in the *bled* I forget to speak *en français*.'

'That's all right. I can understand more Arabic now anyway. I understood you, telling Badou he smelled like a little puppy and must have a bath. Mena is teaching me,' I said.

Aszulay bent over the tub and washed his face and neck and hands with a hard bar of soap. He splashed water over his hair, running his fingers through it. He pushed up the sleeves of his robe and washed his arms to the elbow. Then he emptied the tub into a shallow depression near the cistern and filled the tub again.

'Come, Badou,' he said, pulling off Badou's djellaba and

cotton pants and *babouches* and lifting him into the tub. He splashed water over the little boy, and Badou smiled.

'The water is warm from the sun,' Aszulay said, using a cloth and the soap to wash away the grime. 'Close your eyes, Badou,' he said, and lathered and then rinsed Badou's hair.

I looked around the sun-dappled courtyard, at the beautiful tiles, and suddenly I wanted to feel them. I undid the laces of my shoes and slipped them off. Then my stockings. The tiles were, as I had imagined, warm and smooth. They were spotless from the servant's recent cleaning. I walked slowly around the courtyard, knowing I was hobbling deeply without my boot, but not caring. I walked, revelling in the joy of my bare feet on the beautiful tiles. I hadn't walked outside without my shoes since before the polio, when I had often run about the yard barefoot in summer.

Aszulay and Badou paid no attention, caught up in Badou's bath. And then I saw my reflection in the long mirror. I could see my whole body. The sun and wind, in the last three days, had darkened my skin further. My hair, neatly braided by Aszulay's sister before we'd left their camp, had, after the wind and our overnight stay in the truck, come undone and hung over my shoulders. My eyes, still ringed with the now-smeared kohl, stood out, larger than I'd ever seen. The decorated shawl Aszulay's mother had given me was draped over my kaftan. I stared at myself, from my hair to my bare feet, understanding what Badou had said. I looked, from this distance, surprisingly like Manon. A similar oval face, the same wide dark eyes and curling hair. I had never seen it before.

'The tiles and designs are glorious,' I said, looking from my reflection to Aszulay. The tiles in Manon's courtyard, and in Mena's, were much more pedestrian: pretty, but a limited design, and more subdued colours.

'There are many traditional patterns of *zellij* – the tiles,' Aszulay said, looking from Badou to me. His eyes took in my feet, staring at them for just an instant, but in that brief second I felt as though I had exposed my naked breasts. My breath caught in my throat; there was a strange eroticism – for me – in Aszulay seeing my feet.

I had never let Etienne see them. We had only been intimate from the fall into the winter, and I always wore stockings. When we were in bed, I kept my bare feet under the covers, making sure to put on my stockings before getting out of bed.

I thought of the way Aszulay had held Badou's feet the night before.

'What's this one?' I asked, quickly turning, pointing to one of the black and white designs.

'Hen's teeth,' he said, and at that Badou laughed.

'Hens don't have teeth, Oncle Aszulay.'

'And this series of round ones?' I asked.

He again looked away from Badou. 'That is little tambourine. The rows above are divided tears.'

'What does divided mean?' Badou asked.

Aszulay didn't answer.

'When one thing is made into two,' I said. I thought about Aszulay, and how I had seen both sides of him: the desert man and the city man.

Badou shivered, and Aszulay lifted him from the tub, wrapping him in a long piece of flannel, patting him to dry his skin and combing through his wet hair with his fingers. He slapped the dust from the little boy's djellaba and pants and wiped off his *babouches* with a damp edge of the flannel. As I watched him fit the shoes back on to Badou's feet, I envisioned him tending to his own children.

'Now you look fine, and Maman will not be angry,' he said, and Badou nodded without smiling.

'Can I stay here longer, at your house, Oncle Aszulay?' he asked. 'I don't want to go. Sidonie can stay too.'

Aszulay shook his head. 'You must go to Maman, Badou. And we also must take Sidonie home,' he said. *Home.* I knew he only meant the word in the literal sense, and yet it made me think. Was my low room under the African stars now my home?

He dumped out the water, but filled the tub for a third time. 'Come,' he said to me, and I stared at him. 'Your feet,' he said. 'The water will feel good on your feet.'

I went to the tub. Bunching my kaftan at my knees with one hand, and putting the other on Aszulay's arm, I stepped over the rim of the tub. The water was warm, as he had said. I wiggled my toes, smiling at him. He pulled a low stool to the edge of the tub. Then he picked up the bar of soap. I knew what he was going to do.

I put my hand on his shoulder, to steady myself, while he gently lifted my right foot and washed it, up to my ankle. Then he put it down, and as he began to lift my left foot, I had to hold tighter to his shoulder, to keep myself steady while balancing on the shortened right leg. His shoulder, under my hand, was strong and hard. I let my fingers hold on to him for the extra few seconds when he had finished washing my left foot and I stood with both feet on the bottom of the tub.

Then he took my hand as I stepped out, and gestured for me to sit on the stool. He crouched in front of me and took my feet, one at a time, and dried them.

'Bring Sidonie's stockings and shoes,' he said to Badou, and the boy ran to pick them up and bring them to Aszulay.

Aszulay put on my stockings, and then my shoes, lacing them. The whole time I watched the top of his head as he bent over my feet. I wanted to reach out and touch his hair, run my hand down the back of his head, touch the edges of his ears, his neck.

I kept my hands folded together in my lap until he was done.

We were passing through a small, busy souk not far from Sharia Soura. Aszulay and I walked side by side, while Badou was a few feet ahead of us. I was aware of Aszulay's blue sleeve brushing mine occasionally. I glanced up at him. What did I want him to say? I knew he felt what I felt. I knew he wanted me as I wanted him.

'I have three canvases to work on this week,' I finally said, breaking the comfortable silence. 'I took one of my oils to the hotel, and they said they'd take it on consignment, as well as more watercolours.' I smiled up at him, but he was silent, staring straight ahead as if concentrating on something else.

'Aszulay?' I said, and when still he didn't turn to me, I followed his gaze.

A dark-haired man, his shoulders gaunt and curved

under his linen jacket, turned a corner ahead of us. I had only time to catch a glimpse of his pale profile. But I knew. This time I knew. It wasn't like all the other times I had thought I'd seen Etienne in Marrakesh.

I stopped for one instant, and then, dropping my bag, pushed through the throngs in the square, turning the corner where he had been, but here was a wide street, lined with markets, teeming with people and animals.

'Etienne,' I shouted into the swarming milieu. I snatched my veil from my face so that my voice was clearer. 'Etienne!' Heads closest to me turned, but I couldn't see Etienne. I worked my way through the crowds, calling his name, but my voice was lost, blending in to the rest of the clamour. Panting, I finally stopped in the middle of the street, my hands at my sides, staring at the sea of people and animals milling around me. Alleys ran off this street in all directions; Etienne could have gone down any of them.

Aszulay touched my arm. I looked up at him. 'It was Etienne,' I said. 'You saw him. I know you did. He's here, Aszulay. He's in Marrakesh.'

He pulled my arm, leading me away so that we were standing under the shaded overhang of a locked gate, where the noise wasn't so intense. 'Badou,' he said, reaching into the folds of his robe and pulling out a few coins, 'please go and buy bread. From the stall, there,' he said, pointing.

Badou took the money and ran off.

'I must tell you something,' Aszulay said. I absently noticed that he had my bag over his shoulder.

I nodded, thinking only of Etienne. He was here, in Marrakesh.

'When I came to get you, on our way to the

countryside . . .' Aszulay hesitated. 'I should have spoken of it, even though you asked me not to. Sidonie. Look at me. Please.'

I was still staring into the street. 'Spoken about what?' I asked, turning towards him.

'At Manon's, when I went to pick up Badou just before I came to you,' he glanced at Badou, waiting for the bread, 'Etienne was there.'

He said the final three words in a rush. I opened my mouth, then closed it.

'I should have told you,' he said. 'Even though you asked me not to speak of Manon, and Sharia Zitoun, I should have told you.'

I leaned against the gate. 'Etienne is at Manon's?' I said.

He nodded. 'And I didn't tell you because . . .'

I waited, watching his mouth.

'Because I wished you to come to the *bled* with us. With me. I knew that if I told you Etienne was here, you wouldn't come. And . . . and something else.'

Still I stood there. When he didn't speak, I said, in a quiet voice, 'What else?'

'I didn't want you to go and face Manon and Etienne by yourself. I didn't want to leave Marrakesh, knowing . . .'

'Knowing . . .?'

But Badou came running back then, the round of bread under his arm.

I looked down at the boy, who glanced from me to Aszulay.

'Does he know? Does he know I'm here?' I asked Aszulay.

Aszulay nodded.

'But he doesn't know where I am.' I stated it, rather than asked it.

Again Aszulay nodded.

'You didn't tell him.'

He didn't answer.

'But . . . if he knew I was here, he must have asked you, or Manon, about me, how I was. Where I was. Wouldn't he have tried to find me, over these last few days?'

Again, Aszulay didn't appear to have an answer. I had never seen him like this.

'Aszulay. Has he been looking for me?'

'I don't know, Sidonie.' He took a deep breath. 'I speak the truth. I don't know.'

'Let's go, Oncle Aszulay,' Badou said. 'I have the bread for Maman.'

'You should have told me,' I said to Aszulay, ignoring Badou. 'You let me go off with you, knowing, all along, that this – that Etienne – was the reason I was in Marrakesh. And yet you . . . you betrayed me, Aszulay.' My voice had risen.

'No, Sidonie. I didn't betray you.' Aszulay's voice was low, and his face held something. Perhaps anguish. 'I . . . I wished to protect you.'

I pulled at my bag, and he slid it off his arm. 'Protect me from what?' I said, louder than necessary, then I slung the bag over my shoulder and turned sharply, walking alone back to Sharia Soura.

I went to my room and lay on the bed. Etienne was here; I could be facing him within the hour, if I so wished. But why did I feel more a sense of dread than excitement? As

I'd just told Aszulay, this was why I'd come to Marrakesh. This was why I'd waited all this time. Why was I so angry at Aszulay? Was it really anger, or was it something else?

I rose and looked at myself in the mirror.

Again I saw how I resembled Manon.

Now everything was different. It was so complicated. What had just unfolded between Aszulay and me . . .

I couldn't go to Sharia Zitoun just yet. I needed a little more time, one more night, to prepare myself to see Etienne.

Of course I was unable to sleep at all. My thoughts went from Aszulay's kiss, his touch on my feet, to Etienne, and what I would say to him. What he would say to me.

I tossed through the endless night, and was glad to finally hear the morning prayer. I bathed in the tub in my room, washing my hair. I pulled my best dress – the green silk with cap sleeves – from my case and put it on. I brushed my damp hair back into its usual style, pinning it firmly, and studied myself in the long mirror.

The dress was all wrong, wrinkled badly and hanging oddly on me. Although I could never appear pale with my darkened skin, there was a drawn look about me, as though I had just recovered from a tiring illness. And with my hair back, my face appeared too severe, too angular.

I sat on my bed. Then I unpinned my hair, feeling the thick waves fall over my shoulders. I took off my dress and put on a kaftan. I took my veil and *haik* and went downstairs. I asked Mena for her kohl, and outlined my eyes. Then I called for Najeeb, and went to Sharia Zitoun.

CHAPTER THIRTY-SEVEN

I STARED AT THE *HAMSA* on the saffron gate. I closed my eyes and knocked.

Within a moment Falida called out, asking who it was.

'Mademoiselle O'Shea,' I said, quietly.

She pulled open the door. I stood there, unable to force my feet forward.

'Mademoiselle?' Falida said. 'You come in?'

I nodded, taking a deep breath, and stepped into the courtyard. There were loud voices from within the house, although I couldn't make out what was said. Badou sat on the bottom step of the outside staircase.

'*Bonjour*, Sidonie,' he said, but he stayed where he was, not running to me as he usually did.

'*Bonjour*, Badou. Falida, is Monsieur Duverger in the house?'

She nodded.

'Please go and tell him Mademoiselle O'Shea is here,' I said.

She went inside, and the voices stopped abruptly.

I stood, trembling slightly, and suddenly there he was. Etienne. My Etienne. My initial reaction was shock at his appearance; he was much thinner than I remembered him, the gauntness in his shoulders I had seen yesterday more apparent. And yet his face was somehow bloated, and very pale. Had he always been this pale, or was it that I was used to a darker face now?

He stared at me.

I tried to remember that I loved him. But seeing him standing there, looking so . . . vacant, I felt nothing like love. I felt hatred. I thought of all I'd gone through, coming here, searching for him, having to deal with Manon. Then waiting for him.

I hadn't thought it would be like this. I had imagined him holding out his arms, and me running to him. Or me weeping, him weeping, one of us weeping, both of us weeping. Oh, I'd created so many images.

Instead, we simply stood there, looking at each other.

He took a few steps towards me. He held a glass in one hand; even with the distance between us, I could smell alcohol. I thought, in a detached manner, that his face might be bloated from far too much drinking. 'Sidonie?' he said, frowning, his forehead creasing. I thought of my nightmares, when I stood in front of him and he didn't recognise me.

I pulled off my *haik* and veil. 'Yes,' I said. I thought my voice might be shaky, weak, but it wasn't. And my trembling had stopped completely. 'Yes, it's me. Don't you know me?' I asked.

His eyes widened. 'You look . . . you're different.'

'As are you,' I said.

'Manon told me you were in Marrakesh. I couldn't believe it. You came all this way.' His eyes ran down my body, hidden under the loose kaftan. Surely Manon had told him there was no longer a baby. 'But . . . how? And . . .'

He didn't say *why*. But I heard it. 'Yes,' I said again. 'I came all this way. And I lost the baby. In Marseilles. In case Manon hasn't told you. In case you're wondering.' It came out so easily, with so little emotion. I knew that Etienne would be relieved.

He had the grace to shake his head. 'I'm so sorry. It must have been a terrible time for you,' he said. 'I'm sorry I wasn't there with you.'

But he wasn't sorry. I could see it; it was just his usual way of speaking. He always knew what to say. He'd known what to say to me every time he saw me in Albany. And at that, something rough and barbed pushed through me, something that might have been one of the Moroccan *djinns*, and I ran at him. I slapped his face, hard, on one side and then the other. The glass fell from his hand, crashing on to the tiles and exploding into pieces. 'You're not sorry. Don't say you're sorry, with that simpering look on your face,' I said, my voice loud. I was vaguely aware of a whisper of cloth behind me, the soft pad of bare feet on the tiles.

Badou, or Falida, I thought, but it was only the ghost of a thought.

Etienne stepped back, his hand on one cheek. There was blood on his lip; I had hit him hard enough for his tooth to sink into it. 'I deserved that,' he said, staring at me, blinking. Then he shook his head. 'But Sidonie, you don't know everything.'

'I know that you ran from me, within days of me telling you I was pregnant. You left Albany without even the courtesy of a phone call. A letter. Anything. That's all I need to know.'

'So you came all the way here to tell me that?' Suddenly he listed to one side, but caught himself, and sat down heavily on a stool. 'To slap me?'

'No. I came here looking for you because—'

And then Manon was in the doorway. 'Because she couldn't keep away,' she said. 'And look at your behaviour,' she said to me, shaking her head, but there was something pleased in her expression. 'What do they call this behaviour in America, eh? The woman wronged?' She looked behind me. 'What are you two staring at?' she said then, and I turned to see Badou huddled against Falida, near the gate. She had her arms around him as though to protect him. 'Get out,' Manon said, and Falida took Badou's hand and they ran through the gate, leaving it open behind them.

'I know you're not well,' I said now, breathing heavily. 'Manon told me. What is it? What are the *djinns* she talked about?'

'I can't practise medicine any more,' he said, lifting one hand and looking at it as if it were his enemy. 'I can't trust myself to be responsible for anyone's life.' Now he looked back at me with a tortured expression. 'All I can do is consult. For a while. My life is over. I saw what happened to my father. Now it will happen to me. It's Huntington's chorea.'

The name meant nothing to me.

I took a step towards him. 'I'm sorry for your illness, Etienne. But you should have told me,' I said. 'You didn't have to leave me like that. I would have understood.'

'I would have understood,' Manon mimicked, her voice high and silly, but with something dark underneath.

'Can we go somewhere?' I said, glancing at her, and then

back to Etienne. 'Somewhere where we can speak alone? Just you and me? Don't you have anything to say to me? About us? About our time in Albany?'

'That time is gone, Sidonie,' he said. 'You and me in Albany. It's gone.'

I didn't want Manon to hear anything more; I didn't want her witnessing what Etienne and I had to say to each other. 'Manon, please,' I said, harshly. 'Go in the house. Can't you give us a moment alone?'

'Etienne?' she asked, drawing his name out. 'Do you wish me to leave?'

He looked at her. 'I think it would be better.'

Why was he treating her with such careful consideration? This had nothing to do with her.

She left, her silk kaftan whispering about her. Once she had disappeared, I went and sat across from Etienne. The low table with a brass tray holding Manon's *sheesha* was between us. 'I think I understand, Etienne. I didn't, until Manon told me about an illness that moves from parent to child. The . . what you called it.'

'Huntington's,' he said, his voice low, staring at his knees. 'Huntington's chorea. It only strikes in adulthood, usually after thirty, so it's often that the parent doesn't know of it until he or she has already produced children. There's a fifty per cent chance of it being passed from parent to child.'

We sat in silence. The imprints of my slaps darkened his ashen cheeks.

'Paranoia, depression,' he said then. 'Spastic twitching. Problems with balance and coordination. Slurred speech. Seizures. Dementia. Eventually . . .' He put his face into his hands.

I stared at the top of his head as I had at Aszulay's, only the day before. A surge of pity went through me.

'I'm sorry, Etienne,' I said. 'But now I know that this is why you left me. Because you didn't want me to have to watch you suffer. I know you didn't think it would be a life for a wife. For our child. But that's what people do. People who love each other. They care for each other, no matter what.'

He lifted his head and looked into my face. His eyes were so dark, flat. I wanted to know what he was thinking. Had his face always been so closed?

'But to leave without a word, Etienne. To not even have the consideration to try and explain . . . Well, that I don't understand.' My tone was calm, now. Logical.

He looked down. 'It was cowardly,' he said, and I nodded, almost encouragingly. What did I want him to say? 'And so disrespectful to you. I know this, Sidonie. But . . .'

But what? Say you did it to protect me. Say you did it out of love for me. But as these thoughts came to me, I suddenly knew that although a person might be honourable enough to protect someone they loved, it wasn't Etienne. He wasn't honourable. He was, as he'd just admitted, a coward.

'I came all the way here, to North Africa, Etienne, to find you. That's how much I believed in you then. In you and me. I needed to find you, to try and understand . . .' I stopped. His face was still so closed, so unwilling to let me in. I wanted to slap it again. I realised my palms stung. I clenched my fingers.

'That's how much I loved you, once,' I said. I heard the past tense. *Loved.* 'Was it all a game for you, then?' I asked, surprising myself, thinking of Manon's words. 'Were you only passing time with me, and I . . . I was so naïve, so blind, that I believed you cared for me as I cared for you?'

'Sidonie,' he said. 'When I met you . . . I was drawn to you. You let me forget about my trouble. You were good for me. I had known with certainty, shortly before I saw you for the first time, that I hadn't escaped the genetic roulette. I knew what my future held. I didn't want to think about it. I only wanted . . . I needed not to think about it. To . . .' He stopped.

'To be distracted?' I didn't recognise my own voice. Again I was repeating Manon's words.

'Of course. It's as I told you. He never loved you.' It was Manon, in the doorway again. She came towards Etienne. 'Don't you see the obvious?'

I looked at her, then back at Etienne. 'The obvious?'

Etienne turned his face from me. 'Manon, not like this,' he said, then looked back at me. 'If I'd known where you were in Marrakesh, I would have come to you. I didn't know where you were, Sidonie,' he repeated. 'I wanted to speak to you alone. Not . . .' He stopped, and Manon laughed. A hard, brittle laugh.

'Oh, Etienne. For God's sake, speak the simple truth to the woman.' She came to him, putting her hand on his arm, clutching his sleeve, her fingers, with their painted nails, like a claw. 'She can take it. She may appear fragile, but underneath she's like steel. So tell her the truth. Or I will.' And then she leaned against him and kissed him. A lingering kiss, on the mouth.

I was too shocked to respond.

Etienne pulled away from her hand, pressing trembling fingers against his forehead. Without looking at me again he left the courtyard, through the open gate. I sat where I was, stunned into silence.

'Well,' Manon said. 'Now you know.' She made a tsking sound. 'So weak, poor man. And nothing to do with his illness. He's always been that way.'

'Know what? What are you talking about?' Had I imagined the way she'd kissed him?

'He's having such a difficult time with it all. Trying to come to terms with the truth.' She sat beside me and lit her pipe, taking a long pull. I smelled *kif*. 'He just can't accept the fact that he did what he said he wouldn't.'

I looked at her lips, sucking on the mouthpiece. She had just kissed Etienne. Not as a sister.

'Yes,' she continued. 'He said he would not allow the *djinns* to pass further. He would not perpetuate his disease,' she said.

I opened my mouth. Everything was confused, wrong. 'But . . . he knows . . . there's no longer a child . . .' My voice was distant in my own ears.

Manon shrugged as if only mildly interested. 'But there is,' she said, taking her lips from the mouthpiece for a moment.

I shook my head. 'What do you mean?'

She set down the mouthpiece, holding in the smoke. Eventually she let it out in a long, slow sigh, staring at me. 'Badou,' she said.

Time passed. I simply stared at her.

Finally Manon picked up the mouthpiece of her pipe again. 'I made him want me. That's all. After his father's funeral, when he still thought I was only a servant's daughter, I asked him to help me with some small, insignificant task. Something to make him feel powerful, as though I were a weak woman, needing the help of a man.' She smiled at the memory, an ugly smile. 'An accidental touch, a look held a little too long . . . for me it was just a game.' She smoked again, and her eyelids lowered. 'It was simple, Sidonie. I had to do little to bring him to his knees.' She snapped her fingers. 'Like catching a fish with a succulent worm. I decided, when I saw him at his father's funeral, that finally I would punish him as he deserved to be punished. I would make him want me, let him touch and taste me, and then . . . poof.' Again she snapped her fingers. 'I would send him away. I would drive him mad. I have done it with other men. It's a pleasure for me to watch them squirm on the hook, and then cut them free. But they can no longer swim as they once did. They are damaged.' Her face glowed. 'Poisoned with desire for me.'

I thought of the kneecap and tooth from a corpse. The way she had stuck me with the poisoned sliver of bone.

'Of course I made him wait. I made him want me with such ferocity that he lost his mind. And then, finally, I gave in, knowing that he'd be back. He came to me again, and again and again. He had never known a woman like me. He couldn't get enough of me.'

I tried not to draw a comparison, tried not to think of the way Etienne and I had come together each time. Had there been this fire, the kind of passion Manon spoke of?

'It was as it probably was with our father and my mother. Our father was hypnotised by my mother. He wrote her proclamations of love. I kept them after she died. I read how he loved to take her, in the room next to where his wife read, or entertained friends. It gave him pleasure to know his wife was within hearing; it was the secrecy that drove him. And so it was with Etienne. I made him take me where we might be seen, where he would be humiliated if caught with a servant's daughter.'

'Don't,' I whispered, sickened at her imaginings.

'After we became lovers, I had him purchase this house for me, and put it in my name. I had him draw up a legal document that would afford me a generous allowance every month, in perpetuity. In perpetuity,' she repeated. 'He would always have to support me. Of course that was when I let him think I loved him, that I wanted only him, that we would always be together. That no man could satisfy me like him. He fell for it all. He promised he would stay in Marrakesh, and work as a doctor in La Ville Nouvelle. We agreed there would be no children.

'He did not propose marriage. Of course not. He, the great French doctor, marry a lowly Moroccan servant? Oh no. I would always be his concubine. In his heart I believe he thought no woman worthy to marry. A woman for companionship, for sex, *oui*. For marriage, no.'

I had expected him to marry me.

'But when I had the house, and was secure, I told him. When I knew I was in his head, held fast, with all his thoughts consumed with me, I told him. I waited until the perfect moment, as his face was over mine, and him deep inside me.'

'Manon,' I said, 'please.' Why didn't I get up and leave? Why did I sit, as though I were the one under a spell, and listen to her sordid story?

'We looked into each other's eyes, his so full of desire, of love, and I told him. *I'm your sister*, I said. I had to repeat it. He couldn't understand what I was saying.' Again she smiled, that awful, victorious smile. 'But when I said it for the third time, he pulled away from me as if my body were a flame, and I had taken all his air. Etienne, being Etienne, challenged me, asking me what proof I had. And it was then I showed him my mother's letters from our father.'

I felt ill, imagining the scene. I could see her face, enjoying every moment of it, and I could also see Etienne. The horror and shock. Etienne, always the one in control, the one with the answers, the right thing to say at the right time.

'He became sick, right in front of me. He raged, he wept. And then he left. That's why he went to America. Because he could no longer be in Marrakesh. He could no longer even be on this side of the ocean, so near to me, but never again able to possess me.'

'Manon,' I breathed, shaking my head. 'Manon.' I could think of nothing to say.

'But it was easy to keep track of where he was. Of course I have many influential gentleman friends in the French community. When I realised Etienne had left me pregnant − a complete accident, like you, eh? − I considered getting rid of it. It would have been easy; don't I know enough about these things? I have rid myself of others.' She stared into my eyes. 'But something told me it would be better to keep the child; a further insurance policy. I wrote regularly to Etienne over the years, telling him I was a mother, talking about the child. But I made no accusation. He never replied. And then, last year, my needs grew, Sidonie. So I wrote to him that I was sorry I had used him, that I had changed, and wanted to repent. And that there was a deep secret, something I could only tell him face to face. Of course he suspected, and so because of my urging – and to get away from you – he came back to Morocco.' Then she lowered her chin, looking at me almost coquettishly.

'Did you not wonder why Etienne – a man like Etienne, clever and worldly – wanted a woman like you, Sidonie?'

I blinked. 'What? What are you talking about?'

Manon's face was full of contempt now. 'You idiot. Can you see nothing? Etienne never stopped dreaming of me, wanting me. It's me he loves, not you. Do you not look in the mirror, and see what I see? Do you not recognise that Etienne saw in you something that reminded him of me? Of the one woman he loved? Even the fact that you painted, well . . .' She shrugged. 'He chose a shadow, since he couldn't have the bright light. That's all you were to him. A feeble reflection of the woman he truly loved, but couldn't have; he only turned to you because you reminded him enough, in appearance, of me. And he knew that he could so easily possess you. He could never possess me, but you – don't you see? Every time he held you, every time he made love to you, Sidonie, he was dreaming of me, closing his eyes and seeing me. You never meant anything to him. Nothing at all.'

I stood, knocking over the brass tray; it hit the tiled floor with a clanging ring. In the dying echo I heard Manon's words, over and over, as if holding a mirror to a mirror, all the reflections closing in on each other.

Nothing at all.

CHAPTER THIRTY-EIGHT

I SAT ON MY BED, seeing myself in the mirror across the room. I was exhausted. After all these months of waiting and hoping, now it was over.

What Manon had told me was not inconceivable. If I hadn't seen Etienne, seen him with her, witnessed his inability to speak up to her, I might not have believed her. But I had seen it for myself.

The afternoon call to prayer came, and I looked towards the window, picking up the *zellij*. I thought of Aszulay, remembering his touch as he bathed my feet.

He had told me not to wait in Marrakesh for Etienne. After we had been in the *bled* together he told me he hadn't wanted me to be alone when I went to Etienne on Sharia Zitoun. He knew the truth about Etienne and Manon, and thought that I would be devastated, shocked. He worried about me.

I was shocked, yes. But I wasn't devastated. When I had seen Etienne, I had looked at him as though he were a stranger. He had become the stranger I'd seen in my bedroom, all those months ago in Albany. But had he really changed, or was it me?

I was no longer the woman from Juniper Road.

I had come to Marrakesh to find Etienne. I had found him. I understood why he had left me. It was simple: he had never loved me.

I hadn't known many truths about Etienne. In actuality I had never known the real man. He had only disclosed what suited him. My short time with him had been a fantasy. Perhaps what I thought was love was also part of that fantasy.

It was such an old story, one every woman can see from the outside. But it's difficult to see when one is inside that story, with all its fictions and whimsies and hopes. And now it was completely over. The story had an ending.

I was alone again. But not in the way I had been alone before Etienne, before knowing a man, and before the thought of my own child.

I went to the table where my latest canvas − of the jacaranda tree at Sharia Zitoun − was propped against the wall. I thought of Badou opening my paintbox, so proudly and reverently in the courtyard, and at that I put my fist against my chest.

Badou. As Etienne's child, did he carry the monstrous gene in his small, perfect frame? Now I moved my fist against my mouth, thinking of the warmth of his body as I held him. I remembered my unbearable concern when I thought he was lost in the dust storm. The relief and joy when Aszulay brought him back.

The night in the truck with Aszulay, and what I had felt.

I remembered the words of Mohammed, with his monkey, in D'jemma el Fna, telling me I would find what I searched for under the Southern Cross. Mohammed had been right. I had found something.

But I couldn't keep it. Aszulay was a Blue Man of the Sahara. Badou was another woman's child. I had fallen in love with this country, its colours and sounds and smells and tastes. Its people. One tall man, one little boy.

I thought of my growing friendship with Mena. The protectiveness I felt toward Falida. Badou's hand in mine.

Again, Aszulay.

The best I could do would be to go back to Albany and remember it with my paints. But even there, in the cold of winter, I would not paint Morocco with the detached eye of a tourist, a mere observer. I was no longer an observer, but a participant in this life.

But it's not your world, I repeated to myself.

C'est tout. That's all. The story is over.

I couldn't eat. Mena asked if I was ill.

'No. But I am sad. I go home soon,' I told her, in Arabic.

'Why? You don't like Sharia Soura? Nawar speaks badly to you?'

I shook my head, shrugging. It was too wearying to try to explain, in my simple Arabic.

She licked her lips, and something came over her face. 'My husband? He hurt you?'

'No. No, I never see him.'

Her face relaxed.

'But Aszulay?' she said. 'I think he is a good man.'

'*Na'am*,' I said. Yes.

'Not all men are good,' she added, and unconsciously reached up to touch the back of her neck, and I thought of her scar. Of Manon kissing Etienne.

★

511

I was lying on my bed in the darkness, still in my kaftan, when I heard men's voices in the courtyard. I recognised Mena's husband's voice, and both the sons, and then . . . It was Aszulay's voice. I rose, so swiftly, and hurried to the window.

He was there, sitting with them, drinking tea. They were talking as if it were simply a friendly visit. They finished their tea, and the husband and sons stood.

Aszulay said something further, and the husband looked up. I pulled my head back from the window, but in a moment there was a quiet knock on my door.

I opened it. It was Mena. 'Aszulay is here,' she said. 'He asks to see you. Wear your face cover, Sidonie,' she said, frowning. 'My husband is home.'

I did as she asked. She went down the back stairs, the staircase the women could use to avoid going through the courtyard if a man was there. I went into the courtyard. Aszulay stood.

'Are you all right?' he said.

'Yes,' I said.

'But you've seen Etienne,' he stated. 'I went to Sharia Zitoun earlier this evening. Manon told me you had been there. She told me . . .' He stopped, and I looked at him. 'Now do you understand why I didn't tell you about Etienne immediately? Do you understand what I meant by wanting to protect you? I knew I couldn't stop you from uncovering the truth — Manon would be certain you knew everything — but I wanted . . . I'm sorry. I was selfish. I wanted you to have a few more days . . . I wanted . . .'

I sat on a bench. He didn't say anything more, also sitting down again. Finally I said, 'I understand, Aszulay. It didn't go well at all this afternoon.' As I uttered the words, I suddenly thought of Badou. The last thing he'd witnessed was me slapping Etienne, screaming at him. I put my hand over my eyes, imagining the distress and fear on his face as he ran to Falida; both their expressions as they fled the courtyard.

They would see me as no better than Manon. They would see me as a woman who screamed and hit.

'Sidonie?' Aszulay said, and I lowered my hand.

'I was thinking of Badou,' I said. 'Poor child.'

'It's not been good for him,' he said. 'Still, many children in Morocco . . . in many places . . . He has a roof, and food,' he said. 'I have tried to make life a little better for him.'

I nodded. 'I'm glad he has you. I can't bear to think of him growing up with Manon. And what's so heart-breaking,' I said, tearing away my veil, not caring about Mena's husband at that moment, 'is the thought of what he might carry.'

'Carry?'

'You know. The disease. Huntington's chorea. I know Manon doesn't care; surely she imagines that by the time he's a man and the disease might manifest, she'll be dead. So why should she care?'

'I don't understand,' Aszulay said.

I stared at him. 'What don't you understand?'

'Manon doesn't appear to have it. So why would Badou?'

'But . . . Etienne. Etienne has it.'

'Yes. He's his half-uncle, but it has to come through a parent. Isn't that true? That's what Manon told me.'

I shook my head. 'Aszulay. You don't know? Manon

513

never told you that Badou is Etienne's child?'

Aszulay leaned back. 'Manon doesn't know with certainty who the father is.'

I swallowed. 'But she does. She told me it was Etienne when she talked about her relationship with him. Only this afternoon. That Badou was the result.'

Aszulay stood and walked quickly, once, around the courtyard, as if trying to contain anger. Then he came back and sat across from me again. He shook his head, staring at the wall behind me. I knew him well enough to understand he was composing himself. Finally he looked into my face.

'Manon was with Etienne before he went to America, yes. But she was also with two other men at the same time: a Jew from Fez and a Spaniard from Tangier. And Badou was born ten months after Etienne left for America. His father is either the Jew or the Spaniard.'

I heard the soft coo of a pigeon from the high wall behind Aszulay.

'But . . .'

Again Aszulay shook his head. 'Sidonie. Manon says what she thinks will achieve her purpose. She's told you other lies, and still you believe her.'

'Her purpose?'

'Her purpose is to hurt you. From the first day I saw you – and saw how Manon treated you – I knew what she was doing. She was initially jealous of you for the main reason, but I've seen her grow more and more so, because now you have taken not only Badou's attention, but also . . .' He stopped.

'The main reason?' I asked, when he didn't go on. 'What do you mean?'

514

'She's jealous because she fears that perhaps her brother did love you. Even though she didn't want him once she'd achieved her purpose, she couldn't bear to think of him loving anyone else. She wanted all of his adoration.' He leaned his back against the wall. 'Manon is like this. Surely you see it.'

I watched his mouth as he spoke.

'She cannot bear to be second-rate; she says it's how she was made to feel, always, as she grew up. And so now . . . she must be the most important woman with every man in her life. She does not want a rival, even for her son.' He paused. 'She does not want to share anyone with you. Anyone. You have the evidence.' He leaned forward and took my hand, turning it over and running his thumb over the tiny mark in my palm. 'What she did to you, when she knew I chose to spend time with you. How she harmed you.'

I was still concentrating on the fact that Aszulay had said that Manon was afraid Etienne had loved me.

'He was so weak,' I said, trying not to let hostility come into my voice. 'And if he'd actually loved me, as she suspected, he wouldn't have left the way he did.'

The red cat crept into the courtyard, stopping, staring at something in the bushes, its tail twitching.

'She told Etienne Badou was his so he would give her more money,' I said.

Aszulay nodded. 'That part could be true. She wanted him to provide more for her – in the name of Badou, of course. But I think originally she only meant to play on his conscience, ask him for money as Badou's uncle.'

I thought of her saying that the reason she hadn't

aborted the child was as assurance of an easy future.

'But it was when he spoke of you – I was there – of a woman in America, one who carried his child, that she flew into a rage. He said he didn't know what to do; that he couldn't face it. It was then she told him Badou was his. Like you, he believed Manon; it didn't occur to him she would lie about Badou. He didn't know she had been with other men while she was with him; he didn't know Badou's exact date of birth. For him the circumstances and timing were correct. I heard her, and knew what she was doing.'

His voice grew louder, more indignant.

'She didn't want to be second-best. To you again, Sidonie. She didn't want me to care about you, and she knew I did. And then, when she heard you had conceived Etienne's child – I'm certain that it was at that moment, upon hearing of it – her jealousy became so great that she wanted – needed – to outdo you.'

My mouth opened. 'She would allow her jealousy, her insecurity, to create such a monstrous lie?'

'When she told him, I was so angry with her. I opened my mouth to argue, to tell Etienne the truth, that she lied. But it all happened so quickly. Etienne jumped up; he said his goal was to try and stop it, by not passing on the disease to a future generation. And yet now he had done it not once, but twice; he had already created one child – your child, Sidonie – and now he had just discovered he had created a second. Badou. His face was white as he stood, shaking. I grabbed his arm, telling him *no, wait, Etienne*, but he rushed out into the night.'

I could imagine the scene.

'I argued with Manon, and told her she must tell him the truth. But she said he deserved shame, and humiliation. That there wasn't enough shame in the world for Etienne; maybe now he would know how she had felt, betrayed by their father.' He stopped. 'Manon and Etienne are similar, Sidonie, in their thoughts of themselves. This is their common characteristic.'

I knew he was right.

'Nevertheless, I stayed there all night,' he continued, 'waiting for Etienne to return, in spite of Manon's fury at me. I have seen her do many things I disapprove of, but I couldn't let her do this. Although Etienne has limitations, it wasn't fair to make him suffer further. He would suffer enough with his illness. I was going to tell him the truth, that Badou wasn't his.' He gripped his own hands. I saw the corded veins standing on the backs of them. They were hands that could use a shovel with such strength, and could hold a child with such delicacy. 'But he didn't return. He simply didn't come back. He left his clothes, his books, even his glasses. A few weeks later he sent a letter to Manon – the one I first told you about – saying he had had time to think, and would take responsibility for his child. He would come and see him, every few months. He said in this way he would at least make sure the child wanted for nothing.'

I nodded. Manon thought she had won. In this way she could continue asking for anything from Etienne. And he would provide it, out of guilt. We sat in silence, apart from the occasional sound of the dove.

'And so – have you told him?'

Aszulay shook his head. 'When I picked up Badou,

before we went to the country, Etienne was there, as I told you. But it wasn't the right time. Badou was present, and Manon hurried us out. And he had said he would stay for some time. I knew I would tell him when we returned from the *bled*. And I went there tonight, to speak of it to him, but he was out, Manon said. But she knows what I wish to do, and will prevent me in any way she can. She's told me I'm not welcome any more; to not come back to Sharia Zitoun.'

Was Etienne really still in Marrakesh? I thought of how he'd left this afternoon, and wondered if he'd run off again, the way he ran to America when he found out the woman he loved was his half-sister. The way he ran back to Morocco when I told him I was pregnant. The way he ran to another city when Manon told him Badou was his. This was how Etienne dealt with what he didn't want to face. By running away.

'All I can do is hope, somehow, to see him again, and tell him the truth. But it will be difficult. Manon will see to that.'

We sat in silence.

'And now, Sidonie?' he asked.

'Now?'

'What will you do?'

'I . . . there's nothing more for me here. In Marrakesh.' I looked at him, waiting for him to say what I wanted him to say. Needed him to say. *Stay, Sidonie. I want you to stay. Stay and be with me.*

He didn't speak for a long time, nor did he look at me. I saw his throat move as he swallowed, and then he said, 'I understand. This is a country so different from what you have known. You need freedom. You would be a prisoner here.'

'A prisoner?'

Finally he looked at me again.

'A woman here . . . it's not the same as America, as Spain. As France. All the countries in the world where a woman like you can do as she wishes. As she pleases.'

I wanted to ask him what he meant by *a woman like you*. I thought of my life in Albany. Had I been free? 'I haven't felt that I've been a prisoner here,' I said. 'Yes, at first it was difficult. I was . . . afraid. But that was partly because I was alone, and came on a mission that perhaps . . . perhaps I wasn't sure about, although I convinced myself that I was. But since I've known . . . since I've been part of Marrakesh, lived here, in the medina, I've still been somewhat unsure of my actions, but not unsure about how I feel. I feel alive. Even my painting is different. It's alive as well, in a way it never was before.'

'But, as you say, the reason you came to Marrakesh no longer matters.'

'Yes. Etienne no longer matters.' I turned from Aszulay's eyes, staring at the tiles on the floor. Didn't he know what I wanted him to say? Hadn't he sought me out, invited me to come to the gardens, to his family in the countryside? Hadn't he shown concern about me when he knew Etienne was in Marrakesh? He'd just said that Manon was jealous because she knew Aszulay cared about me.

Had I completely misread him? But the time we'd spent in the *bled* . . . the way he looked at me. The way we'd told each other about our lives. The way he had touched my feet. His mouth on mine.

But he wasn't asking me to stay.

Had I been so wrong?

'Maybe . . . maybe I'll just stay to finish the last canvas for the hotel,' I said, forcing myself to look back at him.

He nodded.

I willed him to say something more. But he didn't. He stood, and went towards the gate. I rose, following him, and put my hand on his arm.

'Is this goodbye, then, Aszulay? Will . . . is this the last time we'll see each other?' I could barely speak the words. I couldn't say goodbye to him. I couldn't.

He looked down at me, his eyes somehow dark, in spite of their light colour. 'Is this what you wish?'

Aszulay! I wanted to shout. Stop being so . . . so polite, was the only word I could think of. I shook my head. 'No. It isn't. I don't want to say goodbye.'

He didn't move any closer to me. 'And . . . do you think . . . could you truly live in a place such as this? Live, Sidonie. Not visit, not stay for a short time. Not wander about the souks, or daydream in the gardens. I mean really live.' He stopped. 'Raise children.' He stopped again. 'And endure the differences between the world you once knew, and this world.'

I couldn't speak. He was asking me too many questions, but not the right one.

'Can you see this life clearly?' he asked then, and again, I was confused by his words, and just looked into his eyes.

And then I opened my mouth. *Yes*, I was about to say. *Yes, yes, I can see it with you*, but he spoke first.

'You don't have the answer,' he stated. 'I understand more than you realise.' He turned from me then, going out of the courtyard, shutting the gate quietly.

I sat on the bench, not sure of what had just happened. The red cat came to me for the first time, rubbing against my legs. And then she leapt on to the bench beside me and lowered herself on to her paws, staring at me.

I heard the throaty rumble of her purring.

CHAPTER THIRTY-NINE

Over the next few days I did what I had told Aszulay I would do. I completed my final painting, delivering it to Monsieur Henri and collecting my payment for the others that had been sold.

'Your work has become popular in such a short time, mademoiselle,' he said. 'The owner of a gallery on Rue de la Fontaine has mentioned he would like to speak to you.' He gave me a card. 'You may get in touch with him at your leisure.'

I sat in the coolness of the lobby, looking at the envelope and the printed card. Dare I think that I could sustain myself by my painting in Albany? Would I find the interest for my work there that I had here?

But I couldn't bear to think of Albany, and Juniper Road.

I walked slowly back into the medina, followed, of course, by Najeeb. As we passed Sharia Zitoun, I instinctively looked, as I always did, at the niche in the wall.

Since that first time, seeing Badou and Falida hiding there with the kittens, I had never seen them there again. But now I made out a shadowy figure.

I went closer. It was Falida, with a small grey kitten on her lap.

'Falida,' I said, and she jumped. She looked up at me, her eyes too big in her thin face. There was something stricken about her. 'What is it? What's wrong, Falida?'

Her eyes glistened. For all I had seen her mistreated by Manon, I hadn't seen her cry. 'I am on the street again, mademoiselle,' she said.

'Manon turned you out?'

'They're all gone.'

'All gone? What do you mean?'

'My lady and the man. Gone. And Badou. I don't want to be on the street. I am too old now. It's not good for a girl on the street. Bad things will happen to me. I'm afraid, mademoiselle.' She put the kitten to her face, as if hiding her tears from me. But her narrow shoulders shook.

I leaned down, putting my hand on her forearm. 'Falida. Tell me what happened.'

She lifted her head. Her lips were dry. I wondered when she had last eaten. 'My lady and the men. They fight.'

'Etienne? She fought with Monsieur Duverger?'

'All men, mademoiselle. Monsieur Olivier and Aszulay and Monsieur Etienne. Always fighting. Badou is very sad. He is afraid. He cries and cries.'

I licked my own lips, suddenly as dry as Falida's. 'But . . . where did they go? And who? Was it Manon and Etienne and Badou? Did they go somewhere?'

Falida shook her head. 'The other one. Monsieur Olivier. He said he take my lady, but not Badou. He don't want Badou. My lady said she give Badou to Monsieur Etienne. But Aszulay talk to Monsieur Etienne, then Monsieur Etienne fight with my lady and goes away and don't come back. My lady . . . she so angry. Badou and me hide. We afraid. She bad when she angry; she hit us. We hide here, but then night comes, and I don't know what to do. Badou hungry, cries more all the time. I take him back to my lady, she give me a paper, and bag with Badou's clothes. She tell me take him to Aszulay, and give Aszulay paper.'

'And . . . did you?'

Falida nodded. 'Aszulay not there. I leave Badou with servant. She tell me go away.' Falida put her face against the kitten, and once more tears shone on her cheeks.

'When did this happen?' I asked.

'Two nights I on street,' she said.

'Do you know how long Manon has gone for this time? With Monsieur Olivier?'

Falida shook her head.

'Come with me,' I said, and she put the kitten back into the hole in the wall and stood, and I took her hand.

We went back to Sharia Soura, and I gave her bread and a plate of chicken and couscous, ignoring Nawar's glares. I had the servant heat water, and after Falida had eaten, I let her bathe in my room, giving her one of my kaftans to put on. When I went to check on her, she was asleep, breathing in deep, exhausted sighs. As my room dimmed, I lay beside her on the mattress, and closed my own eyes.

I awoke in the night. Falida was curled against me. I put my arm over her and went back to sleep.

The next morning I combed Falida's hair for her, braided it into two long tails, and gave her breakfast. As the day before, she was silent, her eyes downcast the whole time. Although she was so thin, I noticed the kaftan was the right length; she was already almost as tall as me. When we'd eaten breakfast, I called to Najeeb.

'Can you take me to Aszulay's house?' I asked Falida. I wasn't sure I could find it from Sharia Soura.

She nodded, and with Najeeb following, we went through the medina until I recognised Aszulay's street.

I went to his gate and knocked.

Aszulay opened it, Badou at his side.

'Falida!' Badou said, in a delighted voice, and grinned at me. 'Another tooth is loose, Sidonie,' he said, showing me one on the bottom, rocking it back and forth with his index finger.

Falida kneeled, putting her arms around him. He hugged her quickly, then pulled away, speaking into her face, his words an excited jumble. 'We were looking for you yesterday. Guess what? Oncle Aszulay said the next time we go to the *bled* I can bring back a puppy. And we're going to teach it to fetch a stick, like Ali's dog. And you can help us, Falida. Isn't that right, Oncle Aszulay?'

'Yes,' Aszulay said, looking at me, not the children. He wore a simple dark blue djellaba. He didn't smile. 'Take Falida into the house and give her some of the melon we've prepared for lunch, Badou.'

I watched the children leave the courtyard. My hands trembled slightly. I didn't know if I could look at Aszulay, didn't know what I'd say.

'Poor things,' I said, still in the doorway of the courtyard. 'What's happened? Falida said Manon went away with Olivier.'

'Sidonie,' he said, and by the way he said my name I had to look at him. 'I didn't know if I'd . . .' He stopped, his face so still, so serious. So beautiful. I wanted to touch it.

He glanced at Najeeb, still standing behind me. 'Will you stay for a while? I don't like speaking in this manner, in the doorway.' His face was still unreadable.

When I nodded, a tiny muscle in his cheek twitched. He spoke to Najeeb, and the boy left. Aszulay took my arm and pulled me inside, shutting the gate. I was suddenly weak, and leaned against it.

'I told Etienne the truth,' Aszulay said. 'I went the next morning, after seeing you at Sharia Soura, and told him that Badou wasn't his.'

I waited, watching Aszulay's face.

'He was relieved, of course. He said he would leave the city immediately; even as an uncle, he had no real interest in the boy. He won't be back to Marrakesh.'

Still I said nothing.

'He asked me . . . he wanted me to tell you that he was sorry. Sorry for the pain he caused you. And to wish you well, and to ask that you will some day forgive him.'

I looked down. I didn't know what to feel, didn't want to talk about Etienne with Aszulay. We stood in silence.

'And Manon?' I finally said, when I could again look at him.

'Manon finally has what she always wanted. She left me a letter. She's arranged to have her house sold, and has gone to live in France. With Olivier. I don't know how long he'll be blinded by her; she has the same hold over him she has with all men, at least at the beginning. But if he proves to be like the others, he'll tire of her moods, her demands. Before too long she will lose her appeal.'

'And then she'll return?'

He shrugged. 'Who knows? But there will be nothing here for her any more. Without her house, without her son, without any friends – I cannot call her a friend any longer, not after her final actions – she will not have . . . what is the expression? When you can no longer come home?'

I didn't answer his question. 'But . . . Badou. Manon simply left him?'

He looked over his shoulder, at the house. 'In her letter she wrote that since I was so concerned about the child's future, interfering and destroying her plan to have Etienne take Badou, now I could take responsibility for him. He was of no further use to her. So she discarded him, as she has done to all those who are of no further use.'

He stood in front of me, looking down at me, and then moved closer and put his hand on my cheek, covering the old scar. 'But of course this is not a hardship.' He stopped. 'I love the child.'

I tried to think of something to say, but was too aware of his hand on my cheek, of standing so near to him. I felt the warmth of his fingers, and wondered if when he removed them they would leave a faint blue stain.

'Twice I went to Sharia Soura to speak to you,' he said. 'Both times I was told you weren't there.'

'But Mena didn't tell—'

'They think we are incorrigible. You and I, Sidonie. They don't approve.' He smiled, so slightly, as he said it.

I waited.

'I am an honest man,' he said. 'Tuaregs abide by a code of honesty, and of bravery.'

'I know,' I whispered.

'I was honest with you, the other night, when I said I

understand more than you realise. I do understand what you want. That you want to stay. And since the night I came to Sharia Soura when Manon hurt you, and you held my hand against your lips, and said you thought of my hands . . . since that night I couldn't hide my feelings from myself. You are different from any woman I've known, Sidonie.'

I watched his mouth.

'You are willing to be afraid, to accept fear, and move with it. But you also made me afraid, Sidonie. And I haven't known this feeling for so long, and it filled me with doubt. I was afraid that if I asked you to stay with me . . .'

He stopped.

'Afraid of what?' I said, or perhaps whispered.

'I thought it would be easier if you said no. But if you said yes, I was afraid that in time you wouldn't be happy, and would want your former life again. Even with your painting. With Badou and Falida, with . . . with children of our own. That what I have to give you won't be enough. Our lives have been so different, so—'

I stepped closer to him. I smelled the sweetness of melon on his lips. 'I can see my life here, with you,' I said.

A bird trilled in the branches overhead.

'You see it? It is enough?' he said softly, his eyes fixed on mine.

I waited until the bird had finished its song. 'Yes,' I said. 'It is enough.'

Inshallah, I thought. *Inshallah*.

ACKNOWLEDGEMENTS

I relied on a number of books for information and inspiration while writing Sidonie's story. *Women of Marrakech* is Leonora Peets' description of life as a doctor's wife in 1930s Marrakesh. Elizabeth Warnock Fernea wrote *The Streets of Marrakech* after her sojourn there with her family in the 1970s. These two first-hand accounts were particularly useful. Also of importance to my understanding of the country was the small, exquisitely detailed *In Morocco*, written by Edith Wharton in 1919, after she travelled through Morocco with the purpose of writing its first English travel guide. Cynthia J. Becker's *Amazigh Arts in Morocco: Women Shaping Berber Identity* was infinitely enlightening.

I also relied on information found in *The Voices of Marrakech*, by Elias Canetti, *Morocco That Was*, by Walter Harris, *A Year in Marrakesh*, by Peter Mayne, *Caliph's House*, by Tahir Shah, *The Conquest of Morocco*, by Douglas Porch, and *A Narrative of Travels in Spain and Morocco in 1848*, by David Urquhart. Paul Bowles' novel, *The Sheltering Sky*, was inspiring and revealing. I was able to unearth a wealth of glorious books depicting Morocco's architecture and the design of its *riads*, the old-style houses within the medinas, with their tiled courtyards and gardens. These books gave me greater insight into the beauty and exoticism of this magical country.

Loving thanks to my daughter Brenna, who twice accompanied me on adventures through Morocco, and made the experiences all the more exciting and wondrous with her presence. Thanks must go to our own Blue Men: Habib, Ali and Omar. Habib drove us from Marrakesh through the High Atlas mountains to the edge of the Sahara, playing Santana and Leonard Cohen and lovely Arabic music to accompany our long and wild journey over the *hamadas* of the Atlas. Ali and Omar led us on camels and drove us across the *erg* – the dunes – and the plains of sand and gravel – the *regs* – of the Sahara to our nomad camp under the stars, where we found the Southern Cross. I especially appreciated Ali's knowledge of life in the desert, and the wonderful stories of his mother, who was a nomad bride at the age of eleven. Omar kept us entertained with his songs and drumming and dancing, and taught us the hand-clapping that accompanies so many of the songs of the desert. Thanks to the unknown Berber woman who decorated our hands and feet with henna, and the accommodating staff at Hôtel Les Jardins de la Koutoubia in Marrakesh.

On this side of the world, thank you to my older daughter Zalie and my son Kitt, for their understanding and great listening skills, and for always making me laugh. Thank you to my sister-in-law, Carole Bernicchia-Freeman, for supervising my French. And a special thank you to Paul for providing so much brilliant colour during the stark black and white realities of the writing life.

Thanks go, again, to my agent, Sarah Heller, for everything from plot discussions to dinners and drinks to both commiserate and celebrate. Thanks to my editor in London, Sherise Hobbs at Headline, for the astute suggestions and gentle direction and patience.

Of course thanks must also go to Peter Newsom of Headline and Kim and all the staff at McArthur and Company in Toronto.

And a final thank you to the rest of my family and friends who have shown endless support during the writing of this book over a rather tumultuous but exciting period in my life.

LINDA HOLEMAN

In a Far Country

THE INTERNATIONAL BESTSELLER IS BACK

Pree Fincastle, daughter of impoverished British missionaries in India, is left alone and destitute when tragedy strikes. She embarks on a journey in search of Kai, the son of her mother's ayah, and the only person she can trust. But Kai is not the man Pree thought he was, and the secrets he holds will unlock the door to another world, another time – and, shockingly, another life.

From the whispering Ravi River to the hidden heart of Peshawar, this is a story of penury and prostitution, tragedy and bloodshed, secrets and love. But ultimately it is a story of hope; a story that, once read, will never be forgotten . . .

Discover the world of Linda Holeman:

'A sweeping, unputdownable saga (think *The Thorn Birds* and *Gone with the Wind*) that you'll want to tell all your friends about' *Woman*

'Sheer bliss . . . A superb read in every way' Lesley Pearse

'A once-in-a-lifetime read' *Globe and Mail* (Toronto)

978 0 7553 4507 6

headline
review

LINDA HOLEMAN

The Moonlit Cage

'I have always been told I was wicked'

The Moonlit Cage is the spellbinding story of Daryâ, a young Afghan girl, cursed, worthless and despised by her husband and her family, who embarks on the journey of a lifetime – one that takes her from the unforgiving valleys and mountains of her homeland to 1850s London, the heart of the mighty British Empire.

Enthralling, unusual and richly textured, *The Moonlit Cage* is a thrillingly realistic evocation of a lost world. It is a novel you will never forget.

Praise for the international bestseller *The Linnet Bird*:

'A sweeping, unputdownable saga (think *The Thorn Birds* and *Gone with the Wind*) that you'll want to tell all your friends about' *Woman*

'Compulsive reading . . . (*The Linnet Bird*) succeeds in being more than just a historical saga' *The Lady*

'Sheer bliss . . . A superb read in every way, epic, moving and unpredictable. I couldn't put *The Linnet Bird* down until I'd finished it' Lesley Pearse

'(Linda Holman) is a master of dramatic tension and of seducing a reader's attention . . . There is a beautiful imagination at work here and a touch of genuine narrative magic that makes the book a once-in-a-lifetime read' *Toronto Globe & Mail*

978 0 7553 2856 7

headline
review

The Linnet Bird

Linda Holeman

'For you, I will write of it all – part truth, part memory, part nightmare – my life, the one that started so long ago, in a place so far from here . . .'

India, 1839: Linny Gow, a respectable young wife and mother, settles down to write her life story. To outside appearances Linny is the perfect Colonial wife: beautiful, gracious, subservient. But appearances can be very deceptive . . .

An unforgettable book, richly descriptive and mesmerising from the start, *The Linnet Bird* is the spellbinding story of the journey of Linny Gow – child prostitute turned social climber turned colonial wife turned adventuress. Frequently disturbing, often moving and always enthralling, it is that rare thing: a once-in-a-lifetime read.

'We use that old cliché "unputdownable" so often that it has little real meaning any more, but I can assure you The Linnet Bird *stands alone, proud and beautiful . . . I turned the final page with deep regret'* Lesley Pearse

978 0 7553 2463 7

headline

Now you can buy any of these other bestselling titles from your bookshop or *direct from the publisher*.

FREE P&P AND UK DELIVERY
(Overseas and Ireland £3.50 per book)

The Linnet Bird	Linda Holeman	£6.99
The Moonlit Cage	Linda Holeman	£6.99
In a Far Country	Linda Holeman	£7.99
The Life You Want	Emily Barr	£6.99
Changing Grooms	Sasha Wagstaff	£6.99
The Return	Victoria Hislop	£7.99
The Heart of the Night	Judith Lennox	£6.99
Luxury	Jessica Ruston	£6.99
Love and Other Secrets	Sarah Challis	£6.99
The Message	Julie Highmore	£6.99

TO ORDER SIMPLY CALL THIS NUMBER

01235 400 414

or visit our website: www.headline.co.uk

Prices and availability subject to change without notice.